The Innkeeper

HOLLY MOORE

The Innkeeper

TATE PUBLISHING
AND ENTERPRISES, LLC

Published by Tate Publishing & Enterprises, LLC
127 E. Trade Center Terrace | Mustang, Oklahoma 73064 USA
1.888.361.9473 | www.tatepublishing.com

Tate Publishing is committed to excellence in the publishing industry. The company reflects the philosophy established by the founders, based on Psalm 68:11,
"The Lord gave the word and great was the company of those who published it."

Published in the United States of America

ISBN: 978-1-62854-174-8
Fiction / Romance
13.10.10

Contents

Chapter 1

I rushed through the room, packing my things as fast as I could, knowing that this was, at last, the right decision. My old life would have to end here and the birth of my new life would begin now. The feelings, the pain, the solitude would all be left behind me now. I passed the table too closely and heard the picture frame wobble and then smack back, showing the family forever printed on the glossy side of the paper underneath the cracked glass. I gently placed the picture in my hands, staring down at it. My breathing started to speed, my chest rising and falling faster than it should have. It all seemed unreal to me now. That family was so long ago, I almost wondered who those people were. They didn't seem as familiar and demanding as they once had. What waited for me now was something new and different. These strangers in the picture would be left behind now, but not forgotten. I had never intended to leave this place, this home of ours. It had now become more of a tomb, holding me down with shackles. I had been afraid to leave, afraid to change for fear of forgetting. I laid the picture back down and zoomed past my sister. Her face was twisted up into a variety of different emotions, disapproval mostly.

"What?" I grunted with my arms in the air, knowing all too well what she was thinking.

"This won't change anything. This won't make any difference," she answered, exasperated.

"Then what difference does it make to you? It is still my life, right?"

"Of course it is. But…to leave…this way? What would they think?"

"What do *they* have to do with anything? This isn't about *them*, it's about *me*." I stormed through the doorway and into the bathroom. I was doing fine until I caught a glimpse of myself in the mirror. The breathing thing came back, and before I knew it, I was grabbing the sink ledge for stability. My sister wasn't far behind me, and I could hear her thrumming her fingers on the doorframe.

"See, you're not ready," she whispered softly.

I felt the coldness of her words whip over me like a crisp winter chill. They weren't far from the truth, but it infuriated me enough to keep pushing on. I huffed again, squared my shoulders, and looked at myself. There I was—too young to be old, too old to be young. Not more than thirty-three years old. I was alone, no husband, no kids. I was stuck in this huge house, all alone with no one but my annoying and loving sister, Mandy, to keep me company. My hair was long and brown; my eyes were dark brown, almost black; and my youth, well, it was fading fast. I wasn't much to look at, I didn't think. I was average in just about every way. After today I would be different; I would be a new person. *Today is the day,* I kept hearing over and over in my mind, charging me onward. I pulled my hair into a messy ponytail and thrust the drawer open. I scooped my hand in grabbing more things out to pack. I wasn't ever planning on coming back here; I was done with the cross I bared. It was time to let someone else take their turn.

Elaina

March 20, 2009

The morning came fast and before I knew it I was lying in bed wide awake. I always hated mornings because they reminded me of how alone I really was. A new day to spend with virtually no one—no noise, no clatter, no footsteps coming down the stairs—just me in this huge beautiful house. The day ahead wasn't anything special, just a meeting with my realtor and best friend, Harris.

Upon hearing her name most people assume she is a he, but I am, without a doubt, positive Harris is a she. Her hair was the first thing I noticed about her when I first met her eons ago. She was standing in the country club bar, one hand resting flat on the bar and the other sat on her hip. She was dressed in some awful tennis skirt that had purple and pink pastel hatch marks all over it; white shoes, white socks, and white shirt. But when I got to her head, I noticed her bright-red hair. It was long and woven into a braid that reached the middle of her back. She was tall and slender, no fat on this woman to speak of. She was talking to a man way too old for her who was standing next to another woman, probably his wife. The wife was giving the redhead a look that should have urged the redhead away, but it didn't. If she had the courage to confront her, she might have killed her; but she didn't say a word or do a single thing, her scowl spoke all the necessary words. The redhead gave the woman no notice and finished her conversation with the balding man and then turned back to her iced tea at the bar.

I was there to meet someone who wasn't there yet, so I decided to wait at the bar, but the only empty barstool was next to the redhead. As soon as I sat down, she turned to me and smiled. It was the type of smile that a person gives you when they understand you better than you think they do. I had never seen or met this woman before, but I was sure she was a member at the country club. She took another sip of her iced tea and turned to me with her hand jetting out.

"Hi, I'm Harris," her voice exploded. She was confident and sure of herself, and I got the feeling that she would be like that no matter where she was. She spoke with a slight southern accent that she didn't try to correct.

I grabbed her hand with as much normalcy as possible. I didn't like human contact these days. Her grip nearly crushed the bones in my hand and fingers. I winced slightly, and she immediately let up on her vice-like clasp of my hand.

"Nice to meet you, Harris. My name is Elaina. Elaina Mur—"

Before I could finish my last name, she blurted out, "Murphy, I know. I've heard all about you." Her smile was genuine and trustworthy, but I was still caught off guard by her already knowing who I was. Why would she know my name? Then I thought about where we were—the best place for housewives to get together and chitchat about everybody else. Why had I ever joined this stupid club? I should have known I would be gossiped about sooner or later. Immediately, I hated this redhead and understood why the other woman had hated her too.

"Well, I guess there is no need to tell you about myself then, is there?" I halfheartedly joked. It didn't bother me that she was pushing her kindness on me, or that she seemed to know more about me than she should have. But as much as I disliked her, I felt very comfortable around her right away; I felt like I didn't need to pretend to be something I wasn't. Everything was already out in the open, so there was no need to dance around the obvious. For the first time in months I felt okay, and not just that I felt I had to *say* I was okay. We sat at the bar for an hour or so. My appointment turned out to be rather late and eventually I decided to forget about it altogether.

She told me about her family, her two divorces, and her work. She was a realtor, one of the best in Richmond. She mainly focused her attention on the bigger homes. She called them "estates" not mansions. Estates were larger than mansions with much more property to maintain. She was good at it, too, and she had made her money on her own. Neither of her husbands had had money until they met her. The country club membership she had here was under her name, her maiden name. She had been a member her entire life since utero with her parents; and when her business took off, she became a member under her own name. I told her very little about me; she already knew my story, as pathetic as it was. She never gave me that undeniable look of pity, which was a refreshing change. Suddenly, I realized I liked this woman.

She was interested in my house from day one of meeting her. It was big and fully furnished, with just little old me living there. When she couldn't convince me to sell, she did have another idea how I could make money.

"It's not renting, Elaina. It's more like a bed-and-breakfast-type deal. They come in for a week, or however long, and you cook for them, clean for them, take them where they need to go, take care of anything they need. It will give you something to do, and you can make a nice amount of money. The people would be screened, of course. Some of them might even be rich with no wives…" She danced her eyebrows up and down about that one—always trying to get me on a date. She never let up, which was fine because I never caved, but the idea that there was someone on this planet that hadn't totally given up on me was comforting.

"Is that for your sake or mine?" I chuckled.

"Very funny." She rolled her eyes. "I don't need another husband, thank you. Will you just think about it?"

"Of course I will. I promise."

I did think about it for a week straight. In the end, I agreed, and I had been letting my house out for almost four years now. Some of them were strangely private and never left the house. But I had a pool and a nice backyard with tons of space, and I didn't need to be there just because they were. Most of the guests were very nice people who usually stayed a week or two and then went back to wherever they came from. Still, there were the occasional funny stories to tell Harris about.

One man had stayed with me while his wife redecorated their house. He decided it was just too much of a mess; and since his wife kept changing her mind over and over, he ran while he could.

Their house was in Charlottesville near UVA. He traveled back and forth to work every day, so all I had to do was keep his laundry up and cook breakfast and dinner for him every day. It was one of the easiest jobs ever. I had my doubts about his faithfulness in the marriage but it didn't bother me at all. I never got involved with my clients. What business was it of mine anyway? I barely even spoke to them most of the time. They seemed to like it better that way. After two weeks, he decided to spend some time with his wife back in Charlottesville for the weekend. When he arrived back home, he noticed the strange car in the driveway. He also noticed that very little work had been done. He walked in the front door and called out his wife's name, but no one answered him. He decided to take a shower so he headed for the master bedroom, that's when he heard the giggling. To him it sounded like two schoolgirls laughing, but when he opened the door he wasn't quite sure what he was seeing. He recognized his naked wife but not the other woman in bed with her. It turned out the other woman was also the interior decorator. After that, he moved to a hotel closer to his wife so he could keep an eye on her, abruptly ending our business relationship. He had told me the story late one night after dinner. It was the same time he informed he was leaving. The poor man was obviously still in shock about the whole matter, and I actually felt bad for the guy. He wasn't old or ugly or even a mean person. I guess in my mind that would have made it close to okay, or even deserved, but he was nice and kind and loved his wife dearly. He just wanted to give her everything and love her; it was as simple as that. Too simple for his wife I suppose.

It was usually just one person at a time, and they were usually on some sort of extended business trip. Why they would choose to stay in my house rather than a hotel was beyond me, but still I had about twenty guests a year. I made a good chunk of money doing it, but usually I just tucked it away in my savings account. Harris was a great friend as well as a savvy investor, which made me lots of money. I trusted her more than anyone else I knew except for my sister, Mandy. My sister was two years older than me and had never quite gotten over the fact that I was an adult now and that I was fine on my own. She worried about me all the time, but I was used to it now.

So today my schedule was lunch with Harris and then probably over to Mandy's to see my two nieces, and then back home to no one and nothing. The restaurant today was the country club, which was nice, as usual. Harris never went anywhere or did anything halfway. She was already sitting at our table when I got there and motioned me over with a martini in one hand and cell phone in the other. I walked over to her and sat down. She was on her phone making another real estate deal, so I waited patiently, quietly rubbing my fingers against the linen napkin at my lap. Most people might be bothered by her incessant phone calls and chattering away into a piece of plastic, but it was really interesting to watch her sometimes—the pride she had in her work, the way she smoothed people over with her silky but stern voice. It was wonderful to see a woman have so much control of her life and never waver in the slightest. Finally, she was done, and she snapped the phone shut and turned it to vibrate. This was not something she ever did, but I let it go.

"Hey, Laina, you're here! I ordered you a martini, I hope that's okay?"

"It's fine, thanks." It was a little early for me but what the hell.

"Vodka, dirty, on the rocks, right?"

"You know that's right, Harris. So what's up with the phone?" I asked her the question like I was asking her about the weather, but she suddenly was caught off guard that I had noticed at all.

"Oh, that. Well, we have a real estate deal to discuss," she answered worriedly, watching my expression change from relaxed to focused.

"Okay, what's with the look?" I asked as her face grew more lined and heavy.

"What look?" she snapped back comically.

"That one." I pointed to her face. "And didn't we already discuss this? No more 'inmates' for the year," I teased.

"Don't call them that; you know I hate that. I think you will like this one, but you should know, this is a *big* one." She was still slightly unnerved. It was different to see her nervous in any way. "What are you gonna do anyway, Laina? The weather is still too cold to plaster yourself by your pool. Besides, it's a lot of moola!" She rubbed her thumb and forefinger together and raised her auburn eyebrows at me.

"So?" I challenged. "Spill it. But I'm not promising I'll do it. Seriously, I was looking forward to some time to myself."

"Time to yourself is all you have—" and then she caught herself. She looked down at her calendar book and obviously noticed the day. Her head snapped up with a look of deep embarrassment. "It's today, isn't it?"

I sighed loudly. "Yes, Harris, it's today."

"I was just so excited about this deal, I wasn't thinking. Are you okay?"

"I'm fine, Harris. It's been four years, not four months. People do get over things, eventually. Now, what's this big deal you keep going on and on about?" I was used to deflecting my pain. There was simply no point in making people feel worse about my past. I put on a very brave face most of the time; but if I was being honest, four years wasn't much different than four months—it hurt just the same.

I could see it in her face that she didn't believe me completely, but she knew better than anyone not to push the subject. She knew that I hated pity more than anything, and I watched her as she reviewed all the prerequisites of being my friend. Don't talk about *them*. It had taken me three months to even mention it to her, and when I finally did, she was quiet—for probably the first time in her life—until I was finished. After that, we only discussed it sparingly. She knew enough to know not to ask and not to bring it up.

She stared at me evenly with one brow arched in perfection across from me, undoubtedly remembering the same thing and wondering what she should say now.

"I don't have all day, Harris. Make me an offer, or you're paying for my lunch too," I teased, knowing full well she always paid for my lunch at these ridiculous places.

She snapped out of her brief lapse in concentration and began pulling out files and sheets of paper with too many words printed on them. I dreaded the thought of having to go through all the paperwork tonight. I was almost positive I would take the job because Harris was right—all I had was time to myself.

"Well, my lovely, today is your lucky day!"

"Oh joy!" I interrupted sarcastically, and Harris frowned again.

"Stop that. I am about to give you the coolest job you have ever imagined, so don't interrupt me again, or I will make you pay for my lunch today." Her brow lifted with analysis all over it, trying to make sure I was done with my antics, for now anyway.

"Please continue. I'm bursting with excitement and anticipation."

Her face beamed with exhilaration, and I could tell she had been waiting for this moment all day. She flicked her red hair out of her perfect face and twisted it behind her shoulders so I could see her dark-brown eyes better.

"His name is Grayson Sparks. Ever heard of him?" she asked like it was a joke, like I should already know who this person was. The name rang a bell but a very distant one. I wasn't sure why I recognized it at all.

"Not really. The name's a bit familiar. Why? Who is he?" I asked, starting to straighten up in my seat.

"He's a really great actor. He's kinda new to the scene. I mean, he's been around a while, but he has just started really taking off in the last few years. You really don't know who he is?" she asked in fake shock and rolled her eyes as she continued on. "But they are beginning filming in a few weeks on his new film, down the road from you. It's a remote place somewhere deep in Powhatan. Apparently they were able to find a secluded place there." She rolled her eyes at that too. Powhatan wasn't really the most crowded place. Lot's of people lived there but there were also lots of trees and land where no one lived at all. I always thought of it as slow-growing and easygoing. I was thankful for it, because everything around it seemed to bloom overnight. I snorted in response with a sneer.

"Anyway, his agent is a longtime pal from way back." She danced her eyes up and down as I rolled mine. "He was looking for a home to stay in, instead of a hotel, since the shoot is going to be about three months, and your name came up. Before I knew it, I was sending pictures to him and they want to book it for his entire stay here!"

I didn't really respond right away, and she waited with her brows lifted, waiting with anticipation for me to do anything, even breathe. I thought about a movie star being in my house, how weird it would be. What about security? Paparazzi? What if some crazed loony tries to break in and kidnap him, or kill him or me? Maybe this wasn't for me. What did I know about film stars? Weren't they all just full of themselves anyway? I shook my head when I tried to imagine cooking for this to-do star, seeing his face curl up at the sight of my simple meals and simple home.

"I don't know, Harris, that sounds kinda weird."

She could hear the hesitation in my voice, so she started explaining quickly. "He will have his own security; you'll never even know they are there. He will have his own driver so you'll never have to take him anywhere. He is not picky or annoying. He is very down-to-earth, I promise. Oh yeah, and he's from Scotland, so his accent is one of your favorites." She danced her brows at me again. She knew I loved accents, and Irish and Scottish were right at the top.

"By the way, the pay is incredible." She slid over an envelope and did a little anxious dance in her seat. I grabbed it and tore my thumb into the sealed flap. It was a check with five figures on it. I felt my heart race and my palms start to sweat. This couldn't be right. Nobody in their right mind would spend this just for my simple accommodations.

"This amount is ludicrous! It's a house not a mansion. This sounds a little too weird for me, Harris. Maybe you should get someone else."

"There is no one else. Your house *is* a mansion, you goof! That's just the down payment, silly. When he returns to LA after shooting the film, you get another check, just like that one." Her smile spread across her face but fell slightly when she realized I wasn't excited about this at all. This was too much for a Monday afternoon. She sighed loudly and then took my hand. "You have a few days to think about it. But Laina, you need this. It will give you something to do with that huge house of memories. You might enjoy his company, you might not, but if you laugh just once while that man is here then it will be worth it." She smiled at me as she gently tried to urge me to do this thing—this crazy, oddball thing that someone like me would never do. The money was great, but it just all seemed too crazy for me. She was right; I needed to make some changes. It was time. It had been four years since my last life-altering experience. I had been content to be distant and antisocial. But even I was starting to get the itch of change. The loneliness was getting to be too much for even me. But I wasn't sure if this was the way to go about making change.

I went home after lunch feeling uncertain about what I wanted to do about my new offer. It sounded too good to be true—too much money, too easy of a job, and way too much eye candy. I had gone straight to my computer and looked up this "movie star.". There was a lot of information about him—not much of it was very gentlemanly—but the pictures were nice, very nice. It seemed Grayson Sparks was thirty-eight, a bit of a ladies' man, never been married and usually only dated younger, taller, more beautiful women. He was a tall, dark-brown-haired, hazel-eyed man. His body was perfect in every way—lean, muscular, bronzed and strong. He was always flipping off the paparazzi, always into something or someone, and most of his movies were pretty darn successful. He made a ton of money for his action movies but did just as well in the romantic comedy realm. Lately, he had been doing some more sinister movies. As I kept pointing, clicking, and reading, I also found out some better things about Mr. Sparks. He was originally from Edinburgh, pronounced Edinburra, Scotland, where he was raised until he was about twelve years old, and then he moved to the States to pursue an education which he completely screwed up. His father had passed away of lung cancer when he was sixteen, fueling his horrible behavior. It turns out he was not private-school material either, and he was booted out of three schools before his mother decided home school was the best route for her gifted son. In every interview, his mother spoke kindly of him and never let on that he had ever been more than she could handle. She said she was proud of him and that she couldn't have asked for a better son, well, besides the other son she had. I learned that after he turned nineteen, he moved back to the small village in his native land and lived there for about seven years. He was in a three-year relationship and briefly engaged to a girl from his hometown before he decided to try acting. They had moved back to the States together. He had gotten a taste of acting while living briefly in New York. He loved the theater and everything it was about—the passion, the drive, the pure love of it was what attracted him to it. He moved to LA shortly after that and started going on castings, and before he knew it, he was the next best leading man as well as suddenly single. I'm sure his success had much to do with his boyish good looks, the incredibly sexy accent and his perfect body, or maybe it was his ability to actually act. I had seen some of his movies before, and they were good. I had just never paid much attention to the name. The whole story sounded like a fairy tale until the part about his mother dying came up. There were two smaller pictures at the end of the article of Grayson and his mother. The first was taken at a movie opening, one of his first leads. She was very tiny standing next to his six foot frame, and she looked tired and weak but very proud. Grayson stood with his long arm around her, his eyes beaming and his smile spread from cheek to cheek. It was from his first big movie premiere. It was easy to see they were both excited. The other was of the two of them posing somewhere tropical with his dog and his brother, Nathan. They were darkly tanned and smiling, with the crystal-blue water behind them as the backdrop. It looked more like a family photo than a press photo. His mother had passed a few months after that, but she had lived long enough to see her screwup of a son finally make something of himself with success.

I stared at the computer and had been doing so for hours when the phone rang. I knew who it was, Mandy. After lunch with Harris, I had dropped by to see her kids and, of course, her. I'm sure she could tell that something was off for me today. My mind was elsewhere, but she had probably thought it was about what today usually meant for me, loss. This new turn of events had surprisingly taken my mind off the bad day I thought I was going to have; I had not even had time to think about it, much. I sighed after the phone rang its course, stopped, and then started ringing again a few minutes later. *Ever-consistent Mandy.* I thought I'd better answer it so she was sure I wasn't hanging from the chandelier or something tall and sturdy enough to hold my weight.

"Hi, Mandy," I answered.

"How did you know it was me?"

I looked over at the clock; it was eleven at night. She was the only one who would call me this late. I simply chuckled and sighed again.

"What's up, Mandy? What's with the late phone call?" I urged.

"Oh, I don't know. You seemed…distant today."

"Don't worry. I'm fine, really," I said with a smile.

"Really? You sure? 'Cause I could come over if you want."

"Nope, I'm fine, just looking on the computer at a new client." I explained as nonchalantly as I could. Another part of this big deal would be secrecy. I could not tell anyone he was there. If I did, it could be a security breach and my contract would be broken. They could even sue me if I leaked one word to anyone.

"He or she?" she asked.

"It's a he."

"Cute?"

"Well, let's see, he's about eighty-two with white hair and…"

"Eww, never mind."

I laughed quietly to myself because of how easily she had been misled. Mandy was my older sister. She had always been protective of me since we were kids. She had a husband and two little girls; her life was complete. A few weeks ago, she had informed me that she was expecting another baby. I was shocked when I heard but only because I thought she would wait a little longer, not just because she was having another child. She would have ten if her husband let her. She usually got her way, so she may just have ten someday. I had wanted a bunch of kids once upon a time, but fate had other plans for me. Mandy was only about two years older than me, making her thirty-five, but she treated me like I was five years old sometimes. She worried all the time. Since my mom had moved to her summer home on the water permanently, she was always coming over and checking on me to make sure I wasn't drinking liquid plumber. She was annoying, but she made me laugh a lot, and I knew everything she did for me and to me were out of love. Besides, all we had were each other. My mom was gone and never coming back for either of us. Sometimes I think that bothered Mandy more than she let on. I had always known what my mother was; and while biologically she was our mother, she was no mom. I know Mandy held out hope for her to change, but not me.

"Are you okay, really? I know this day is always hard for you," she whispered with a bit of sadness to her voice.

"I'm fine, really. You and Tim can sleep soundly. I don't have any sharp knives or prescription pills to gobble down." I laughed again but she was silent.

"That's not funny, Elaina."

"Sorry, Sis. I just wish you would stop worrying about me so much, that's all." I felt bad immediately. It was too soon for jokes I guessed. It may never be time for joking about that. "I'm pretty tired. Can we talk tomorrow?"

She sighed out loud knowing I was giving her the cue. "Sure, Laina, tomorrow. Love you."

"Love you too, even though you are the most obnoxious sister in the world." She finally laughed, and I knew she would rest a little easier than before.

Suicide

The night of my suicide attempt had been a bad one. I had spent weeks mourning *them*. My father had also just died, and my mother had just moved away out of her disgust for me. Mandy and my mother couldn't get me to do anything. Mom had been unsuccessful at getting me out of the house or my bed. Defeated and full of annoyance, she gave up and decided to move as far away from me as possible. She always blamed me for what happened. Her leaving wasn't what upset me; we had never had the mother-daughter relationship that most people have. We were mostly estranged my entire life, and I had become indifferent to the whole situation over time. She was trying to be something she wasn't—caring and nurturing. It was no surprise to me that she failed at showing love to me. It was what it was, and nothing was going to change the way things were between us. After my loss, she had become even more annoyed with me. She blamed me for what happened constantly, and I had a feeling that my other family did too. There were days when the phone rang constantly. I never answered it. Eventually people got the hint. I was as dead as *they* were now.

The day my mother left gave me an opening to end it all. Now that she was gone and out of my way, I could do what I had been planning to do for months. There really was no point to be here anymore. All my dreams were crushed and gone like dust. Like *them*. My doctor had given me Vicodin for my injuries from the accident, which had been pretty bad. I hadn't needed them after coming home from the hospital, but I filled the prescription and kept them anyway. I knew there would be a use for them eventually. I had known what I would probably do since the day I left the hospital.

My mother left that morning, yelling and slamming the door behind her taking her fury with her, thankfully. Mandy rushed after her, trying to get her to come back. After all, my sister couldn't stay with me and babysit me all day and night. She was pregnant with her first child and completely overwhelmed with everything. My mother never came back, and I was relieved. Mandy was at a loss as to what to do. She had left with the promise of being back first thing in the morning with some sort of plan of action. That left me with plenty of time to take care of my unfinished business.

I waited for an hour or so, because Mandy almost always came back after forgetting something at my house. The hour came and went and she never returned. I remember being a little sad that I wouldn't get to see her again before I died.

I took a long bath, scrubbing my battered body. Weeks after the accident, I was still in pretty bad shape. I still had wounds to nurse and my body was stiff from not moving much. I tried to slit my wrist first, but every time I tried, I only scratched the razor across my skin and *their* faces would appear in my mind with heavy disapproval. Even though it was only in my mind, I couldn't do it. I got out of the tub, wrapped my towel around my bruised body, and walked over to the sink. There was an old medicine cabinet over the sink, and I gripped the side of the mirror with my fingers. It creaked open slowly, and there were the pills I had tucked away for an opportunity like this. The bottle glared back at me, daring me to pick it up.

Take two pills every 4-6 hours for pain as needed is what I read, but what I saw was, *Take every last pill until the pain is gone...*

It was almost ten at night by now—too late for Mandy to come back. I had to be sure this was what I really wanted. It was. There was nothing to live for anymore. I took each pill, one by one, until the unused bottle was empty. With thirty pills sloshing around in my stomach, I made my way to the couch in front of the fireplace to watch the flames slowly burn down and go out like I was hoping my life would. My body got heavier and heavier with each struggled breath. My vision was fading and I was cold, even though the fire was still burning. I gripped onto the stuffed animal that *she* loved so much and closed my blurry eyes. I wasn't scared, I was ready to die. I *wanted* to die. Without them there really wasn't a point to being here anymore.

I must have drifted off. My body was trying to die like I was asking for it to do. I have no idea how long I laid there, with my breaths becoming slower and slower and more shallow. There was no pain at all—nothing—just numbness. The more shallow the breaths became, the more numb my fingers and toes got. It spread to my arms and legs and I waited for it to reach my lungs and heart. As I drifted further and further away, I saw visions of them coming to embrace me. We were in a strange place; not home, somewhere else. It was wet and rainy where I stood. We were outside standing next to a huge fireball. The grass around us was tall and brown, and it blew in the breeze, swaying back and forth. I could see them but they were more like blurry figures that became weeds as well, swaying gently back and forth. The slower my breathing got, the foggier they became. I walked over to them with my arms extended and my hands reaching for them, but they shook their grassy heads no at me. Then they screamed no at me over and over like a chant rather than a rant. Suddenly I felt pain on my chest and heard faint screaming in my ears. When I looked back to them, they were gone as well as the fields of blowing grass, and I was all alone with the huge fireball. I tried to run but my legs didn't work anymore. There was something pulling me back and away from searching for them. I struggled as hard as my mind would let me, but in the end I lost.

I don't remember anything else until I woke up in the ICU weeks later. There were tubes and lines coming off my body in every direction. My throat was dry and achy, and when I tried to swallow, it burned all the way down my chest. Every breath hurt and felt forced. I opened my eyes and saw Mandy sitting there beside me. Her eyes were open but she looked exhausted, like she hadn't slept for days.

When she saw that my eyes were opened, she sighed and smiled but there was only deep concern set in her eyes with a trace of pity. She gripped my hand in hers and cupped my face with her other free hand. There were tears in her eyes and her face was red and puffy. She had been crying a lot, and for a long time.

"Not the ending you were expecting, huh?" she asked through swollen, tightened eyes. "You should be dead, you know?" she whispered with a tight throat.

There was a tube in my throat so I couldn't talk. I tried to sit up but she gently forced me back down. I looked at her with confusion and sadness. Mandy tried to ignore my disappointment in the obvious outcome. I could see that she was still wondering if I was really that desperate to die and get it over with. She was still hoping that I had been scared straight this time.

She sighed loudly and readied herself for the breakdown of information she thought I needed to hear. "You've been here a couple of weeks. They were feeding you with the tube since they induced your coma. You lost a lot of weight and you're gonna be really weak, but you'll live." Her voice drifted off and I could hear the sobs start up. She turned away from me so I wouldn't see her cry. Through the sniffles, she continued. "I found you, did you know that? Do you remember that?" she asked through tears of anger and sorrow. "I had to drag you to the floor and pump your chest until the paramedics came." She stopped talking suddenly, not able to continue. She collected herself like the lady she is and started again with hopeful eyes, "They'll take the feeding tube out as soon as you start eating again."

I made a hopeful face thinking there was still another way, but she saw me and immediately knew what I was thinking, what I was planning. Her face turned bright-red as her blood pressure went through the roof with fury, and her hand slammed down on the table beside my hospital bed. She leaned over real close to my face so that she was sure I heard every word. Her eyes leveled on me like a lion staring down a helpless animal, then she started in on me with a threatening voice that snarled through her clenched teeth. "You *are* going to eat, Elaina. You *are* going to get better and leave this place. Then, you *are* going to a place that can help you." There was no question about her intentions to keep me alive. She wasn't going to allow me to die, and I knew it right then that she would never leave me alone again, and I would never get the chance to try to off myself again. "Someone has to help you because I can't." She cut away from me again, feeling the weight of it all again. She rubbed her pregnant belly as if it soothed her.

I smashed my eyes shut in embarrassment and anger again. This is not what I wanted. I didn't plan on waking up; I hoped I wouldn't. I had been so sure it was finally over but I was still here and I had no other choice but to "face the music," as my father used to say. I narrowed my eyes back at Mandy stubbornly.

"What were you thinking?" she asked with her softer, more recognizable tone. "Why would you do this? I knew you were having a hard time, but why this, Elaina? What would *they* think if they saw this? You can't be with *them* that way, you know?" she whispered softly. "Please don't do this. First dad and now you; I can't bear it. We'll get through this together. I won't leave you alone again. I'll do whatever it takes," she vowed.

She had no idea that alone was exactly what I wanted.

A few days later, I was heading home; well, not exactly home. "Transitions" was going to be my new home for a while. I was going to learn how to cope there and deal with my loss. The rooms were small, and I had a roommate after a couple of days. They put me on suicide watch for the first forty-eight hours just to be on the safe side. Everything was pretty much taken from me—mouthwash, belts, shoelaces, sharp objects, my razor; they even removed the shower curtain from my bathroom. I wasn't allowed any visitors or phone calls. They didn't want me getting my hands on any pills or drugs to finish the aborted mess I had made of my crumbling life. After two days, they deemed me safe enough to have a roommate and gave me my shower curtain back. My razor was returned to me only under supervision as I shaved my legs and underarms; everything else, well, forget it. It was humiliating but necessary, obviously. I constantly thought of ways to end my life and they could see it. I was relieved that I could shower in privacy now, not that my roommate cared. She was doped up on some kind of crazy pills.

Eventually, we started having group meetings that included all suicidal patients. It seemed a little dangerous to me to put all of us suicidal people together in one room at the same time. We could have most likely stapled ourselves to death or even paperclipped each other. At first, I will admit, it was a complete joke to me, but after a few weeks I slowly came around and started talking. I had no other choice but to talk. Silence only fuels the thoughts and the needs that you dream about. The building was cold and chemically cleaned with astringents that burned your nose and throat from the strength of them. I had one window in my room with parallel bars across the view. My roommate snored and talked in her sleep, sometimes she screamed. The counselors, however, were kind and gentle and seemed to understand. Many of them had been through similar experiences like mine and it made me feel hopeful to know that one day I would be okay again. After three months of meetings, one-on-ones, exercises in self-readiness, and bad food, I felt stronger and more capable of dealing with what had happened. I was ready to come home and move on, whatever that was.

I was coming home to many unresolved things though. When I got home, the same problems were still there like before. It took me a while but things slowly started to come together. It was a slow process, but at least I was alive. Weeks later, I met Harris. She was exactly what I needed. Someone who didn't know me at all, my own little personal godsend to the light of life.

Chapter 2

I slept pretty good in my empty king-sized bed. When I woke up, I slid off the bed and dragged myself into the bathroom to the sink. There I was, a thirty-three year old woman; no husband, no kids, not even a pet. I was tired of being alone, tired of not caring, and tired of trying to make everyone feel more comfortable around me because I was the elephant in the room. I was ready for something new and different. No more mourning for me, I hoped. I brushed my teeth with fierceness as I thought out my words for Harris carefully. I made my coffee, poured a cup, made myself a bowl of fruit and sat on the back deck looking out over the woods. My phone sat beside me like it was my breakfast guest. I stared at it for a long time, slowly sipping the hot coffee and nibbling at a piece of pineapple. I had the same breakfast every day. I pulled my knees to my chest tightly as if I were hugging myself to find some strength or maybe some nerve. Finally, I grabbed the phone and sped through her phone number. It rang only once, I'm sure she had been expecting me.

"Good morning, killjoy," she snickered. I could hear someone talking in the background but her focus was totally on me. "Made up your mind yet? The agent has called three times this morning wondering if there was any news. Apparently this client really wants to stay there."

I was silent for long moment.

"Oh, damn. Laina? Did I lose you? This stupid phone!" she shouted, adding a slur of a dozen expletives.

"I'm here, Harris," I shouted back at her over her rant. "Tell the agent I'm in, but I'm gonna need more money. Three months is a long time to put up with someone. Tell them to double the offer and I'm in." I didn't know what I was thinking. What did I need more money for? The initial offer was more than enough. This wasn't like me at all. Usually people played hardball with me, not the other way around. I was suddenly feeling tough, and I liked it.

"Did you just say double their offer and you're in?" she gasped while trying not to laugh.

"Yes. Double or nothing," I answered flatly.

"Geez, Laina, who peed in your fruit bowl this morning?" she cackled. "I will let the agent know. I'm sure it won't be a problem. But you do realize that's eighty-five thousand dollars right? US dollars?"

"Yep."

"You're sure this is your only offer? They may walk away, you know," she countered.

"Take it or leave it," I answered.

She laughed again. "I'll call you when I hear anything, Mr. Trump."

It didn't take long to get the answer I was waiting for. They agreed to my counter offer and the paperwork was faxed minutes later. I signed, they signed, Harris smiled and smiled. This was the most money I had ever made doing this type of thing, ever. I got my first check and then was told that my money was not intended to be used for Mr. Sparks. There would be a separate account for anything he needed. A few days later, his agent faxed over a list of his food likes and dislikes. I was happy to see that he didn't like anything too weird that I didn't know how to cook. He liked simple food and lots of it. He also asked that I always have fresh fruit of any kind and natural peanut butter. That made me smile, thinking of someone I used to know.

After a few more days, the boxes started arriving. I was instructed to get everything ready for the movie star before he got to town. Having the boxes sent early was just a precaution so that security would not have to deal with them and that the media didn't get word that their big-time movie star would be so easily accessible. He was coming a week early before shooting began to prepare, have meetings, fittings, and most importantly fool the press into thinking he wasn't even here yet.

He was booked in a magnificent suite at the Jefferson Hotel downtown—a suite that he would never see. They did about ten background checks on me as a security measure. The types of questions I was asked to answer were ridiculous. Basically they wanted to make sure I wasn't some cuckoo bird that was going to chop of the actor's big toe while he slept and then sell it on eBay.

As I went through the boxes, I noticed how many clothes he had. There were outfits for every occasion and shoes, tons and tons of shoes. Everything was labeled exactly how he wanted it to be. He would be sleeping in my room; I would be sleeping upstairs in the guest suite. It took weeks, but I had gotten all of my things moved out of my room and moved upstairs. My old room was all ready for him. His clothes were hung and folded perfectly. His shoes were stacked neatly across the floor of the closet. His belts and ties were hung perfectly, in the order best for him to pick and choose. The white billowy bedding that was sent over was already on the bed, along with his specific pillows that came in another box. I couldn't help wanting to vomit a few times as I wondered how he would be. If he was this picky about his clothes and bedding, how horrible would *he* actually be? I tried to push negative thoughts away as I cleaned the pool, poured in the chemicals until the levels were perfect, and pulled every weed from the backyard. I was not told his exact date of arrival; instead, I was going to get a phone call when he arrived at the airport, then I would go to meet him and his driver to take him back to my house in my car. Of course, security would be following us, but we would never know they were there. It all seemed a little *007* to me, but whatever. I was getting paid, and if these Hollywood snotballs thought they really needed all these extra precautions then who was I to judge.

Time moved slowly as I readied the house for his big arrival. Harris came over almost every day to make sure I had done everything to the specifications of the contract. Of course, I had always done things just a little too simply for her taste. She would change a pillow, or move a lamp, but when she left I put it back the way it was. If Grayson Sparks didn't like my house, he was free to leave it anytime he wanted. I had gotten more than enough money for doing very little and the contract had clearly stated that the first payment was non-refundable. It was mine whether he liked it here or not.

On the last day of preparing, I went through the whole house and removed every picture and then hung them back up three times. I finally decided to leave my personal pictures in the house, but not in his room. I was glad that I had moved upstairs weeks ago so I would never accidentally enter his room from habit and see something I shouldn't. I felt pretty confident that I wouldn't even go in his room except to make the bed or change the sheets.

I was nervous about him coming now. With nothing to do except wait, I felt like a ticking time bomb. Spring was in full motion, the tulips and daffodils were starting to bloom, the green was starting to come back to Richmond. It had been about a month since I had first heard Grayson Sparks' name mentioned. While I tried to pretend that I wasn't excited, I would find myself lurching to the computer, looking up his name and seeing what he had done the day before in LA. The pictures were immediately plastered all over the Internet every time he did anything, but for the past few weeks, there hadn't been any new pictures or stories on the nightly gossip shows. When I went back to check the dates of the other pictures, I saw that they were dated from almost six months ago. I assumed he had been too busy with work to go out in public. It never dawned on me that he might actually like the quiet life.

I had only one thing to do today after my shrink appointment, and that was meet with Harris for dinner. She promised it was fun only and nothing about the client would be discussed. For the entire day before that, I had decided to sit by the pool and enjoy the day. It was almost May and the weather was perfect—not too hot, not too cold, and there was still a constant breeze that smelled like flowers and green grass.

I got up early and readied myself for the day. My therapy session was at nine in the morning. I hated going to see my therapist. It seemed like such a waste of time after all these years. I only went because of Mandy. She insisted I go after the "attempt." Dr. Linda Macy was a pretty good psychologist as psychologists go. She was older than me, but not by much. I had insisted on seeing someone older than me; it was just too weird talking to some infant who hadn't gone through anything yet. She had jet-black hair that was to her shoulders and she had big, round glasses with dark-red frames. She was petite—shorter than me—and her voice was sort of babyish, but she was tough as nails. She got right to the point and dealt with things at the core of the problems. As much as I hated coming to see her, I was grateful to have her in my life. She had been very important to me in those first few months home from my stay at the psycho ward.

I parked in front of Henrico Doctors' Hospital where she worked and took the elevator up to the second floor of the separate medical building. I could have taken the stairs, but nobody ever does. It seems kind of stupid that most people take the elevator because they are in a hurry for an appointment, even though the stairs are sometimes faster, and you usually end up sitting in the waiting room for twenty minutes anyway.

Dr. Macy's waiting room was very nice and soothing. The walls were this soft-green color and she had magazines about happy things and happy people scattered all over the place. She specialized in failed suicides, divorce, fatal disease and basically anything having to do with loss or death. She shared her office with another psychologist that specialized more with children. I was just settling in with a *Cooking Light* magazine when she popped her head around the door and motioned for me to come back.

Her office was very plain and pretty empty. There was a desk, a chair, a chase, and a few lamps. I could always smell smoke whenever I walked through her door of which she always apologized for. Smokers always apologize for smoking, even in their own office apparently. It didn't bother me but I did notice it.

"So, Elaina, have a seat. How are things going?" she asked as she walked around her desk to sit behind it and face me.

"They're going, I guess. My new guest is coming any day now. I think I've gotten everything ready for him," I answered, slightly bored.

"How are you feeling about having a new person in your house?"

"Fine."

"How is the 'eating more thing' coming along?" she asked with more seriousness.

"Fine," I answered flatly. I hated talking about my weight. I had never really gained much of it back since my suicide attempt, and it had made everyone worry a bit. I wasn't anorexic or anything, but I was a little too thin even for my taste.

"Elaina, stop blocking me," she chastened.

"I'm not. I eat healthy and I run. Maybe I'm just supposed to be thin." I rolled my eyes and turned away.

"Something's got you rattled. What's going on?" she asked again.

"I'm not rattled, I'm just fine."

"How was the anniversary? How did that go?"

"Fine. I had lunch with Harris, and we talked about my new client coming, and that's about it."

"Tell me about him," she asked.

"I don't think I can."

"Why?" she asked, confused.

"He's, umm, kinda famous. I'm not supposed to say anything."

"This is confidential, Elaina. You can tell me." She reminded me of her code of ethics she was sworn to uphold.

I sighed and lowered my chin. "His name is Grayson Sparks. He's an actor," I answered, feeling guilty.

"Well, that explains your aloofness today. That's pretty exciting. How do you feel about it?" she asked again, this time with more of a push to her voice.

"He's just a guy, nothing more. He's gonna be with me for three months though, much longer than the usual."

"Does that bother you?"

"No. Not at all." I shrugged.

She stared at me for a long moment. Her eyes narrowed and her lips were mashed together with irritation.

"Maybe today is not a good day for you to talk. Tell you what"—she stood up and grabbed her day planner—"Why don't we plan to meet sometime next week?"

"No," I answered quickly with a bit more volume to the word than I planned on.

Her head snapped back at me. "Excuse me?" she asked, surprised.

"I mean"—I cleared my throat. I had wanted to end the sessions for a while now—"I'm not coming back anymore, Linda. I think I'm done."

She was silent for a while, and then she smiled and nodded her head. "I guess I knew this was coming. It has been over three years now. If you think you are ready, then I will support your decision." She stared at me as if she was studying me and my intent. "If you need me for anything, please call me, okay?"

"I will." I stood up and shook her hand. "Thanks, Dr. Macy. I really appreciate everything you've done for me."

"You did it, not me." She smiled gladly giving me the last bit of confidence she could.

I drove home feeling a little bit liberated and relieved. I wasn't sure how Mandy would take the news. She relied heavily on Dr. Macy, and my appointments made her feel like I was safe. I went home, made a celebratory drink, and sat out by the pool.

Getting ready for dinner was a pain in the guest suite. There wasn't nearly as much room as I was used to having downstairs, but I managed. Harris called three or four times to confirm the place and time. I was allowed to choose tonight, and we were going to Brios for dinner. It was one of my favorite places to go—great food, great people, and a great place where we could also sit outside. We were taking separate cars because Harris had a meeting before dinner. I assumed she would be late but was happily surprised when she was already sitting at the table when I got there.

"You look thin, Elaina. What have you been eating? Or should I say what have you *not* been eating?" Her brown eyes narrowed at me teasingly.

"It's nothing. I've been busy that's all." That was twice today about my weight—enough already.

"Oh, wait a minute. Are you trying to look good for the actor? Laina, you devil you," she teased in an overdone Song of the South accent.

"Shut it, Harris. There is nothing wrong with trying to look your best, is there?"

"Not at all, honey. You do your thing! You look great. I just wish I saw you like this more often, that's all. You are a beautiful woman, Lain. You're young and smart and available. It's time you started realizing that. I'm glad to see it. By the way that dress makes your boobs look phenomenal!" She smiled her genuine smile at me. I couldn't help but smile back at her. Harris was tough and to the point, but I loved her honesty. It was pure and never wavering. I trusted that I would always get the truth from her. Mandy was more of a pleaser. She wanted to make me happy because she felt bad for me. She was scared I was going to off myself someday. She loved me, of course, but sometimes never challenging a person is the wrong thing to do.

Dinner was great. We had lots of food and lots of drinks and, as promised, Mr. Sparks was never mentioned. The only way we could talk about him from now on would have to be almost in secret code. We couldn't risk having his location leaked to the press. No one knew who I was and no one cared who I was. That is why I think he chose me; no one would ever think to look for him with me.

Chapter 3

May 1, 2009

The morning I got the call was a rainy one. I was trying to find some clothes to put on other than the swimsuit and cover-up I had been wearing for the past few days. The weather had been beautiful for days, and now that there was a real-life movie star coming to Richmond, it, of course, had to rain. I don't know why I even cared, but bad first impressions were usually the ones that stuck. I was annoyed that this would be his first view of my town.

I was suddenly very antsy. I thought about taking a Lexapro, but I decided not to. I could do this on my own. I was determined. I didn't need any medicine anymore. I headed for the shower to get cleaned up before I was supposed to meet one of the most handsome men in the world. I wasn't worried if he would like me or not. He was not my type at all. I was just nervous about having someone new around; I always got this way before a newcomer arrived.

My house wasn't close to any others in the neighborhood. I had a double lot. It used to be my dream house, with the wooden beams through the ceiling and the hardwood floors. The house was beautiful and had been awarded justly so in the parade of homes when it was built. It was an honor, not really for me, but still it was nice to be recognized for the work. Even though my house was beautiful to most people, I always wondered if it was as beautiful to the visitors that stayed here with me.

I never tried to make relationships with the clients who stayed with me. I simply cooked their meals, cleaned their rooms, made their beds, and tried to be as accommodating as I could. Conversation was something I left up to them to start. If they wanted to talk I would respond, but not very long; and it seemed as soon as they had struck up a conversation, I was politely ending it and pushing on to another imaginary chore. I wasn't rude, just not very chatty; closed off, even, but always nice. I smiled at their bad jokes and silly stories. This new person coming would be the same, I assumed.

By the time I had gotten dressed in a little black sundress, Harris was waiting for me in the den. She had made herself a cocktail and made me a smaller version of what she was drinking. Her face was determined but gentle. She took one look at me and could tell I was nervous. Hopefully she was right about what I was nervous about. Harris had been trying to get me to date for years now, to no avail. I had a sinking feeling that she was putting more into this Mr. Sparks than she should have.

"I thought you could use this." She raised my tinier glass and shook it. The ice clanged back and forth in the glass. Bourbon, just a shot full. She knew she shouldn't have opened the bottle, but I could see in her face that this was an emergency. I grabbed the glass and pushed my feelings about the bottle she had opened aside.

"I really shouldn't drink, you know. I do have to drive a very important person home today."

"Yes, yes, very important indeed." She rolled her eyes at me and took a swig from her glass. "So, I forgot to mention one thing about your new guest."

"Oh great, now you tell me…what?" I asked her.

"It seems the movie man has a dog." She answered with her eyes smashed together tightly, knowing how I felt about dogs.

"A dog," I answered. "Really, a dog? You know I don't like dogs in my house, Harris." I was ready to chew her out, but I saw that she was sorry.

"I know that, but it was a last-minute thing from his agent this morning. It's housebroken and everything. I am going to pick her up while you are gone getting him. She will be here when you get back."

"No, Harris. You can kennel the dog. I don't want another dog here. When Hermit died, I told you that was it. No more dogs. Besides, how can a person just forget to mention they have a dog? That's just…stupid." I sighed with irritation.

Hermit had been my old dog. He was a goofy-looking mixed breed that I had for years. He loved children and licking faces. Even though he was over a hundred pounds, he still thought he belonged on your lap and in your bed. I loved him anyway. When he died, it was hard. He was the last thing I really had left of… them. I swore to myself no more dogs.

"You aren't keeping the dog, Laina. She is just visiting. No dog—no money," she teased.

"Fine, but if it pees on my floors, it's out of here." I shot back the bourbon in the glass and grabbed my keys. It was time to go pick up Mr. Movietime.

"Good luck." Harris chimed behind me. "Macbeth will be here when you get back."

"Mc who?" I snapped.

"The dog, hello?"

"Oh, for pity's sake." I grumbled and headed out to my huge SUV in the garage. It was enormous, I knew it, but it was safe—safer than the other car I had had. Even if a car hit me, it wouldn't bother me in this massive thing. I turned the key, and the car shuddered under my feet and came to life.

Who in the hell names their dog Macbeth? What a goofy name (although I had named my dog Hermit). Well, I guess we can't all have normal dog names.

The meeting place had been decided weeks ago; I had gotten to choose it since I was from around here. We were meeting in a park with tons of children. No media would come there; at least, I couldn't imagine anyone coming there. The park was down behind James River High School near my house. It was named that because it was located close to the James River. People hiked, jogged, walked, canoed, and played volleyball there. Sometimes the nearby elementary school would have walking field trips to the river when the weather was nice. No one would be looking at us or paying any attention to us there. It took only a few minutes to drive there, while they were coming from the airport about thirty minutes away. I admit it was a little sneaky, but I hated driving for too long with someone I didn't know with me. I would like to be uncomfortable for as short a time as I could.

I was there early, on purpose. They had requested that if I saw anything strange, I would call them and find another meeting place, just in case word had gotten out, but there were just a few kids and moms here today. The ground was still wet from the earlier rain, and the sky held heavy black clouds with the threat of more rain. It was still early, too, only about eleven in the morning, so we should be safe from prying eyes. The big black town car pulled up slowly, almost hesitant. I raised my arm slowly and motioned him over to where I was parked, and he started toward me. The car parked and out the driver jumped, reaching for the back door, but it opened before he could get to it. I froze, unable to move as I watched him open the door all the way, kick one of his feet out, then two, and finally step out of the car.

He was taller than I imagined he would be. It's hard to judge height from pictures. As soon as he stood, he stretched his back and moaned a little, then threw a baseball cap over his rich brown hair and looked over to me. The rain started again, and the few people at the nearby playground screamed and jogged back to their cars for cover. The driver scurried around the car to get a few smaller bags from the trunk and then zoomed past me to put the bags in the back of my SUV. For a long moment, we stood there staring at each other in the rain. I was still frozen when he suddenly broke out a huge Hollywood smile. When I didn't react, his huge smile dissipated into a shyer, boyish grin. That more natural smile put me at ease, and my nerves were gone.

"Am I late then?" he asked with his Scottish accent. He was much more attractive in person, but I was still annoyed that he had tried to charm me immediately with his goofy movie-star smile. *Why couldn't he have just smiled like a normal person would?* I thought to myself.

"No, you're not late," I answered curtly.

He noticed my tone and his face fell slightly, but he walked up to me and stuck out his massive hand. "I'm Grayson Sparks. You can call me Gray though, only my mum calls me Grayson." He smiled his more endearing smile. I shook his hand. "And you must be the lady of the hour, Elaina Murphy. It's a pleasure to meet you." His eyes met mine naturally, and I noticed for the first time how incredibly beautiful they were. They were stunning—a light greenish grey and genuine—and I realized why he was so busy working in the movies.

"And you, Mr. Sparks—"

"Ah, please call me Gray." He waved his hand as if he were embarrassed.

"All right then, Gray, if you are ready, we can head off to the house so you can get settled in. I think your driver will be back around two this afternoon to take you to a final fitting, so I can make you lunch while you get unpacked." I spoke evenly with little emotion. I was trying to be professional. It was important to set a boundary early.

His smile fell even more as he seemed to realize this wasn't going to be buddy-buddy relationship. I was doing a job, not a friendship.

"I'm ready whenever you are, Ms. Murphy."

I didn't correct him like he had me. I didn't want the closeness here; I wanted to be more professional. He would call me Ms. Murphy, even though it reminded me of how old I was and the fact that he was gorgeous and he would forever see me as the "Electric Grandmother"; it made me want to vomit.

The drive to the house was very short, as I promised him, and I was incredibly relieved to get back home to my comfort zone.

"This is a big car for just one person," he stated.

"I like big cars," I answered.

"You must like to feel safe then, 'cause this thing is huge." His voice elevated in a humorous tone.

"Safety first," I muttered.

We pulled into the driveway. Relief came over me but then I heard the dog bark, and I was angry all over again. I had managed to forget all about the damn dog.

"Your house is beautiful. How long have you been here?" Before I could answer, he went on about the timbers along the front that made a triangle, then the absence of any neighbors. The house looked more or less like a huge log cabin, only it was no cabin. It had three floors of living space, four fireplaces, two huge decks in the rear, and a twenty by eighteen swimming pool in the back. Everything behind us was woods and would always be, since no one could build there, ever. It was about seven thousand square feet of house. I always thought it was too big even when we were building it, but sometimes it's too much fun to realize when you are in over your head.

"The house was built in 2003, so since then, I guess. Take a look around if you want. I'll take your bags in and get your dog some water."

He had gotten toward the backyard but suddenly turned and jogged back to me. "I can get my own things, Ms. Murphy. You don't have to do that. You don't have to be so serious either; just treat me like you would a friend, okay?" Then he hit me with those damn eyes and crooked smile again. I looked away quickly to grab my keys from the ignition.

"Suit yourself, Gray, I'll be in the kitchen making lunch. Is Cobb salad okay? Your agent sent me a list and that was one of the tops on it."

"Sure. Can I help?"

"No," I blurted then calmed it down a bit. "No, thank you, Mr. Sparks, I can manage. Please go get settled. Your room is on the first floor. Go on and take a tour."

He nodded, finally relinquishing control of the moment, and scuffled into the house. Moments later I heard barking and howling from Macbeth. I rolled my eyes and headed to the kitchen.

I watched Gray play with his dog outside by the pool, throwing the ball he had packed in his bag into the pool and watching Macbeth dive into the water to get it. It had been a long time since I had seen a man in my backyard playing with a dog. From the back, he even sort of looked like…

The door rushed open from the backyard, and there he was again, only this time standing in my kitchen, leaning against the doorway. I continued to work, but every time I looked up he was already looking at me, studying me. I would catch him looking just as he looked away with an embarrassed smile. I had prepared everything in advance for his salad, since I knew he liked them a lot. There was enough stuff here to make them all week if he wanted. Having someone watch me in the kitchen as I cooked was something that never bothered me. I had always loved cooking, and I was a little happy that I now had someone to cook for for a change. I quickly tossed the salad and placed it in front of him beside the linen napkin and fork. He looked up at me strangely, and I gazed back at him, not understanding his confused look.

"Is that not how you usually have it?" I asked, suddenly self-conscious, wondering what I had done wrong.

"Oh, no. The salad looks great, but—"

"But what? Oh, yeah, I forgot. What would you like to drink?" I felt my breathing come back down, realizing what I had forgotten.

"Umm, water is fine, but that's not it either."

"Well, what then?" I asked, a little sharper than I should have.

"Will you be joining me then?" he asked bashfully with his furrowed brow.

I hadn't expected this from him. I had always assumed that he—the big-time movie star—would want to be alone, that he wouldn't want to talk to me or spend any kind of time with me, and that he would definitely not want me to join him for lunch just twenty minutes after arriving. He was not turning out that way at all, first with all the smiles and conversation, and now he wanted me to eat with him too.

"Oh…well, would you like me to? I mean, you don't have to invite me to join you; it's okay really. I don't really like boiled egg whites either," I teased. This one weird request was too much even for me. According to Gray's agent, he only ate egg whites, no matter how they were prepared.

"What's wrong with egg whites? They're good," he answered, surprised.

"They're gross," I replied through my chuckle.

"I like them."

"Nobody *likes* egg whites, Mr. Sparks. They just say they do."

Having said that, he suddenly shrugged his shoulders awkwardly and flashed a look of disappointment as he grabbed his plate. He seemed to realize that I wasn't interested in eating with him, or I would have already made a plate for myself. I quickly tried to make up for my awful manners.

"Eating outside is lovely this time of year. Maybe I could join you for a bit out there, and we can talk about your stay here."

He smiled and seemed relieved that I had said something. "Please join me then, Ms. Murphy." He answered with a smile, but I could tell he was a little depleted as he walked to the table outside under the umbrella. I grabbed a huge bowl from the cabinet and filled it with water and opened the door. Macbeth, a cute little white boxer with two black ears and black nose, was lying on the patio, sunbathing. When she saw the water, she bounced up to her feet in one swift movement and began lapping up the cool water immediately. I went back inside, grabbed some water for myself, and headed out to socialize with someone I never thought I would ever talk to.

"It's weird, I know," he said suddenly after we had been sitting in silence for a few minutes. I was letting him eat without bothering him. We gave each other the smiling nod every so often. After ten minutes, I was starting to wonder what the hell I was doing out here.

"What's weird?" I asked.

"Living in this big house all alone." I looked at him strangely, not knowing what to make of his comment. "That's why I got Macbeth; she's my number one lady," he continued as he patted her loudly on the back. Macbeth turned over on her back and started kicking her feet out toward him. It was cute to see a man so in love with his dog. I hadn't realized that he must have brought Macbeth because he didn't want to be alone; that she was his companion. I immediately felt bad for slightly hating the dog earlier and was glad he never knew how annoyed I was about it.

"I know you didn't want her here. Your realtor friend told my agent this morning." My face must have been fire-engine red. "But I promise, she won't be any trouble. She'll be with me on set so you won't have to fuss with her while I'm gone."

I cleared my throat. "It's really not a problem; it's just that I haven't had a dog here since—"

"Hermit? Yeah, she mentioned that too. Goofy name, by the way." He chuckled.

"Oh, I see, and Macbeth is so much better?" I responded.

He nodded his head with a smile as he dove into his salad. "Fair enough then," he mumbled.

He chomped away for another few minutes, and I watched him closely. He had been taught proper manners. His napkin was in his lap with his other hand. He ate slowly and took normal-sized bites, not like other men do. He didn't speak with food in his mouth either. He was very pleasant to talk to and, of course, to look at, but that is as far as my fantasy went about him. He was way too pretty for me, and who in their right mind would want me—screwed-up old me. I was sure he wasn't interested in the least in me; he just wanted to break the ice and feel more comfortable. I assumed he was doing all this stuff to make himself feel more at ease.

"So what are the house rules?" he asked, lifting one eyebrow.

"Rules?" I asked, confused.

"Yeah, you know, like curfews, drinking, smoking, friends or no friends allowed—that kind of stuff."

I thought for a moment. "How about you ask me what you want to know and we'll go from there?" I offered. This wasn't an invitation for him to ask me anything; I assumed he would keep to the subject of house rules, but I was wrong about him, again.

"Do you drink?" he asked.

"Yes," I answered curtly.

"Smoke?"

I hesitated for a moment, unsure how to answer. "Sometimes, when I drink," I answered sheepishly.

"Me too." He laughed, putting me at ease. "Can I smoke in the house?"

"No."

He laughed louder at my response because I must have given him the look, the look that all women give men when they are very serious and not willing to negotiate.

"Okay." He chuckled. "No smoking in the house then. Drink of choice?"

"Martini, vodka, dirty, on the rocks." His eyebrow raised at that answer. "What?" I asked.

"Nothing. I just didn't think you were a hard liquor kinda girl, that's all. Next question. How old are you?"

I rolled my eyes. "That's not something I'm going to answer. But I do have an older sister and technically I will always be younger than her." We both had a chuckle and he continued on.

"Ever been married?"

I stared at him with narrowing eyes and tight mashed lips. My chest started to tighten as I caught my breath, but then I remembered that it wasn't his fault. He didn't know anything about me. He was just trying to be polite. I hadn't been asked anything like that in a while, nearly four years. He was staring back at me with a furrowed brow, probably trying to figure out what was wrong with me. I grabbed my wrist searching with my fingertips for my watch to twist it around so I could read it. It was past two in the afternoon, and my body went into panic mode.

"Oh, wow. You better get going. Your driver will be here any minute." He started grabbing his plate and glass of water. "No, no, I'll get that. You go ahead and get ready," I ordered. He smiled his indisputable smile and shuffled into the house, scratching Macbeth before he disappeared inside, still chewing on his last bite of food.

When the driver arrived, he handed me a booklet with Grayson's itinerary for the next month. He said nothing much and mostly just stared blankly at me. Back inside, Gray looked to be in deep thought. I'm sure he was trying to figure out why a person would do this, but it really wasn't any of his business. I ignored him and started cleaning the kitchen. I finally relaxed when he was out the door, asking him only what he wanted for dinner that night. He had requested grilled chicken and roasted vegetables. Perfect, I already had those things at the house.

When I went into his room I could smell his cologne in the air. He hadn't unpacked his little bags from the plane, and Macbeth was asleep on her doggy bed he must have brought. His dirty clothes were laid out on the bed, so I grabbed them and took them to the washer to clean them. Before throwing his shirt in, I paused to smell the collar. I don't know why I did that.

When he returned home again, I was already preparing the veggies, chopping them up and throwing them onto the baking sheet. I had made a dip with some sliced celery and peppers to munch on while I cooked.

"It smells great," he said.

I paused and smirked. "I haven't started cooking yet," I answered, confused.

"I love the smell of peppers and onions, raw or cooked," he explained.

"Oh." I smiled and kept chopping.

When I turned around to wash the onion smell from my hands, I heard the cabinet door open and then close. I started rubbing my hands together under the warm water of the faucet. The soap was slimy in my hands. I heard two glasses clanging against each other and then the ice dispenser going for each glass. I spun around to see him making two drinks. When he saw me he froze, putting his hands up.

"You said, martini, dirty, on the rocks, right?"

I put down my chef's knife and peered over at him. "I don't know what you think this is, but I—"

"I think this is two very uncomfortable people trying to get more comfortable, that's all." He smiled again, and my heart skipped a little. "I need a drink. It's been a long day, and I thought you might want one too."

My eyes didn't ease up though. I stared back at him evenly, my eyes narrowed tighter. He chuckled and his lips pulled up to one side. He was having fun and enjoying himself.

"I promise, that's all. Can we just have a meal together and talk and get to know each other a bit. I think it would make this a little easier."

Suddenly I realized that I had already eaten and this was his dinner, not mine. "Umm, Grayson, I already ate earlier. I'm sorry. I just didn't know when you would be back, so I ate when I fed Macbeth."

The look of disappointment that came over his face again was horrible. I tried to fix the uncomfortable air as fast as I could. "But you've made me a drink, so I guess we can share this dip and veggies while I drink my martini, if that's okay?" I tried to smile warmly as best as I could. I'm pretty sure I failed miserably.

This seemed to ease his displeasure a bit. We talked for a while about his day and what his meeting was about, just the average and expected small talk. It was more natural tonight than it had been earlier in the day. As I turned the grill on, he stood to the side with his hand covering his mouth. I suspect he was interested to see if I knew what I was doing. "You know, I can cook my own food, Ms. Murphy."

"I'm sure you can, Gray, but this is my job, remember?"

He said nothing, only nodded his head, and I walked back to put the veggies in the oven.

"So, you said something today that made me think. You probably need a schedule from *me*. I cook breakfast at eight thirty every morning; unless you need to eat earlier than that, just let me know. I will have lunch ready for you by twelve most days, if you're here, but if you are hungry you can help yourself to anything in the pantry or fridge. If you are not here for lunch, well, I guess I could pack you something if you wanted. Dinner is usually at seven, and I usually have a cocktail every night before then."

"Sounds simple enough, Ms. Murphy," he answered, grinning at me again. It reminded me of the other thing I wanted to mention to him. Not really a house rule but a statement.

I sighed and started again, "I know that you want us to be friends and that it sounds more normal to try to be friends, but I prefer not to be. I don't know you and you don't know me, so let's not pretend that we want to really know each other." When I turned around, he was sitting at the island looking at me, crunching down on a pepper. He was hurt, I could see that, but he simply nodded his head and let it go. I immediately hated myself for saying anything. He hid his feelings better after that.

"Whatever you prefer, Ms. Murphy, he answered softly.

Chapter 4

The Month of May

For the first week he was with me, it seemed like we were always together with the awkward silence that built up more and more every day. I tried to stay busy and be as accommodating as I could, but he never stopped trying to get me to talk. He would make a drink every night when he came through the door. We would chitchat with the same weirdness as a first date, and then once his dinner was ready, I would serve it to him and retreat back to my chores or my bedroom. There wasn't anywhere else I could run to; he was everywhere. His personality filled the room like perfume and intoxicated me over and over. I began to look forward to him coming home every day even though I knew I shouldn't. My mood seemed to lighten up when he was in the house, whether I was in the same room with him or not. It didn't matter; I knew he was there, only feet away. He smiled all the time and told lots of jokes, most of them dirty jokes, but I liked them and they made me laugh. He was much more comfortable with me than I was with him. Sometimes I would catch him staring at me with the strangest look on his face. I never asked him what he was thinking for fear he would tell me about some blond beauty he was working with on the set every day. I didn't hold out any sort of ridiculous hope that he was interested in me. I knew who I was and what I looked like. I was an average person with an average life with very little expectations left in me.

One day, when I came home from grocery shopping, I found him already home as I followed the sound of his singing into the kitchen. He was cooking…dinner…for two. I was amazed, not that he was cooking, but that he had managed to find something to cook since we had no food in the house. He hummed happily as I stood in the doorway, still undetected. My drink was on the island, waiting for me—martini, dirty, on the rocks. When I walked into the kitchen, his eyes flitted up to see me standing with groceries. When he saw the bags in my hands, he immediately grabbed them from me and set them on the counter, then started out to the car to get the rest. That didn't surprise me either; he was a gentleman and had been since he got here. He had been sneaking me help all week. For three nights in a row, his dinner plate was cleaned and tucked in the dishwasher before I could shuffle to the kitchen to clean. He never left a mess and even cleaned out the sink after brushing his teeth. What had me off kilter was the fact that he was cooking a dinner for two, which meant him and me. There was no one else here or coming over as far as I knew. Maybe it was for someone else. I tried to convince myself that it was for him and some date. When he came back in, he looked sheepish as I stared at the spread he was fixing—lobster and filet mignon with green salad and grilled peppers. This was one of his favorite dinners, I knew, because he had told me days ago during some distant conversation we had had over cocktails by the pool. It had become our usual to have drinks while I cooked his dinner. The only difference for me had been that he was with me; this was something I did every day before he came here, and would do again when he would move back to California.

"What is all this?" I asked in an annoyed and slightly irritated tone. Whatever he was doing, I was going to have to clean it up later. It didn't bother me, cleaning, but I wanted him to think it did. I knew I was playing a dangerous game, but something inside of me let it keep going.

"Now, don't get angry. I just wanted to make you dinner for a change. I can eat mine outside and you can eat inside, but I'd much rather we ate together. I know it's last minute and you may have plans—"

"I don't have any plans," I answered quickly.

He smiled, cocking his head to one side like a curious animal, "Well then, would you mind sharing a meal with me?" he asked finally.

I didn't know what to say. It was a shock that he did all this. I knew it was wrong to say yes, but he had gone to so much trouble. How could I say no to that smile, those eyes? That's what I was afraid of.

I sighed a long exasperated sigh from being worn down and answered, "Well, I am hungry, and it does look good. When do we eat?" I knew enough to know when I'd been beaten.

I went upstairs, with the drink Gray had insisted I take with me, to have a shower and change clothes. He had promised that I had all the time in the world to get ready and comfortable. I rinsed in the shower without washing my hair, just enough to wash away the heat from the day. I pulled my hair back in a loose bun, pulled on some ripped-up jean shorts and an old concert T-shirt and headed downstairs. If I was gonna get roped into having dinner with this guy then I refused to look my best.

He was finishing up the peppers for the grill when I came back down, and the way he worked his chef's knife across the round vegetables told me he knew what he was doing in the kitchen. I was in a trance while watching his hands move over the pepper and hold it just right before slicing into it with the razor edge. Then my eyes moved from his hands to his forearms around to his arms, studying the bands of muscles that worked as he moved the baking sheet beside the pile of green and red peppers. I turned my direction to his shoulders and around his neck, then his face. His face was more than handsome—it was beautiful. His skin was tan from the West Coast sun, which made his hazel-grey eyes stand out even more. His chin and jaw were covered with tiny bristles of hair. Usually he was clean shaven; he must have been growing it out for the movie he had begun filming. I didn't care; it made no difference to me. He was nice to look at but I could also tell he knew a lot more than just cooking in a kitchen. I assumed he was dangerous, maybe even predatory. I had known men like him in my lifetime. Men like this were simply not equipped to be anything more than a good time and a quick good-bye. I'm sure he had broken more than a few hearts in his lifetime; and mine, if I let him, was no exception. But the view, for now, was more than enough for me.

Without looking up from his chopping, he spoke. "I hope you don't mind"—he motioned his knife toward the back of the house—"I was sorta hoping you would say yes to dinner, so it's all set up out back. If that's okay." When I glanced back at him, his expression looked unsure as he studied my face searching for any sign of annoyance. I simply nodded and went to the bar to refresh my drink. Without even thinking, I grabbed his empty glass and poured him another Jack and water. He tried to hide his smile but couldn't; I guessed that it pleased him to see me being social and more comfortable. I guessed that he felt he had finally won me over, but he was wrong.

"Thank you," he said in a surprised tone.

"You're welcome, Gray." I answered flatly.

"So, I guess you're wondering why I'm even here this early?"

I have to admit I was a little curious. He had been getting in around ten every night for the past two days since shooting had actually begun. I lowered my gaze at him and arched an eyebrow, urging him to continue. He smiled a crooked smile, pleased that I was willing to chat.

"Well, the day was a total bust." He continued with his thick accent. The word *bust* sounded closer to the word *boast*. "Everything seemed to go wrong. Sometimes I wonder if this director knows what he's doing. And that woman they've got me working with, Cody Ramsy, that woman needs to pull that long pole out from her arse."

I laughed under my hand for a minute, and he looked up at me, surprised that I was laughing and unable to figure out what I found so funny. His brow furrowed slightly.

"Her what?" I asked.

"Oh, sorry, my accent gets a little thicker when I talk fast." He apologized but laughed with me. He tried to talk slower, but it didn't help much with his accent; I was glad for that. His accent was sexy, no doubt about that. Talking with Grayson Sparks was an experience. His hands were animated along with his eyes. Every now and then, his eyes seemed to light up during his stories. I asked him about acting and how he had gotten into it. He admitted that he had fallen into acting and that it really wasn't as fun as it used to be. He talked for a while about how he didn't even find himself that talented, and he was pretty sure he had been successful for his backside and not his acting chops. He gazed longingly toward the woods as we sat outside by the pool. I could see that he wasn't fishing for a compliment but that he actually thought of himself that way. I immediately felt protective of his feelings for some reason.

"That's ridiculous; you're a great actor, Gray." This comment shocked him completely, and I thoroughly enjoyed watching him squirm in his seat. He lit a cigarette and turned to me, mystified, while clanging the ice in his glass around. His lips pulled to one side and he scratched his nose with his thumbnail.

"You've seen my work then?"

I froze for a moment, trying to figure a way out of this topic. *He thinks I have been watching his movies, or that I'm a fan. How embarrassing.* I didn't know what to do or say. A few more seconds and he would think I was some mental idiot, so I decided to play it cool. "Of course, hasn't everybody?" I answered emphatically.

He raised an eyebrow as his thought engine turned over and over. When he was deep in thought like this, it made me nervous like a little girl again. I found myself hanging on for dear life, waiting to see what he would say next. I felt like an idiot—like a class A idiot. This time, my body seemed to lean in closer with my mind. I realized the closeness of our faces and pulled away. He noticed this, of course, and shook his head with a smile.

"So, let's hear it then?"

"Hear what?" I asked, confused and slightly flushed.

"What have you seen of my movies?"

"Oh, no. I'm not going there, come on…" I begged.

"You said you had seen some of my work, right? Tell me then, what have you seen?"

"I'd rather not." I started to play with my hair more, trying to find something else to concentrate on. I wished I could pull it over my face and run away.

"Oh come on, you can tell me. Unless…you were lying just then?" One of his eyebrows popped up, and he turned those gorgeous eyes on me again. I was in a daze, just for a second, before I started to get angry.

"I don't lie, Grayson," I snapped.

"Then tell me," he challenged in a playful manner. His face fell slightly when I shook my head no at him. "Oh great, it's one of my old movies, right? The ones that really concentrated more on me arse than me acting. The ones that really sucked, by the way!" He was laughing, but I was still staring down at the ground twirling my hair, wishing I could disappear. He saw my face and quickly stopped pressuring for an answer. "I'm sorry, I was just curious." He got up to check the steaks, and I felt my stomach drop. *Just tell him, what's the big deal?* He was getting farther and farther away, and as the distance grew I felt worse and worse. Every time he tried to get to know me in a genuine way, I shut down. I could hear him huffing and sighing, obviously frustrated with me.

"Okay," I shouted from across the patio. He stuck his head from around the grill to make sure I had really said something at all. "It was *Break of Day*, all right? That's the one I saw."

"Really? That was one of the good ones, I thought," he answered, looking pleased.

"Me too." I smiled at him as nicely as I could. It had been a romance flick that I dragged *him* to.

When he came back around to sit, I could feel him watching me again. Why did he do that? I was nothing special, and it really made me uncomfortable. As he sat down, my eyes leveled at him again. His brows rose in fear.

"What?" he asked, not knowing what he had done wrong.

"Why do you do that?" I asked.

"Do what, Ms. Murphy?" he questioned.

"Study me like that. Why do you do it? Why are you trying to be friends with me anyway?"

"Wow!" he answered.

"What?" I growled.

"If I tell you the truth, are you gonna hit me or eat me head off?"

I laughed briefly then tightened my lips again. "I don't know."

"Hmm, well, let's see. I probably look at you so much because you are…umm…stunning. I obviously don't seem to have much of a choice either, for that matter. I want to be your friend because you seem like a clever woman and someone that I want to know better. You're a great cook and you make a mean bed, and when you smile your whole face seems to light up. I wish you would smile more, because it's truly a sight to see. But I think the question should be 'why wouldn't I look at you?'"

His words came out fast and there was a lot of accent mixed up into words that were hard to get, but I knew what he was saying. I wasn't quite sure what to say. He thought I was stunning? Why me? Why not some other young, gorgeous girl? I looked back at him with red cheeks and realized that he was waiting for me to say something.

"Thank you." That was all I could muster.

He smiled at me, "You are very welcome"—his brow pulled together again in deep thought—"although you don't seem to believe that I find you attractive, and I can't figure why."

"For someone who was educated, you seem very dense sometimes," I attacked.

He laughed. "Thanks for that, but I still don't get what you mean."

"You date girls from Hollywood; I'm just a simple southern girl from Richmond, Virginia. You date girls in their early twenties; I'm getting closer and closer to my mid-thirties every day. You are way out of my league, truthfully. And me, well, I missed your league altogether years ago."

"I guess I date girls that I'm around," he explained softly.

"Exactly. Women like me don't get noticed by men like you," I told him.

He was silent and still while what I said sank in. His eyes were focused on his thumbs as he twined and untwined his hands together. I thought for sure I had blown it. I must look crazy for sure now. But he stood up and walked over to me, shoving one of his hands into his jeans pocket, leaving the other hand free. I watched his hands because I didn't have the courage to look at his face. He knelt down in front of me and gently lifted my chin with his free hand. He was touching me and part of me was terrified but another part of me, a deeper part, couldn't wait to see what he would do next. When I looked into his eyes, I was done for. I knew that look; it had been four years, but I remembered it. Desire and need were always a clear signal that I never misunderstood, but before I could turn away, he spoke, "You have no idea just how perfect you are, do you?" His eyes were liquid fire and filled with determination. "You are beautiful." I had no choice but to get lost in his eyes, and then without much warning, he pressed his lips to mine very gently. I could taste the bourbon and salt of his mouth. He moved closer as his lips moved over mine and I could feel his warmth. His hand moved from my chin and cupped my jaw; his fingers gave the slightest pressure to my jaw, urging me closer to him. His lips parted mine, gently, and then I could feel his warm tongue sliding across my bottom lip. When I responded with my mouth and pressed my body closer to him, he gently pulled me from the couch and down on his lap. His hands slid up my back under my shirt, caressing my skin with his fingertips. The kiss lasted far too long, but I couldn't gather the strength to pull away just yet. His touch was warm and tender, and his lips were soft and endearing. I felt the familiar tender heat glide over my body like a slow fire burning. I wrapped my arms around his neck and wrapped my legs around his waist tighter.

It wasn't until Macbeth started barking that I shot out of my Grayson coma. Both our lips froze, and I pushed back away from him so that I could see into his eyes. The desire and the urge were still there, but when he saw my face his expression changed. My lips tightened together and I could feel the tears coming from somewhere I had kept hidden for years. His eyes turned apologetic and he opened his mouth to say something, but I pressed my finger to his parted lips. He waited for me to speak, still hopeful that I would say what he wanted to hear.

"Don't do that." The words whispered from my mouth in a rush, and they were all I could say to him. I stood up and picked up my empty glass as the front doorbell rang. As I walked back through the house, I saw him sitting on the couch with his head in his hands.

Harris stood at the door, tapping her fingers on the doorframe. I gazed back at her and suddenly picked up on the fact that she was annoyed with me.

I shrugged my shoulders. "What's with you?"

"What's with me? What's with *you*. Where the hell have you been?"

"Here, working." I answered, looking at her like she was crazy. I shrugged my shoulders again. "What?"

"So you're too busy to call your best friend and tell her the Grayson gossip?"

I heard the back door open and close behind me, and my head turned to see the blurry sight of him in my peripheral vision.

"It's really not a good time, Harris, really. Tomorrow?" I asked. "There's really nothing to tell anyway." I promised.

"Oh my God, is that him?" she whispered, almost snarling, trying to see past me and get a good look.

"Harris, please, not tonight. How about I cook out tomorrow and you can come and meet him then, if he says it's okay."

She stopped fumbling and rolled her eyes, "Fine, Laina, but you can't keep him to yourself forever, you know. It's been nearly two weeks already. What's with the red cheeks?" she teased.

"Tomorrow, Harris. Good night." She stuck her tongue out at me and turned and walked down the stone stairs back to her car. I shut the door and went straight to the kitchen where he was waiting.

"I'm so sorry, Ms. Murp...ahh, bollocks, I'm gonna call you by your first name, all right?" He stood there looking at me, searching for a feeling or an emotion to go with. "Elaina, I don't know what got into me, I just couldn't help myself."

Suddenly I felt my temper flaring up, trying to explode. "You should really try harder! I'm a married woman! You can't just kiss people like that whenever you want to. There are rules! This isn't some Hollywood party!" I stormed off and headed upstairs. As I climbed the last few steps I realized what I had said and sighed and froze. *I guess the cat's out of the bag.* I turned around to see him standing at the bottom of the stairs with his mouth hanging open. He looked completely confused and caught off guard.

I threw my hands up in the air. "Yes, I was married. I'm not anymore. Sorry if I confused you. I'm just upset." I turned back to the stairs.

"Hey, wait a minute! That's it? That's all? 'I was married but I'm not anymore?' What does that mean? If you aren't married anymore, then why can't I kiss you?"

My brow furrowed. His voice was hurt and desperate. I felt bad for yelling at him. I had, after all, kissed him back. I mashed my lips together and shook my head angrily. "What do you want from me?" I begged.

"I just want to get to know you, that's all. You excite me and yes, I'm attracted to you; and if the truth be known, I can't wait to get back here every day just so I can see you. So yes, getting to know you is necessary!" he shouted.

I suddenly felt bad for him. "You don't want to know me, Gray," I whispered while shaking my head.

"Jesus! What did he do to you? What kind of hell did he put you through?"

"What?" I gasped.

"The guy that ruined you for everyone else. The guy that took out your heart and tore it to pieces. That guy Ms. Mur…Elaina!" he fumbled out.

"That's not fair!" I shouted, getting angry and territorial.

"Oh no? I know you like me too! I know that you wanted to kiss me as much as I wanted to kiss you! How's *that* for fair? I'm on to you Elaina, and don't think for a second I don't know how you feel now, because I just felt it back there. I felt you and it felt great! It was the best feeling I've had in a long time!" He lowered his head and softened his voice. "But I'll be respectful. I won't ever kiss you again. I'll stay away and keep my distance." He was quiet for a while as he gathered his thoughts. "But I won't deny that I like you, that I think you are probably perfect for me in every way. You are like no other woman I have ever met, and I won't deny that you scare the hell out of me because you make me feel like myself again." He added much more calmly, "Good night, Elaina."

That night, I cried for the first time in a long time. I held my bedside picture close to my heart. The shivers came all over my body, remembering them, wishing they were here. I was sad because I was alone. I was sad because I knew I really liked him too. I was sad that I was too scared to even try, too scared to take a risk with my heart that I had tried so desperately to put back together again. I was too chicken to admit something so horrible. I guess the time had finally come. It was time for me to let someone into my deep and dark cave of pain and hope they didn't turn and run away.

He had been here only two weeks, and I knew I was attracted to him and he was attracted to me; the kiss we shared was proof of that. I knew we liked each other. I knew it would only get harder to stay away from each other; and that kiss, that was something else. Just thinking about it could take up a whole day; the way my body felt when my lips touched his was incredibly strong and undeniable. A jolt of excitement and newness had rushed into my body with his touch. Gray was a great kisser, and the way his hands grazed my skin left goose bumps all over my body. He was also a good person and always a gentleman and courteous. He made me laugh more in the past two weeks than I had in the last four years.

Every day was a struggle to do the one thing I said I would do from the beginning—stay away. I kept very busy and cooked and cleaned away the days. At night I kept a distance and so did he, but the way he looked at me didn't change. He was neither angry nor happy but a numb in between. He mostly read his script and played his guitar outside at night while I cooked. I would listen to him strumming along, and it turns out he was good at that, too, no surprise there.

By the end of the second week of May, I was running out of steam. His stares and smiles kept coming. When we did talk, it was about the movie he was shooting. He didn't try to get close but I could still feel his eyes on me all the time.

The cookout with Harris never happened, I had decided it was a bad idea, but I did meet her for lunch a few times. She was always pushing me for information, but I felt it was wrong to discuss something so private. In many ways, I was having a weird and warped relationship with Gray, but I couldn't put my finger on just what kind of a relationship it was. We cooked together, ate together, drank together, cleaned the kitchen together, and wanted each other but tried to stay as far away from each other as we could. Harris was no help either with all her silly fantasies. It was rather ridiculous, some of the things she would come up with. I told her nothing. During one of our lunches she actually was helpful, and it turned out she had given me the piece of advice that would forever change my life.

"So your new 'friend'"—she held up her fingers in quotation marks—"Does he know about…you know?" she asked.

"No. Why? Why would I tell him that?" I answered.

"Well, you guys see each other every day, and you are not the most forthcoming person in the world, Laina."

"So? What's it to him?" I asked, getting slightly flushed in the face. I could feel the blood rushing to my cheeks.

"He might surprise you," she encouraged.

I said nothing and only narrowed my eyes at her.

"You should tell him." She huffed, throwing her arms into the air in annoyance. "Jesus, tell somebody that you're hurting and that what happened sucked, and you will never be the same again. You won't talk to me or Mandy. Maybe you should try and talk to him," she growled.

I waited for her to calm down. I knew I was difficult—beyond difficult—but she had been patient with me for so long. I felt like I owed it to her to listen to what she was saying, even if I hated her saying things like this.

"Is that all you have to say about it?" I teased, trying to make her smile.

"I won't say anything else about it, I promise. Not today anyway."

"Thanks." I sighed and pretended to sweep my forehead free of fake beads of sweat. Harris rolled her eyes and I could tell she wasn't done. "Okay, Harris, just say what you want to say; you will eventually anyway." I smirked.

Her eyes cast down as she rolled her fingers against her fork and knife. "It's just that sometimes…I don't think you see what other people see when you look in the mirror. I don't even think that you ever really see yourself at all. I just wish you could see what everybody else sees."

"I do see myself," I snapped. "I'm a woman in her thirties, struggling with life and trying to get on with it. End of story." I answered.

"You are such a fool, a class-A moron. Nobody's story is ever over till it's over," she replied with deep sarcasm.

"Thanks," I chuckled.

~~~~~~~~~

Driving home, I realized she may be right, maybe I should tell him. I tried to go back to the months afterwards; tried to conjure up the pain and the mourning that seemed to last forever. I spoke to no one and hid away in my room. I was all alone and I hated it. I despised the distance I kept everyone at. I wasn't living any kind of life at all, it was obvious. I slammed my hand on the steering wheel, willing back the tears. It was time to talk, even though I was going to hate every minute of it. He needed to know why I was so angry and hurt. I made my plans and preparations and waited for him at home.

When I had heard him coming in, I had frozen on the stairs and hadn't moved yet. All my body allowed me to do was slide down and sit at the foot of the stairs. He wasn't expecting to see me awake when he got home that night. It was a late night of shooting and it was coming up on one in the morning, but when he saw me, he smiled his perfect smile, and poured a drink for me and one for him.

"What's going on, Ms. Murphy?" he asked as he slid in beside me on the hard wooden stairs.

I turned to him so I could look him in the eyes and saw the worry on his face. It may have been confusion; it didn't matter because once our eyes locked on each other, I felt a familiar shudder and a deep burn. I closed my eyes so that I could concentrate better. It didn't do much to calm my nerves, so I decided to open my eyes and muddle through the most awkward conversation I would probably ever have. When I opened my eyes, he was still there, looking like the movie star he was. I sighed loudly and reminded myself to focus.

"I owe you an apology for my behavior. I know it's not your fault because you don't know certain things about me. So for being impatient and for totally overreacting, I am sorry, Gray."

He nodded his head. "Apology accepted, Ms. Murphy, although it wasn't necessary."

"There is something I need to show you, it's in my room." His eyes suddenly bulged in shock and I chuckled. "Not that. It's a picture that I think you need to see." I stood up and took his larger hand in mine and lead him up the stairs. I opened my bedroom door and turned on the light. The picture sat upright on my bedside table where it had for four years now. I picked it up and brushed off the new dust that had managed to collect on it in one day and handed it to him.

Grayson focused on the picture for a long time, and then as he seemed to get what I was showing him, his eyes softened and then started to water, but he quickly rubbed them and the moisture was gone.

"That's a…beautiful family. Where are they, Elaina?"

"You are the first person who has ever asked me that, most people already know the story." I answered as I forced a smile.

"What happened?" he asked and then sat on the bed, pulling me down to sit next to him. "It's okay, you know. I promise, I won't…run away."

"I was married in 1998. We were happy as hell; too happy, I guess. We bought a little house, fixed it up, and then saved our money and bought the land that this house rests on now. We couldn't afford to build anything on it right away so we waited, saved our money, and took our time. In 2003, our daughter was born. The next year, we finally came up with the money to build our dream home. We were set to move in April 2005, but we never did. I wanted to take John and Georgia out for a celebratory dinner since the house was finally almost done, and we were set to move in just a few weeks. I should have taken the car in to get it looked at, since the car's warning lights had been flashing on and off and acting funny for a few days, but John promised he would take it in the next day."

I could still clearly see Georgia fanning herself with paper paint samples and having to touch each piece of fabric we used for her bed and curtains. The memory made me smile but with the happy came the pain. I was happy, because I could still remember those moments so vividly. The pain was only having my memories to hold on to now.

"Georgia was so excited about her new room in the new house! It was pretty amazing, actually. It took me forever to get everything just right for her. She was my only child and would always be because of complications I had giving birth to her. I had to have an emergency C-section and then they couldn't stop the bleeding. It all happened so fast. John was so scared that he would lose me, he gave the doctors permission to take my uterus, and that was that."

I slapped my hands down on my legs and sighed. "But we had Georgia—sweet, little, perfect, brown-eyed Georgia. I can see her chocolate-colored curls falling down around her face." I stopped, suddenly feeling the tears choking me. I took a deep breath and continued without looking at Gray. "John and I loved her as much as we could, and we tried to be the best parents for her. We were planning on adopting when she turned three. We wanted a lot of kids, and just because I couldn't give birth to anymore didn't mean we wouldn't have our large family. That was the plan, you know, the plan that never played out."

As I realized I was nearing the harder part of my past my hands started to shake. I hadn't told this story for a long time, but I had never told Gray. He had no idea what had happened and the idea that he had somehow misconstrued my high and unbreakable walls with something my husband might have done to me was more painful. My husband had been a remarkable man, and it wasn't his fault that he was gone.

"On the way back from dinner, the car started acting funny. I was driving so I tried to see which light was coming on. I remember being annoyed with John that he still hadn't taken the car to get fixed. I was annoyed that he hadn't bought me the new car he had promised months before. I was so stupid. When I looked down at the light, I felt John's hand on the wheel suddenly, jerking it to the right forcefully. When I looked back to the road, I saw why he had. A huge black Hummer had wandered over to our lane and nearly hit us. Before I got over the shock of what John had done, I realized the car was still coming over toward us, fast. We were going about seventy miles an hour down 288; it was the regular speed limit. I mean, everyone drove that fast."

As the moment of impact approached my hands clasped together and tightened as if I was back in that damn car again. My nails dug into my skin and the pain distracted me long enough to continue.

"When the car slammed into us, I heard Georgia scream, then John shouting to her, 'It's okay, baby!' But…it wasn't…okay. The car flipped after impact, crossing over the road parallel to us. I don't remember much after the first time the car slammed into the ground. I don't remember hearing the crash or being hit or even slamming to the ground seconds later. I just remember their scared voices."

I stopped talking at that point and tried to will the tears away. I had gotten so very good at pushing them away. The images still came back in flashes for me every now and then. The screaming and the sound of twisting metal would haunt me in my dreams.

"When I woke up in intensive care and saw my sister, Mandy, sitting next to me, I knew it wasn't good. Her hand wasn't the one I wanted or needed. Her being there instead of John told me he was hurt and unable to be with me."

I blew out another deep gulp of air. "I never imagined that it would be as bad as it was, though. They both died from the accident. John…suffered sever trauma and died the next morning, but my Georgia held on for three days before slipping away in the ICU in the middle of the night, while I slept. She never woke up, but Mandy was there when she died. I wasn't."

My body shivered automatically, and I felt Gray's arm wind around me and tighten. "When I first came home, I couldn't stop hearing Georgia screaming. It just played over and over in my mind. That was the last noise I heard her make. It just wasn't fair— none of it was. I mean, children aren't supposed to die. Everyone tried to get me to sell this house; everyone except Harris. The day I met her I was supposed to be meeting an interested buyer, but there was something about her that convinced me to pretend like I didn't see the man when he walked into the bar. That was that. I moved in a few weeks later and I've been here ever since. Harris reminded me today that I needed to trust people again and be honest with you."

"She sounds like a good friend," he added in a softer tone.

I took another deep breath. "Her room is just as it was supposed to be. I never changed it. I have never let anyone see it, ever. I haven't been in there since the day I moved in, but I was thinking, now that I'm telling you this, maybe it's time to see it again. So, would you like to see Georgia's room with me?"

Gray was taken off guard. "Are you sure?"

"One hundred percent."

He took my face in his hand and wiped the tear away from my cheek with his thumb. "I'd be honored, Elaina."

When I opened the door, it was a shock at first. The room was dark and lifeless. Her white four-poster bed was in the center of the room, with a white netting cascading down from the ceiling and around the bed. I flicked the lights on and then the lavender walls woke up to brighten the room. Behind the head of the bed and hanging from the wall were white painted letters that spelled her name. The room was huge, bigger than I remembered. Some of her toys were set in the corner that I hadn't been able to part with when I moved in. The worse part came when I spotted her favorite stuffed animal on the daisy-printed comforter that laid across her princess bed. It was a monkey but flat, not fluffy. So she could cuddle it. It was worn and tattered, but I knew why the sight of it upset me so much—I knew that her scent was probably still all over it. I crossed the room as Gray carefully followed, and I snatched up the tan monkey. I hesitated for a moment and shot Gray a look. Somehow, he knew what I was asking. *Do I dare?* He shrugged his shoulders and his eyes turned sympathetic. I lifted it to my nose and immediately I could smell the dust and the age of the toy, but then I caught the faint scent of her soap, and her fruity shampoo that she loved so much. I felt my legs shaking, and I felt Gray's hand grab my arm to steady me.

"Laina? You okay?" he whispered.

"I can still smell her, see."

He obliged me and sniffed the toy with his eyes closed. When he caught the smell, his eyes opened, and he smiled. For the first time in a long time, I felt the weight of it all; the loss and the pain somehow were still there. The feelings had been hibernating inside of me for four years. As much as I missed John, I seemed to miss Georgia even more. John had lived a life—he had seen the beach, the sea, been on a plane and traveled, found love, become a husband and a father, and lived a great life. Georgia never got to do anything with her life. The joy of her life had been mine and

John's, but now it was mine alone; I was the only part of her left. Then I realized that I had not been honoring her life at all—I had been wasting mine. John would want me to live and love again—to see the things he never saw, to do the things he never did. Hiding wasn't something he would like at all, and that's what I was doing—hiding from everyone: my old friends, any thought of love or sex. I was a shell; a hermit. I felt a rush of adrenaline spark through my body.

"That's it," I whispered as I put the monkey back on the bed gently, as if it were a baby bird.

"I don't follow," Grayson answered.

"Come on." I motioned with my hand to leave her room. He followed me downstairs and out the back door and stood watching me in complete confusion.

"Do you swim?" I asked.

"Of course."

"Well, then…what are you waiting for?" I asked excitedly. I ripped my shirt over my head and pulled my shorts down and kicked them over to the lounge chair. I unhooked my bra and scooted my panties down so I could kick them over with my other clothes. The heat felt so sweet over my naked body. I ran and jumped into the pool with a scream. The water hit my skin like ice, but it was refreshing in the heat of the night air. I surfaced and smoothed back my hair. I found him still standing there with his jaw hanging wide open. "You coming?" I asked breathlessly.

He smiled back at me with his eyes still bugging out of his head. He still wasn't sure if I was insane or not. He stripped down to his boxer shorts but stopped short. His hesitation and shyness caused him to burst into laughter.

"Should I turn around? I know I'm not the first to see *it*, Grayson," I teased, but when he stood motionless, I turned around and waited with my arms resting on the side of the pool. I heard and felt the splash a few seconds later. When I turned around, he was treading in the water looking at me like he had been since he got here. He was bewildered but unable to turn away.

"What?" I asked.

"Are you a little cuckoo then?" he asked, teasing me again as his eyes gazed over my body through the water.

I thought for a moment about that question. I caught his eyes admiring my body and smiled. I knew I was more than a little cuckoo. "I guess I am." I laughed.

He made his way over to me from across the pool, his eyes intent on me the whole time. It was the same look he had given me right before he had kissed me a few days ago. I could feel something burning down through my body, almost like an aching desire and need. It had been years since I had any physical contact with another man. He came right up to me but didn't touch me. With his eyes, he was already touching me, kissing me, loving me.

I looked at him and cocked one eyebrow up. "What are you waiting for, Grayson? Do you want an invitation?" I chuckled.

"Just following orders," he explained with a smile. "You told me not to kiss you again, remember? I always do what I'm told." He was very cool until I moved closer to him this time. When I took the initiative, his eyes widened.

I wound my hands around his neck and pulled myself right up to his naked body. He grinned a devilish grin and chuckled, "I think you are about to break the rules, Ms. Murphy."

"Somebody's got to," I whispered. My lips gently touched his. My hands moved down his back and pressed him to me even further. His arms came around me as his lips pressed down on mine more forcefully than they had with the first kiss.

He pulled me over to the wall where he made love to me for the first time. He was so intuitive that I could have wept with pure satisfaction. There was nothing he wouldn't do, no unsaid instruction he would not take. He aimed to please me, and I tried as hard as I could to please him back. Everything felt right, finally.

I never thought of my sweet John once that night. He had given me his gift already, his love. I knew now no matter what I did, or whom I loved from hereon, he would be there. Without him I could have never recognized a feeling like this. I tried not to think about tomorrow and only tried to think of Gray and wanting him more and more every time he touched me or grazed his lips across my throat.

Chapter 5

When I woke up the next morning, I knew right away I was not in my bed. Well, I was, but not the guest bed where I was supposed to be. I could feel Gray's fingertips gliding up and down my spine. Every so often he would stop and draw circles softly. His hands were more rugged than I thought they would be. I guess I figured he was manicured, buffed and polished on a regular basis. Not so. He looked like a real man, he loved like a real man, and he felt like a real man. I sighed out loud and turned over, letting the sheets fall away, exposing my breasts to the dimly lit room. Gray's hands drifted up past my chest to my chin, and then ran back down my neck, down to my bellybutton. I refused to open my eyes, still remembering his touch, his moans, and his breath on my skin from last night. The cool breeze of the fan above washed over me, causing tiny goose bumps all along my skin.

"Good morning, Ms. Murphy." His voice was low and rough with the morning.

I giggled, thinking about last night. We were a little bit past the titles. "I think you can call me Elaina now."

He laughed lightly and kept drifting his fingertips around my waist and bellybutton. When my eyes found his, I noticed that he seemed to be waiting for me to look at him. His brow was slightly furrowed when he gently spoke, "Are you…all right?"

"Yes, I am. What time is it? Don't you have to leave soon?"

"Shortly. I just wanted to see your eyes before I left. To make sure you were okay."

I laughed nervously. "Is this real? Am I really here with you, in bed?"

"Well, I'm afraid so," he assured me.

"It does seem real, doesn't it?"

"I hope it's not too disappointing." Gray snickered and laid his head down beside mine.

"I'm not disappointed at all," I answered.

He smiled widely and then popped up and headed for the shower. I watched his bare buttocks walk away toward the bathroom. "I'm gonna get cleaned up before Jason gets here. I got a love scene with 'Mrs. Cody Smart Arse' today." He rolled his eyes and then suddenly froze in his tracks, realizing what he had just said. "I'm sorry Laina, that was stupid of me."

"What? It's just work, right?" I answered coolly, trying not to look or sound bothered in the least. He was on to my game and he snuck back over to the bed.

"Look who's jealous!" he teased.

"I'm not jealous, Grayson, stop that. It was just one night. It's not like we're serious or anything. We're adults here." I shoved him away playfully, but I could see that something I had said had wounded him. "What? What did I say?"

"Elaina, perhaps my feelings for you were not made clear the other night and last night, especially. This was not just a 'one-night thing' for me."

"Well, no. You are staying with me for a while longer," I teased, placing my hand on his chest.

"No, Elaina, that's not what I meant. I like you. I mean, I *really* like you. This"—he pointed to himself and then me—"is important to me. Do you understand?"

"I think so. But I think it's too early to talk about this now, and you're gonna be late. You know Jason hates to wait for you."

He shook his head, knowing I was right but wanting to talk more about the subject at hand. After a moment, he nodded his head with a sigh and headed back toward the shower. In a goofy voice, he broke out his best leprechaun imitation: "You know, Ms. Murphy, I could use your skills in me shower this morning."

I laughed and waited for a moment, thinking, *What did he mean I am important? What did important mean? Important for now? Important because I am here and no one else is?* Did I really care that much how important I was to him? Yes, I was sure that I cared. I knew there was a huge probability that when the movie was done filming, we would be done with whatever this was. He would return to LA and I would stay here, alone. I knew it was going to hurt pretty bad to say good-bye to him. I shook away the thoughts and heard Grayson singing the Lucky Charms cereal commercial, "They're magically delicious…" I laughed out loud in spite of myself. The temptation was too strong; I wanted him all over again. I joined him in the shower and then again when he got dressed and then undressed. I wasn't sure of anything that morning except for the fact that Grayson Sparks was forty-five minutes late to work that day, and he left with a smile on his face.

Although nothing had been discussed between Gray and I, I thought it was best that no one know about our "fling" just yet, maybe not ever. So at lunch with Harris and Mandy that afternoon, I said nothing about it. I'm sure I overcompensated in covering up my news by drilling the two of them relentlessly about their lives and seeming way too interested in Mandy's day-to-day life with her kids and her husband. Mandy's pregnancy was going along fine, and Harris was going on and on about this out-of-towner who was looking to plank down a bunch of money on a house in the west end. She was too pleased with herself to really notice the permanent smile plastered on my face, at least for the first half hour of lunch. I listened attentively to the two women go on about their lives. Mandy was sick of being pregnant already and hated her swollen feet. She had gained more weight than she thought and was crying into a napkin about the scolding her ob-gyn had given her about it. Harris was getting sick of a competitor trying to take all of her clients. To make matters worse, this "stealer of clients" was about ten years younger than Harris. Our food came, finally. I was starved and I felt relieved to just eat and not talk for at least ten minutes or so. My wish was not granted.

"What's with you, Lain? You haven't stopped smiling since the waiter brought the water," Harris questioned.

"Yeah, what's up with that? You never smile about lunch in these snotty places!" Mandy stuck her finger to the tip of her nose and pressed it up in the air, teasing Harris about the restaurant pick.

Harris politely flicked her the bird and turned her attention back to me. "Well, Laina? What's the story?"

I sat paralyzed with fear. What was I supposed to say? There hadn't been time to discuss anything before he left. We had been too, umm, busy to talk.

"Nothing really. I'm just in a good mood today. Is that okay with you, guys? Is it a crime to be in a good mood?" I snapped.

"Well, yeah. For you, I mean. *You* are never in a good mood and you never smile this much." Harris pointed out in a rather contemptuous tone.

"Shut up, Harris," Mandy chimed, trying to protect me as usual.

Harris threw her hands up in the air. "Hey, if she wants to be happy, more power to her. All I can say, it's about damn time!"

"I agree!" Mandy added.

"Gee, thanks," I muttered sarcastically.

We ate our salads and the conversation dragged for a bit. Mandy started again about her weight and how scared she was that she would never get back to her pre-pregnancy size. I thought I was home free until Harris mentioned something she knew she should not have.

"So Elaina, how's the new house guest going?" Her brows twitted up and down knowing she was being a pain. I kicked her under the table and her eyes bugged at me in fake pain. I felt bad for her a little bit, knowing that baby and pregnancy talk bored her to tears.

"What guest?" Mandy asked.

"I told you, remember? The older man." I answered thick with boredom.

"Oh yeah. He's still there?" she asked through her bite of lettuce.

"Yes, for three months; maybe more." Suddenly Harris was the one kicking me.

"Oh, that sounds awful. How boring!" Mandy continued.

"Not really. He's nice enough and pretty much keeps to himself."

"Oh, well. That's okay I guess." Mandy started stuffing her mouth again.

I looked up to see Harris narrowing her eyes down at me from her high horse. She pointed to her mouth and then pointed back at me. I immediately realized I was smiling again and pulled it back in a bit. It was too late, Harris was on to me. Her little fantasies about us were probably hitting an all-time high.

She mouthed the words "I saw you."

"What?" I mouthed back. I pulled my finger to my lips trying to silence her. For now, anyway.

Mandy suddenly popped up. "I'll be right back. Baby bladder," she muttered as she flitted away to the restroom.

As soon as she was gone, it was just Harris and me. I took a deep breath and squared my shoulders toward her.

"What are you up to, Elaina?" she taunted.

"Stop it, Harris, please. I'm not doing anything." I rolled my eyes.

"You slept with him, I can tell."

"No, I didn't. Stop it, someone will hear." I technically wasn't lying; we didn't exactly sleep.

"You do know he will eventually have to go back to LA, right? she reminded me, and my happy balloon of a heart deflated slightly.

"Yes, that *is* where he lives," I answered.

"Fine, I won't ask you anything more. But, just so you know, I *know*. Just be careful, Laina. He's a big leaguer."

"You are wasting your breath, Harris. Nothing is going on," I hissed back. I wasn't sure what annoyed me more; her total lack of faith in me or the fact she was worried about me.

"Okay. Whatever you say." She grinned and then nodded her head in Mandy's direction. "Here comes the warden," she taunted.

"Don't call her that. You know I hate that. She's my sister; be nice, please."

"Fine, only because she's your sister. But I swear if she pops one more kid out, I'm moving to another state. I mean, what is she trying to do, populate the entire country?"

"Shhh," I hissed with a grin.

She dropped the Grayson subject after that, as she promised, but I knew I couldn't keep it from her for much longer.

On the way home, I wondered what tonight would be like. The day had separated our last moments together long enough to bring us to our senses, especially him. Even if he dumped me or came to his senses, I would still be thankful that he had been able to prove to me that I was still alive and capable of loving someone again.

It was a late night for him; he would be gone until close to two in the morning. I had left a note on the counter for him to find his turkey sandwich in the fridge. Then I fed Macbeth and headed upstairs for a shower and then sleep. I was pretty tired after not getting much sleep the night before, and I wondered how he could go and shoot movie scenes all day being so exhausted. Then I remembered how exhilarated I felt this morning and wondered if he had too. My shower was long, and I could feel my legs swaying back and forth with sleepiness. When I came out of the bathroom to get into bed with a good book, I found I was not alone. Macbeth had made herself comfy at the foot of my bed. She raised her head when I approached, waiting for me to wave her away, but I was too tired. We made eye contact; her eyes darted from mine and then to the wall a few times, hoping that I didn't notice that she was lying across my bed. I chuckled at her silly fear. "Just for tonight, goofball." She put her head back down when I was settled into bed. While I was reading, she slowly worked her way up to the pillows next to me. I knew what she was doing, but I was too engrossed in my book. When I finally did look beside me, her head was resting on the pillow like a little child. She looked too cute to push away, so I let her stay. I turned the light out and drifted to sleep quickly.

Sometime later, I could feel arms around my back and legs. I wasn't sure what was happening, but I had been moved and I was not alone. I turned my head to see what was happening; that's when I heard his voice.

"Sorry to wake you, but I don't like to sleep alone, and you did take my dog."

"Oh, you're home," I answered groggily. "Where are you taking me?"

"To my bed, of course. I was rather disappointed when I didn't find you there."

He lay my body down on the bed. He had already pulled the sheets back before he had gone searching for me. He pulled the blankets up and over me and I felt him lie down beside me. "How was your day, my little innkeeper?"

"Long. I was tired all day," I whispered, half awake.

"I guess you should have tried to sleep more last night then." He chuckled darkly. "Go to sleep. I just wanted to feel you beside me."

"Good night," I sighed.

"Good night, Elaina."

Before I knew it, I was under again. I knew he would be there when I woke up, unless this was another dream. For now, his warmth beside me was wonderful, and the way I fit up against his body with his arm wound around me was perfect.

Chapter 6

The Beginning?

When I woke up, Gray was already in the shower whistling away. I rolled over to see the daylight break into the room in long, narrow strips. I could smell his shampoo and soap as it drifted in from the bathroom. Macbeth was lying at the foot of the bed. I guess she didn't like to sleep alone either. I sat up and she turned her head back to me. Her eyes seemed to smile at me.

"Good morning, you little bedhog," I whispered as I stroked her head and rubbed her ears.

Gray walked into the room, completely naked. I guess he wasn't shy anymore.

"Oh, I'm sorry. Did I wake you?" he apologized.

"Your whistling is very nice," I teased.

"Was I whistling? Sorry, I didn't even realize." He smiled.

I slid off the side of the bed and stood as my silk nightie slid back down into place. "Hungry?" I asked.

"Actually, I'm starved. I was too tired to eat my sandwich last night, but thanks for making it," he answered while pecking my neck with his eager lips. He kissed me again and then again, and then his lips stayed and moved up my throat and back to my lips.

"Good morning, you," he whispered with his rugged accent as his arms wound around my waist again.

"Good morning," I answered as a feeling of terror washed over me. *Do not get too comfortable, Elaina. Do not fall for this guy.*

I was frying his eggs and crisping his toast when he came into the kitchen with his call sheets and notes. The blue T-shirt he wore accented his biceps—not too big but just right. His face was scruffy and he rubbed at his chin, scratching the prickly hairs taking up residence there. He dashed into the fridge and pulled my fruit out and set it on the table. He grabbed a bowl from the cabinet above me; and as he moved across me, his scent filled my head. He spooned out the same amount I always ate and poured me a cup of the coffee, I assumed, he had started before his shower.

We ate breakfast across from each other at the kitchen table. Our eyes rarely left one another's. Every now and then we would both chuckle. We were like two high schoolers just starting a romance—shy about what the daylight brought after the night.

"I work late tonight but after that I get a day off." He threw the bait out and let it sit for a bit.

"Oh?" I answered as if I couldn't care less and stuffed a pineapple slice in my mouth.

"I would like to spend some more time with you, if that's all right. I don't want to foul up any plans you already have or anything." He backtracked, misreading my aloofness. I felt badly about being so nonchalant a second ago, but my fears got the better of me and suddenly I was speaking without thinking.

"What are we doing, Gray?" I demanded calmly.

"Having breakfast," he answered with that crooked smile that I loved.

"You know what I mean. What's happening here?"

He smiled wickedly. "I'm not really sure but I think... something great is happening here."

I sighed and narrowed my eyes at him. "What does that mean?"

He looked at me warily. "Look, I know this is crazy, totally crazy, but I really love being with you. I know there is a lot we need to discuss. We'll have all day tomorrow to sort it out, all right?"

I twisted my lips up the side. "Sure. Tomorrow," I murmured and rolled my eyes.

"Let's be patient with everything, all right. I want to do this right for a change."

I smiled at his attempt to calm my rattled nerves.

"Is it too much to ask for a kiss before I head out, or would you rather keep eatin' me head off instead?" He tried to hide his smile but it was useless.

I stood up and moved over to him and planted a light kiss on his waiting lips.

"Anything else you need?" I asked sincerely.

He raised his eyebrow and suddenly grabbed my backside.

"I meant, are you still hungry, Gray?" I chuckled.

His eyes still playfully wicked, I felt his hands lift me suddenly and force my legs around his waist. He kissed me passionately for what seemed like forever. We were starting to get carried away on the kitchen table when we both heard the car horn blasting out front. He groaned on top of me and slowly unraveled me from his body.

"I can't be late two days in a row. Or could I?" he deliberated in his mind while looking incredibly sexy as he scratched his head and messed his brown hair with his hand.

"No, get going," I chastened.

He slowly backed away, watching me on the kitchen table. His hazel eyes fell down to my legs that were still slightly parted. "Hmm, if you go to sleep before me tonight, please sleep in my bed. I don't want to have to go looking for you again."

"We'll see," I teased.

~~~~~~~~

It was hard to find something to keep me busy during the day. I kept finding my thoughts turning to Gray more and more. Thinking about what we would do tomorrow, and the next day, and next. What he would say about us and how he felt. What I would admit and what I would keep hidden from him. Then I would worry about where this was going and how this could ever work. I found myself chastising my thoughts of having anything more than a very sexual summer fling with this man—this man that I hardly knew but that I felt more at ease with than anyone in years. I cleaned the house, changed his sheets and mine, and prepared food to cook for dinner. The rest of the day I plastered myself by the pool, reading and thinking. Around three in the afternoon, I ran some errands taking me out to the bank, then to the Fresh Market for stuff we needed—mainly fruit, because it turned out Gray liked it, too, with just about every meal. I grabbed some fresh flowers for the house and then headed home. Gray would be late tonight so I would eat without him and leave his dinner in the fridge. I stayed out back until pretty late, around eleven, before walking wearily into his bedroom. I was here last night and the night before that, but it felt weird coming in here without him, almost as though I was an intruder there, so I turned around and headed for the soft, leather couch instead. Macbeth was already there in her usual spot in the corner of the sectional. I grabbed a blanket and turned the TV on. Eventually I fell asleep. When I woke up, I was cradled in his arms again. He was mumbling something about being stubborn when he gently laid me down on the bed, just like he had the night before.

"Who are you calling stubborn?" I grumbled.

He laughed quietly. "You."

I rolled over on my stomach and I could immediately feel his fingers trailing around my shoulder blades and then down my spine. I sighed with satisfaction. He wasn't so tired tonight. Suddenly his fingers were replaced by lips kissing my back, neck, and shoulders. I tried to turn around to face him but he gently urged me to stay on my belly. I could feel him behind me, sliding his fingers up and down my legs so lightly I could barely feel it. His hands rested on either side of my ribcage. He was never forceful, always gentle, but I always knew exactly what he wanted from me. The night was shorter than it had been the first night, but it was somehow even better. We knew each other better now, the unsure feeling was gone. The unknown about how we felt about each other had disappeared.

~~~~~~~~

The morning came too soon for me. My head was laid out across his chest, and he was dancing his fingers across my shoulders and back. I wasn't sure but I think this was his way of waking me up.

"Good morning," I whispered through my sleepiness.

"Mornin'," he rumbled with his deep scratchy voice. I could feel his mouth moving against the top of my head. "It's today."

"Really?" I asked teasingly.

"Yes. Today I get you all day. No more wondering what you do all day."

"That is highly overrated, you know," I sighed, "I'm pretty boring."

"Elaina, you are anything but boring," he growled. "I speak from personal experience." His hand slid down to my backside.

"You like that, don't you?" I teased.

"What?" he asked playfully.

"My…rear end." I giggled.

"Yes, I really, really do." He laughed.

While he showered, I cooked breakfast. He came out in a pair of jeans with no shirt. His body was pretty close to perfect. He wasn't a big muscular man, but he was fit, lean and strong, and tall, over six foot.

"And what are we having this morning, Ms. Murphy?"

"French toast, bacon, juice, and coffee." I answered.

He sat on the barstool at the counter and watched me work. "Are you gonna eat any of this?" he asked, honestly unsure if I would actually eat anything.

"No, I already had my fruit while you were in the shower. Eat up." I slid the plate over to him. "I'm gonna go shower and get dressed. Sundress okay for your whole day with me?"

"Perfect. I plan to eat a meal with you today, so you'd better be ready."

"We'll see," I shouted as I flew up the stairs.

When I came back downstairs, he had cleaned the kitchen already and packed a picnic lunch for us. He had promised we would eat together, but I never thought he planned on leaving the house and venturing into the public eye. I braced myself for what was about to come. Unsure, I took his hand and headed to the car.

The ride was strange. The last and only time we had been in a car driving together was the first day he came here, and *I* was the one driving. I wasn't sure how he knew where to go, but he seemed comfortable with his directions. I didn't distract him with questions while he drove. I was still amazed at what he seemed to remember and retain. He had been here three weeks and already he drove around the area like he was born and raised here. Was there anything he couldn't do well? I started panicking about what would happen if someone saw us or saw him. What would happen then?

He stopped at a light, a familiar light, and he was getting ready to turn onto a familiar road. We hadn't gone far. I turned to study him as we sat at the light waiting for the red to turn to green. When he saw me, he smiled and then turned back to the wheel and pretended to concentrate on his driving.

"You know, in Scotland, driving is whole other ballgame," he teased.

"I'm sure it is." I sighed.

The light turned green and he turned left onto the next street. I watched out the window as we passed by the elementary school, then the high school, then watched the road narrow and turn into a one-lane road. The speed abruptly changed down to fifteen miles an hour and suddenly all kinds of pedestrian signs started popping up. When we reached a fork in the road, he turned left again and followed the road around, and then finally parked facing the playground. It was the park where we had met that first day. He had remembered it and taken me here again. He cut the car off and looked over at me, waiting for my reaction.

"Well, that's impressive," I complimented with surprise.

He smiled and laughed as he pulled on a baseball cap and sunglasses. He opened his door and stepped outside, wandering around the back to check on the basket in the car. I was stunned that he would do something like this: First, that he wanted to spend his whole day off with me, and second, that he brought me to an average park with a picnic basket lunch to the first place we ever laid eyes on each other. He was good, really good. He was at the door opening it, but I kept staring at the playground, smiling in spite of myself.

Then I thought to myself what Harris had said the other day: *He's a big leaguer,* she warned. I froze with doubt. Suddenly I felt like a bit of a fool. Did her comment mean I was a minor leaguer? I guess that meant I was done a few days ago then. I sat in the car with a scowl, wanting to smack Harris.

"You coming?" he asked as he extended his hand to me. I shook the snarl from my face and turned to look at his perfectly happy face. He was a good person, that I had seen first hand.

Take a chance, I told myself. I took his hand and he began leading me toward a path.

"I thought we could walk a bit. I've never been here before, outside of the parking lot. I just like the idea of walking by the river. Jason said no one would notice me here, so we shouldn't be disturbed."

"Sure," I answered, not knowing whether to let go of his hand in public or not. When I tried to loosen his grip, he clamped his hand back down on mine, letting me know he wasn't going to let go.

We had a ways to walk before getting to the river, but he strolled along and admired everything about this place that I had always thought was average. He was in love with the trees which were everywhere. He admitted that was one of the things he liked most about my house—the trees that surrounded us there made him feel safe. Halfway to the river, he got comfortable enough to take his sunglasses off, and I thanked him for that, at which he laughed.

"I know it's stupid, but sometimes it's just...necessary...to hide," he explained.

"You mean you don't want anyone to see me with you, right?" I laughed quietly at his side.

He halted in the middle of the path. "What? Why would you ever say that?" His expression was one of hurt.

"'Cause I'm me and you're you. We're not exactly from the same, well, universe," I mumbled out, trying to explain myself.

"Do you know how ridiculous you sound?"

"No. Do you know how ridiculous you look in your sunglasses and hat? It only makes people look at you more, you know," I teased.

He laughed but still didn't let go of what I had just said. His face turned more serious. "I know this is all different for you and a bit sudden. I don't blame you. I used to be just like everyone else, too, just taller than most. The acting thing...it's not what people think it is. It's great, don't get me wrong, but it's lonely." He gently pulled me onward down the path but kept talking steadily. "People think they are getting the movie star when they meet me. Women; they're all into you until they see you're not a god or some mythical creature; you're just you. They reject you when they see the real person is just that, a person."

"Sounds painful." I smirked.

"You have no idea what it does to the ego," he answered with a laugh, allowing me my fun at his expense, but he continued on, "It strips you down and hollows you out, and then you realize the only way you're gonna get company is if you play the role they want you to play. You have to be what they expect, or you are always alone. Before you know it, you're always acting and no one knows who you really are, even you. It's lonely, believe me. I had given up on ever meeting anyone who didn't already think they knew Grayson Sparks the actor. No one ever wanted to see or get to know me, just simple old me. The day I got out of that car—no wait, it was before that—the day my car pulled up and I saw you standing there for the first time, waiting for me, something inside me turned back on. It wasn't your beauty, although God really loved you when he made you. It wasn't your long brown hair blowing all around your face or the way the early sun lit up your tan shoulders and made your skin glow. It was your reaction to me—nothing. When I gave you the predictable million-dollar smile, you rolled your eyes. You wouldn't look at me; most people stare at me like I'm going to turn into a blasted cow with bat wings."

"Well, that would be worth seeing…"

He grinned, but I couldn't sidetrack him. "You never wanted anything from me except for me to leave you alone. You weren't already impressed by me like most people are. You challenged me to be myself again. You frustrated me more than any other woman I've met. It wasn't until I acted like myself that you gave me the time of day."

"I'm sorry."

"Don't be. You made me pay attention and memorize every detail about you: The way you twitch your lips when you're about to yell at me. The way your eyebrows smash together when you're scrubbing the counter for the third time in thirty seconds. All of your one hundred different smiles and mannerisms. Like the way you always rub your fingers across your fingernails when you are nervous."

I listened to him as he rambled, searching for a point, and I knew there was one. So far this could go good or bad.

"I know what you want to know. Where is this going? Where can this possibly go, when I'm leaving in a few months? Right?" he asked.

"I was wondering about that, yes." I answered, unsure if that was really it.

"But that's not all, right?" I shrugged my shoulders. "Okay, Elaina, I don't know what this is or where it's going, but I know I want to find out. I want to spend every minute with you while I'm here and then, well, let's just see what happens. Fair enough?"

"That's fair, but what about the other women?"

He laughed out loud, but when he saw the seriousness on my face, he stiffened in front of me.

"Are you serious then? Women? What women are you referring to?"

"I read magazines, Gray. I watch TV. I see the pictures of you with all the different girls every night. Please, don't take me for a fool."

He smirked at me and twisted his mouth up to one side. "Of course I would never take you for a fool, but there are fools out there who actually believe that garbage. I just didn't think you were one of them." He started walking again but let go of my hand.

I tried to keep up with him but it was hard, seeing how his legs were much longer than mine.

"You're telling me that everything in those magazines, everything *they* say is wrong, a lie even? Everybody's lying, is that it?" I asked.

He suddenly turned back to me with his eyes narrowed and his lips tight. "What is it that you want to know, Elaina! Just ask me then!" he growled, angered by my accusation.

I couldn't say anything that I wanted to say. He was angry but also obviously hurt deep down. I could feel my eyes welling up with tears, ashamed of what I was thinking. I couldn't get the words out at all. He shook his head slowly back and forth and started walking again. The space between us grew and grew, and with every step he took I lost a bit more of my foolish pride.

"Okay, I'll tell you!" I shouted, glad that no one was around. I stormed up to him and faced him head on. "What happens if for some stupid reason, I…I fall in love with you and we have the most amazing three months together, but then you have to go because your job is over? We see what happens. Then I see you on some talk show or some awards ceremony, and you're there with some…teenager? Then what for me? What do you think happens to me when you go; when you leave me? I've been in love before, Gray! I gave him everything—every single part of me—and then he left…well…died, not much difference! I'm thirty-four years old! I'm no competition for the countless women waiting for you in LA or around the world even! For you, this is a let's-just-see kinda thing; for me, when you leave…I really will be alone!"

I wasn't sobbing but the tears were streaming down my face. I was completely embarrassed for my outburst. My pride was completely gone and I stood alone, stripped down with all my feelings. He watched me carefully and stepped toward me. His face was sad as he reached for me. His hands cupped my face and his thumbs rubbed my tears away from my bright-red cheeks. He rubbed his nose against mine and sighed before kissing me under the tree-shaded path. I could hear the river water rushing behind us and people laughing and shuffling around us, but I didn't care about them. When his lips were free, he spoke softly into my ear. "I'm scared of losing you, too."

"Really?"

"Yes, you crazy woman! Can't you tell?" He chuckled softly. "Look at me! I'm a complete mess whenever you're within a hundred feet of me. My hands get sweaty, my brain starts spinnin' in me head; I can't get anything I say right. I knew when I first kissed you that I was well on my way to loving you."

"Love?"

"There is no other word I can use to describe you. And the women you are so worried about; weren't you paying attention before? They don't care about me, they don't know me. Once I got to know who they really were, I didn't care about them either. As soon as I realized what they were hanging around for is when I was out the door. They'd probably have a heart attack if I brought them to a park for date. Those girls have no substance; they're fake. You are a woman; you know what you want and what you like. That's far more sexy than some bimbo in a club after money or fame. You are the one I want to be with—no one else but you."

"Me too. I can't fill my days up enough when you're gone," I mumbled.

He laughed softly.

"What so funny?"

"It's not funny; it just sounds like me when I'm actually at work with something to do. It's like I can't get through the day fast enough to get home just so I can catch the sight of you singing in the kitchen while you chop vegetables."

"I don't sing in the kitchen," I protested.

"Yes, you do, and I love it." He smiled crookedly with his eyes cast down at me and sighed softly. "I do love you."

I smiled at his profession and leaned onto his chest to hide my face. He had said what I never thought I would hear. He loved me, and I was positive that I loved him.

We walked hand in hand passing strangers that never even noticed Gray. It was strange, but by the end of our walk, as we got closer to the car, I had completely forgotten why he needed the baseball cap in the first place. The man I knew was an ordinary man taking a walk. He could have been half a dozen people that passed us on our walk, but I knew he wasn't. He never would be; he would always be Grayson Sparks, the movie star, and I would always just be the widowed Elaina Murphy. Somehow though, after today, it seemed possible that we could actually work out. Stranger things had happened.

As we ate the lunch Grayson had prepared, he could tell I was thinking about something before I said anything at all.

"What is it? What are you thinking over there?" he asked warily.

"That this is the best peanut butter sandwich I have ever tasted." I giggled while covering my mouth with my hand.

"Are you making fun of me then? I know it's simple, love, but I like simple things. They taste better." He danced his eyes up and down teasingly.

I liked the way he said things so innocently and honestly. There was nothing untruthful about him at all as he ate his regular, everyday-guy, peanut butter sandwich. He was lying on his side with his legs stretched out and feet crossed. His chest was slightly turned toward the sun but more so facing me. His head was propped up by his free hand and he was smiling into the sun under his navy-blue hat. I'm sure he was hot under that thing; I couldn't wait to get him home and throw him into the pool to cool him off. He turned to me and saw my thoughtful look.

"What's wrong now?" he teased. "Want another one of me famous sandwiches?"

"I was thinking about the fact that if we are going to be seeing each other for a while, then what about the press? Do we just hide out in my house?"

"Of course not!" he said as if he were cursing. "Besides, does it look like we are hiding?" he asked while opening his arms out to the trees around us.

I shot him a glaring look and huffed, "Then, what if someone sees us? What if the press finds out where you are staying?" I asked.

He answered quickly as if he had already thought about this before. "Then I guess if someone sees us and if they find out where *we* are living, then *we* will move to a hotel together."

"What if the press asks you about me? What will you tell them?" I pressured impatiently.

He thought longer this time and turned to me with his brow furrowed. "Well, I guess that depends on what you want me to tell them, love. What would you have me say?"

"What *should* be said? I don't really know how all this stuff works," I grumbled. In truth, I was confused as to how this was going to work but eager to hear his theories at least.

He laughed again as he threw a few grapes into his mouth. "Well, if anyone asks, I hope you don't mind if I refer to you as my lady. Is that okay with you, Elaina?" he answered while chewing on the juicy fruit.

"Yes." I answered, and he leaned over to kiss me gently for a moment. I could taste the grape on his lips.

"Grand. Okay then, next question?" he knew there were more coming, and he seemed to be enjoying himself as I prepared myself to ramble through more questions.

It was something that we needed to talk about, as unnatural as it was. This wasn't like we were just two people that met and found that we enjoyed each other's company. It wasn't like this was going to be the usual courtship of a relationship or even friendship. There were going to be rules and regulations to this affair. It really felt like the romance was being let out of our romance tires as we tried to figure everything out. It was necessary, like many things I was about to learn. His privacy and safety were always going to be an issue. He was really famous, and I needed to be ready for whatever that brought my way. For now, we had both agreed that we would try to keep our relationship a secret for as long as we could—which meant "no comment." He explained to me that the longer we were able to keep it to ourselves, the more time we would have between just the two of us. Once things went public, our relationship would be for everyone to judge and dissect. I agreed completely that secrecy was best for now. It was easy for him to move around Richmond without anyone noticing him, by Gray driving my car or Jason driving him in the Lincoln town car, so we would be able to go to lots of places without detection for a while. Most of our time, however, would be spent in my house. It was the safest place since no one knew he was there, not even my neighbors. I could tell my friends—he didn't mind at all—but they couldn't tell anyone else. That was easy; I only had two friends and one was my sister.

After lunch, we lay out across the blanket on our backs, letting the late spring sun beat down on us. He turned to face me and lightly traced my jaw with his finger. Gray liked to use touching as a way of communication. Today, this was his way of letting me know he was ready to leave. The rest of the day we spent by the pool or in the pool drinking margaritas and listening to music. Gray laughed at some of the songs on my iPod, while others he seemed to like. Some of my favorites were his too.

For dinner, Gray had had Jason drop some steaks off in the fridge while we had been gone earlier; always the sneaky planner. I made the salad and he grilled the fillets. We lit candles all around the pool and he started a warm fire in the smallish chimney. It was still May and the nights still carried a bit of a chill with them. It was a perfect end to a perfect day. Of course, Gray was not tired when we headed to bed; and as we lay across the bed in the dark afterwards, he told me breathlessly, "Thank you. I've wanted to do that to you since this morning." We both laughed out loud and found each other under the blankets. The sheets were cool as they skimmed our sweaty bodies, and it felt good as the thin linen slowly drifted down onto my overheated skin. I didn't cuddle into my usual nook under is arm, I was too hot tonight, but when I woke up somehow I had managed to sneak my way into my favorite spot, and the first thing I felt when I woke up were his arms around me.

Chapter 7

I was in the kitchen looking through my planner for any upcoming things I would need to prepare for. Then I saw it in red permanent marker: *Lunch w/ Harris @ Bakers Crust 1pm!* I had obviously picked the location. The importance of the red letters was further pressed with three red lines under them. It had been a week since Gray and I had decided what to do about everything. I was planning on telling Harris about us today, but despite hours of thinking and rehearsing what I would say, I was blocked.

I was early today and waiting for her to arrive. I ordered a martini and stared down the glass door entrance. I watched the cars hurrying by down Cary Street, hoping I would see her approach so that I could attempt to control my nerves. Suddenly, there she was in the doorway pushing past an old grey-haired lady that was exiting through the entrance door. She must have come from a different direction. Immediately I was anxious, nervous, speechless, and nauseous. She crossed the room and sat down in front of me looking at me strangely.

"What is with you, Laina?" she asked as her left eyebrow lifted with an investigatory arch. "You keep wrinkling your forehead like that and Botox won't be able to help you." She held up her hand in front of my face and waved it back and forth. "Laina... where are you?" she teased.

"What? Oh, hey," I answered, stunned.

"What, no smiles today?" She smirked.

"Sorry, I've got a lot on my mind."

"I can see that." She waved the waiter over, quickly glanced at my drink, and ordered a martini of her own. "So…what's new with you? Any news?" she asked, half interested while squinting at her Blackberry before stuffing it into her bright-yellow hobo bag.

"Not much. You?" I asked, kicking myself mentally for my lack of courage.

Harris took the bait and began telling me about her awful past few days. The big money spender was much more difficult and picky than she had anticipated. I started tuning her out when she left less and less time for me to speak in between her complaining. It's not that I was scared to tell Harris about Gray; there was nothing to worry about from her. I knew she would be happy for me. I just worried about her worrying about me getting hurt. She had made it pretty clear that she didn't trust Gray's type. She thought he was a love-'em-and-leave-'em sort of guy that would surely love me and then leave me when he was tired of me. I was scared of not being able to convince her that this was for real and not just fun for him. I was worried about how I would be able to convince her that Gray was a good guy and that this wasn't just a fling, when most of the time I needed Gray to convince *me* of his feelings for me. I was sure that she would be less angry about my being with Gray and more upset that I had kept it from her for so long.

"Elaina? Are you even listening to me?" she demanded, interrupting my thoughts.

"What? Yeah, of course. The man turned to you and said it was hideous." I answered, thankful that my overrun mind had allowed me to hear the last few words of her story. She rolled her eyes and continued talking. I didn't hear the rest of it but pretended to pay more attention.

Her drink finally came and she immediately took a long sip from the tall, delicate glass. "Wow, I really needed that," she cooed. "So, what's with your wrinkly forehead today? What has you so uneasy?"

I took a sip of my drink and cut my eyes at her. My forehead wasn't wrinkly. She was five years older than me anyway. I set my glass back down on the table, taking my time and nodded to her purse.

"I like the bag. New?" I asked with little enthusiasm.

"Cut the crap, Laina. What's going on?" Harris demanded.

I laughed at her consistency. Harris was always Harris, whether you wanted her to be or not.

"Okay. There is something I need to tell you, but I'm not sure how you will respond."

"You won't know until you tell me, so get it over with already. I'm getting older over here."

I cast my eyes down and then to the side pretending to watch something far off from our table. I was buying time, trying to get the words right and suddenly feeling a choking sensation in my throat. I cleared my throat, attempting to loosen the tight feeling that was threatening to cut my words off.

"You were right before"—I started and then paused, unable to continue. Harris stared at me with confusion—"about Grayson and I."

Her eyes bulged and she took another sip of her cocktail. "That's what you were afraid to tell me? That you and him are, well, sleeping together?"

I nodded my head yes. "I wasn't sure what you would think about it." I answered, ducking my head down, refusing to look her in the eye. She was quiet for a moment and then she sighed with a wispy giggle.

"Well, Laina, I'm not surprised at all."

"You're not?" I asked, confused.

"Of course I'm not. You're gorgeous and so is he. Something was bound to happen. I must admit, I wish it were me and not you, but I think everyone does."

I smiled at her jealousy. I always had and still thought she was way prettier than I could ever hope to be.

"He is a lovely person, Harris. You should meet him." I smiled.

"What for? He's not staying, is he? I mean, he is still leaving when shooting is done, right? It's not like you two are gonna get married or anything." As she spoke, I conjured up the image of saying good-bye to Gray. It left a pit in my stomach.

I lowered my head again, embarrassed. She had jumped way ahead in the conversation, and as much as I should have expected this, I was caught off guard. My silence must have clued her in to my pain because she sighed.

"Laina? How serious is this? How long has it been going on anyway?" she inquired.

When I raised my head back up, a smile peeked out through my sad demeanor. She smiled and shook her head realizing she had been snowed for longer than she imagined. "Laina," she whispered. "It's serious, isn't it?" Her smile widened, and she waited impatiently for me to tell her about it. "How long?"

"A while, almost a month now," I burst out.

"You've been keeping secrets for a long time! Why didn't you tell me sooner?" she teased with bright eyes.

"I don't know. I didn't think you would understand. He's not what you think. He's so much better than anything you would have thought. He's a normal guy; he likes peanut butter sandwiches and walks in the parks..."

"He is anything but normal, Laina. Just be careful with him," she warned.

I narrowed my eyes at her and thought long before I spoke again. I wanted to make sure I said this with conviction.

"He loves me, Harris."

That stopped her from continuing on with her orange cone warning speech. She looked at my eyes for the first time and saw that I was not stupid or naïve; I was in love, and she was ruining this moment for me.

"Do you love him?" she asked, raising one eyebrow.

I swallowed hard and nodded my head up and down. I was amazed that I had managed a nod at all. Love wasn't something that I said or expressed much anymore.

"Have you told him?" she asked.

"What?" I answered coyly.

"You know what, Elaina," she answered flatly. "John and Georgia, that's what."

"Yes, I told him," I answered while straightening up in my seat, clearly uncomfortable with where the conversation had gone.

"And?" she asked.

I was amazed that she was still asking me these things. Couldn't she see my warning signs? Fidgeting in my seat, looking away…Why was she pressuring so hard?

"And what? He knows. End of story," I snapped.

The waitress came back to take our order. She was slightly uncomfortable as she watched Harris and I have a stare-down contest. "Umm…are you guys ready to order?"

"I'll have the tomato soup, the cheesy one," I answered. Harris was swiftly studying the menu trying to figure out what to order.

"Bread bowl or cup?" The waitress asked.

"Cup, please." I answered, looking over to Harris again. She was still studying the menu. I rolled my eyes and looked up to the now-impatient waitress.

"She'll have the same," I finally said.

Harris cut her eyes back to me, obviously annoyed at my ordering for her. The waitress took one look at Harris and made a beeline to another table.

"Sorry! She was just standing there waiting," I apologized halfheartedly. I knew that she would order the soup anyway.

Harris sat across the table, and if looks could kill, I would be bleeding out on the floor. She was stewing, waiting for me to answer her about the family I had once had.

"Why does everything I do have to be about John and Georgia? They have been gone from my life for over four years. This thing with Gray and I has nothing to do with them."

"Oh no?" she hissed.

"No."

"What do you plan on doing when he leaves? And he *will* leave."

"No, he won't!" I snarled.

"How do you know he won't?" She cocked one of her eyes up to peer down at me in judgment.

"Because I just know. He's not like that," I assured.

"How do you know?" she pressured again.

I could feel the tears welling up in my eyes. This was what I was afraid of most of all. I knew she would make me say the words she knew I needed to say. I took a deep breath and steadied my breathing.

"Because if he leaves, I'll die inside just like last time, all right!" I blurted out.

She leaned over and grabbed my hands and pulled them to the center of the table, her eyes saddened by my pain. She was guilt-ridden about making me so upset, but she felt it was necessary.

"Laina, look at me," she whispered, but I wouldn't. I couldn't bring myself to look at her because I knew deep down that she was right. "Please, Laina," she pleaded in a whisper. "Look at me."

When I finally did look up at her, her eyes were tearing up now, too. I felt a ping of pain in my heart. I knew that Harris cared, that she was my dearest friend. I knew she would never hurt me and I trusted her more than anyone, even myself. She had been the one there for me who had pulled me from the ditch I was settled in years ago. I owed her my attention, my full attention.

"If you love him, then let yourself love him. I won't judge you, not ever. If he leaves then he leaves, but you will be okay. You need to know that. You need to be sure of that. Him leaving will not kill who you are. If he has found a way to make you live again, then I love him too already. I know that any man that could bring you back to life again is worth my respect, but if he breaks your heart then I'll kill him."

I snorted through my tears and managed a laugh. The rest of our lunch, I told her everything about Gray; how wonderful Gray was and how down-to-earth he really was. She was sold by the time the waitress came around to try and sell us a dessert.

"I'll take the cheesecake," Harris replied.

"I'll have the fruit tart," I answered.

The waitress nodded while jotting down our orders and then disappeared back to the kitchen.

"Now, next things next. Does Mandy know yet?" she asked, and I suddenly felt my stomach drop again.

~~~~~~~~

When I got back home, I still had hours before Gray would be home. It was another late night again. I was used to his schedule. He was usually gone all day, and it gave me time to look forward to seeing him. The pollen season was nearly through, but Gray's allergies were not. We had been trying out every possible allergy medicine known to man, but nothing had worked so far. There was supposed to be a huge thunderstorm tonight, so hopefully most of the yellow death powder would be washed away and gone until next year. I wondered about next year; where I would be, what I would be doing. I wondered where Gray would be and who he would be with. Gray would be close to starting promotions for the movie he was still filming now. He wouldn't have any time for me and my boring town. Our relationship would be over by then and he would be dating someone else—someone most likely considerably younger. For now, I was content with the way things were and determined to deal with him leaving when the time came, and not a moment sooner.

I was sitting on the couch folding clothes when I let my head roll back, stretching the muscles in my neck and shoulders. That's when it caught my eye. The delicate urn that sat on the mantel all alone. I had placed it there a long time ago, unsure if I would ever really be able to follow through with John's wishes. For years I had dusted it every day carefully and sometimes even talked to it, foolishly thinking they were listening when no one else was around. Harris had asked me at lunch what I would do when Gray left. I'm sure she was talking about the fact that I honestly hadn't dealt much with John and Georgia's passing. I had them both cremated and had combined their ashes together; that is what John always said he wanted just in case something like that ever happened. It was funny now to imagine that he may have known that someday something like that would happen, that we would be separated somehow, and I would be left to follow through with his decisions. He wanted his remains to be taken to our river house and scattered from his boat under the Tappahannock Bridge at sunset. This had been his favorite place because he loved fishing there; but this was also Georgia's favorite place because she knew, during car rides to the river, that when we crossed this bridge, we were close to home. I had never been able to bring myself to do it. I imagined their souls sitting in that damn urn, waiting each day to be let free. I felt horrible about it but it was just something that scared me. If their ashes were gone, then so were they, forever. It was a selfish thing on my part and it caused many arguments with my family and his, but it was my decision and mine alone. My mother wasn't talking to me and neither were his parents. Both had long since given up on me seeing their reason. It was my life, my business, and they had never given me the time to deal with things right after my husband and child died. They wanted me to sell the house and move on somewhere else. They wanted me to move on and try to live my life, but I just couldn't. Moving into this house had been the last straw for them. For four years, my beloveds had sat together on my mantle waiting patiently for me to do the right thing. For four years I had failed them.

If I couldn't let go of them or even say a proper good-bye, how would I be able to say farewell to Gray when the time came?

The thunderstorm hit just as predicted by the weatherman. It was a real bad one too. The lightening was spectacular and then the rain came down in sheets. The pool filled fast and I had to go out during the storm to try draining some of its water out. I loved the pool but also hated it with a passion. John had insisted that it be big enough to swim laps in. It was big all right—downright huge—and an enormous pain in the ass. I cursed him as I turned knobs and it started to force the pump to expel the extra water. When I came back inside, I was soaked through and through and felt like a wet poodle. Macbeth stared at me like I was an idiot for going out there in the first place. Her head cocked to the side as I flipped my head over and wrapped my hair into a towel. "Don't look at me like that," I snipped at her with a grin. She came over and sat beside me, holding her furry head right under my hand as usual, waiting for me to pet her. I groaned under my breath and scratched her ears and then headed upstairs to take another shower. It rained for hours and was still raining when I went to bed in Grayson's bed.

~~~~~~~~

In the morning, I woke up to him staring at me, and I started laughing hysterically.

"What are you doing?" I asked through chuckles as I covered my mouth.

"Nothing, just waiting for you to wake up," he answered unapologetically.

"Do you do this every morning?" I asked with curiosity.

"No. Usually I can't see your face 'cause it's lying right here," he answered and pointed to his chest. "I got to get a shower, love. Join me?" he asked.

"No, I don't want to get up just yet." I lay in the bed thinking about my day and what I needed to get done. And then I suddenly remembered a request from Harris yesterday. I was abruptly nervous and questioning whether or not it was a good idea at all to even ask him. But I did anyway.

"Harris wants to come over for dinner tonight. She wants to meet the famous Grayson Sparks."

I didn't hear anything for a few seconds and I started to worry that maybe my initial feeling of just not telling him was the right one.

"I guess that'd be okay. I do get off early tonight…and I do want to meet your friends," he answered warily.

"Is that a yes then? Should I call her?" I asked in a hopeful voice.

The shower cut off and I could hear him grabbing his towel and drying off. "Sure, give her a call. I should be home by nine. She can keep you company until I get here."

He walked into the room. His hair was still dripping wet and he was smiling his crooked smile. He looked tense and his shoulders seemed tight and uneasy. It made me anxious wondering what he was thinking.

"Are you sure? 'Cause I can call her and tell her that you're working late and you can't tonight," I offered.

His lips tightened and he turned to me with his head tilted to one side. There was something strange in his eyes, something I didn't recognize. It was the first time I ever felt like he didn't trust me. It felt odd and uncomfortable.

"What did you tell her, Elaina?" he asked. His eyes were cold and tight.

So the roles had been reversed. In just two minutes I had ruined the easy, carefree air between us. It was now tainted with doubt and mistrust. But, I hadn't done anything that we hadn't discussed was "okay." I wanted my friends to meet him; there was no crime in that. I squared my shoulders and narrowed my eyes at him. "I told her that we were seeing each other."

"Did you tell her that it was a secret, like we discussed?" he asked, still way too serious for my liking.

"Yes. Did...I...do something wrong, Gray?" I asked in barely a whisper. His cold eyes suddenly broke from some weird trance. He seemed to realize that I was scared of his reaction. His eyes softened and a gentle smile spread across his face. It was as if he had caught himself reverting back to an old habit. I remembered what he had told me about the girls he had, for a lack of a better word, dated; and how they had used him and his fame. Then I remembered what I had said just a minute ago, right before the weirdness erupted. *She wants to meet the famous Grayson Sparks.* I was an idiot. I caught him studying me again and his eyes turned sympathetic.

"I'm sorry, Elaina. It's just that I'm not used to people wanting to meet just me. I'm not used to trusting anyone, because everyone usually has their own personal angle or agenda. It wasn't fair to even think about you or your friend that way. I'm sorry."

As he spoke, he moved slowly over to me with his towel still wrapped around his waist. He was sitting beside me, and he reached his hand out and slid his fingers across my face and rubbed my cheek with his thumb. His eyes searched mine, looking for forgiveness. When he seemed to find it, he pulled me to him and kissed my lips softly. My reaction, of course, was more than it should have been. There was something about him being this close and this exposed. He had to pull away this time. He laughed softly and kissed me once again on the forehead.

"Work," he whispered like it was a job.

"Work," I repeated like it was nuisance.

Chapter 8

The Friend Meets Lover

I had tried to keep busy all day, but nothing seemed to help my jitters. I had cleaned and cleaned the house a few times, even though it was already clean. I made and remade Gray's bed. I folded and creased the sheets down perfectly. I scrubbed the shower and found myself obsessing over a small spot in the grout that wouldn't come clean no matter how hard I scrubbed. I gave up finally and cursed at it as I fumbled out of the shower. The first stop was the mall to get a new black sundress. Next I went to the Bon Air Seafood market and got some fresh crab and then headed to the grocery store to get the rest of the ingredients needed for crab soufflé, my very own creation; some fresh salad fixings and, of course, some fresh fruit. I headed to the ABC store and got some tequila and some margarita mix. When I finally got home, it was after five, and I found that Harris had already called the house twice looking for me. My cell phone was turned off. I checked the messages to discover that she was planning on getting here at six, if not earlier. *Great.* I ran up the stairs to the shower and raced through the process of getting ready, cursing Harris the whole time. I hated being rushed, it unnerved me, and that was the last thing I needed tonight. When I got back down stairs, Harris was already there, making us margaritas. When she smiled at me, I rolled my eyes.

"What? Didn't you get my messages?" she asked.

"I told you he won't be here until after nine, remember?" I hissed.

"Sorry, I had a cancelation, so I figured what the hell."

"Yeah. Well, you're helping me with dinner then, so get an apron on. I can't have you ruining your Donna Karan ensemble," I huffed.

Harris was about as helpful in the kitchen as she was with cleaning it. Dinner was finally prepared and ready to cook after a bunch of whining from Harris. It was about eight, so there was plenty of time for drinks on the patio by the pool. I had a feeling I was going to need a few to get me through this strange night. Harris seemed completely normal with not a bit of nervousness about her. I was drinking like a fish and smoking like a dragon. I warned her not to do or say anything crazy. By the time nine o'clock rolled around, I was pretty tipsy but relieved when I saw the car lights illuminate the side yard. Gray was here, finally. This was a weird feeling indeed, trying to act normal around a friend meeting a star who didn't want to be treated like a star. I was hoping Harris would be able to contain herself when she saw him. I could feel my fingers fidgeting, as my thumbs smoothed over my fingernails. The slick feeling of my fingernails soothed me for some reason—I didn't care why—I was just glad that I could control my anxiety.

When he came through the back door to find us, I could tell he had had a long day. He searched around looking for us. His charm was still there, and when he found us sitting by the shallow end of the pool, he smiled and began walking a bit faster toward us.

"You're home," I called.

"I'm sorry I'm late, love. Jason drives like his grandmother." He laughed and kissed me on the cheek, then turned to Harris. "You must be Harris. It's nice to meet you." He stuck out his hand and she took it hesitantly.

"Likewise, Mr. Sparks. I've heard wonderful things about you."

"It couldn't all be good; I'm a bit of a slob with an obnoxious dog, I'm afraid." He laughed. "And please do call me Gray." Harris smiled and tilted her head to the side, and I knew she liked him right away.

When he got back from his shower, he looked more relaxed than before. He was carrying a pitcher of freshly made margaritas with a cigarette dangling from his lips.

"I thought you could use another round." He beamed. "I have a late morning tomorrow, too, just found out this afternoon." He sat down beside me, rubbed my thigh, and kissed my cheek. "You look lovely tonight," he whispered into my ear. I blushed slightly but when I caught Harris's eye, I stiffened up immediately. She rolled her eyes at me and turned her attention to Gray. The smell of him was intoxicating. He moved his hand from my leg and wrapped his arm around me, pulling me closer to him.

As the evening wore on, Harris got more and more tipsy. Her words were slurring and she was saying things she normally wouldn't. I was hoping that dinner would sober her up, but it did little to counteract the alcohol. After dinner, Gray started a fire in the outside fireplace and helped me clean the kitchen. Every chance he got he touched me—whether he was resting his hand on my bottom as I washed the dishes, or he was standing beside me and his finger drifted down my arm. It was a constant reminder that he was here with me and totally present. He was enjoying himself and that made me happy. He never mentioned how drunk Harris was even though it was clearly obvious. He only said that he liked her and thought she was a riot. While I finished in the kitchen, he snuck back out to Harris to keep her company. I thought nothing of it, but when I came back out I could hear Harris's voice; it was muffled like a whisper. I could barely make out the words she was saying.

"What's with the whispering?" I asked, pretending not to care as I took my place by Gray on the couch by the fire. Gray seemed unsure of what to say, his face was strange again like this morning, but it was more of a confused expression than mistrust this time. "What?"

He cleared his throat. "Harris was telling me about your river house on the Rappahannock River. She was surprised that you had never mentioned it before. I agreed."

I looked at Harris crossly. "Well, I haven't been there in years, I barely think about it anymore. It was really John's place anyway. He had it before we were married. His grandparents handed it down to him."

"It sounds lovely. I'd love to see it sometime." He dropped the bait.

Harris cut her eyes back to me and raised an eyebrow. "You'll never get her to go, trust me. I've been trying for years," Harris answered for me.

Gray turned to me, confused again. I could tell that he sensed something was being kept from him, something between Harris and I. He stiffened and leveled his shoulders.

"Why is that?" he asked.

Harris chuckled and took a sip of her margarita. "Ask her. I'm surprised she hasn't already told you. I was under the impression she had already."

Gray smiled uncomfortably and turned his head to me and waited for an answer. But I wasn't looking at him, I was seething at Harris.

"Stop it, Harris," I hissed.

"I'm not doing anything, Laina," she exclaimed with mock shock.

"Yes, you are. Stop it," I growled, growing more and more irritated.

"Am I missing something, ladies?" Gray asked peacefully.

"I think you've had too much to drink, Harris. Let me take you to the guest room. You can stay here tonight." I tried, but it was useless.

"You can't just put him on a shelf when it's over, you know," she snapped.

"Damn it, Harris! What are you doing? Why?" I shouted.

"Hey, girls, easy. I thought we were having a good time," Gray interjected again.

"Someone has to say it to you; no one else will! Your sister won't, your mother won't, and if he never knows then he certainly won't!" she growled back.

"Harris, stop it, please," I begged. Tears were filling my eyes getting ready to roll down my face. She finally saw me through her drunken fit and she stopped. After a few minutes of awkward silence, she slowly got up and put her glass down.

"Gray, it was nice to meet you. I'm sorry about this. I never intended to ruin the evening. I honestly thought you knew. I apologize. Good night." She turned and walked into the house.

After a few seconds, I heard the sound of her car starting and pulling away. I took a huge breath and slumped down on the couch by the pool and lit another cigarette.

"What was that about?" Gray asked, stealing my cigarette from me.

My blood was boiling and I could feel my heart trying to pound out of my chest.

"That was pressure, to do the right thing I guess. She's not very subtle, is she?"

"What's the right thing?" Gray asked, suddenly very interested.

I turned to him. I could feel the tears gliding down my face. How would he ever understand? What would he think about me, knowing how wrong I was?

"She thinks I should say good-bye. She thinks it's time."

"I don't follow, love," he answered, furrowing his brow.

I stood up and gently took his hand in mine and pulled him into the house, through the doorway and into the den. I pointed to the mantle, surrounded by a rock wall.

"I was supposed to take them to the river and scatter their ashes, but I couldn't. The river cottage was their favorite place. I haven't been there in four years because…I know they aren't there. What's the point?"

He stared at me, trying to think of what to say. I had stumped him again.

"Harris thinks if I get too close to you and then you leave, that I may not recover. I tried, you know, to kill myself after they died. My sister, Mandy, found me. She dragged me from the floor all the way to her car, by herself. She gave me mouth-to-mouth and screamed for me to wake up. I remember bits and pieces, but I can't remember her face, thank God. That would have really… killed me. She has been extra protective since then. Harris thinks you should know about my suicide attempt, so you know what you're getting into with me."

"Why didn't you tell me any of this?" he asked.

"Because I didn't want you to look at me like you are now. I didn't want you to think that you have to be with me because you're scared of what I might do to myself if you leave. Because I don't want to think about you leaving when I know you will. I was different then, I was dead inside. I had nothing. I want you with me because you want to be here. When it ends, it ends. I'm prepared for that when it comes."

"Why would I leave you? I told you how special you are to me. Why won't you believe me?" he asked with worry.

"You can do better than me; you know it as well as I do. I have way too much baggage to be good for you," I whispered.

"You are good for me Elaina, don't think that," he begged.

"Can't you see me? I'm a sinking ship. You don't belong with me. I'm no good for you. I'm broken and I always will be." I cried, determined to make him see that I was right even if I prayed he would refuse it.

He grabbed my face in his hands, shaking his head back and forth and looked deep into my eyes. "What's it gonna take for you to believe me, love? You're not getting rid of me that easily. Your past is in the past. You have to leave it there, love, in the past." He stopped me from talking any more by keeping my lips very busy for the rest of the night.

~~~~~~~~

When I woke in the morning, he was gone, but there was a note beside me on his pillow where I was sure to see it.

My dearest innkeeper,

I went out for a bit. Coffee is ready and waiting in the kitchen, and so is your friend.

Love,
Gray

When I shuffled into the kitchen, Harris was still sitting at the kitchen table, spinning her finger around her mug, waiting for me. At first I was angry and I could feel it seething through my body. My first thought was to smack her across her beautiful, sorrowful face, but it passed in seconds. She was upset—more than I had ever seen her. She had been right; my suicide attempt shouldn't have been kept from Gray, but I was going to tell him. I just hadn't gotten around to it yet. The fact that their ashes were still sitting on my mantle was wrong, and I should have told him about that too. There was something wrong with me, or different. For the first time in a long time I was intent on holding on to another human being. I had allowed myself to get attached—to love again. I knew I had been angry at her because she was right. Everyone was right but me. The more I thought about it, the less fury-filled I became. She was only trying to help, in her way. She was trying to protect me from myself. It was probably very hard for her to say the things she had said last night; and now here she sat, getting ready to grovel because that was what she thought she should do. My shuffling feet alerted her to my presence. She snapped her head up at once with a look of apology.

"Laina,…I…I'm so sorr—"

I lifted a finger up and closed my eyes. This confused her momentarily and she abruptly stopped talking.

"Please don't, Harris. I really can't bear it," I whispered. Harris said nothing, only stared at me with bewildered eyes. "You don't need to apologize, really."

She was quiet for a while and nodded her head, but then she began shaking her head back and forth angrily.

"No, no, no. I came her to apologize and that's what I'm gonna do!" she snapped. "I had no right to say those things to you, especially with Grayson here. It was horrible and there is no excuse for my behavior. I am so sorry, Elaina. Please except my apology."

"No," I answered.

"No? What do you mean no? No, you don't forgive me?" She gasped.

"No, I don't accept your apology."

"Why?" she questioned, confused again.

"Because there is nothing to say you're sorry for. You said the truth. You said what I was too afraid to say. Now, it's out there for him to know, so thanks, I guess." I explained.

"Don't you dare, Elaina! Please don't say thank you! He's leaving, isn't he? You're thanking me for scaring him off, aren't you?" She trembled.

"Nope, he went to work this morning as far as I know," I answered.

Harris sat and stewed for a few minutes. I worked around her silent statue making my cup of coffee and preparing my usual bowl of fruit. At some point, she stopped giving me the death-ray eyes and decided she was done pouting. When I came to sit next to her at the table with my coffee and fruit, she sighed loudly. I ignored her as usual. But then I looked up at her staring at me with her hard eyes.

"What?" I asked, annoyed.

"Why do you always eat fruit for breakfast? Every damn morning, fruit, fruit, fruit. Don't you like anything else? Cereal, muffins, toast, eggs maybe? Just same old, boring fruit," she huffed.

I chuckled and dove into a strawberry with my fork and stuffed it in my mouth. I smiled at her annoyance of my daily ritual. I truly loved fruit, but that wasn't why I ate it every morning. I couldn't tell her that the smell of strawberries reminded me of Georgia's hair after her bath. I couldn't tell her that John's favorite gum was Juicy Fruit and that the taste of grapefruit reminded me of his breath when he kissed me. It also could have been that Georgia only ate fruit for breakfast every morning when she was alive. John could never pass a pineapple in the grocery store without grabbing it. There were a few reasons that I ate fruit every morning, but I wouldn't tell her any of the real reasons. I couldn't. It would almost feel like telling her a secret that they had asked me to keep—an inside story or family joke between the three of us. I smiled again.

"I just really love fruit," I answered, still smiling to myself.

"Whatever. You should really try something else some time." She was defeated and she knew it. I hadn't meant to, but I had thrown a wrench into her entire day of worrying and stressing over what to do to make last night up to me. It felt good getting under her skin and rattling her for a change.

Chapter 9

What to Tell Mandy

A few days later, I was starting another day. It was going to be a long one and a lonely one. Gray was heading back to LA for a few days to handle some business; and even though he had asked me to come with him, I knew I wouldn't be comfortable going.

He woke up early and just lay there in bed beside me. He huffed and puffed and finally slinked out of the bed and into the shower. While he was in the shower, he continued his huffing and puffing, making me smile at his unhappiness for having to leave. He moved much slower than usual, and when he finally came back into the room, instead of getting dressed he got back into bed. He slid over to me under the covers and found me in the dark of the morning. His arm moved under my pillow and his other arm wound around my waist, pulling me closer to him. His face pressed into my hair and he sighed. I started to laugh quietly.

"Stop laughing," he ordered playfully. His voice sounded deep, rough, and tired.

"If you don't want to go then just stay here," I offered with a wicked smile.

"I wish I could see your face, Ms. Murphy," he chuckled. "You're quite enjoying this, aren't you?" he teased.

"Not at all, but if you don't stop huffing and puffing, you're gonna pass out, and this whole conversation will be pointless because you'll miss your plane."

He muffled another laugh and squeezed me closer to him. "I just don't want to leave. I like it here." His tone was more serious now, and I knew no more jokes were necessary.

"I like you here," I whispered.

"How much?" he asked the question as if he were snooping for information.

"What?" I laughed.

"Well, do you like me here or do you love me here?" His voice was a bit shaky and unsure.

I turned to face him; I needed to see his eyes. "Well, if I had to pinpoint it, I would say...*love*. I love it when you are here," I answered, hoping my answer would please him.

He smiled but didn't allow any other emotion to show through. I got the feeling I had just missed an opportunity to tell him how I felt. The moment was gone now. Even though he seemed to not be affected by my evasive maneuver, I could tell that he was a little sad.

"That's good to know then." He lightly chuckled beside me. I pressed my head into the curve of his neck and snuggled in. I could feel my hair getting caught in the bristles on his chin. "I gotta get going, love."

"I know." I sighed.

Grayson stayed beside me for another fifteen minutes before dragging himself out of bed and getting dressed. He was ready when Jason the driver pulled into the driveway and honked the horn. He kissed me again and again as I sat on the edge of the bed with my legs dangling down and around his. There was a sadness in the way his lips touched mine.

"I'll be back in two days, I promise. I'll call you when I get there." He kissed me as soon as he finished talking.

"I'll miss you," I whispered into his ear. When I spoke the words, the breath hit his ear just right and goose bumps erupted all over his arms. His intensity grew and he gripped my waist harder and more forcefully. His hands knotted in my hair, pulling me closer. Suddenly, he tugged my hair back in his hand with enough force to pull my head back. His lips searched my neck and throat. He found my lips again and kissed me passionately until I couldn't breathe. When he pulled away, we were both panting and breathless. His eyes smoldered. They were so beautiful. I could see the specks of green and brown mixed in with the grey in the early morning sunlight. "I love you, Elaina," he whispered.

My heart stopped, and I could feel the air being choked off deep inside my throat somewhere. I couldn't say anything, and he didn't give me a chance to. His lips quickly found mine again. "I'll see you soon, love."

He kissed me on the forehead and then hurried out to the impatiently waiting Jason.

I was speechless and exhilarated all at the same time. He loved me, I knew he had for some time, but now, the way he had said it—I could see that he really meant it for the first time. He had put his heart out there again, and I hadn't said anything. Well, I kind of couldn't say anything. Maybe he had planned it that way, maybe not. In his fear of my response, he had kept my mouth busy so that I couldn't say anything at all. This beautiful and wonderful man loved me. How was this possible? After everything he knew about me, how could he love someone like me? I had killed my family in a stupid car accident that could have been avoided. I had refused to go to the funeral because I was afraid to say good-bye. I still hadn't followed John's wishes and scattered the ashes in the river by the bridge. I was a horrible person. I didn't deserve any of this. I wasn't supposed to get another shot at love and happiness, was I?

~~~~~~~~

This afternoon, I was going to see Mandy and stay for dinner to spend some time with my nieces. That would sufficiently distract me, I was sure of it.

When I got to Mandy's house, I was reminded once again of her perfect life: Two daughters and another one probably on the way. A great husband with a great job. A beautiful home with the best furniture and decorations. We had once been very much alike. Everything was perfect, and I suddenly realized that everything was perfect here except for me. I was dressed in a simple black sundress. My hair was pulled into a messy bun. I didn't look at all as glamorous as the Kindrick family. Mandy had dressed the two girls in matching poufy sundresses with a tropical flower print. These dresses weren't for the sun though and definitely not for playing around in. I could tell Mandy had slaved over their hair because the two girls were walking around as if their hair was made of blown glass. They were cute though, one five and one three, both with white-blond hair and perfect tans from playing in their backyard pool. Mandy came in with her hair perfectly coifed into a french braid and wearing a bright-purple sundress and gold sandals. Her toenails matched her fingernails with the same purple hue for polish. Her face lit up when she saw me sitting at the island in the kitchen.

"You made it. I wasn't sure if you were still coming. Harris told me you might be going out of town for a few days." She beamed.

Harris and her mouth. I cursed her under my breath. "No, I decided to stay here." I seethed while trying to sound normal and upbeat.

"Good, 'cause we got lots of food here, and Bill is working late so it's just you, me, and the girls."

"Oh, sure, that's fine."

When Mandy turned to the side, I caught a glimpse of the belly. It was pretty big for four months, but not too big that people would see it right away. She had camouflaged it perfectly with a sundress that focused on the all the great things about being pregnant.

"So, do you know what you're having yet?" I asked, happy to talk about something she was interested in.

"Oh, yeah, it's another girl. Can you believe it? Oh well, maybe next time we'll get a boy."

"Next time? Is Harris right about you? Are you becoming a baby factory?"

She rolled her eyes as she stuffed huge red peppers with some sort of sausage-looking mixture.

"You know, some of us need more out of life than work, Elaina. Some of us enjoy having a family. We can't all be robots like Harris," she scoffed.

"She's not a robot, Mandy. She is just different, that's all"—I chuckled softly—"and I think it's great you guys are having lots of kids." I wasn't just saying that to her either. I was happy for my sister and everything she had. It was just that sometimes being around her was a soft reminder of what I had once had, and every now and then it stung a bit.

She rolled her eyes again, realizing her hormone-laced attack on Harris. "I know, I'm sorry. That wasn't fair of me to say."

Dinner was great as usual. She had grilled chicken and made fresh salad with basil and tomato and goat cheese. The weather was perfect. The air had turned cool for June as a rainstorm approached, and the breeze that had been barely alive strengthened and swirled through the trees. The warmth hadn't gotten too moist and sticky, and everywhere I looked there was green.

Mandy was a great cook. Like me, our mother had taught her to cook as a child. My mother wanted us to be able to take care of a man and our families. It was important to her. She was hard on us and never complimented us for anything. We never did anything right or near good enough. She was a cold woman that never touched or smiled. I can recall the few times she actually hugged me in my life: Graduation from high school was the first, then college. Next was my wedding day and then the last was the day Georgia was born. Years later, Mandy and I had talked about mom and her inability to hug or show affection. We both compared notes and both found it comical that she had hugged us almost the same number of times for the exact same things. My father was a caring and loving man. He was incredibly emotional. My parents fought most of the time. They were so different that it wasn't possible to get along. They spent most of their time apart; and when they were together, they didn't speak to each other unless it was necessary. Mandy and I were lucky to get my dad's heart.

My nieces had retired inside to watch cartoons on the couch. I was sure they opted for that choice so they could get out of the bridesmaidesque dresses their mother had put them in. I didn't blame them. They looked completely different now in comfortable pajamas and more like little kids.

Mandy poured me another glass of wine and sat back down. "So, anything new with you now that we can talk without the PG rating attached?"

"Were we supposed to be PG? I didn't know that," I teased.

She laughed at herself and then pointed to me. "You know they hear everything…and repeat everything too."

Yes, I knew that. I smiled to myself thinking of one of the times I had come over for dinner. I had said the word *crap* in front of Sammie, her youngest. I didn't think *crap* was that bad, but to Mandy and Bill, it was horrifying when Sammie went to preschool the next day. The kids were in the middle of an art project when Sammie stated, "This crap is for babies!" From then on, I was asked to use a PG sensor while the children were around. They even asked me to apologize to Sammie for using such a "yucky" word and explain to her that I had not meant to say such a gross thing.

"Well, there is something I've been meaning to talk to you about." I grinned tightly, trying to stay calm while wondering what her reaction would be. Telling Mandy things like this were always dangerous. I never knew what she would think, and that made me nervous.

Her eyes brightened and grew the size of apples. "Really? What's that?"

I felt bad for her suddenly. She had been out of the Grayson loop while Harris had been way too involved. Her feelings would probably be hurt at first, but now was as good a time as any.

"I've been seeing someone for almost two months now."

Her eyes bulged. "You mean dating?"

"Yeah. He's really great. I like him a lot." I nodded with a girlish smile.

"That's great, Elaina! Who is he? Anyone I know?" she asked enthusiastically.

I felt really bad for her now. I really should have told her sooner.

"Yes, you probably do actually."

"Really? What's his name?" she asked excitedly.

I closed my eyes and swallowed hard, then I said his name, "Grayson Sparks."

Mandy sucked in a huge gulp of air and started coughing. This was not a name she expected to hear. Maybe someone from the country club or a friend of Harris's, but definitely not Grayson Sparks.

"You mean *the* Grayson Sparks? The movie star? From Hollywood?" she blurted out.

"Yes, that's him."

"Stop pulling my leg, Laina. That's not funny!" she warned.

"I'm serious." I answered, unfazed.

"But...how? Where did you meet him?"

I raised one eyebrow at her and waited to see if she would make the connection. It didn't take long at all. Her face turned serious with deep thought trying to figure it out. Then suddenly her face lit up like a lightbulb.

"He's the balding old man? Grayson Sparks is living in your home? Now?"

I laughed a little. "Well, technically he's in LA right now, but he will be back Friday."

Mandy started panting and waving her face. She caught her breath after a few moments, then her face turned more serious. "Laina, he is a total lady's man! You better be careful."

I had known this would be her reaction, so instead of trying to convince her of our true feelings for each other, I simply agreed.

"I know. Don't worry, it's not serious, I assured her gently.

Her face relaxed and then she allowed herself to get excited again. "Grayson Sparks! Really? Wow!"

The rest of the evening she asked me countless questions, most of them about Gray. I told her just enough to give her something without telling her anything. It was sort of sad how our relationship had changed. We had been very close once upon a time, but now she was more like my mother than a sister. The mother I never really had that nurtured me and protected me no matter what. At the same time I couldn't tell her everything anymore. I knew if I did she would inevitably dissect it and analyze everything I told her. It was easier to edit as much as possible and leave out most of the details. I told her to keep it quiet and not tell anyone anything. She agreed, reluctantly. Mandy was probably dying to tell her country club friends, but she would keep quiet, I was positive. She was someone I could trust; I knew that.

That night, I was in bed watching TV when suddenly there he was.

And on to some more exciting news, Grayson Sparks has returned to Los Angeles for a few days on a break from shooting his latest film, *I Found You*. Shooting began in the beginning of May and should resume in two days when he returns to Virginia. He is starring alongside new and up and coming Cody Ramsy, and the rumor mill is working overtime trying to hook these two stars up. Sources have described their working relationship to be more than just friendly and the two are reportedly spending lots of time together off set as well as on. Sparks, who arrived in LA late this morning, was all smiles when walking through security checkpoints but had no comment when asked about his relationship with Ramsy.

I tuned out the rest of the news after that. I knew that this story was a fabrication; he hadn't had time to spend time with her outside of work. At least that's what I thought. I wasn't going to allow this news report to upset me. If I planned on being with Gray for any amount of time, I would have to get used to the lies from the media. I put my head down and tried to go to sleep, then I remembered he was going to call me when he got in. I shot up, grabbed my phone, and dialed voice mail. There was a message, and it was from him.

"Hey, love. I just got in. The press is already hounding me at the airport. Anyway, I'll try to call you later then. And umm"—he cleared his throat before he whispered into the phone—"I miss you like crazy already."

The phone hung up. So weird how he was there talking to me and I was just watching it on TV. If the media had been there a minute before or a minute later, they may have had him calling me on the news. It was nice to see his face even if the report was total crap. He sounded so happy and energized on the phone. I snuggled over to his pillow and breathed in his scent and drifted off to sleep.

The next morning, Gray was all over the TV again doing the morning talk show circuit. He walked across the stage and my heart skipped a beat. He looked good, really good. I felt prideful of the fact that he was mine, for now anyway. He walked across the stage in a dark-grey suit with a navy-blue shirt underneath that was unbuttoned at the collar. He was smiling his megawatt smile, obviously playing the movie star part. The questions were typical inquiries about the new movie about to come out and what it was about. They asked him how it was working with some of the actors, and he answered graciously as usual. The questions starting drifting to more personal topics. Before I knew it, they were asking him about his personal life. So I put down the laundry and walked over to stand in front of the TV.

"So, Grayson, are you seeing anyone special these days, or are you still playing the field?"

I stopped breathing.

He smiled widely as if he had been waiting for this question to come. "Well, there is someone. She is very special," he answered.

The crowd went crazy with screams and whistles. He laughed, and for a moment his face graced his genuine smile that I love.

"Is this special woman acting with you on your new film?" the interviewer asked coyly, trying to dig up some dirt and obviously assuming the woman was Cody Whatshername.

"No, she is not an actress. She's fantastic and I'm proud to call her my lady!" He beamed again and his face seemed to blush.

After the crowd quieted back down, "So, is this serious?"

He smiled again and shrugged his shoulders. He looked uncomfortable for the first time. "I certainly hope so!"

The crowd went crazy and the interviewer yelled over the audience to go to a commercial.

My stomach was filled with butterflies. I was overjoyed and excited. He had actually done it. I never thought he would actually talk about us, but he had. Not only that, he was excited about it and not afraid to show it to the whole country. I fell back on the bed and screamed into the pillow.

The phone rang as I was screaming, and I jumped about three feet into the air.

"Hello?"

"There you are. Where have you been? Busy catching up with your friends?" he teased. Gray always teased me about having only two friends, but I tried to assure him that it was easier for me.

"Gray! How are you? Where are you? I just saw you on TV."

"Did you now? Was that okay what I said then?" he asked.

"Of course, I just didn't think you would say anything, but yeah! Of course, it's fine!" I answered like a schoolgirl with a crush.

I could hear him chuckling on the other end. "Well, I've only got a few minutes. My agent's got me slammed for the time I'm here so…can I call you later?"

"Sure. Of course."

He laughed again. "I miss you, Elaina."

"I miss you too, Gray."

"By now, love."

"Good-bye."

The interviews continued on most of the morning. Some were on the set, others were on the phone. One interviewer actually asked for my name, but he declined to answer. He thought it was too intrusive on my privacy. It was strange to watch him on TV; the Gray I knew was so normal and everyday. This man was different. He was larger than life on the screen, but here with me, he was just Gray—my Gray.

That night, there were more reports of Gray and Cody having an onset affair even though Gray had already admitted that he was in a relationship with someone else. The media was relentless with him. They never seemed to let up, but he took it in stride. Another day passed and I was eagerly awaiting his return. I kept finding myself tapping my fingers on tables or drifting off into thoughts of him. For some reason, his admittance of our relationship had stirred newer and stronger feelings for him inside of me. The idea of falling for someone was exciting and terrifying at the same time. I feared that my broken heart would fail me somehow; that it wouldn't be able to handle anything or anyone else. Every time I thought this way, a pain would start in my chest and then I would imagine his face—him—standing in front of me. Then he would smile his simple smile. Then the pain in my chest would move south and my body would begin to burn a slow, smoldering fire. Thank God I wasn't driving today because I'm sure I would have wrecked my stupid, oversized car—a car I bought out of fear of getting hurt again, or even losing another loved one. There was no one left to lose though, a fact that had always been painfully obvious and at the same time moot to me.

He was supposed to be back late tonight, Friday night. Macbeth followed me all over the house that day. It was as if she knew he was coming back, too, and she was just as excited as I was. I didn't need to cook dinner for him which left me with one less thing to do to take up more time in my day.

I decided to take Macbeth for a walk in the same park Gray and I had gone to that wonderful afternoon. She was full of energy and dancing all around the water. She would bound left then right and then duck her head down on her paws, sticking her butt up in the air with her little nub of a tail wagging furiously. I wished I could get out my energy that way. I wondered how ridiculous human beings would look if that was acceptable for us to do. Then I tried to imagine couples wagging their butts in the air at the sight of each other. How simple would life be then, when only a wag of a butt cheek could show someone how much you really love them and enjoy their company? I chuckled to myself, but Macbeth turned to me and cocked her head to the side, seeing something I hadn't. I should have noticed the man standing behind me, but I didn't. I had been too busy imagining people behaving like dogs in more ways than one; then suddenly, by the time I did notice him, it was too late to flee.

"That's a nice dog you have there!" he shouted from the path up the bank, only twenty feet away.

I turned unexpectedly to see the man standing there with a camera in his hand. My first thought was that he was taking pictures of the river, but it was a real nice camera, with a long lens attached to it, and he was wearing long pants and a button-up shirt. It was summer and he looked out of place, more than I was comfortable with. So I was careful with my answers.

"Yeah, she's great." I nodded but then in a split second decided to turn the tables on him. "Did you lose your dog or something?" I asked, raising an eyebrow with fake concern.

"Me? Oh no, I don't have a pet. I'm here looking for something else." He scoffed. "That dog looks very familiar." He pointed to Macbeth. "Had *her* long?" he asked with a slight grin that was neither friendly nor honest.

"Oh, I've had her for years," I answered quickly, becoming more and more sure of what this jerk was doing here.

"Really? 'Cause that dog looks just like someone else's dog that I know. He's working in town for a while." He smiled and exposed his yellowing teeth.

"Oh. Well, have a nice day." I ended the conversation and hurried Macbeth out of the water and to the car. It wasn't easy getting her to walk away with me. I could feel her pulling toward the man, and a low grumble was escaping her chest. The man was still watching me as I drove off while he spoke into his phone.

As soon as I got home, I called Gray. He didn't answer and I figured he was probably in the air and couldn't use his phone, so I left him a message.

"Gray? It's me. Look, you can't come home with Jason tonight. I think a paparazzi spotted Macbeth and I at the park today. I'll get Harris to come get you instead. Call me when you land, Okay? Okay, bye."

I hoped that I was wrong. I hoped that the guy at the park was just a weirdo that liked carrying a camera around for no good reason. I hoped that if he was who I thought he was, it wouldn't ruin the rest of the time Gray and I had together. If anything, I was sure that we were going to have to be very careful from now on. The press obviously wanted to know who the new girlfriend was, and they were already searching for answers.

Chapter 10

Harris brought Gray back to the house around one in the morning. She didn't come in to say hello, and I'm pretty sure she was angry with me for making her pick him up so late, but I was consumed with other worries for the moment. It was a rather severe precaution, I admit. As worried as I was, Gray was like a livewire, and as soon as he came through the door, he rushed to me, putting both of his hands on either side of my face to kiss me. He didn't have to say anything at all; he said it all with his hands and his tender lips. When he pulled away to look at me, his mouth pulled up to the side and he chuckled.

"Hi," he whispered.

"Hi," I answered.

He leaned in to kiss me again, but I stopped him short. He didn't like that at all; his mouth dropped and his brow furrowed in frustration.

"We need to talk about that jerk at the park."

"What about him? He's just some pap; nobody cares about them."

"He was weird, Gray. He recognized Macbeth. He had a camera. He may have taken a picture," I explained.

"And?" he asked with his eyes about to roll.

"He could've followed me home! That's what!" I snapped, getting more frustrated with his lack of seriousness.

He stuck his hands in the air as if to surrender. "Okay, I understand already. He scared you, is that it?" His hands fell to his hips and his eyes narrowed to look me straight on.

"Yes."

"Elaina, we talked about this, remember? I can't hide forever, right? We can't hide forever, right?" His voice was low and controlled. No matter how hard he tried, he could not mask his blasé attitude about it. Then his eyes narrowed and his face turned red with fury. The bored face was gone and in its place was anger; fury. "Did he speak to you?" he spoke through his teeth, and his voice was barely audible, straining to control his temper.

Suddenly, I was scared. I didn't understand why he was so angry with me all of a sudden. I couldn't figure out what had happened that was so terrible in the last few seconds.

"That's what I was trying to tell you. He was creep—"

He put his finger to my lips, stopping me from talking. His breathing was faster than normal and his eyes were smashed closed in anger.

"Did I do something wrong?" I asked in a small voice, much like a child's. His eyes flashed open in horror with apology.

"You didn't do anything, love. I'm sorry. I'm not mad at you. It's him. That guy is always crossing the line." He took another steadied breath. "Let me guess, he was sort of heavy, stupid pressman hat on, and he was dressed like an accountant, right?"

"Umm, yeah, how did you know that?"

"He follows me everywhere in LA. He is at every single event and every non-event I attend. He works with one of those trashy celeb magazines. He is always looking for dirt on me. He even showed up at my mother's funeral."

"Why? Does he not like you or something?"

He grinned devilishly. "I accidentally…knocked him over once when I was leaving the airport." My mouth dropped open, and he immediately put his hand up to stop me. "He practically ran over this kid—she was probably no more than six—all just to get a photo of me leaving the airport. Such an idiot! The mom started yelling at him and he called her some nasty name, so…I bumped him onto the baggage claim carousel. He lost his shot at the photo. I guess he hates me or something."

"Oh," I answered.

"Anyway, who cares if he got a picture of you and Macbeth? You can't let them control your life, Elaina."

I scrunched up my face, not sure of anything he was telling me. This was too close. He was too close to my home, my life. Gray knew how to deal with this stuff, I didn't. He gently placed his hands around the tops of my arms. "Relax, love. You'll get used to it. I promise nothing will happen; they just want a picture. That's not so bad, is it?"

I sighed loudly, allowing my face to relax a bit. "I guess not."

"Good. Now can I get back to fondling you now?" he teased with one eyebrow lifted.

I smiled in agreement, and I was abruptly lifted over his shoulder and carried into the bedroom, where he gave me the greeting he had wanted to before.

~~~~~~~~

It was mid June. It was getting hotter every day, but the humidity had stayed away so far. I was grateful because that meant I could be outside almost all day. I didn't take Macbeth with me to the park again, but I went often. The creepy camera man was there usually whenever I was. Gray was working around the clock, at least that's what it felt like. He was exhausted when he got home late at night and he was up at five in the morning the next day to start all over again, sometimes earlier. I tried to stay busy. I walked, I ran and swam, I shopped and cleaned. I met Harris for lunch and met up with Mandy every week. Both of them questioned me nonstop about Grayson. Mandy was still in the dark about how I really felt about him, and Harris knew almost everything. Juggling the two of them was getting exhausting.

Then when Gray was home, he pressured me about my feelings for him, always gently tugging at the question of whether or not I loved him. I hadn't said it yet. I could tell it was a source of annoyance for him. He didn't say it often, but when he did say it and I didn't say it back, his face fell a little more each time. It was getting harder for him to hide his disappointment. The strange thing was, the longer he was here, the more I did fall in love with him, but the easier it was to deny him that information. I didn't take pleasure in it at all; seeing him upset, even if only for a second, was physically painful for me. I couldn't understand why he kept trying or why he loved me. It still was wrong to me. Why had he chosen me? He had told me all the reasons why so many times, but still I held back. I refused him entry into my heart.

Gray started to change. It was a subtle change, but I noticed it. His usual lighthearted ways grew darker. His good moods lessened. He was still loving and attentive, but I could feel his determination starting to waver. The time was flying past us. Still he pushed in his own subtle way to get me to tell him how I felt. He wanted something more, and I just wasn't sure if I was able to give any more.

The urn sat day after day on the mantle. I looked at it every day and thought of John and Georgia every day. Sometimes I would catch Gray staring at it, but when he realized I saw him, he shifted his eyes away and toward something else in an awkward motion. Still, there were wonderful times as well. The times when he let things go and let us be us were the best times: the skinny dipping in the pool late at night, the late mornings, the all nighters. The way he would look at me when we were making love. I don't just throw that term around. I know there is a big difference between having sex and making love. Gray and I had our fair share of great sex, but then there were the other times too—the times when he stared into my eyes and I back at his, that moment when you are with someone and everything feels right and perfect; you feel safer than you ever have before; the arms around you aren't just someone's arms, they are his arms and they are arms you never want to live without and have no idea how you ever did for so long—those moments were the greatest for me. His face was never wrinkled with worry or fear, just tireless love. As much as those times were so very precious to both of us, I felt things slipping.

By the beginning of July, things were changing again. Gray was more impatient now and getting tired of the charade. He had been cranky since getting home that night. We ate dinner outside by the pool. He barely spoke while we sat across from each other. I tried to get him to talk; I asked him questions about his day, but he gave me nothing but short answers. He finished before me but sat silent and waited for me to finish my dinner. He stared at me, studying me, maybe even judging me. My stomach was in knots as I tried to force myself to eat. When I finished eating, I poured some more wine for both of us and shot him a smile. Gray had had four glasses already. He didn't have to work the next day, so he was drinking more than he usually allowed himself. I looked up from my glass and smiled at him again, but he didn't smile back. The silence and the unknown of his mood was more than I thought I could take. I started to rise from my chair and head into the house.

"Are you still in love with him?" he muttered.

"What?" I was shocked. I didn't know what to say or think. I slowly sat back down, lowering my head to hide my face from him. I was embarrassed and unsettled; I couldn't figure out why. Asking me about John was something he never did, ever. I could tell by his tone that he was just as uncomfortable with this subject as I was, but he wasn't backing down this time either.

"You are, aren't you?" He slammed his hand and napkin down on the table and took a gulp of wine. "That's why you don't love me, isn't it?"

I couldn't answer him; I didn't know exactly how to answer his question.

"Elaina, please just tell me. I deserve to know." His voice was softer this time but still with a tint of displeasure.

"Gray, please," I begged, trying to avoid eye contact. Up until now, John and Gray had been two very separate things in my mind and my heart. To think of them as the same or even in the same way was uncomfortable for me.

"Answer me, Elaina. Am I wasting my time with you? 'Cause if I am, please just tell me, and I'll go."

"Is that a threat? If I don't say I love you, you'll leave?" I snapped, getting angry now. I stood up and stormed into the house with the dinner plates. He stayed outside. After I finished cleaning the kitchen, he was still outside. I wanted to go to him and tell him I was scared, terrified really. I wanted to tell him that I loved him, but I couldn't. Was this what my mother went through? This internal struggle between what she wanted to do and what she was actually capable of doing. Had her genes finally emerged inside of me; stopping me from showing love or even giving love? I had been able to give myself to John so easily. Why couldn't I do that now? Now that a man wanted me, wanted to love me and give himself to me. I knew the answer to all of this. I had given every bit of myself to John and then Georgia, and they had left me—no—they had died. I couldn't take that again, not again. Even though Gray could leave and would leave, I couldn't say the words he wanted me to say.

I decided to let him cool off, and I went to bed. He never came to bed, but I knew he was inside somewhere that night. He stayed away and I finally had the first taste of the pain that would come when he left.

In the morning, he was passed out on the couch. I slinked past his sprawled-out body on the couch and started making breakfast. I didn't hear him get up, but I heard the shower door slam as he stepped into the stall. When he came out, he looked embarrassed, maybe even mortified. He seemed scared to talk to me. He sat at the island and silently watched me fry up some bacon and eggs. I had refused to look up at him, letting him stew a little more, but I knew I had to eventually face him. I knew I would crumble at the sight of him so I had taken my time. I looked up and he was staring at me, like he always did. His eyes were bloodshot and puffy from too much wine, and his hair was still damp and messy.

"Elaina, I'm sorry. I had no right to speak to you that way last night."

"You're right! You didn't," I answered.

"I know," he mumbled.

"I'm trying really hard, okay? I want to trust you; I want to be with you and...love you, okay?" His eyes shot up in shock. That word, that little word that he had wanted so badly to hear last night was finally spoken. "Yes, I can say it. I just don't say it unless I'm sure."

"You think I'm not sure of my feelings for you then?" he questioned with a tinge of anger. I pushed my hands down hard on my hips with a loud huff and waited. "I know how I feel about you; I just don't know how you feel about me. Every day I wait and hope that you will tell me, that you will give me some sort of...something! But you don't. You never do. I just want to know how you feel. Is that so bad? Is that too much to ask?" He rubbed his temples with his hands, roughly feeling the hangover pound away. "Do I just enjoy this time with you, knowing I will have to go in the end? Or maybe I should try to make a go of it then? What am I supposed to do? Please, just tell me?" His voice crackled and his eyes burned into mine.

"I thought we were just gonna wait and see," I whispered. I could taste the poison on my lips as I tried to convince him not to love me, not to stay.

"That was then, Elaina. Things have changed for me! I want you! I want all of you! I want you with me, forever. That I do know for sure!" His voice thundered through the room. Maybe he had reached his limit, finally. He looked down at the ground and spoke softly now, and his lips turned up at the sides. He seemed to admit his defeat and was willing to retreat for a bit. He shook his head gently and smiled with a sigh, then he looked at me. "But if you can't give me that, then I'll take what I can, I suppose. I'll love you while I can, and then I'll leave, if that's what you want."

"That's not what I want, Gray. I don't want you to leave," I whispered.

He smiled gently at me. "But you can't love me?"

"It's not that I don't love you or that I won't; I don't know if I can…give you what you need. I don't know if I can ever have that again with anyone." My voice broke, and I could feel the tears creeping back into my eyes. I heard him hop from the stool and shuffle around to me. He paused a few feet away from me, unsure of what I wanted him to do. I stepped the few feet to him and pressed my face into his chest and started to cry.

He sighed and wound his arms around my waist, pulling me toward him. He held me, tightly, for a long time. When he started to pull away, I held on and pulled him back against me. He laughed quietly.

"Okay, we will just wait and see, like we said. But I do love you, Elaina. I can't pretend that I don't, okay?"

"Okay." I sighed.

Chapter 11

The Photo of July

July was hot as hell, and there was no escaping the humidity that swallowed up the air and spit out more heat. Gray hated the weather now, and it seemed to annoy more and more every second he was stuck in it. He was not used to this kind of sticky, nasty air. Air conditioning was a wonderful thing and Grayson quickly learned to appreciate it.

After our talk, things had been much better. Gray was more at ease in knowing that I at least wanted to be with him and love him. He was more reserved now than he had been, and he tried to hold back just enough so as not to pressure me. Outside dinners were no more, and we had to move inside to the dining room table. It was actually romantic eating at the massive table. It could have sat ten easily, but we sat across from each other at one end of the table.

Macbeth hated the weather as well and spent most of her days panting at the door, pleading to come in, or swimming around in the now-warm pool. I had grown quite fond of Macbeth. She was a cute dog that loved to cuddle. If she wanted you to pet her, she would lower her head right under your palm and wait with big brown eyes. She was fiercely protective. I was more than starting to like her; I was growing very attached to her.

After dinner, she had been abnormally agitated. Gray had gotten so annoyed with her that he had put her outside. Once outside, she rushed to the back of the yard and paced back and forth, all the while facing the woods, then she sat in one spot and stared. We could hear her low growling from the kitchen.

"Something's got her spooked," Gray muttered. "She never acts like this, does she?"

"Never. You wanna go have a look? It might be another dog or a cat, a deer maybe."

"I'll go. You stay here, just in case it's a...well...I'll be right back."

He walked right up to Macbeth and patted her on her head and rubbed her blackish-brown ears between his fingers. She was still totally alert. He couldn't get her to relax. I stepped just outside the door. "You see anything?"

"Nothing," he answered as he stared into the dark trees.

I walked over to him and put my hand on his back. He turned to me and automatically kissed me. That's when I heard it, the clicking noise. The creepy guy's camera had made the same noise that day at the river. I froze and so did Gray.

"Did you hear that?" he whispered.

"Ah-huh," I answered.

"What do you see? Don't let him know you hear him," he whispered around my lips.

I looked instinctually in the direction of the clicking and then, finally, I could barely see him sitting there, perched in a tree stand.

"I see someone," I whispered. Gray grabbed my hand to get my attention. "Go call the police. Tell them there is a strange man in your backyard. Don't let him see you panic or use the phone. Act like nothing is wrong," he whispered into my ear as if he was kissing me. He was a good actor, I wasn't. I turned and walked normally into the house and pretended to clean the kitchen. The house phone was sitting on the counter so I slid it off and lowered my hand down below the countertop to dial 911. I calmly walked to the laundry room where the man couldn't see me on the phone.

"911. What is your emergency?"

"There is a man sitting in a tree stand in my backyard," I fumbled out, hardly believing it myself.

"Excuse me?" she asked as if she didn't believe me.

"There is a strange man in my backyard, taking pictures of my friend and I. Please send someone."

I gave her the address, and she promised someone would be there and asked that I stay on the phone with her. I couldn't walk around with the phone in my hands, or the photographer would see that I had called the police, so I pressed the speaker button and placed the phone back on the counter. I turned my back to the yard. "I'm not gonna talk to you, but I'm here. You're on speaker phone."

"Okay, Ms. Murphy, just keep your phone on. The officer is coming down your street now with his lights off, so you won't be able to see him, but you may hear him. Okay."

"Yep."

When I looked back to the pool, I could see Macbeth still standing in the same spot, and Gray was tirelessly trying to get her to play fetch. He acted normal as if nothing was wrong at all. My heart was pounding and my hands were trying to go numb on me, but I continued to clean the kitchen. My heart was pounding in my chest. I imagined the worse. I wanted to be with Gray, not in this damn house all alone.

"One of the officers is there now. He is going to the backyard. There will be another officer there in a minute at your front door. Do not answer your door until I tell you to, okay, Ms. Murphy?"

"Yep," I answered quickly so I didn't give myself away.

I heard some yelling and then I saw the flashlights find the man in the tree stand. Macbeth was barking her head off and growling viciously at the man through the fence. I was tempted to let her out and let her attack the man, but the police were there now so there was no need. He climbed down slowly from his tree and the officer placed him under arrest and handcuffed him. Then the doorbell rang.

"Ms. Murphy, that is the other officer; go answer your door. When I know the officer is with you, then you can hang up. All right?"

"All right."

Gray flew past me while grabbing my hand. The officer was there at the door, as promised by the operator.

The man was arrested and taken away. Gray and I were asked a ton of questions. The officers immediately recognized Gray and tried to be as helpful as they could.

"Do you know that man?" one of the officers asked.

"He's a paparazzi from LA, where I live," Gray answered. "He's been around town for the past couple of weeks. He even approached my girlfriend at the park recently." He wound his arms around me proudly but his expression didn't change. He was furious. It took me a second to realize what he had just said.

Girlfriend? That felt weird. The officer raised his brow and I couldn't be sure whether it was because of the crazy man's antics or the fact that Grayson had just called me his girlfriend.

"Well, we can keep him until tomorrow. Most likely then we'll have to release him. We can charge him with trespassing since Ms. Murphy owns the property all the way to the creek back there. We're talking about a small fine and a ticket though. If you need anything else, just call." He handed Gray his card with all his numbers on it. I had never had a cop give me their personal card before. I rolled my eyes at the butt kissing that was going on right in front of me.

"Thank you, officers. I'm sure we'll be fine. Thank you for all your help." Gray sighed but was very gracious as he walked the policemen to the door. He turned to me waving the card in his hand and rolled his eyes. I chuckled under my hand. He looked so funny whenever he rolled his eyes. He was very animated, but I laughed because we were thinking the same thing—overkill.

Once the cops were gone, he came over to me and put his arms around me. "You okay?"

Surprisingly I was. I had been terrified but now that I knew that jerk was going to be sitting in jail tonight, I felt much better. Hopefully, when he was released, he would go back to LA. "I'm fine. It's just that was my first trespasser."

"Sorry, love. He probably got some pictures. I should call Freddy."

"Sure."

Freddy was his agent. He was extremely high strung. Harris had told me all kinds of things about him. He was apparently very meticulous and by the book and had been a thorn in her side through the whole contract business with Gray staying here. I let Macbeth back in and she shadowed my every move as I finished the kitchen. After a few minutes, Gray was back with his laptop in hand.

"What are you doing?" I asked.

"That jackass got some photos out before the cops got him down. He must have been sending them off as soon as he was taking them. Damn Internet. I'm just gonna have a look real quick."

I nodded, not really caring to see the pictures. That was fast if they were already up. I started to wonder what he had gotten pictures of. I wondered how many nights he had been out there taking photos. I started retracing the last week; what we had done and where. We had never felt like we needed to lower the shades or close the curtains. I thought about the many times both of us had walked around the bedroom naked or run into the kitchen to get water with not much of anything on at all. My stomach dropped and I started to panic again. I scrubbed the counter for the fifth time and waited anxiously for Gray to say something. I was hoping he wouldn't find anything, but he did.

"Oh no," was all he said.

"What? That bad?"

He waved me over. "Come over here and see for yourself."

There were tons of pictures. He had been here a while and had pictures of me and Macbeth at the park that day. He had photos of Gray and me in the pool, eating, then in the pool again, then kissing, then taking our clothes off and well…you get the picture. Every day seemed to have been chronicled and detailed. Every move I had made in the last two weeks was documented in vibrant colored photos. It was obvious that he had wanted to break the news about Grayson Sparks' new girlfriend. He would stand to make a small fortune.

"Can he publish these?" I whispered.

Gray didn't answer; he just shook his head back and forth.

"Grayson!" I shouted.

"If he was not on private property when he took them, then… maybe," he conceded.

"What! Those are naked pictures! We are…the whole world… you can't let him go public with these, Gray! You can't!" I yelled without even realizing that the pictures were already public.

"Calm down, love. Freddy is calling the lawyers tonight. We will do everything we can. I promise." He reached out and hugged me tight, but it didn't do much to calm me down.

The rest of the evening, Gray was on the phone with Freddy off and on. How had this happened to me? I'm just a girl from Richmond, Virginia; I'm nobody special! Months ago I was just normal, like everyone else, and now…I'm a side freak show on the Internet with my boobs out for all to see. This is not my life, not at all. I started to feel anger, not at the "peeping tom crazy" but at Grayson. Even though I knew deep down it wasn't his fault and he felt terrible about it all, I was mad. The more I sat with the possibility of this happening to me, the angrier I got! It was all I could do to contain my feelings while I watched Grayson work his magic with Freddy. I hoped that it would stop the publishing of the pictures—the naked pictures—of me and him.

Every now and then, Gray would look my way and give me a hopeful grin. The fact that he didn't seem to worry about this made me even more angry. Then again, I also understood that this was his life; he was used to this sort of thing. I begrudgingly grinned back what must have been the fakest smile ever because he snorted in laughter at my attempt. I rolled my eyes and poured a drink and sat and waited beside him for any news at all, all the while watching the minutes tick by as they cemented my fate as an Internet porn star.

By morning, the photos had hit the Internet everywhere, and by the time the evening entertainment shows came on, the pictures were all over TV too. They knew my name, they knew my age, and they knew I was the new girlfriend. The TV shows had to black out certain parts but the Internet didn't. There were photos of Gray and I making love all over the Internet, and the TV shows had hinted about a possible video as well. It was a nightmare. Gray promised me that the lawyers were working on it and that hopefully the photos would be removed before morning. The damage, however, was done. This had been one of the longest days of my life of which I drank through mostly—a Bloody Mary for breakfast, another for lunch, and a stiff cocktail for dinner.

> Grayson Sparks reportedly has been having a secret affair with the woman who owns the home he chose to stay in while filming his latest film. The mystery woman has been identified as thirty-four-year-old Elaina Murphy of Richmond, Virginia. Murphy was made a widow after losing her husband and child in a car accident just four years ago. Sparks has cryptically claimed recently that he is in a relationship with someone, but has not verified who this woman is…

"Did they have to say my age on television?" I moaned.

"So sorry, love, really I am," Gray spoke through his teeth.

"It's not your fault." I drank the last of my drink and the ice rattled against the empty glass.

"Do you want another then?" Gray asked with a sad smile. I could tell he was tired and that he felt like a monster for bringing this into my life. He looked helpless as he rose up from the couch and headed to the kitchen.

Grayson's phone rang. It was his agent again. He had been on the phone with him for most of the day while he went into work for a few hours to tie things up and ever since he had gotten home this evening. Freddy seemed more concerned about Gray's portrayal in the present movie he was filming than the world seeing nude pictures of his client and his girlfriend. I didn't know if that was a good thing or not. My first instinct was to hate Freddy for being so insensitive, but when I realized that he was behaving that way because he wasn't worried, it calmed me down a bit. Of course he wouldn't be as upset as Gray or I; there weren't any naked pictures of him on the Internet; but if he wasn't worried, that might mean that this was something that we *could* make go away as fast as it had come on us. That is what I was hoping for anyway. I waited and waited for any news. I found myself praying for the phone call that would tell me this was finally over. Still, days passed without anything being done.

~~~~~~~~

The house phone rang and snapped me out of my fury.

"Hello?" I answered timidly, not knowing if it was more press.

"Did they really just say your age on national television?" Harris hammered away.

"Oh God, you saw it," I grumbled.

"Umm, hello, Laina, everyone did! What the hell is going on over there?" she demanded.

Gray turned to me and mouthed the words "who is it?" I mouthed back "Harris" and rolled my eyes. He grinned when I pulled the phone from my ear as Harris ranted on the line. My hand opened and closed as I mocked her.

"Some jerk took some pictures of us here at the house; he's been here since right before Gray got back from his trip to LA. It's a mess. His lawyer is trying to get the photos taken off the websites…it's just taking some time."

"Websites? Naked pictures? What has that guy gotten you into, Laina?" she shrieked, and I could hear her fingers tapping away on the keys of her computer. It didn't take long until she found the first of many sites with the posted pictures. "Oh… my…God…" then silence again as she looked through the photos. After a few moments of her sucking in air through her teeth, she took a deep breath. "Well, at least you look good, Laina."

"Are you serious, Harris? That's all you're gonna say?"

"What do you want me to say?" she asked warily.

I calmed down and tried to find my nicest tone of voice. "Nothing, it's fine. Look, I have to go."

"Sure. Have you heard from Mandy yet? I bet her country club buddies are gonna love this…" she teased.

"It's not funny, Harris, and no, I haven't heard from her yet…" just then the other line beeped in.

"Crap!"

"What? What is it? Ohhh." She realized who was on the other line. "Hell hath no fury like a woman booted from her country club…" Harris cackled away.

"Bye, Harris," I hissed.

After trying to get Mandy to breath regularly again and convince her that Gray and I had no idea that the photos were being taken, she started to come back down to earth. She was devastated to say the least. Her daughters had been watching TV while she was cooking dinner, and they had seen the pictures of me. Her husband had called her from his game of golf to ask why my butt cheeks were all over the Internet. It was a very bad day for Mandy. Eventually, she was able to stop thinking about herself and ask if I was okay. I assured her that I was and ultimately convinced her that everything would be all right.

When I hung up with Mandy, Grayson was talking to Freddy again.

"Yeah, Freddy. Let me talk to her first. All right. I'll get back to you within the hour, all right?" He hung up his phone and sighed loudly.

"What now?" I asked through my own sigh.

"Damage control. Freddy wants to know what to tell the press."

"Tell them to fu—" I started, but he placed his hand over my mouth.

"Ah, careful now, love. Don't get personally involved with them. This is all just business."

I scrunched my face up again and pouted while I narrowed my eyes at him.

"Why do you have to tell them anything? It's your personal life; it has nothing to do with your acting!" I yelled at the ceiling.

"I know, but Freddy thinks I need to make sure my fans know that this was not some slimy thing I did. He thinks we should do an interview together or at the very least make a joint statement."

"You're kidding. I'm not doing any damn interview, Gray."

"I thought that's what you would say." He grinned back.

I sat there as his comment sunk in little by little. Slowly the anger started to surface. A new reason to be angry—Gray wasn't interested at all in my feelings; he was more worried about his image. I glared at him and his eyebrows flew up, and he leaned away from me feeling the onslaught coming.

"This is not about us or anything remotely close to us! This is about you trying to look good! You need to repair your image so you can keep your career! That is all that matters, right?" I shouted.

"Easy, Elaina. That's my arse out there on the blasted Internet as well!" he argued back.

"Sorry." I spit the word still angry. "Hasn't everyone already seen yours anyway!"

That was a low blow and he pressed his lips together tightly and took a deep breath before he spoke again. I had gotten under his skin for the first time. I shouldn't have said that about him; it was a cheap shot and really mean.

"Honestly, I don't really care about what the public thinks about me. I don't even think I want to do this anymore," Gray admitted as he let his head fall back on the couch cushion.

"What?" I was suddenly nervous and unsure of what he was tired of.

He turned to me and rolled his eyes. "Acting. It's just not fun anymore. I've been in this business for twenty years almost, it's getting old."

"Then quit! You don't need the money, let's face it." I offered.

He gave me a bewildered look. "Someone's been googling…"

All of a sudden, I was embarrassed. He had caught me. Even though I had only looked him up the one time, before he even came here, he knew a secret that I didn't want him to know. I tried to cover myself but I knew it was too late.

"Doesn't everyone on the planet know how wealthy you are?"

"It's not the money, Elaina. I have more than enough to retire. Everything I have is paid for and done. It's just that; so I quit or retire, then what? Just sit around and get fat and old. No thanks."

"You mean be a normal person. Be just Gray for a while? What's wrong with that? You don't have to get fat either, just older," I teased, suddenly finding myself offering him comfort.

He stared into my eyes, agreeing with me. Somewhere he was remembering saying the same words just weeks ago. Longing after some life he never had. He shook his head. "Enough of that for now. What do you want me to say to the press? I've got to call Freddy back before the hour."

"Say whatever you think is best for us, but I'm not doing any interviews. This is your show, okay."

"All right then, I will give him a call and come up with something, I suppose," he grumbled.

Later that evening on the entertainment news, his statement was released. It was the top story of the night on the media hoar of a show.

The official press release was simple and to the point:

> The pictures released last night were taken by a trespasser. My girlfriend, Elaina Murphy, and I had no idea we were being photographed, and we plan on taking this breach of our private lives to the proper authorities. We have been in contact with lawyers and plan to take immediate legal action. Thank you to all of my fans for your continued support and to the officers who arrested this stalker. We ask that you respect our privacy at this time. Thank you.
>
> —Grayson Sparks

The comment did little to satiate the media's desire to break new information about the pictures or Grayson Sparks new girlfriend. Since the pictures had been released to the public, my home had become a prison. The media had descended upon us, and I was stuck at home. At least Gray could go to work and get away, but he promised it was just as bad on set. The media sharks had already had their first taste of blood and they were circling for more. I couldn't understand why people seemed to care so much about who Gray was dating and that he actually was carrying on a normal relationship with someone. Maybe the fascination was with my being an average person who lived out of the limelight. Maybe they were just interested to see him naked or caught in the act of being with a woman. All of it seemed incredibly intrusive, and I felt more and more violated every second. Gray seemed to get calmer as things progressed. He was used to this crap. After all, he had told me about how the media got everything wrong and made things up to create stories when they couldn't find anything. He had told me how some of the stories were laughable and some were incredibly hurtful, like the ones about his mother when she was dying. Some trash mag had actually printed that his mother had AIDS and was at death's door shortly after her first round of chemotherapy. Grayson sued them and won a modest settlement as well as a retraction from the editor. Sadly, his mother never lived to see it.

Chapter 12

Good-bye

The last few weeks with Gray here were hectic. Security was immediately upped and production on his present film was sped up to get Gray out of here sooner. Thanks to Freddy, Gray would be gone almost a week before I had thought he would. My stomach was in knots, but Gray was still here now. The time we had together was short, but we refused to think about it ending. We closed our blinds now and pulled down the shades, of course, but our lives went on as they had.

A week after, *Photogate*, the Internet site, removed the photos and put out a four-page apology. A few days later, they offered Gray and I two hundred thousand dollars. The deal was done by the end of the day, and Gray, with my permission, donated the money to a fund for cancer treatments for children in honor of his mother. It was amazing to see how fast things were worked out. I realized how powerful Gray's lawyers had been and why he had never worried about things being handled appropriately. He knew how to ride out the storm and had done so beautifully. But there was a new storm ahead for me in days.

The last week Gray was here was not long enough. We spent almost every minute of our time together holding each other, kissing, and talking. Gray never asked me the question that I knew was coming before he left. By the middle of the week, however, I noticed a change in Gray. He was still loving and affectionate but the intensity had changed, lessened. He looked at me with pained eyes now, knowing the end was getting close. It was as if he knew what I would say and how it would end. He seemed to have wrapped his mind around our future and was preparing himself for the end. Every time Gray looked at me with his sad eyes, I felt a little bit of my heart break. By the time the last night came upon us, my heart was filled with tiny fractures and was waiting for the final blow to undo my heart at last. It would be my doing—my heartbreak. It would be this way because I was unable to love him the way he needed to be loved.

We were having dinner here tonight; the other attempts to go out had been a disaster. By the time we arrived, the press was everywhere and we were photographed going in, eating, and coming out again. The other patrons hated it and by the end of our meal, they hated us too. We were the cause after all. We decided it was best to just stay in and eat here at home, where it had all began. Since the paparazzi stunt, we hadn't eaten outside, but tonight we were.

It was the end of July. August was upon us and the air was hot, and the breeze had all but died. Tonight, however, brought with it a fantastic breeze. We were lucky. Not just for the breeze, but for everything that we had gained this summer. I was not ready to say good-bye to Gray; I did love him, deeply. I was hoping that he would ask me to come with him, hoping that he would try one more time to convince me to go home with him. I had thought a lot about it this week, day after day. He was what I really wanted; he was the man I had been waiting for. He had brought my heart back to life and shown me that I could love again. I wanted all of him, and I wanted to give him all of me, but I was prepared for him to say good-bye. I knew, somehow, that what I had to offer wasn't enough for him. He deserved better—far better than me.

Gray had made arrangements for a chef to come to the house and cook and clean for us tonight. I was doubtful that the chef would be able to clean as well as me, but I went along with his plan.

Our dinner of filet mignon and roasted carrots with garlic butter sauce was simple yet delicious. Everything had been wonderful, so far. I sensed Gray's uneasiness throughout the night. I tried to pretend that I didn't notice. We took our drinks to the poolside couch. I rested my head against his neck as he sat with his arm around me, his fingers sliding up and down my arm and shoulder.

"This feels wrong," he said quietly.

"What do you mean?" I asked, confused.

He turned to face me and then pushed me away far enough so he could look into my eyes. I stared back for a moment goofily, but then I realized he was serious. His expression was sad and unwaveringly resolved. When his eyes broke away, I could see the tear clinging to his long lashes. I knew then what he was doing and I tried to sturdy myself.

"I don't know how to say this..." he fumbled. He looked back to me with kind eyes. "I don't want you to come with me, Elaina."

I sighed and smiled gently. "I know."

"It's not my love for you; that will never be broken, ever. It's just that I love you with all of my heart. I would marry you right now if I could—if you only would. I know that's never gonna happen. As much as I love you, I deserve what you had with John. I deserve to have the love of my life with no other man involved. I know that you are still in love with him, maybe you always will be. I had hoped that I would be enough for you, but I know now that I'm not. I deserve all of you, and I will take nothing less than that." The tear fell from his eye and rolled down his cheek. "You won't even bury their remains. You are holding on to a ghost, Elaina. They are gone and they're not coming back. I'm here, now, and I'm alive, and I want you—every part of you."

"I know," I sighed softly.

"I can't wait forever. If I can't convince you now, then I never will be able to." He waited for me to fight or for me to beg, but he could see that it wasn't going to happen. His eyes pleaded with me to let go of the past and move forward with him. I could see this was his last effort, and he must have seen it in my eyes that I couldn't let go yet.

"I know," I moaned. Tears of my own were now pouring down my cheeks. "Please, Gray," I asked him, hoping that he would make it quick.

He took my face in his hands like he had one hundred times before and looked into my eyes. "All right then." He sighed. "If you ever change your mind, you know where to find me." He pressed his head to mine. I nodded my head and sucked in a breath as my hands found his face. His gentle lips found mine and he kissed me softly, his lips barely touching mine. I felt a shiver run down my spine covering my arms and legs with goose bumps. I felt his jaw tighten under my hands as he grabbed them and pulled them away to place them in my lap. His finger found my chin and lifted my face to his. "I do love you, my Elaina." He kissed me fiercely this time with an intense passion. I could feel his tears on my face. Then he moaned and pulled away. "Goodbye, Elaina," he sighed. Then he did what I feared he would all along—he let me go. I knew that it wasn't for him or even what he wanted. He had done this for me.

He left that night. He had already packed all of his things. He took the redeye to LA and had left me all alone. I felt empty, like a shell. He took everything with him. I cried myself to sleep, wanting to hold him. I wanted to hear his voice or call him just once. He was right, he deserved more from me. I was blinded by my own fear. Now that he was gone, I realized he was the man for me, he had always been the man for me. As soon as he had walked up to me that day in the park, I knew. Now he was gone, just like I had feared since the first kiss.

The next few days were terrible. I could barely do anything. I couldn't sleep. Nothing seemed important anymore. Each day, I would walk past the urn, and with each passing morning I grew more and more disgusted with it and myself. I was mad at John and Georgia—mad at them for dying and leaving me here all alone. Furious that John had left me after promising to love me forever. I had felt safe with him and secure. I hadn't felt that again until Gray had come into my life.

It had been two weeks since Gray had disappeared from my life. The photographers, one by one, returned to Hollywood to follow the bigger story. I watched Gray on TV doing interview after interview. His eyes were dead and lifeless, obviously just going through the motions. Interviewers asked him about me, or his "girlfriend," but he declined to comment. One reporter had gotten so obnoxious that Freddy had to step in and pull the plug on the interview altogether. Gray was a gentleman, as always. After days of questioning and relentless photographers, he never told the media anything.

Harris showed up around one in the afternoon that Friday. When she saw me, her eyes bulged. She knew I was depressed but she had no idea how bad, and neither did I until I saw her expression. My stomach dropped at the sight of her, and I tried to muster some energy to deal with my best friend.

"Have you been eating anything?" she asked with her hands placed firmly on her hips.

"What are you doing here?" I asked, annoyed by her presence.

"I'm your friend. I came to check on you." She looked me over again and sighed, "How long has he been gone?"

"Two weeks." I whimpered as I slumped down into a chair at the kitchen table.

"Why are you sitting around here pouting and moping?" she demanded.

"Leave me alone, Harris," I begged, unable to look at her. I knew I was being pathetic, but I didn't need to hear from her too.

"No, I'm not gonna leave you alone." She growled. "When are you going to wake up and accept that they are gone? You are wasting your life away in this stupid house. You pretend that you're fine, but I know you're not." She paused and jabbed her finger at the fireplace. "You think that urn is alive? You think John and Georgia are gonna come flying out of that thing one day?"

"Shut up!" I screamed, grabbing my ears.

"You think you owe them your life because you lived and they died? You don't! You were just sitting in the right seat, that's all! It was their time to go, not yours! That's it, Elaina! Let them go!" she yelled back, breathless. I could tell she was scared to tell me these things; scared of what I would do with a mirror put up in my face.

The rush of pain came down on me; it was crippling, and I felt my body slump to the floor. I couldn't feel anything or see anything. I bawled and bawled. My throat stung from my wailing. "You're right, you're all right. I know! I'm…I'm just…broken. I just can't fix it, nobody can!"

Harris crouched down beside me and put her arms around me. "Just let them go. You know how. Let them go and what is broken inside of you will heal itself again."

"I can't," I promised her, but I knew that there was a way. People managed to say good-bye to loved ones every day and get on with their lives.

"Yes, you can. You're ready, Laina, you are," she whispered to me.

"I know. I have to do this. I can't wait anymore. Will you help me pack?" I asked while wiping my face and nose with my hands.

"Sure…but, Elaina, where are you going?" she asked in confusion.

"Lancaster. I have to say good-bye to them the way John wanted."

While we packed, I gained more and more energy. I now had a mission in front of me. I was focused and ready. Harris excused herself to make a phone call, and when she returned, her expression was strange.

I threw my arms up in the air. "Now what?" I asked, exasperated.

"I have to tell you something. You might not like it. Ah, hell, I know you're not gonna like it."

"What?" I sniped.

"It's about John's parents, Janice and Richard."

"What about them?" I asked, surprised to hear those names but worried now about why she was bringing them up again after all this time.

"They have been taking care of the cottage since John…died. Mandy told me a long time ago, but she made me promise not to mention it to you. They've been keeping the yard under control and making sure the house doesn't fall apart. They weren't trying to overstep; they just didn't know when you would be back, so they took…the initiative."

"Great," I answered sarcastically.

"I just got off the phone with Janice to make sure they weren't there. She knows you're coming, but I told her you wanted to be alone."

"You knew all this time and you didn't tell me?" I asked, half caring about her answer.

"Mandy told me after your suicide attempt. She was upset and didn't know what to do. She wanted to commit you or something. That wasn't easy talking her out of, believe me. She was worried about you; we all were, even Janice and Richard."

"Just keep her away from me, Harris. I had to put up with that woman long enough when John was alive. Tell her to return her key, too!"

Chapter 13

The River Cottage

The drive down was shorter than I remembered: down 360, to Tappahannock, cross the bridge and through the long narrow street until I hit Route 3. Route 3 had always been my favorite part of the drive down here. It was the first indication that we were almost there. I turned at 354 and kept going until I saw the little sign—the green-and-white street sign that read Old Airport Road. I turned right and kept going down the paved road until it turned to gravel. I smiled when my tires hit the rocks and I saw the dust cloud up behind me. I remembered this—all of this—the smell of the field to my left and the lush trees to my right; the rabbits hopping alongside my car trying to avoid getting run over; the deer lying in the middle of the field, smashing the cornstalks down to stay hidden and cool; the road wound around the field like a big *U*. I passed the old gray horse stables I used to take Georgia to. The horses were still there grazing in the middle of their fenced-in field. Then, up ahead through the broken trees, I saw the water. The sun was dancing around on top of the small waves that rolled in. It was beautiful, just like I remembered.

Out of habit, I turned around to see Georgia's face. She always got so excited when we could finally see the water. She, of course, wasn't there, but I imagined her sitting there. She was smiling a huge smile and her eyes were wide with excitement. She was clutching her monkey in her chubby little hands, and her feet were dangling from her car seat. "Look mommy!" she said pointing to the water. I smiled, but when I blinked her image was gone. Suddenly I was reminded again of why I was here and what I was trying to finally do. The urn sat beside me, buckled in the seatbelt with my purse worked around it to protect the ashes. I could see the house now. The rancher hadn't changed a bit. The dark-green paint had faded a bit but the red shutters were still bright red. Under the carport was the boat—John's boat. It had been his most prized possession. He loved nothing more than riding around the river and fishing in that thing. Georgia loved it too. When they were down here, they were inseparable. He had made so many plans for that boat; he never got to do them.

I parked the car, hopped out, and stretched my back for a long second. The smell of the freshly cut grass was the first smell I caught. Everything was exactly the same. I knew that the inside would probably be the same as well. John's parents had been coming here since he died to keep the place together. It angered me to imagine them here. This was our place, not theirs. I did, however, appreciate their efforts in taking care of the old place since I wasn't capable of doing so. My stomach twisted and I was suddenly acutely aware of the internal struggle my mind and body were having. I wanted to go inside, but my heart raced as I got closer to the door. My mind told my legs to stop, but my legs ignored my head. I pulled the silver key from my pocket and walked up the side stairs to the door. It was locked, which meant my past in-laws were not here, not yet anyway. I fought with the lock a bit but finally got the door opened.

Walking in was like walking back in time. The smell of the house was the same; I hadn't expected that. John's scent was everywhere. A few things had been moved and taken out, but it was still the same little place it had always been. The house has only two bedrooms with a nice-sized den and kitchen. We had redone just about everything. I had tirelessly painted the entire house when we bought it ten years ago. The floors were hardwood with hardly any rugs throughout. I took off my flip-flops and pressed my bare feet to the floor as I closed my eyes. They felt the same. There were still pictures of John, Georgia, and me all over the walls; seashells on every table that Georgia had collected. Maybe John's parents hadn't been able to take them down. The front porch that went across the entire back of the house was still in winter weather lockdown. Everything was covered and placed away from the screen and up toward the house, stacked up neatly. I picked up my bags and started toward the master bedroom where I would be staying. I deliberately passed Georgia's old room without looking in it. I knew her things were still in there, and that was just too much for today. The door to my room was stuck, probably moisture, so I gave it a shove, and it cracked open suddenly. Again, the smell of John was everywhere. The bed was neatly made. John's fishing poles and lucky fishing hat were leaning up against the wall in the corner. He had planned a fishing trip the weekend before he was killed. I sighed out loud and lay down on the bed. I shoved my head directly into John's old pillow and breathed in strongly. His smell was still here, too, somehow. It was probably all in my head, but I didn't want to know whether it was real or not. I drifted off to sleep soon after that.

The next few days were filled with thunderstorms, the kind a person welcomes in the heat of the day. The temperatures had soared to the 100s. The smell of salt and dead fish filled the air. Salt water and dying stinging nettles filled the river. The winds blew a hot and thick air of new and old. I sat on the porch for hours, watching the storms make their way across the river; at first just a haze across the way and then a blanket of gray mist upon the shore and the water's edge. Then they hit like a giant wave. The thunder was loud and the lightening cracked across the water and in the yard. With the storms came a cooler air, but it didn't change anything. I was still alone and drunk.

I woke the next day to more rain and thunder so I slept again, maybe the whole day. When I woke up three hours later, there was a different charge in the house. I heard footsteps and shuffling in the kitchen. I sat up in bed and tried to listen better, but I didn't hear anything else. Thinking it was strange and definitely creepy, I got up, wrapped my thin knit robe around my tired body, and walked back into the kitchen. That's when my stomach dropped and my breath froze. I hadn't seen John's mother in almost four years, but there she was sitting at the kitchen table with her paper coffee cup. When she saw me, her eyes widened in shock. Then her face fell slightly. "Oh, it is you," she whispered.

"Janice?" I questioned weirdly, crossing my arms over my chest.

She smiled, realizing she had surprised me but proud of herself for doing so. "I know, I know. Your friend Harris told me you were coming and not to bother you, but I just had to come. I'm sorry." She answered with an uncomfortable tone to her voice.

I didn't answer her. I just grabbed the plastic bag full of new curtains for the den and started pulling them out to hang. I had bought them on a whim, not knowing why at the time but sure I would need something to do while I was here, so why not hang new curtains. I needed a project if she was going to be here for any amount of time. We had never really gotten along. She had always been too involved with John and my marriage for my taste. After the accident, she had tried to take over everything. She had tried to tell me what to do; she had failed miserably. She knew this routine as well as I did, and even though she knew I didn't want her here, she wasn't about to leave.

"New curtains, huh? They look nice. Be careful hanging them, you don't want to fall."

I snapped my head back to her in annoyance, but I could see she meant nothing by the remark and that I had overreacted. It was weird how things seemed to have evolved between us over curtains.

"What are you doing her, Janice?" I snarled.

She bowed her head down and concentrated on her coffee, tracing the lid with her finger. "Harris tells me you are here for a reason. Is that right?" she asked quietly.

I shot my eyes at her again, narrowing down at her. She took that look to mean yes. She nodded her head, letting me know she understood.

"So you are planning on...scattering the ashes?" She sighed loudly this time.

I was trying to slide the curtains down the rod to hang them, and I sighed too. "Yes, I'm going to try," I answered curtly. "Why?" Just after snapping at her, the curtain slid back off the rod and puddled on the floor at my feet. "Shit," I hissed.

"You want some help?" she offered.

"No. I got it, thanks." I snapped and went back to my task.

"Look, Elaina, I know you don't want me here. I know you are angry with me and that I did and said some things I shouldn't have, but we are still family. I just want to ask you one thing and then I'll leave you alone here."

I turned around and met her awaiting eyes. She was nervous and it showed horribly.

"What is it, Janice?"

"I...I would like to come with you...when you take Johnny and Georgia. If...if you do decide to do it."

I said nothing in response. I couldn't. I had not expected to see her or to have her ask me something like this.

"I still feel like they're here. I never really felt like I could properly say good-bye, knowing they were still waiting...on your mantle like that." Her eyes furrowed, showing a glance of her anger at me for waiting so long. "I need this; it's all I ask of you. Please, let me be there with you?"

I knew it was hard for her to beg, especially with me. I understood what she said and I sympathized with her. I closed my eyes tight, annoyed with myself for what I was about to do.

"He hated it when you called him that, you know?" It was true that John had hated being called Johnny. It had made him feel like a child and his mother was full aware of it. Although he never asked her to stop calling him Johnny, it was obvious to me that he hated it. At first I had found it funny that his mother got under his skin too but after years of her antics it had just become another reason to dislike her for a stupid reason. I sighed loudly, but in my mind I knew I was just trying to make this whole thing harder for her. I felt bad for that immediately. After all she was here, she had made the first move, and I owed her more than some nasty comment about her choice of nickname for her dead son. I sighed out loud. "I'll call you if I decide to do it. Okay?" I whispered.

Janice nodded her head with her eyes closed and stood up. "Thank you, Elaina." And then she walked out through the kitchen door, letting the screen door slam after her.

~~~~~~~~

The days were long here. I tried to answer some questions in my head and my heart. Gray was right; he deserved more from me than I could give. He was a great man. He was perfect for me in every way, but I had pushed him away again and again. What if he was my soul mate and John had just been part of my journey to get to Gray? That sounded terrible to me, but also very possible. Maybe I was never meant to be with John forever. That couldn't be right, because then Georgia…well, her life was not a mistake and was definitely meant to be. Maybe I was only supposed to have had them for that short time. That must have been why it was so wonderful—that was all I was allowed to have. In order to be who I am now, I had to experience the pain of losing them. No, no, no. Nothing made sense anymore.

I tried running, walking, swimming, shopping, cleaning—all to no avail. At the end of the day, it was still just me, alone in an empty house, staring at an urn and heat lightning. It was no different than at home. Two weeks had flown by and still I had not mustered up enough courage to do what I came here to do.

When I woke up that next morning, something strange happened. I rolled over and reached for someone who wasn't there. Since I had been down here, I had done this same thing every morning, reaching for John. This morning when I reached over, I was thinking of Gray. I shot up immediately when I realized what had happened. Maybe I had been waiting for a sign and this was it. Though I never really believed much in signs, this definitely felt like one to me.

I looked over at the picture of John and Georgia on the wall. They had been fishing that day and had dragged me along with them. I was determined to get a picture of them together, so when they were reeling in a fish I shouted at them to smile. They had, and for that brief second I took the picture of the two of them. Now they smiled back at me, happy. I smiled and blew a kiss to them. "Thank you," I whispered.

I was getting the boat ready when Janice pulled up. When she got out of her car, her face looked as bewildered as she had sounded on the phone early that morning. She walked over to me with her hands in her pockets.

"Need any help?" she asked.

"There's some sandwiches inside on the counter and some water. Do you mind throwing them in the boat?" I asked with way too much energy. I was only on my fifth cup of coffee.

Everything was ready, and when we climbed into my car to drive to the boat ramp, Janice noticed the urn in the backseat, safely buckled in with the seatbelt. She turned back to me and raised an eyebrow.

"Safety first, right?" I explained.

She smiled and then turned back to the road. When we got to the ramp, she was no help at all. I asked her to carry everything to the boat while I unhooked everything. Getting the boat into the water was trickier than I remembered, but I did it and after parking the car, I was behind the wheel of the boat and puttering out from Greenville Creek and toward the river.

The ride wasn't too long, about forty-five minutes from here. The water was calm today with hardly any waves at all. This meant it was also as hot as a fried egg in cast-iron skillet. I drove the boat fast to create our own breeze. Janice didn't talk at all during the ride to the bridge; I was grateful for that. When we got to the Tappahannock Bridge, I slowed way down and finally cut the motor off. I dropped anchor at about the halfway point of the bridge. This had been John's favorite spot. Janice was watching me closely as I grabbed the picnic basket and pulled the plastic tub of night crawlers out. She glanced over to the side of the boat and spotted the fishing rods. Her eyebrow flicked up in an arch.

"I thought we could fish for a bit, if that's okay," I stated.

Janice smiled and held her hand out for the bait. "I'll bait your hook. I know you hate touching slimy things."

We didn't really catch anything; a few small catfish, nothing worth keeping. I studied Janice when she wasn't looking. Her hair was grayer and her face was more wrinkled than I remembered. The last four years obviously had not been kind to her. Her eyes sat a little deeper into her face and her cheekbones were much more prominent. She was thinner—a lot thinner than the last time I had seen her. She hadn't eaten a thing all day. I was starting to think she was just anxious about today. She grabbed her stomach a few times, but I assumed it was motion sickness. But when she grabbed her bag and popped a few pills, I had had enough of the charade.

"What's going on, Janice?" I finally asked.

"What do you mean?" she tried to spread a naïve look across her sickly face.

"You've never been this thin in your life, and you love turkey sandwiches. What's going on?" I asked again, more sternly this time.

She sat across from me with an angry look on her face. We stared each other down for what seemed like forever. Finally, she nodded her head and turned to look out on the water rather than me.

"I'm sick. Stomach cancer. They haven't given me much time either."

The boat rocked gently back and forth as her words drifted around me in the light breeze.

I swallowed hard. "How long, Janice?"

"A few months, maybe. I guess you came around just in time. I was worried for a while." She laughed quietly, trying to make light of the situation.

"Why isn't Richard here?" I asked.

"He thinks I'm getting another treatment, but…I've told the doctors that I'm done. If nothing's worked by now, then really there's no hope left."

"You don't know that!" I chastened as I rolled my eyes. Then I thought, *Who the hell am I to judge?*

"Yeah, I do and so do the doctors. But I get this nifty little pain pump." She lifted her loose shirt up to show me the square box on her hip and then she pointed to the tube that ran up toward her chest to a catheter. "It helps a lot."

"I'm sorry, Janice, really I am." I smiled softly at her and then wound my line in. She followed my lead and waited to see what I would do next. I grabbed the urn gently and placed it in my lap. I took a deep breath and thought of what to say. In the end, I decided to just to talk to them, so I did.

"Well, guys, here we are. I'm sorry it's taken me so long to say good-bye, but it's time. John, Georgia, take care of Grandma J. I love you both so much, and I'm so sorry that I couldn't protect you. I should have been paying more attention." I stopped trying to choke back my tears. I wanted to be strong for them for once. "I think about you every day…every minute. Even though you won't be with me anymore, I will still be here. John, you were the first love of my life and I will always be thankful for the time we had together. You taught me how to love and be loved. I miss you every day. I love you so much. Georgia, you were my sun, my moon, my sunrise and sunset. You were the most beautiful creature I have ever seen and known in my life. Mommy will always love you, my sweet angel. I'm so sorry I couldn't save you, baby." The tears were coming, and I knew I had to act fast or I would not be able to see what I was doing. I gently slid the lid off the urn and waited for the breeze that was sure to come. Somehow I knew that John would make sure of that. When I felt the wisps of my hair begin to tickle my neck, I knew it was time. I stood up beside Janice and let my family go. The ashes whirled above me and blew over toward the bridge. They dropped to the water and swirled down and around the boat. "Good-bye, my loves," I whispered so softly that I was sure Janice could not even hear me, but I know they could.

Janice wound her thin arm around me and squeezed me as tightly as she could. "Thank you, Elaina."

We headed back to the cottage and got there close to dusk. The sun was setting behind us as we got closer to the house. The colors were in layers of purples, hot pinks, golden yellows, and bright oranges. Slowly but surely, the sun faded into the water horizon and nightfall was upon us. Janice watched the sunset in awe, and I got the sneaking suspicion that this could be her last sunset on the river. I docked the boat on the pole at the end of the pier. Janice sat still in the boat, still facing the sunset that was now gone and over.

"Janice?" I whispered, trying not to disturb her.

"That's really it then, huh?" she answered.

"What do you mean?" I asked, feeling the exhaustion of the day beginning to weigh on me.

"Life and then death. One day you're here and alive, and then you're gone. Just ashes in the wind." Janice spoke, but I sensed that she was really talking to someone else.

"I suppose so," I answered, unsure if that was the right thing to say.

"They didn't have enough time. It's not fair. I've lived so long. They didn't get enough time, did they?" she argued in a reproachful tone.

"No, they didn't," I agreed.

"I shouldn't have given up on you so quickly, that was wrong of me. I'm sorry, Elaina. You were a wonderful wife and mother, and John and Georgia loved you dearly. John's father and I... loved you dearly. I saw how this hurt you. I saw how you fell apart." Her eyes cast down to the water. The sound of regret was strong in her voice.

"You don't have to do this now," I begged.

"You're right. Now is not the time."

"No, I mean you don't owe me anything, Janice. You were upset. Everyone was, and you were all right. I should have stepped up and handled everything better."

I tried to assure her but it felt unlikely. She didn't say any more after that though as we drove home and then later when we walked up to the house. She didn't stay for dinner either. She gathered her things and headed out shortly after that.

"Take care, Elaina. I wish you nothing but happiness."

"Thank you."

I reached out and hugged her, and she wound her arms around me oddly and uncomfortably. The hug was brief and a bit cold, but I felt better having done it. She turned, got in her car, and drove off. I watched her headlights brighten down the road and then turn out of sight.

That was the last time I saw Janice Murphy.

The next morning, I packed the stuff I had brought, closed up the house, and headed home to no one and nothing. Not even a pet would welcome me home. I drove home, sure of at least one thing: John and Georgia were at peace, finally. And for the first time, so was I.

Chapter 14

Home Alone Again

The house was dark when I pulled up with nothing but the patio lamp post illuminating the front walkway. I dragged my suitcase from the car and shuffled inside. When I turned the lights on, I saw the empty house. It was not welcoming at all, and it seemed almost cold even though it was a scorching ninety-eight degrees outside.

Gray had been gone nearly five weeks, and I had still not changed the sheets out of fear of his pillowcase losing his scent. He had taken everything with him when he left—everything but his blue T-shirt that I loved. He had once told me I looked sexy wearing only that and told me I could have it. I recounted the weeks we had spent together, but even that didn't bring me any comfort.

Day after day, I wandered around the house cleaning, organizing, and for some reason, I found myself packing things away—things that I didn't want around anymore: pictures and clothing, even some furniture; things that belonged to John that didn't belong here anymore. More and more, my house no longer felt like mine. I began to feel like the visitor here. Something was pulling me away from my safe and comfortable home every day.

~~~~~~~~

Mandy's baby shower was another delightful event I had to attend in the weeks after I returned from the river. I managed to shower, get dressed, and drive over to her house for the party. It was awkward to say the very least. As I walked in, there were baby decorations all over the place. Above the kitchen island hung a baby-pink pacifier swag, and in the center of the island itself was a huge diaper cake. This was so out of my comfort zone that I wanted to run.

Even when I had been pregnant with Georgia, I had demanded no baby decorations. Mandy had happily obliged me, fearing that pushing me further would only cause me to cancel the whole thing. She was shocked when I had agreed to it at all. My baby celebration was simple with just a few close friends—friends and family I hadn't seen in four years; friends and family that would be here today for sure. I made my way through Mandy's immaculate house, to the patio out back. I spotted Harris immediately, who looked like she had been cornered by Bethany Kane, the most annoying woman at the country club to date. Harris saw me and immediately made a faux face of boredom. I grinned and kept right on past her. I was not about to get caught in Bethany's tentacles.

As I looked around, I saw some familiar faces and some new. My cousin Grace was there with her friend Jenny. I had been close with Grace before the accident and had gone out with Jenny a few times for cocktails. After my family died, Grace grew tired of me like most of my friends. She had called me and left messages, trying to get me to move on, like everyone else did. Sadly, she was one of the first to give up. I guess cousins aren't as close as I once thought they should be. Or maybe my mother had gotten to her. Either way, I hadn't spoken to her in years. I glanced over to her and she was staring at me with a bewildered look on her face. She must have been surprised to see me, and I could see her internal wheels turning over trying to think of the perfect and most appropriate thing to say to me. I grinned at her hoping to make her feel less awkward. She grinned back, stiffly, but made no other move. Jenny was beside her, tugging at her arm to meet another new person. I sighed as I stood alone, searching the layout for Mandy, who was nowhere in sight. Then I felt an elbow nudge; I knew who it was.

"So, Bethany wants to know when I'm having a baby of my own," she laughed shyly. "She thinks I should hurry up before my eggs go bad. Can you believe that stuck-up little b—?" Harris stopped herself from saying what she wanted to say. It was a baby shower after all and not at all the time or place.

I snorted through a chuckle without even looking at her. Harris was always a godsend at parties. She usually hated the people there almost as much as I did.

"Cindy Langly was hoping you would bring Gray with you. I told her, 'Yeah, that'll happen.' Geez, what an idiot."

I chuckled again, trying to find Cindy in the crowd of rich housewives. I finally spotted her in a deep whispering match with Bethany, both of them looking at me with peculiar expressions.

Harris nudged me again. "It was good of you to come, honey. I'm sure it will mean a lot to Mandy. Maybe next time she won't invite me. At least, that's what I'm hoping for."

"Next time?" I hissed.

I had missed Mandy's last baby shower. I was too busy feeling sorry for myself to attend. I thought I might skip this one, too, for the very reasons I was experiencing now, but I couldn't skip another one. Mandy would get over it, but there was simply no excuse for my missing something else. It just wasn't right.

"Ooh, speak of the devil, there's Little Miss Preggers now. She's gotten huge, wow! When is she due anyway?"

"October," I answered.

"I was thinking about getting her some condoms as her gift, but I didn't think she would get the joke."

"Probably not, Harris," I answered flatly.

"I got her some of those baby thingies instead. You know, the ones that are shirts and pants in one."

"I believe the word you're looking for is *onesie*," I sighed with a smile.

Harris laughed at the word, or maybe she was laughing at her own blissful ignorance of children. "Whatever."

All in all, there were about thirty of Mandy's friends and family present. My mother was nowhere in sight. It didn't surprise me; she had probably made some weak excuse to get out of it.

Women were gossiping all around me, and I could hear their lips buzzing about Gray and I. News about the pictures hadn't escaped their attention as well as the rest of the world's. It felt strange standing here with these people. I remembered a part of my life being this way; sitting around at parties with these same women. I'm sure if nothing had ever happened four years ago, I would be sitting here with these very same scants, talking about everyone else too. I would never have met Harris or Gray. My life would have been so different. But I had met Harris and then Gray. My life had changed, and I was a better person for it.

Later, when Mandy was opening her gifts, I had been stuck next to Bethany Kane. Even though we had been assigned seats, she had managed to sneak in between Harris and I. I admired her skills but wanted to get as far away from her as possible. Her perfume alone was overwhelming, and I knew it was just a sign of things to come. Bethany was a bit older than most of the women at the shower, including me. She was tall, slender, and looked like she had been a very attractive woman once upon a time. She had obviously overdone it in the plastic surgery department, and it didn't help at all that she was one of the most unpleasant people to ever have been around. Still, she seemed to be enjoying being herself while making everyone miserable. Her hands were covered with jewels and gold. Her dress was designer, and her shoes and bag most likely cost more than her clothes. Her hair was brown and thin, slicked back into a perfect ponytail. Her lips were a dark burgundy red that matched the wine she was so delicately holding in her hand. While she was thinking deeply, I could see that her forehead was in desperate need of another Botox injection. She bided her time before saying anything. She dodged eye contact as if I were a wild animal ready to pounce at any minute. Bethany was giving me my space and feeling me out. The thought of having a conversation with her made my skin crawl. When Mandy ripped into her third gift, Bethany turned to me and I tried to mentally prepare for anything that would come out of this monster's mouth, but instead I recoiled a bit.

"So, I hear Gray is dating his costar now and that he's back in LA."

You could hear a pin drop in the room. All the women shifted their bodies and eyes from Mandy to me. The entire supply of oxygen was sucked out from my sister's living room. I sighed as if I couldn't care less.

"Really? I hadn't heard that, Beth," I answered while shrugging my shoulders. I could feel Harris inch closer to me protectively. It wasn't really necessary. I could handle Bethany; she was all bark and no bite.

"I'm surprised it was all over TV last night," she answered, very pleased with herself.

I didn't say any more. I just nodded my head, and soon the ladies turned their attention back to my sister.

"So who dumped who anyway?" she blurted out.

I turned to her with a snarl and gave her a look of annoyance with my brows furrowed. "I'd really rather not discuss that, Beth. I'm sure you understand," I insisted. With my eyes, I silently pleaded for her to stop, but I knew it was in vain.

Her lips came up to the side and she rolled her eyes. The women in the circle were still watching Mandy, but I could tell they were all still listening to Bethany and I. It has always intrigued me how women are the first ones to insist they can't do everything at once; but when there's juicy gossip to be heard, they can split their brains in two very distinct pieces and concentrate on two things at the same time effortlessly. I tried to focus on Mandy and her enthusiasm for her gifts and forget about Bethany, but I knew she wasn't close to being done.

"How much did you get for those pictures? The club was pretty outraged, you know?" she asked. I cringed away trying to hide.

"All right! That's enough, Kane, leave her alone already. They broke up, end of story. Okay, everybody?" Harris explained sternly as Bethany stared her down. "Now, if no one else has any more inappropriate questions, can we get back to the woman of the hour that is growing a child inside of her body, please."

"Thank you, Harris," Mandy added, as I stifled a shocked giggle.

"Well, I was just curious," Bethany muttered under her breath.

After that, everyone treated me like I had some sort of incurable disease. Bethany left me alone, but everyone continued talking about me behind my back, even though they were still within earshot. You would think that women, with the privileged kind of upbringing they had received, would have better manners. I started getting angry. The more I thought about things, the angrier I got. Not just about Bethany but about everything. Gray had opened something inside of me and then left. He had given me such a wonderful gift by giving me himself, and I had tossed it away like garbage. I had given him up so easily. Why?

If I had just been stronger and dealt with things better, I wouldn't be the outcast anymore or ever again. Not that being the outcast bothered me—being around idiots bothered me. I was at the mercy of these cruel women because of the way I portrayed myself. I was soft-spoken, usually, and had very few friends. Most women categorize that as snobby or superior—not the best personality trait. I had lost my husband and child in a horrible accident which people either pitied or blamed me for. I was not the kind of person people wanted to hang out with, and now, to top it off, I was envied and/or hated for snagging the most talented and gorgeous movie star in the business today, only to be "dumped publicly" after naked pictures of us surfaced on the Internet. This was not my finest moment to say the least. It all looked bad, and I looked like a complete fool. If only people knew the truth, if only people looked a little deeper. My anger slowly turned to pity and sadness. Pity for the moronic women I was surrounded by and sadness for how I treated Gray. Gray, who had been my light when I couldn't see, was now my darkness.

My thoughts quickly became consumed by him, and eventually I fazed back into my happy place where Gray was always there smiling at me. Sometimes, if I concentrated hard enough, I could almost feel his hand in mine. I knew that I experienced something that maybe none of these prudes ever had—real love. I was sure that most of these women had married for money or something close to it. I had had all the money a girl could think of in the man that loved me. I didn't care about that. I looked around the room at them all. None of them was smiling or had the glow of love on their face. They all looked tired and angry, except for the ones with Botox. This baby shower was the highlight of their day. They had woken up early and put their best makeup on, done their best hair, and picked their most flattering outfits. They had probably planned out the perfect conversations in their minds and searched endlessly to find the best gift of the day. Everything for these women was a competition. It suddenly all seemed pathetic to me—to have it all and never realize how lucky they were. To have it all and know it, now that would be something.

That night, as I lay in the bed we had shared for so many nights, I couldn't sleep. I couldn't stop thinking about Gray. Whenever I closed my eyes, he was there with his simple smile. After I had said good-bye to John and Georgia, I had hoped for something to happen. Maybe a flip of a switch in the universe would happen and make me feel whole again. But without John, and now Gray, I felt more alone than ever. The obvious started to sink in. I had done this to myself. Losing John and Georgia was out of my control, but losing Gray had been completely by my own hand. I rolled over and screamed into my pillow.

The days that followed seemed to run into one another; each morning brought with it a new level of emptiness. I thought about him more than I should have. I missed him much more than I ever thought I would. Every now and then, I would hear his voice coming from the television, and my heart would sputter. I was becoming, well, pathetic.

~~~~~~~~~

I didn't hear Harris come in at first. I was blaring music all over the house in a deep-cleaning mode.

"Hello!" she shouted with her hands in the air on either side of her face. Her hands were curled like claws, and her face was contorted into a monster-like scary face.

I turned around terrified and screamed loudly, hiding my face in my hands. I frantically grabbed the remote and turned down the music. Harris was staring at me oddly. Her face made a disgusted look and her nose was crinkled.

"I did knock and ring the doorbell and shout," she explained with a little softness in her voice.

"Oh, sorry, I must have been in a daze or something." My voice was shaky and my heart was still pounding away from the fright of surprise.

"Yeah, that or a John Mayer coma. By the way, you look like crap, Elaina. What are you doing?" She grabbed the cleaning bottle and rag from my hands and headed into the kitchen to make a drink.

I rolled my eyes and moved swiftly to the kitchen after finding another rag and spray bottle on my way and started cleaning again. "I'm cleaning and straightening up. This place needs to be…cleaned."

"Have you showered today?" she asked after using the ice dispenser.

"No," I answered, suddenly aware that I probably didn't smell too great.

"Yesterday?" she asked with her brow furrowed again as she poured some vodka into her glass.

"No. Why?" I snapped.

"Umm, 'cause you look like crap and you kinda... smell...a little. What is wrong with you?" she answered with her nose wrinkled up.

"Nothing is wrong. I'm just...just...I don't know. What are you doing here anyway?" I growled, still annoyed about the bad smell comment. I knew I didn't smell, well, not that bad anyway.

She watched me closely, narrowing her eyes, and then sat down at the kitchen table and motioned me over with her hand. I reluctantly went over and sat with my best friend with a huff.

"What is this, Elaina? You never clean this much?"

I tried to put on my best poker face, but I'm sure it was laughable. "I'm just trying to stay busy, that's all, and this place, this whole house just feels like it's...it just doesn't feel like I belong here...anymore." My face dropped in defeat, realizing my pretend armor had failed.

Harris nodded her head in understanding. She gently pulled the dust rag from my hand and squeezed my hand in hers. Then she slid her drink over to me with her free hand. I took a swig and scrunched my face as the straight vodka burned down my throat.

"How long has he been gone now?" she asked.

I took a deep breath and exhaled slowly before answering. "Over a month. Six weeks, maybe more. Why?"

"Elaina, why don't you call him?" she encouraged softly.

"Stop it, Harris! I mean it!" I snapped. "It's over!" I yanked my hand from hers.

"Apparently not. Have you seen yourself lately? It's not pretty," she snorted.

"I already told you, it's not fair to him. He deserves better!" Even though I spoke the truth, it still stung having to say those words. He deserved way better than me.

"There is no one better than you, Elaina. You two are each other's match. You know it as well as he does. Just call him," she urged again.

"No." I crossed my hands in front of me as if I was a ref calling safe at a baseball game.

She growled quietly and huffed a few times. "You know it will make you feel better. Just call him! I know it's driving you crazy not knowing what's going on with him! I saw you at the shower. Bethany hit a nerve, didn't she?"

"Yeah, it would. And no, she didn't," I grumbled.

"You know how to reach him, don't you?"

"Of course, I do!" I snapped at her, suddenly feeling very territorial.

She handed me the phone and narrowed her eyes sternly down at me. "Do it then. If not for you then for me, please. I can't take another day of your moping. If you get any thinner, I'm jumping off a cliff. And this not showering thing is just, gross Elaina," she teased.

I rolled my eyes directly at her this time, not even trying to hide my contempt for her. "Fine," I snapped as I snatched the phone from her hand. I dialed the number quickly as if I had been practicing for weeks. She raised an eyebrow. It rang only a few times before Grayson's agent answered the phone. I couldn't stand him.

"Hi Freddy…this is Elaina…Murphy. Grayson gave me this number in case I wanted to contact him. Could you pl—"

He spoke so fast that it was hard to follow everything he said.

"Oh…really? Okay then. No, no. Please don't tell him I called then…Please, Freddy, don't tell him. Really, it's nothing." Another long rush of words and information from him. "Really, he did?… Yeah, he mentioned that before. I know the place, sure…Thank you, Freddy…I'll let you know…Good-bye." I hung up the phone and stood motionless. It took me almost a minute to realize that I hadn't taken a breath since I last spoke.

"Well?" Harris's voice blistered into my ears.

"He's on an extended vacation until next year," I blurted out, still not believing what I had heard. "He said that Grayson needed a break because he couldn't concentrate. He said Gray may not come back. He asked me what happened before he left," I rambled on.

"Next year? Where the heck did he go?" Harris questioned.

I didn't respond. I was trying to remember a conversation that Gray and I had had weeks ago. It seemed that it had been so long ago, even though it really wasn't.

Gray:	I always go there every year to clear my head. It's beautiful there—the salty air, the clear water. The people there are wonderful. My mother left me the place when she passed on.
Elaina:	Sounds wonderful.
Gray:	Maybe I'll take you there someday.

"Elaina? Hello in there? Where did he go?"

Finally I snapped out of my Grayson coma and shot my eyes straight into hers. "I need a first-class ticket to Belize."

"Where?"

"Actually, Belize City."

"Why would you want to go there?" Harris asked stupidly, then she understood. "Oh. I see. Are you sure?"

"If that's where he is, then yes, that is where I need to be!" I answered matter-of-factly.

She smiled her devilish grin at me and dashed out to her car to get her computer and credit cards. On her way out, she nearly collided with Mandy at the back door.

"Woah! Geez, Mandy, why don't you lose some weight already!" Harris teased passing by her.

"What's going on?" Mandy asked, stunned, trying to shake off the fat joke. "I'm pregnant, Harris. What's your excuse?" she shouted back.

"Elaina is going to get her movie star!" Harris rang out.

Mandy snapped her head to me and followed me to my bedroom as I packed.

"After what that jerk did to you? Are you crazy?" she asked, bewildered.

I rushed through the room, packing my things as fast as I could, knowing that this was, at last, the right decision. My old life would have to end here, and the birth of my new life would begin now. The feelings, the pain, the solitude would all be left behind me now. I passed the table too closely and heard the picture frame wobble and then tilt back, showing the family forever printed on the glossy side of the paper underneath the cracked glass. I gently placed the picture in my hands, staring down at it. My breathing started to speed, my chest rising and falling faster than it should have. It all seemed unreal to me now. That family was so long ago, I almost wondered who those people were. They didn't seem as familiar and demanding as they once had. What waited for me now was something new and different and real. The faces in the picture would be left behind now, but not forgotten. I had never intended to leave this place, this home of ours. It had now become more of a tomb, holding me down with shackles. I had been afraid to leave, afraid to change for fear of forgetting. I laid the picture back down and zoomed past my sister. Her face was twisted up into a variety of different emotions, disapproval mostly.

"What?" I grunted with my arms in the air, knowing all too well what she was thinking.

"This won't change anything. This won't make any difference," she answered, exasperated.

"Then what difference does it make to you? It is still my life, right?"

"Of course it is. But…to leave…this way. What would they think?"

"What do *they* have to do with anything? This isn't about *them*, it's about *me*." I stormed through the doorway and into the bathroom. I was doing fine until I caught a glimpse of myself in the mirror. The breathing thing came back, and before I knew it, I was grabbing the sink ledge for stability. My sister wasn't far behind me, and I could hear her thrumming her fingers on the doorframe.

"See, you're not ready," she whispered softly.

I felt the coldness of her words wash over me. The truth wasn't far from what she said, but it infuriated me enough to keep pushing on. I huffed again, squared my shoulders, and looked at myself. There I was—too young to be old, too old to be young. Not more than thirty-four years old. I was alone, no husband, no kids. I was stuck in this huge house, all alone with no one but my annoying and loving sister, Mandy, and my only best friend, Harris, to keep me company. My hair was long and brown; my eyes were dark-brown, almost black; and my youth, well, it was fading fast. I wasn't much to look at, I didn't think. I was average in just about every way. After today, I would be different. I would be a new person. *Today is the day,* I kept hearing over and over in my mind. I pulled my hair into a messy ponytail and thrust the drawer open. I stuck my hand in and began taking more things out to pack. I wasn't ever planning on coming back here; I was done with the cross I bared, and it was time to let someone else take their turn.

Harris was back before I could find my passport and wallet. I wouldn't need much after all, it was a beach.

"So what's in Belize anyway?" Harris asked while typing away on her computer.

"It's an island called San Pedro. It's supposed to be beautiful," I answered mindlessly.

"Your going to a third-world country for a man that may or may not want you there? Are you crazy, Elaina? What's gotten into you?" Mandy demanded.

Harris rolled her eyes from across the room. I sighed loudly and answered her, "My heart, Mandy. My heart has finally gotten back into me. And I'm not letting it go to waste anymore. Okay?"

"You love him?"

"Yes, I do!"

"He loves you?" she asked warily.

"Yes, he does."

"Still?"

"I hope so."

Before I dashed out the door, I yelled out to Harris, "Put the house on the market while I'm gone. Either way this turns out, I'm moving."

Harris' eyes bulged and her mouth dropped. I grinned and slammed the door behind me, hopefully for the last time.

Chapter 15

Gray

First of all, I should say that I never loved anybody like I love Elaina. It was never my intention to leave her, ever. I had planned to stay with her as long as I could and then take her with me, wherever that was. For years now, I had been growing weary of my career. It had been movie after movie. The money was great, don't get me wrong. It was the lifestyle that I was tired of. The inability to ever have a real friend that I could trust that wasn't my agent. I remember when I had first come here from Scotland. I knew nothing about how this business worked. It was easy back then to get a gig. I was young and eager. Now, I was just tired. I was tired of traveling all over the place. Really, I was tired of being tired of what I was doing. I was sick of the women throwing themselves at me and treating me like a toy. Don't get me wrong about that either; I had a great run—tons of beautiful women, a new one every night if I wanted. I never even thought about loving any of them or even liking them for that matter. The older I got, the more I noticed how empty they all were. Their hearts were as blank as their brains. The more famous I got, the worse they seemed to get.

My mother asked me once how I could sleep with a girl when I didn't even like her. After that, I started paying more attention to details. She would always tell me that I was special and talented. She was one smart lady. Like all mothers, I suppose she was a bit biased, but she was really the only person who told me those things that I actually believed. I realized I was getting closer to forty fast and had never had a meaningful relationship with anyone. Even me engagement years ago was meaningless. I had gotten engaged because she wanted to not because I wanted to get married. That girl cut her losses and got the hell out before I could ruin her. For years I just assumed it wasn't for me, marriage that it is. I had all but given up until I saw her.

I had expected a little old lady when we pulled into that park parking lot, but as she stood there with the wind blowing her hair around, I was simply stunned by her beauty. I have seen thousands of beautiful women, some natural, most fake, but God had made this one perfect. Her dark-brown hair that hung down to the middle of her back matched her dark-brown eyes. She was shorter than me, but I was used to that, being over six foot. Even though she was perfect in every way, it wasn't her looks that caught my attention, it was her expression. I tried to smile at her, but she frowned when I did. I had never had anyone do that before. Even though she frowned, she was still beautiful. She was also the first woman to deny me before getting a chance to speak. I knew right away that I liked her. She was so cute how she tried to be so professional but she kept peeking glances at me in her rearview mirror. She was trying not to look at me but she was still curious. When I tried to make conversation, she avoided me. Mr. Sparks this and Mr. Sparks that. Normally, that would have annoyed me; but when she did it with her quiet voice, it just made me like her more. When she asked me to call her Ms. Murphy, I thought I would melt. Saying her name became a game for me. It turned me on so much to refer to her that way. I knew that she hated me saying it, that hearing it probably made her feel old. If she only knew how crazy she drove me those first few days.

She resisted and avoided me like the plague. Strangely, everything she did seemed to pull me closer to her—the way she cut the peppers with her huge knife in the kitchen, the way she beat the eggs with her whisk in the morning, the way she made fun of me for liking egg whites. That had been the first time she had dared to have a real conversation with me. I was sitting at the bar early in the morning, watching her prepare my breakfast. It was the hottest thing in the world watching her move around the kitchen with such precision and focus. She always wore that little apron around her waist. I would imagine tearing all of her clothes off, but that damn apron I would leave on. When she cracked the egg in the frying pan, I cringed and narrowed my eyes at it crackling in the grease from the bacon. She must have seen me 'cause she quickly explained, "Don't worry, this is for me. I know you only eat egg whites, although I don't know why. They're pretty gross." She laughed to herself and shrugged her shoulders. Her lip lifted a little at the corner and a strand of her long brown hair fell from behind her ear. It took me a minute to say anything because I had been so focused on her beauty.

"I like egg whites," was all I could say, and I immediately felt like an idiot. She looked up at me with her brows crunching together and blew the loose strand from her face. "Nobody likes egg whites, Grayson," she answered me like I was an annoying man at some bar that wouldn't leave her alone. Her voice was still kind but her face said a different story. This woman should have been an actress for the amount of stuff she kept hidden. I smiled at her, and when she saw me smiling, she quickly turned away from me with red cheeks.

"Have you ever even had a real fried egg before?" she asked, trying to get my focus off of her.

"No, I never have. They look like big orange eyeballs, not very appealing. The cholesterol isn't very pretty either, you know?" I loved teasing her.

She rolled her dark-brown eyes. I loved it when she did that. She was so sexy without even knowing it. "Well, you should," she insisted like a mother would do to a child. "They're much better."

"Maybe I will some time," I answered with a wink. When she saw that, she dropped her knife and nearly speared her own toe to the ground. I loved flustering her. It was fun.

She seemed to hate me or spending any kind of time alone with me. She had no idea that I was thinking about her all day and counting down the hours until I could fawn after her again. I began to fixate on her, the way she moved around the kitchen and the house like an angel. She would do the smallest things but I watched her as she mindlessly poured herself more coffee without even looking for the pot or making sure she got the coffee in the cup and not on the floor. She chopped onions that way too, without even looking at them. I couldn't watch that for very long for fear of her chopping off a finger. She never did, thankfully. I figured if she was this talented in the kitchen with her hands…

I started wondering about what she was doing in the day while I was gone. Did she think about me at all, or was I really just a nuisance to her? What would she have on tonight? Would her hair be up or down? Would she ever eat with me? Would she be as nervous around me today as she was yesterday? I realized I knew nothing about her, and so then it became my mission in life to try to get to know her. I wanted to ask her a million questions. The more she drove me away, the more I wanted her. The more she avoided me, the more I wanted to hear her voice and touch her perfectly bronzed skin. I knew very little about this woman that I easily fantasized about eight hours a day. She was a real woman with a brain, and she could cook like nobody's business. Whenever she got out of the shower and came downstairs with her neck still damp, the smell of her filled every room she entered. It wasn't some stupid perfume, it was simply her. Honey, that's what she smelled like. It was intoxicating and it easily fueled my next day of fantasizing. I noticed the way she sat down and cross those legs, the way she walked in the room and the way she walked out of it, the way she would clean over and over. She rolled her eyes at me a lot, I liked that. Then it was the kind things she did, even though I knew it annoyed her to do them. She was always so kind to Macbeth, even though I knew she didn't want her here. She did unexpected things all the time—the way she folded my shirts and pants after washing them every day. She made my bed the same way every morning. She was always up before me, from the beginning.

As the days passed, I learned more about her. She was slowly letting me into her world. I could tell there was still so much she wasn't saying though. She liked martinis, which I found extremely sexy. She liked the real stuff. I was always disappointed when a woman ordered some crappy fruit drink on a date. She smoked, too, sometimes. That was a surprise since she had seemed like such a health nut with her fruit every morning. She allowed herself a fried egg with bacon only once a week. That was cute. It drove me crazy not being able to figure her out. She was constantly surprising me with her little quirks and the funny things she would say. When I noticed that she was more comfortable with Macbeth than me, I knew I had to make a move. For most girls that acted this way, it would be a game for them. I could tell that Elaina was just aloof and unreachable for the most part. It was also beginning to become more clear that she was just guarded. There was a sadness behind her eyes that worried me. I knew there had to be some way to get to know her and talk to her. She knew everything about cooking, and she could tell me anything I wanted to know, and I asked her every night after dinner how she made something so wonderful. I didn't ask her because the dinners were so incredibly tasty, even though they were. I asked her because she would talk about it at great lengths. Her face was more animated when she spoke of the thing she obviously loved. She knew about herbs, spices, and seasonings. She knew all kinds of vegetables that I had never heard of and even grew most of them in her backyard. I listened to her voice and held her eyes attentively. Even the way her lips moved was becoming an erotic experience for me.

I made my move by way of the kitchen. I had gotten off early from filming. It was nice to get away and it was perfect outside for grilling. So I decided I would make her dinner and try and force her to eat with me. I had a perfect plan, I thought. When she came through the door, she was caught off guard. I guess finding me in the kitchen was weird for her. She glared at me, and I thought that I had blown it for sure. I tried to ease the moment with some silly rambling, and she took the bait and her drink. Everything had been going well until she asked me why I always looked at her; I think *stare* was the word she used, and she would be right. I had no idea I stared at her so much, it was weird. When she spoke about what she thought about herself, it was sad. She had no idea what she looked like or how perfect she really was. It was endearing and refreshing to hear that from a woman. I couldn't believe that a woman that looked like her was so completely blind of her beauty. It took me by surprise, and I couldn't stop myself from kissing her.

Her lips were soft and fragile. She didn't resist me at all, and I must admit I got a little carried away. I had been imagining kissing this beautiful creature for far too long. I wanted to touch every part of her body with my mouth. Her skin was so soft, and the smell of her was overwhelming for me. The closer I got, the harder it was to control myself. She was something I had never experienced. Macbeth ruined that moment with her protective nature. Then later, I ruined it with my big mouth. I should never have said anything; I should have just gone to bed and let it be. The pain in her eyes was hard to take. I did learn something new about her that night though—she had been married once before.

The next night, she told me more. I don't know how she got through it. I was hypnotized with the way she showed me their deaths with her words. I could still hear the pain in her heart as she spoke. She showed me their picture. Her daughter was beautiful, just like her mother. The resemblance was uncanny. Her husband was young and handsome, I suppose. I felt competitive right away. It was her daughter that tore at my heart though—the youth and beauty that had been lost. When I looked up to Elaina, she was crying silently. She made no noise, and I could clearly see her pain and her broken heart. It was then that I finally understood her great sadness. I wanted to hold her and take care of her. But I wasn't prepared for what she did next.

When she stopped at the poolside and gently pulled her clothes off, I was unable to move or look at anything else. Her body was as perfect as I had imagined. Her skin was tanned, even her breasts, and I knew right away that she was a topless tanner. My thoughts went right to her lying beside the pool with no top. So sexy, but again unlike the girl I thought she was. Her legs were long and lean; my eyes followed up the curve of her calves, then up to her backside. My eyes stayed there a little too long but then headed up her back, and I could barely see the slight curve of her breast behind her upper arm as she tugged her hair out of its ponytail, then I drifted up to her shoulders and neck. Then she jumped in the water. I could still see her naked body in the pool, but I was bewildered. I couldn't move. She laughed. The way she looked at me made my blood rush to my head and somewhere else as well. When I got into the pool, she was smiling at me. She was waiting for me, but I still couldn't make a move. I had promised I would never kiss her again. I was confused by her. She swam over to me and kissed me, and that's when I fell in love with her. I couldn't deny it anymore. I was hooked.

That night had been incredible. She really was perfect for me in every way—the way she moved under my hands, the feel of her tongue tracing up my neck. My body felt like a livewire every time she touched me. This wasn't like the other women I had been with. For the first time, this meant something to me. I gave every part of her my full attention and took my time with her, just like I had imagined for so long. I opened my eyes to find her looking back at me. I looked into her eyes and really saw her. I was different with her. Something about her had changed me. I didn't want any of it to end. Later, in the middle of the night, her body was next to mine. Her back was to me and the sheet was resting over her hip, leaving everything else exposed. I watched her ribs expand and then drop as she slept. I saw the scars that graced her body from the accident. I couldn't help but touch her. She was intoxicating to me. I traced my finger down the side of her body, raising goose bumps along her skin, and when I got to the sheet, I pulled it off as I dragged my finger down her leg. Her breathing changed, and I knew she was awake. She rolled back toward me to face me. Her eyes were smiling as she touched my face with her hand. My hand found her waist, and I pulled her over to me. It wasn't until my lips touched hers that I realized what I had been wanting. I could not resist her, in any way.

She refused to sleep in my bed with me, so I had to find her every night for three nights. After that, I tried to get any kind of feelings out of her. It was impossible. She acted like she was doing me a favor by never telling me how she felt. I knew how I felt about her; there wasn't any doubt of how I felt about her. I wanted her, I loved her, but I knew that she was still in love with him. Her heart was broken, and even though she seemed to care for me, I knew I wasn't the one she was in love with. I watched her stare at that blasted urn on the fireplace every day. It hurt me more than anything that she still loved him the way she did. It was hard to watch the way she looked at it. It was a look of loss, the look of defeat and hopelessness.

When it was time for me to leave, I thought long and hard about her and what I knew I needed to do. I knew that leaving her would hurt her badly, but I also knew that she had opened me up to something that I realized I had been living without for far too long—love. I wanted more than anything to have her love, for her to be the one that I got to keep forever, but I wasn't willing to share her. I was too young to give up like she was. I couldn't watch her die anymore. It was the hardest thing I have ever done, but I said good-bye and let my Elaina go.

The whole plane ride, I was filled with a fury I had never experienced. So many times I wanted to turn around and go to her and hold her. The result would have been the same. She would never be able to love me the way I loved her. The anger slowly turned to disappointment. I missed her terribly. How could she let me go so easily? I guess I hadn't meant as much to her as she had to me.

By the time I got back to my house in LA, I was just sad. Macbeth was miserable back at home, just like me. She hated being back at the house just like me. To make matters worse, I was slammed with work for the next two weeks straight. It was good for me, bad for Macbeth. My new film was about to be released, so I was in interviews and red-carpet events all month. The busier I was, the less time I thought about her. Even though I was busy in the day, at night I dreamed about her. I could almost feel her skin on mine. I could almost smell the delicious honey scent of her.

Freddy had me doing interview after interview. Mostly, they asked about the photos of Elaina and I, which I had no comment on. They didn't even ask about the movie I was about to release, or the one I had finished filming. It didn't surprise me that they could care less about the new movie and were more interested in my personal life. Every time they mentioned her name, it was like a knife to my heart, and the anger came bubbling back. Gradually, I began to develop a complete hatred for the press and their stupid questions. I started asking myself why I was even doing this crap anymore. In the beginning of my career, I felt lucky to get any work at all, but now that I had made it, I was less and less excited about acting. I had made more money than I knew what to do with. I would never need to work again, and I was beginning to like the idea of just disappearing.

I never told Freddy what I was thinking. He kept trying to get me to take speech classes to rid myself of my accent. I thought that was complete crap. I was Scottish, that is where I was born. My mum would have turned over in her grave about that one. I knew Freddy was trying to get me more money, but when you make fifteen million a picture, what's the point? How much money can one person make? Each day, I grew less and less interested in my job and more intrigued with actually living my life. The last interview I did was the worst. That fella had no idea how close he'd come to getting decked.

"So, Mr. Sparks, tell us about the recent photos taken of you with your girlfriend."

"I already told you I'm not commenting on that."

"You too are still together, right?"

"No comment," I returned flatly. I could see Freddy in the wings waiting for my signal.

"Wasn't she a little old for you? Don't you usually go out with younger girls?" he barked at me like a rabid dog. I just sat there wanting to rip his bloody head off. I tried to gain control back. What he said brought me back to Elaina's fears. She had never fully felt like she was my type, and it had angered me so.

"If you want to ask me about the movie, then ask now, or I'm leaving," I warned him. "And if you say one more thing like that—"

Thankfully, Freddy grabbed me and we left the room. "No more questions today. Thanks for coming, Ted," I heard him excusing me.

When we were in the hall and far enough away from everyone and their cell phones, cameras, and voice recorders, he lit into me. "What's with you, man? Why don't you just tell them it's over. Tell them you dumped her already?"

"It's not like that, Freddy!" My voice must have been really loud 'cause the people we were still close to turned to stare at me all of a sudden. It may have been over, but I didn't want to accept it yet.

Freddy gave me a look that I recognized. It meant tone it down. "Look, I just don't know why you're getting all bent out of shape over this chick. She didn't want you, case closed. You movie stars think everyone wants you...Jesus Christ." He walked away shaking his head. *Just quit then,* she had said to me that night. I had wanted to so badly right then; to call up Freddy and tell him to screw off. Now seemed as good a time as any to break the news.

"I'm leaving, Freddy," I shouted.

He stopped in his short little tracks. Freddy was so slimy, I had known that about him before I hired him, but he was good at making me money. He had made me plenty of it as well as for himself. This partnership was over for me though. Freddy was still young enough to find another shark to leech on to.

"What do you mean you're leaving? We've got eight more interviews today," he barked again sounding more like a Chihuahua.

"I'm done, Freddy. After this press junket, I'm leaving. That was my last film."

He didn't look like he could hear for a second. It was kinda hard not to feel sorry for him, but I really didn't care.

"You can't do this. Please, don't do this to me. You've got two films to promote. You've got contracts."

"Yep, I do. I'll honor the contracts, but I'm not doing any more interviews. I'm leaving this place as soon as I can. I need a break. Call me when you've got my schedule."

"Where the hell are you going? Gray! We've got work! Are you insane? All over some woman?"

"Watch it, Freddy. Be careful," I warned him.

"You're throwing everything away for her; *you* should be careful!"

"Save it! I'm done."

"Gray, please, man. Don't do this!"

"I'm going to my vacation home as soon as my obligations are done here. Get Macbeth ready to leave the country." I walked off and got in my car and drove off. It felt great to be free. Sure I would be back for the press tour for the two films I had, but I was done with acting. I smiled thinking about what she would think if she knew, but then I remembered she probably didn't want to hear from me. Sadness sunk back in.

Two weeks later, I took a private jet to Belize City. A few hours later, I was back in my mother's old beach house in Ambergris Caye staring at the ocean with a drink in one and cigarette in the other. It seemed like the perfect place to retire. It was only missing one thing—her.

Chapter 16

Longest Trip Ever

My flight out of Richmond airport was the following morning at six. I had opted to stay in an airport hotel the night before and have the hotel drive me over in the morning. It was easier, and I wanted to get out of that house; the sooner the better. My flight was on time, and by the time we took off, the sun was trying to come up. It was raining hard and the takeoff was more than bumpy. The plane was pretty small: only three seats across, two on one side, and one on the other. It was hot sitting right beside the engine, but I had a window seat with no one beside me, so I was happy. The flight was a little over four hours from Richmond to Houston, Texas. Once there, I would have a twenty-four layover. I landed in Houston a little after eight in the morning, gaining two hours on my journey. I checked into my hotel, ordered some food, and waited to fall asleep. I returned to the airport the next morning to catch my nine o'clock flight from Houston to Belize City, Belize. This flight was exactly one hour and fifty minutes. This plane was much bigger, a Boeing 737 with six seats across, three for each side. I saw the landscape as we started to descend. I wanted to see tropical waters and islands, but I did not see anything of interest. Belize was surrounded by two countries: Mexico and Guatemala. There really wasn't much to look at from the plane at all, just green.

The landing was terrifying, and still I saw no crystal-blue water, just ugly browns and dead-looking greens. The airport could have fit inside of Houston airport about twenty times, maybe more. The people were all smiling even through customs, and I suddenly realized that I was almost there. The customs line moved fast, almost as if they weren't really checking your passports as much as they should have. I got my luggage and then immediately rechecked my bags, simple enough. Their security, however, was a different story altogether. Because of my need for lighters, I had somehow managed to collect quite a few in my oversized purse. When it went through the machine, I was given a stern look and asked to empty out all of my lighters. I dug my hand through and pulled out three and then put it on the belt to go through the machine again. This time, my purse was taken from me and emptied out on the table. The security guard collected eight more lighters from my bag content pile and handed my purse back to me with an evil expression on her face. "No lighters!" she yelled.

"Sorry," I whispered like a scorned child.

The next part of the trip was not something I was expecting. The itinerary claimed another flight, only fifteen to twenty minutes. But I didn't see any planes; just one tiny plane with the words "Tropic Airways" written on the side. There were maybe eight windows down the side. I knew I was flying with Tropic Airways, but this could not possibly be my plane. I had about fifteen minutes until my flight, so I wandered around looking for any sign of a big plane, but I found nothing. I checked my ticket, my gate; everything was right. That microscopic plane was mine. Suddenly, there was a female voice over the intercom. She spoke fast with a thick accent. I couldn't understand a word of it. It may have been my flight being called, I had no idea. I knew that since the plane was so small, I might miss boarding altogether. Sure enough, people started to wonder up to the gate, asking if they had been called. Her voice was much clearer and easier to understand without the intercom. I heard her announce that it was my turn to board the tiny aircraft.

Walking out to the plane, I was shocked at how small it was again, but I got on anyway. There was a bench seat that sat three across the back of the plane and then three rows of seats after that toward the pilot seat; two on one side and one on the other. Thirteen seats including the one next to the pilot. All I could think about was Gray. I was so close. I had been so preoccupied with the flights and trying to get here that I hadn't allowed my mind to wander over to him and how nervous I was about seeing him again. The engine started and the plane immediately started to vibrate and lift off the ground a bit. Suddenly, the plane felt light and uncontrolled. My stomach dropped realizing that it was too late to jump off and run. I could've taken a boat. Why didn't I take the boat?

Takeoff was swift, and the faster the plane ran down the runway, the more out of control and wobbly it felt, but we got off the ground. After that, every breeze that hit us tilted the plane from side to side. After a few seconds, we were flying over the most beautiful water I have ever seen—finally, the beauty Gray had talked so lovingly about. It was the brightest blue with lines of bright greens and dark shadows. You could see the bottom from way up here. I was no longer scared but instead in total awe of the beauty of this place. The Caribbean Sea is what the pilot called it, and on the other side was the mouth of the Corozal Bay. I stared out my window, in a trance from the sparkling waters we were soaring over. We passed one island that I was sure was ours, but it wasn't. Most of the people around me were couples or people that lived in San Pedro. All of them were happy and smiling. I was getting more and more nervous as we started to come back down to land. It had been about fifteen minutes since takeoff. While we were going to San Pedro, that wasn't my last stop. I had one more to go after that. This is where my plan was going to get tricky.

The landing was bumpy but steady, and the runway seemed too short but at last was accommodating. We disembarked, and I headed to the Tropic Air airport only feet away from the end of the actual runway. The town looked dusty and small. I quickly remembered we were only in the airport, I hadn't seen anything yet. I decided to hold any judgment until I could see more of this smallish island. I waited for my bags and decided to ask some people there how to get a boat or find someone willing to taxi me further down the island coast by boat. They smiled at me, twitching their lips trying to hold back a giggle, like I was an idiot; little did I know that going by boat was pretty much the only way to get anywhere here. A taxi drove me to the end of Front Street in San Pedro. That was where I would catch my water taxi. Where I was going was called Ambergris Caye. This place was where some of the world's best scuba diving was—the Barrier Reef and the Blue Hole especially. I had read it on the brochure while I waited in the small airport in Belize City.

I knew that Gray owned a house and he was not on resort property. I knew that his place was only about a ten-minute boat ride from the town of San Pedro. I also knew that his house had a dark-blue roof and that it was the only one like it—that was all I knew—and now that I was here, it was really beginning to sink in that I was in a third-world country with absolutely no traveling experience and no friends to guide me through. I had no idea where I really was and what exactly I was going to do here. I had made a huge trip on a whim for the person that I loved that I hoped still loved me. One thing was for sure; this was going to be a search mission, and he may not even be there when I arrive. With my luck, he was already gone. With my luck, he had come here with someone else. He had said this was where he went to think and clear his mind. He had also said that he loved me and that I would know where to find him. Thanks to Freddy, I knew where to find him today. But would he still want me? Would he even still be here?

I fearlessly crossed the street filled with speeding golf carts and motorcycles clipping at my heels. I jumped from the street to the sidewalk and tried to steady my pounding heart. My hands fell to my knees as I tried to calm myself. There was obviously no traffic laws here or legal-age requirement. The strange people here drove as if they didn't see other drivers, and if you didn't move out of the way quick enough, you would get hit. As I lifted my head and brushed back my hair from my frazzled face, I watched the town around me, the way other people seemed to already understand the "traffic laws" here. I suddenly wished there had been a brochure on that instead. A few men were smiling and pointing at me as I grabbed the handle of my suitcase and pulled it behind me. I searched for the beach, and finally I saw the water that I had gotten a look at from the plane. The water was the most beautiful I had ever seen anywhere; of course, I hadn't really ever been anywhere besides Richmond, Virginia in my whole life, but still I had to assume it was up there on the "perfect beaches" scale. I wheeled my suitcase through the powdery sand and up the wooden deck ramp. There was a small office on the end. I had brought enough money to bribe someone if I needed to. I was told that most Belizeans preferred American dollar bills over their own Belizean money, so I felt pretty secure in getting someone to take me where I needed to go. The American dollar was worth twice the Belizean, so it made sense to me. There weren't any people at my window, so I waited for the woman to see me. I hadn't thought about the San Pedro state of mind, where five minutes actually meant more like thirty, and Belizean time meant "don't even bother wearing a watch, 'cause it will do you no good."

"Do you need a pass?" the woman at the counter asked in an almost Jamaican accent. Her skin was dark-brown and it almost glowed under the sun that cut through the wooden roof of her makeshift office cubicle.

She startled me; I hadn't even noticed her over the sparkling blue water in front of me. "I need to get to a house; it has a dark-blue roof. Do you know it?" I asked with a hopeful tone.

Her lips lifted slightly as if she wanted to smile, but she didn't. "Yeah, I know the place, but you can't go there." She turned to do something else as if the conversation was over for her.

"Huh? Umm..why?" I asked, confused. I started shuffling toward her now.

She turned back to me with the same smile. "There is no admittance. It is private. We can drop you at the pier before that one though, but you will have to walk the rest of the way with your bags." She pointed to my small suitcase and my even smaller overnight bag.

"That's fine," I assured her with a warm smile, hoping to get one in response.

The woman smiled, but not warmly, and nodded to her friend behind her. "That's twenty Belize dollars. George will take you when he gets back from his run. Just sit and wait over there." She pointed to the end of the pier. It was hot here. I had stupidly worn jeans and was baking in the sun. Still, the view was perfect enough to help me forget the sweat rolling down my neck and back. The water lapped in slowly and leisurely along with a wonderfully full breeze. It was perfect here. I had no idea what time it was, or really where I was. Somewhere on some island in a third-world country. For all I knew, this driver of mine was going to murder me and take my stuff. I was a woman and I was alone. I couldn't have been an easier target. The woman watched me sweat at the end of the dock.

"Hey, miss. You can leave your luggage here if you want to check out town. George will be a while. You bought your ticket; you can leave your things," she called out.

"Really? 'cause I'd love to change. How much time do I have?"

"About half an hour," she said with another weird twitch of a smile.

I walked back down the dock, reluctant to leave my stuff but for some reason trusting this stranger of a woman at her word. I took my purse and all the important stuff I needed to get back to my life—my passport and wallet—plus a swimsuit and strapless sundress to change into. I went to the end of the pier and turned right onto the sand. There were children playing all around, all with the darker mocha skin and bright, kind smiles. I saw a sign that read FIDO'S, so I turned left and walked up the wooden steps. The inside resembled a tiki hut and the bar was huge. I saw the sign for the bathroom so I bolted to it, realizing that I needed to use it. After changing, I shoved my clothes into my purse and sat down at the bar. The bartender came around and stood in front of me and placed a napkin on the bar. "What would you like?" the same weird accent that I couldn't quite pinpoint. He was really tall and dark-skinned with buzzed hair and a bright-blue shirt that read FIDO'S across it.

I thought for a second and then ordered a mai tai. I figured this was the place to have the fruity stuff. He smiled and turned to start making my cocktail.

"You comin' or goin'?" he asked, but it didn't really sound like a question, more like a statement.

"I just got here," I answered shyly.

"Ahh, welcome to Belize. Where you staying?" he asked.

"Umm, I'm not really sure." His eyes furrowed with a confused expression. I smiled back at him.

"I know where I want to go, but I'm not sure if that's where I'll be staying."

He laughed at me. "Where is it that you want to go?"

"The house with the dark-blue roof. You know it?"

"You want to go the movie star's house?"

"Yeah, I guess. His name is Grayson Sparks."

"I know. He comes in here sometimes, usually alone. He doesn't use that name though—Sparks—it's something else. His boat was just out there a bit ago. You just missed him."

My stomach jumped. "Really? He was just here?" I was briefly distracted from the different name thing.

"Yep, with his funny-looking dog." The tall man chuckled to himself as he wiped a clean glass dry with a rag.

Macbeth? She was here? I guess she would be. He took her everywhere he went.

"Thanks," I offered.

I finished my drink quickly and started back for the dock. When I reached the end, my bags were all still there, untouched. The drink had been large and strong, and I already felt a little more relaxed. I smiled in disbelief of the beauty of the water again, sat down and waited, much more comfortably in my lighter clothing.

"You changed!" the woman shouted.

"Yeah, it's hot here!"

"Yeah it is," she answered. "George will be here soon."

"Thanks."

I shoved my warmer clothes into my suitcase and my heart started to pound furiously. He was just here, just a while ago. Even though I had come all the way to a country I have never been to and used my passport for the first time, I hadn't thought about what I would say to him when I saw him. What do you say to a man who tried to love you and failed? How do you apologize for hurting someone like that? All I could see in my mind was Gray standing in front of me with tears in his eyes like that last night I saw him. Would he still want me that way? Had I hurt him too much?

A small black ray glided in the water under my feet, and I watched it scoot along. I watched the tiny fish swarm around in their tiny groups. I decided to lay back and sunbathe while I waited for the boat. My feet dangled in the clear water, and I wondered what was swimming around my toes.

Just then I heard a motor and sat up to see a long, skinny boat pull up to the dock.

"That's him, that's George!" the woman shouted from her small enclosure. I turned back to the man in the boat.

"You the lady that wants to find the movie star?"

"I guess so, that's me."

He grabbed my bags and gave me a helping hand aboard. "It's about a five-minute boat ride."

"Okay!" I shouted. He backed the boat up coming incredibly close to a sailboat anchored out behind him. Then he revved the motor and off we went headed toward Ambergris Caye. The houses we passed were mostly small. We stayed close to the shore, no more than one hundred fifty feet or so. On the way, there was a puffer fish floating on top of the water. George had slowed the boat and told me that someone must have caught it and thrown it back. It was still alive, but the fish had to wait to go back down to its normal size before it could go back down in the water. The water couldn't have been more than four feet here. The bottom was clear and the water was even more turquoise-colored further from shore.

Up ahead I could see the house with the dark-blue roof. The house itself was light blue in color like the sky. It wasn't small but it wasn't huge either. It looked like it belonged here, nestled amongst the palm trees and low-growing shrubs. The boat slowed down again and George pointed to the dock where we were going to. It was at least two hundred feet away from Gray's house. My heart began to race again at the sight of the place. It was simple but perfect, and I wondered if I would ever see the inside of it. I was excited but nervous. This could either be the end of my trip or the beginning of another long haul home. I gripped the side of the boat, feeling the waves tilt us from side to side.

"You will have to walk the rest of the way. I can wait out here for you in case he isn't there. His boat *is* there, see?" He pointed to a sleek-looking boat that looked fast and expensive. It was much bigger than ours; white, with racing lines down the side, and on the back were four motors.

"Do you need any help with your bags?"

"Uh..no, thanks, I got it." I only had two bags. I heard barking and I looked back up to Gray's dock to see Macbeth sitting on the end staring at me and cocking her head to the side. The sound of her got me excited and I grabbed my bags hastily as we got closer to the dock. I had missed Macbeth dearly. She wasn't just a dog, she had become my companion too when Gray had worked long hours. I wondered if she would remember me. I also knew if Gray was here Macbeth would not wander off too far from him. My heart skipped again. George pulled up to the dock and I hopped off with my bags. "I'll wait for you here; if you need me just wave."

"Thanks," I sighed.

"Good luck, ma'am!" he shouted.

I waved and continued on my journey. The dock wasn't long, probably close to fifty feet. There was another house at the end of it that looked empty, but it was much smaller than Gray's. The sun was high in the sky now and it was nearly one in the afternoon. I looked over to see where Macbeth was; I spotted her walking parallel to me, only very far away, sticking her nose up smelling the tropical scents in the air. She reached the end of her dock as I reached mine. She turned in my direction and headed toward me slowly, keeping up at my pace. I had another two hundred feet to walk through the sand. I kicked my flip-flops off and shifted down to the water so I could walk through the harder sand.

The water was cool but comfortable as another roll of sweat fell down my neck and back. You wouldn't get a shock from jumping into it. The palm trees were filled with green coconuts and covered with large, dark-green leaves rippling in the breeze. I saw no sign of Gray anywhere but his boat was still there. I started to question myself as I walked toward the unknown. Something inside of me pushed me ahead. If anything, I had to know if he still loved me. I needed to know if everything he had said to me was real—if he was real. I longed for him to hold me and to hear his laugh. I missed the richness of his voice whispering in my ear and the way his mouth twisted up to one side whenever he was in deep thought. I missed his breathtaking eyes that burned deep down to my soul to wake me up from death. He had saved me from wasting away; he had been my light in all my darkness.

At the halfway mark, I froze in the sugary sand. I was almost there now, and the thought of losing him again had paralyzed me with fear. My heart started to race now, knowing I was only moments away from the best day or one of the worst in my life. Of course it couldn't possibly be the worst day of my life; that day, I was positive, had already happened to me. All I could think of was his face, his smile, his eyes…everything about him consumed me. I finally decided it was worth the pain if he rejected me, just to see him one last time. My feet began to move again toward the dock that was now about one hundred feet away.

I reached the house. It was perfect, just like he had described. There was a concrete sundeck across the front and a small pool off the side. There were pink and red flowering bushes surrounding the deck and the sides of the house. I looked up the steps but no one was there. I didn't dare walk in his house; that would be rude. I dropped my bags at the start of the pier and took a deep breath of the island air and stretched my back. Suddenly, I noticed Macbeth at my side licking my hand and then nudging it over her head.

"Hey, Mac. Not much of a guard dog, are you?" I teased while I rubbed her ears and head. She nudged a little closer and nearly knocked me over. Her little nub of a tail was wagging as fast as it could, and her dark-brown eyes seemed to recognize me fully. A month or two hadn't allowed her to forget the extra treats and scraps I had given her back home. She looked up at me and seemed to smile with her mouth as she wiggled her butt from side to side.

"Where's Daddy?" I asked excitedly. "Where is he, huh?" Macbeth jumped around kicking her paws out but never hitting me or jumping on me. She, of course, told me nothing.

The end of the pier looked nice. I could jump in the water and swim for a bit. Even if Gray rejected me, I would get a swim in before heading back to Richmond. I left my bags and walked to the end of the dock and peeled off my clothes and jumped in the water. As my body contacted the water, I heard someone yelling behind me. My head went under the water and the noise was gone. There was only silence until I popped back up.

"Hey! You! What the hell are you doing?" the deep rusty voice yelled.

I grabbed the end of the pier with my hands and raised my body enough to see Gray running toward me with an angered look on his face, but he suddenly saw who I was, and he slowed down and then stopped short, panting. His brow was furrowed, not in anger now but in confusion. He lowered his head and shook it back and forth slowly. He put his hands on his hips and took a deep breath. Oh no, he was mad, this was a mistake. I should have never come here. I was worried now and I didn't know exactly what to do or say. This wasn't the way I had planned on seeing him, hanging on to a pier. Macbeth lowered her belly down to the decking boards and dropped her head on her front paws so she could lick the salty water off my face.

"Elaina?" he shouted out. "Is that really you?" he asked with his head still lowered, not looking up at me yet.

"Yes, it's me!" I shouted, breathless from paddling my arms and feet in the water.

"What…are you doing here?" he asked while raising his head to see me again through his sunglasses. I wished I could see his eyes; they would tell me everything I needed to know.

What was I doing here? What was I supposed to say now? Even I hadn't gotten that far. I decided to go with honesty.

"Well, there is…umm…something I needed to say to you," I answered breathlessly as I paddled my way back to the dock to hold on for dear life.

He grinned. "You came all the way down here just to tell me something? You know they have phones here, right?" He started walking toward me but hesitantly, his arms were crossed across his chest now closing himself off from me more.

"Of course, sure I know that, but I needed to see your face when I tell you this because it's very important. You did say I could come find you…and I thought I could use a vacation. What the hell." I shuddered at my choice of words and the insecurity of my voice. If I could hear the weakness of my voice, I was sure he could.

"Did you now?" His lips lifted to one side. "So what is it that you need to tell me then?" He was finally at the end of the pier and he was looking down at me in the water paddling with one arm and holding on to the deck with the other. He squatted down to see me better. He pulled his sunglasses off and dangled them in his hand. His eyes were wary and he looked like he wanted to smile but he was too afraid to. He waited patiently for me to catch my breath.

"You were wrong…when you said I didn't love you."

His eyes narrowed and his head cocked to one side as he shook his head in confusion.

"I was an idiot. You were right about deserving more than I was giving you. I was denying myself happiness and in doing that I…I hurt you, because I lied to you. I pretended not to love you and it was stupid, because I ended up hurting you. And because… I do love you, Gray. I'm in love with you. From the moment you got out of that car and smiled at me, I knew you were…going to be someone special. You deserve better than I was. I know I'm ready now because…now I know that I deserve to be happy too."

He stared down at me. His eyes were softer now and his mouth was tight. "Are you sure? I'm never gonna be him, Elaina, not ever," he whispered. "We can have a great life together as long as it's about you and me, just you and me."

"I don't want you to be him. I love you. I want you, all of you, every part of you!" I shouted breathlessly. "For Christ's sake, I came all the way here! I used my passport for the first time! I flew all the way to a third-world country just to see you! I'm scared to death and I'm treading water at the end of your pier like an idiot while your dog slobbers all over me." I laughed.

He smiled his crooked smile at me and shook his head but never took his eyes off me. He lowered his body down on the pier until his stomach was lying flat, with his feet out behind him and his face just inches from mine. He placed his finger on the top of my head with a smile and pushed me down under the water. It was easy for him to do, since I couldn't stand. I went down, half surprised. My feet suddenly hit the sandy bottom and automatically pushed off and then popped back up gasping for air. "Why did you do that?" I gasped while wiping the salt water from my eyes.

"That's for making me wait almost five months to hear those words. You stubborn woman." His lips pulled up to one side again, and I felt that tug inside my stomach. He was so close to me now and I wanted to stretch up to him to kiss him, but I was paralyzed with fear. He grunted as he shot back up to his feet, pulled his T-shirt off over his head, and kicked his dusty flip-flops off. He jumped in the water, executing the perfect cannonball inches from my flailing arms and legs. The splash was huge and the waves that rippled from it hit me immediately, making it harder to keep my head out of the water. Once he was in the water with me, he grabbed my waist and wound his arms around me. He could stand here since he was nearly a foot taller than me. He wrapped my legs around his waist and dragged his fingers up my back to cradle my neck as he pulled me to his face. His lips pressed against mine softly at first and then with more intensity.

I immediately felt at home. His lips slid from my lips across my cheek to my neck. "I missed you," he breathed into my ear.

I laughed silently. "By the way"—I whispered in between kisses to his lips and face— "I'm selling my house."

He chuckled under his breath. "That's good, 'cause I think I'm retiring." He sighed happily. "What do you think of living here, permanently?"

"I think it's a great idea," I answered as I wrapped my arms around his neck and pulled him closer to me.

"That's really good, 'cause I was thinking it was time I settled down." He kissed my shoulders and neck.

"Oh?" I teased.

"I was thinking I would need an innkeeper here for...oh... ever." He lifted me from the water so he could kiss my breasts and my chest.

I gazed up at the sun and closed my eyes, basking in the heat. "Well, I'm sorry. I think I'm retiring too."

"That's good, 'cause I just hired one from the island so that my wife can spend all of her time with me." His lips got more and more urgent and more passionate as he pressed his mouth along my jaw and my throat.

"Who's your wife?" I asked in fake shock.

"I was kinda hoping you would want to be." He smiled and kissed my neck and shoulders. "If you'll have me."

"I didn't come here to clean houses," I teased.

"Is that a yes, Ms. Murphy?" he asked in surprise.

"I think so, Mr. Sparks."

His eyes were filled with joy and shock, then he laughed, shaking his head. "Actually, it's MacNally; Sparks is just my stage name. I won't be needin' that anymore."

"Elaina MacNally." I spoke it out loud to hear the two names together. "I like that."

"I like you," he whispered.

"I love you," I whispered back. He pulled me back to him and kissed me again, exhilarated with the sound of the words he had finally heard. I could feel his smiling lips on my neck and throat as I gazed up at the sky. Behind us, I could hear George puttering away back to town. I guess he figured I was okay. I was more than okay—I was happy, finally.

Chapter 17

The Beginning?

Almost a month later, I was more than settled into our life together in Belize, and we were set to get married. I had no reservations about it at all. Gray and I had decided that it would be just us on our wedding day. We didn't need anything fancy or contrived. We just needed the two of us there. I was ready—more than ready, actually.

I had found a simple white silk dress for the big day. It was long with thin spaghetti straps that crisscrossed in the back. My hair was swept up into a side messy bun with beautiful tropical pink flowers nestled into the twisted strands. Gray had decided to wear a beige linen suit with a white linen shirt underneath, unbuttoned, of course. Neither of us wore shoes, and our aisle was the pier in front of his house. This was not the place for overdone and glamour.

When I began my walk down to meet him, the sun was setting on one of the most perfect days we had had in Belize since I got there. There was a slight breeze and the air was warm with a floral scent. There was no music as I walked down the dock, no noise at all, except the ocean and the waves lapping into the shore. There were no bridesmaids or groomsmen. No family or friends attended this wedding. It was just him and me. Gray stood with his back to the sun with his arms hanging down at his side as he gazed back at me. How could I ever rationalize this moment in my mind? Of all the things I had imagined doing in my life, this was not one of them. This perfect man was mine for now and forever. How could this be? I smiled in my deep thought, too happy to ruin the moment with my tedious overanalyzing ways that he somehow seemed to love.

When our eyes met, he smiled his soft smile and chuckled a bit. He looked at me as if I was the most beautiful woman on the planet. I laughed quietly to myself and tried to stop my cheeks from flushing crimson. If only he knew just how ridiculous I really was. When I reached him and the minister, he stepped forward and gently wound his fingers with mine as we spun back around to face the setting orange-pink-colored sun and the man that would marry us.

We never looked at the minister, only each other. Most of the words spoken were technical ones, and he did most of the talking while we simply smiled at each other like two teenagers in a newfound love. The only important words I heard were, "Do you take this man to be your husband?" and "Do you take this woman to be your wife?" My yes was a softer and more reserved I do, but Gray's was a booming, assured I do!

When we were given permission to kiss, I should have known Gray would make it memorable. His hands cupped either side of my face and instead of pulling me to him he came to me this time. His lips barely touched mine as they shaped their way around my fuller lower lip. It was a delicate kiss, but long. He paused and pulled away just inches from my face as if he were waiting for something. I opened my eyes to see my husband in front of me.

"Hello, Mrs. MacNally," he whispered in his thick Scottish accent that I loved to hear.

"Hi," I whispered back. He lifted my chin with one finger and kissed me again.

~~~~~~~~

Days passed by and then weeks. Weeks soon turned into months and still nothing changed. The freshness of our relationship and now our marriage was still perfect in every way. Nothing had shaken our vows or our happiness in the slightest. We were blissfully unaware of anything that didn't involve us. We filled our days with snorkeling, scuba diving, and swimming. We went to town almost every day to try new restaurants and hang out with the few friends Gray had made there over the years. All four of them were from England and all of them had the same story of coming here on vacation and never leaving. Timothy and William were best friends who came to San Pedro for the first time five years ago, and inside their two-week-long vacation decided that they didn't want to be lawyers for one of the top firms in London. They wanted to stay here and open a bar on the beach with live music and Belikin beer. Jackson had come here to escape his ex-wife and her greedy parents. During the divorce settlement, she had taken almost everything. It was a fact that we now laughed about since two of his best friends had been excellent divorce lawyers once upon a time. Last but not least, there was Jonathan. He had been a doctor back in London, but when he came here on vacation and saw the poverty and the need for better healthcare, he decided that the Belizeans needed him here more than the Londoners did. We saw the guys once or twice a week. I liked them all, but we mostly stuck to ourselves. Gray and I moved around town with ease. There were no paparazzi or media here, just wonderful people with smiling faces. We shopped, looked at local artists' work, met new people, and enjoyed our new life thoroughly. I couldn't help but always wonder if someone was hiding in the bushes with a camera and every now and then pictures of us would surface back in the US. They were always taken from very far away and never of anything inappropriate. We knew they were there but we never saw them. I understood the need for them to come here to find Gray. He had all but disappeared months ago after doing his last interview for the movie he had already completed when we met. His fans missed him and wanted him back. The businessmen movie makers missed their cash cow too. Freddy called a few times after the wedding, but all Gray told him was that we were married and not leaving Belize anytime soon.

We busied ourselves in the day so we could relax at night. There was nothing better than falling asleep, curled up beside Gray under the stars while listening to the waves lap in. The sky, totally clear, with countless stars shining above us, was so beautiful. I was sure this was what heaven must be like.

We did have our arguments and disagreements. It turns out my husband wasn't as neat as he tried to make me believe and was notorious for leaving the seat up. He left his clothes all over the house, and whenever he went into the kitchen, there was a mess where he had been. I had fallen in the toilet one too many times and I wasn't afraid to wake him up in the middle of the night to express my anger about a wet butt. We had a maid service but I had never been okay with it. Having strangers in your house is an uncomfortable feeling for anyone, but with Gray being who he was, I felt like I was always worried about what they would find. Gray could yell; he was loud with a thicker accent when he got angry, but everything, no matter how angry each of us got, turned into a laughing match. Every time he got flustered and started rambling on in his sexy Scottish tongue, it was impossible not to giggle like a schoolgirl. One thing was for sure; fighting was way worth it when you could make up for hours.

Still, I could feel the inevitable looming over us. He was contractually bound and obligated to return and do press for his last movie. I knew it was only a matter of weeks before Freddy would call with the press schedule. We hadn't discussed any of it yet; avoided it is more like it. I knew he would have to basically travel the world in two months' time; do interview after interview all day long; be on plane after plane and not get much, if any, sleep; answer the same questions over and over; and, oh yeah, hate every minute of it. More than anything, we would be apart for a long while. I thought that Gray would probably start to miss his old life—the fame and the fans—but he seemed perfectly content being with me and lying in the sun.

We had been living in Belize for six months when Freddy called and left the message:

> Hey, Gray. It's Freddy, your agent…remember me? Anyway, I've got your schedule here and I'm ready to send it whenever you give me the fax number. You need to be on a plane in two weeks. The movie is opening in four weeks. Two weeks of prepress, then opening night, then onto every damn country you can think of. From what it looks like, you've got a full two months coming up, so get some rest and stop eating, 'cause you have to be camera-ready, man. Please call me back ASAP.

I heard the message first. Gray had gone diving with his island friends, and I had opted to stay home and relax by the pool. For some reason, I played the message over and over; and even though I was tempted to erase it, I knew that he had to do this. We would have to go and do this thing and be done with it for good. Freddy's call had come at an opportune time because Harris had called earlier that morning to tell me my house had finally sold. I would have to go back soon to deal with that most likely anyway. She had sold most of the furniture, but there were still things I needed to deal with personally. Still, I didn't want to leave. I liked it here, not just because it was beautiful but because this was our safe place. This was our home.

That night, we stayed in and I cooked dinner. I made fresh lobster with salad and threw the champagne in the fridge to chill. Even though I would lose my home in two months' time, I was still happy that my house had sold and this would, after all, be the last time we would ever have to do anything with the media.

"What's the occasion?" he asked as I poured his glass full of the sparkly stuff.

"Well, I have some news…actually. I have two things to tell you. One is great, the other is…not so great. Which one do you want first?" I asked with one brow raised.

"Good news first always, love." He grinned, having no idea what I would tell him.

"Harris called this morning after you left. She sold my house!"

"That's great! What did she end up getting for it?"

My face fell slightly. "A little over a million. The property isn't worth what it used to be." I shrugged my shoulders.

"That's still great love, cheers." He held out his glass and tapped it to mine and then leaned over and kissed me gently on the lips. "Congratulations."

"Thank you." I smiled.

"Now, the not-so-good news?" he asked while his face changed from happy to serious.

"Freddy called today." His face fell even more now and the light mood was gone. "He left you a message. You have to leave in two weeks."

Gray's face sunk and his eyes cast down. He let out a loud and defeated sigh. Then his eyes snapped up to mine and with heavy accusation in his tone, he asked, "Don't you mean *we* are leaving in two weeks?"

"Yes, of course. I meant us, of course." I felt awkward and upset. The thought of really leaving here made me nervous. The idea of being in front of cameras again and loud shouting people and photographers terrified me.

He smiled, obviously seeing my fear. "Well, I had hoped that it would be another few months away yet, but now is as good a time as any, I suppose. Did he say where we are going?"

"He's got a package for you. You need to call him with the fax number." My lips turned down and I sighed.

He leaned over to me. "What is it, love?" he whispered, pulling my chin up with his finger.

I smiled back trying to hide my true feelings from him. I knew that if I said I didn't want to go, it would only make it worse. Telling him that I was terrified of his lifestyle wasn't going to change the fact that we had to go. Instead of saying what I wanted to say, I sighed and answered, "It's just going to be strange leaving that old house. I never thought it would sell, I guess." I shrugged softly.

Gray watched my face intently, searching for any hidden emotion. He seemed satisfied with my answer, but he knew why I was quiet and it wasn't about the house. This was where we were safe and neither of us wanted to leave the safety of the island at all. "Don't worry, love, it's only for a few months, and then we can go anywhere you want to go—Italy, Paris—anywhere, I promise."

I had never thought about traveling anywhere before. It always seemed completely out of my reach. I had money, plenty to support myself, thanks to John's life insurance, but it felt wrong to spend that money on vacations. It was meant to take care of me, not go crazy with expensive trips and cars. Then I remembered that Gray had money to spend. He was one of the wealthiest actors on the planet, and now that I was his wife, I was also very wealthy. A shudder slid down my spine and a chill iced over my skin. This was going to take a lot of getting used to. I cleared my throat trying to hide my uneasiness. "I guess Italy sounds pretty great."

He nodded his head with such a confident certainty. "Italy it is then."

Chapter 18

The return flight was long and edgy. I was cranky the whole day because of my nervousness. Gray knew what was wrong with me. He knew I was acting out because I didn't want to do this; I didn't want to get followed by photographers and fans. I didn't want to leave Belize. Most of all, I didn't want to lose Gray to the lifestyle that consumed him. Everything had been so perfect in Belize. I knew now that it had been more of a cocoon. I liked it there because I felt safe there, and where we were headed I would never really be safe. I hated feeling like a lost child that couldn't do anything for herself. Being incompetent was a feeling that did not sit well with me.

Gray chuckled beside me and then I felt his hand on top of mine.

"Don't get too excited now," he snickered.

I pursed my lips and frowned at him which only made him laugh again. Gray was not as annoyed as I was about the trip we were about to begin. He was used to it. It was his job. He had done this many times before. He seemed extremely calm as we landed in Los Angeles.

The media frenzy didn't begin until we began our walk through the airport after customs and security. Once we passed through the checkpoints, we were toast. Luckily, Freddy was waiting there when we crossed over the line of safety. We were escorted to a large room with no windows. Our luggage was retrieved while we waited and then another man, a very tall and large man, began giving Gray and I instructions on how we would get from the airport to the car. It was funny how I had never had to worry about getting from one to the other before. Gray nodded blankly as if he had heard the instructions a thousand times before. I tried to listen to everything he said. Gray pulled his bag off his shoulder and began digging around in it. I cut my eyes to him a few times, annoyed that he was breaking my concentration from the very serious directions that Very Large and Tall Man was giving us. He grabbed the small black items from the bag and zipped the duffel back up quickly. He handed me my sunglasses. As I timidly took them and put them on, he winked at me. It was his way of saying everything's okay. On any other day, this simple wink of his would have worked. It probably would have caused me to throw my arms around his neck and kiss him until he gave in to my unsaid desires. Not today. Today, I was so uncomfortable that my stomach felt like a rock. Now, suddenly, I was faced with the terror of what and who were outside the doors. My head began to feel light and fuzzy. I tried to smile back at him, but whatever face I gave him must have been terrible because his eyes widened and then he burst into laughter. When he saw I wasn't laughing, he stopped immediately. He grabbed my arms and gently shook me, bobbling my sunglasses up and down around my eyes. "Elaina? You okay?"

"Huh?" was all I could say. The blood was draining from my brain and settling into my feet making them feel a thousand pounds each. My head suddenly felt all tingly in a very bad way.

"Look at me, love. It's okay. Everything is gonna be fine. We just go through the doors and we are gone. Simple, just like we talked about. Remember?"

I tried to search my mind for the conversation we had had a few days before. I had finally expressed my fear of people following me, the fear of the unknown, the fear of losing his hand from mine in the rush to get away from the photographers.

"Elaina? Are you in there somewhere? Darlin', if you can hear me, say something, please." With his arms around me, I started to feel the blood return to my face and hands. The feeling crept back in through my fingers and toes. "Please, love, you're freakin' me out here," he begged. Then he placed his hands on either side of my face and pulled me to him. His lips were right at my ear and he whispered, "Only us, that's all we need, remember?" Then he kissed my ear and then my neck, then his face was at mine again. "Only us."

Chill bumps erupted all over my neck and shoulder. He was too close, way too close for me not to have a response. He chuckled, feeling the goose bumps on my neck, then he gently pressed his lips to my ear, then they slid down to the nape of my neck. My head fell back onto his waiting hand and I let out a sigh. I could hear the big, scary guard from across the room when he cleared his throat unceremoniously. It shook me back into the here and now.

"Only us," I croaked softly. "I hear you." I took a deep breath and then allowed myself to look Gray in the eyes. I tried to smile as genuinely as I could, and he smiled back.

"Ready?" he asked warily.

"Sure," I answered.

"If I could carry you, I would," he told me with total seriousness.

I laughed sharply. "I know, but those jerks don't need a great picture like that!"

He laughed again and then grabbed my hand. "Don't let go," he chuckled.

"Not on your life," I griped.

The door opened, and immediately there was a crowd waiting for us—well, for him—all of them shouting his name and yelling a million questions. We were flanked by two bodyguards as we passed through the doorway of our safe room. I was glad that Gray was used to this because I had already forgotten the important instructions from our scary bodyguard. Gray tugged me along, trying to shield me with one arm while holding his other tightly around my body. "Keep your head down and then you won't get blinded by the flash," he muttered under his breath so only I could hear him caution me. I never looked up and allowed Gray to maneuver me through LAX International Airport. It felt like we were moving through a maze, and the voices grew louder and more frenzied as we walked on without speaking. Gray tightened his arm around my waist and I realized that he was almost holding me up off the floor. My legs were moving and my feet were making contact with the ground, but his feet were the ones that moved us forward. After what felt like a marathon, Gray whispered again, "We're almost there, baby." We went through the doors and walked a few more steps, then he guided my body into a car while ducking my head down for me so I didn't hit the roof of the sedan. Finally it was quiet. Gray's angry voice startled me.

"Damn it, Freddy, you said maybe a few paps! That was a damned circus! Why didn't you get more security?" He snarled while he gritted his teeth. I touched his hand that was still around my waist and he snapped his head from Freddy to me. Suddenly his tone was much softer now. "Sorry, love. Are you okay? I didn't know there would be so many," he promised. I looked in his eyes and I could see that he was just as rattled as I was.

"It's okay. I'm fine, Gray," I answered mousily.

His lips lifted to one side into a grin as he shook his head. "No, it's not, but I can yell at Freddy later," he whispered; then he kissed my forehead and pulled me closer to him. I looked up to Freddy who was sitting in the front seat. There was no love lost between us. I didn't hate him, but I certainly didn't like him. He was a good agent, I knew that, but he was not a good person. I realized that I had never met him before; I knew he had blond short hair from the pictures I had seen of him. Now that I was closer to him, I could see his bright-blue eyes and his Malibu

Barbie physique. He was attractive, if you like the slime-ball, fake-tan, plastic type.

"Sorry, Gray. I didn't know that the—"

"Stow it, Freddy. Where is my damned schedule?" Gray snapped. Freddy handed Gray what looked like a college term paper. I swallowed hard and tried not to let it bother me. He opened it and began reading as his finger traced the words down the page.

Freddy turned around again and stuck his hand out at me. "It's nice to finally meet you, Elaina. Gray has managed to keep you under wraps for a long while."

"Freddy…" Gray warned as I reached out my hand to shake his without speaking.

"What? Don't you think she should know why all those people were there, waiting for you guys today? They want to know who your secret wife is. Everybody is foaming at the mouth to get a shot of you. Freddy looked back at me and cracked a fake smile. He knew that the public knew very well who I was and that they had seen enough of me already. It was pretty obvious that he had made some calls to the press and that he was proud of the turn out at the airport. He was walking a thin line, and he wasn't afraid to admit it at all. I must say, Grayson, you have really outdone yourself this time." Freddy's blue eyes ran up and down my body, and I suddenly felt like I needed a shower.

"Eyes forward, Freddy. Believe me, she is way too good for you." Gray's iron lock around my waist tensed and then released. "Is the house ready for us?"

Freddy snorted like a pig and rolled his eyes. "Of course, Gray, everything's ready."

The ride home was long and tense. Freddy did a load of talking about going here and there. This country is set for this date, and this is set for another. Gray seemed comfortable and right at home. Home, for me, however, now seemed unknown. I guess because I had never been here before. I had never seen where Gray lived and worked his days before meeting me. He had promised that it was nothing like my house back in Richmond. My house, he explained, was much warmer and homier. I was going into the unknown. Macbeth had stayed behind in Belize with some island friends because of the traveling that was to come. So I had no one to relate to at all. Every person I would meet here was new and completely unknown to me. The anxiety came back but not as bad as it had been at the airport. The plan had been to come to LA for a week and then head back to Richmond to handle the paperwork for selling my house and see my sister and best friend. It seemed way too far off now. In the week we were here, Gray was booked for countless interviews, booked for three TV tapings and endless meetings. He had asked me to come along with him, and I agreed to come. It was a choice I had regretted but was sticking to regardless of my level of nervousness.

The house was spectacular and I was confused by what he had said about it being inferior to mine. It was a two-story beach home with glass all across the front exposing the ocean and beach view. It was stark and very bare but it had the potential of one day being a homey place to live in. I could make it work if I had to. The only thing getting me through this sudden intrusion into our life was that we would be leaving it all behind soon. No more photographers or people hiding in the trees or bushes. No more cruel news reports about us that were totally fake and fabricated. No more meddling in our lives—just us.

I tried to settle in the day we got there. Our stuff had been delivered before we got there and put away already in closets and drawers. Everything was ready for us as Freddy promised. I stood in the foyer astonished at the view and the idea that I was actually here, living this nightmare. Gray tried to act normal but there was nothing normal about any of this for him or me. I hoped that maybe it would be, somehow, eventually. Gray put his keys on the table by the front door and shut the door behind him as Freddy was speaking in midsentence. He closed his eyes and took a deep breath. When he opened them again, he had tried to cover his stress with a tight smile; it didn't work at all. I got the sense that he had maybe hoped he would not be returning to this place ever again. I felt comfort from that because at least I knew we were both at odds with the situation but still trying to make this work. It was clear to me that he wasn't happy to be home.

"So, this is the place," he said as he clapped his hands together and began rubbing them together like a mad scientist. "Let me give you a tour then."

He took my hand gently and tugged me through the entryway into the house. The foyer led into the den or living room which was huge with tall beam ceilings. It was all painted white with bleached-out wood everywhere. The furniture was big and comfortable leather with a fireplace to the right and a bar to the left. He led me into the living area and passed the wall-to-ceiling windows and into the kitchen to the right. It was huge, white, and full of grey marble countertops. It looked like it had never been used, and I stifled a chuckle already knowing that Gray usually never cooked. The kitchen looped back around the entryway and we went to the other side of the house to the left this time. We entered a huge bright room. It looked like an office with his movie awards and other accolades. I remembered seeing him win a few on TV, and it was weird to see them now in his house and displayed but not where anyone would likely ever see them.

"This is the office where I never go." He smiled and pressed his thumbnail against his temple, seemingly uncomfortable.

"You have so many awards," I said with a bit of shock. I was proud of him and his accomplishments. I wished I had known more about them, and I suddenly wondered why he had never told me about the trophies he had won. Then again, it wasn't his style to brag or gloat.

"Well, you know, I've won a few, I guess," he answered with an almost embarrassed tone.

We backed out of there and headed up the open staircase by the front door. It led up into a large hallway with only two directions to go, right or left. His hand tightened around mine. "Mine is to the right, the other is just the guestroom. They're both the same size." He seemed nervous having me in his home, almost like he was ashamed of some of the things he had done here. I tried to pretend like I didn't notice, but he saw my confusion. His arms turned me to the right and he led me into his room. Right away, the view caught my attention. The ocean was right outside the floor to ceiling windows that filled the wall. The bed rested on the wall directly across from the windows. It was huge and white with beige-colored details woven into the duvet that hugged the sheets underneath. There was a table on either side of the bed with its own lamp. When I saw that, it made me wonder why he would have a table on either side. I forgot about that completely when I saw the enormously tall dresser with a big red bow around the front. I froze and Gray chuckled. He let go of my waist and walked over to it, turned, and faced me with a grin.

"It's a surprise, for you. I wanted to make sure there was enough room here for your things as well as mine. I asked Freddy to handle it, but ah"—he tilted his head up to see the top of this huge piece of furniture—"I guess he went a little over the top though. The beside table is new, too, for you."

I nodded in shock. "All this for me?" I asked.

He grinned again and sighed as he walked back over to me. He grabbed my hands and pulled them around his waist. "I wanted you to feel comfortable here, for however long that may be."

He studied my face and seemed nervous again. "You think it's too much? I know things were way simpler in Belize…"

"It's fine, Gray. Thank you, it's very thoughtful." I kissed him gently and hugged him so I could hide my face. "Your place is really beautiful, baby. The view is just…spectacular." I felt strange and uncomfortable. It felt like we were strangers again. It was hard to find the familiar here in this room.

I could feel his chest shake as he chuckled again. "Thanks, love, but it's your place now too." He tried to pull me back so he could see my face, but I held on tight. He seemed to already know what I was feeling. He sighed deeply but squeezed me back. "It's only temporary, love. I promise."

"It's okay," I whispered. "It's really pretty here; it's just the idea of someone watching us or taking photos or videos—"

"Don't worry about that now, Elaina," he interrupted me. "Let's just try to get through this one day at a time, all right?"

I sighed quietly. "Where's the bathroom?"

"Straight through there." He pointed to a hall beyond the bed that led to the master bathroom. I took one step in that direction but he yanked my hand and twirled me back around to face him. "You all right, Mrs. MacNally?"

"Fine," I answered as I stretched my neck up to his face to kiss him. I wasn't really okay, but he was right. We had to take this one day at a time and get through it.

Chapter 19

Gray

Things were getting off to a rocky start back in LA. The airport fiasco nearly gave Elaina a heart attack. I hadn't expected her to fall right into things, but the immediate change that happened with her was surprising. She dove into things head on. She went to every interview and event I had here. Freddy kept her hidden from the media, but still people knew she was there. Freddy had been right about the public being more than curious about her; there was definitely a buzz that surrounded us. Every interviewer asked about her and wanted to know when the world would meet her. She was always sitting just off camera from me. I swear I could feel her squirming in her seat. I just laughed and shrugged my shoulders. People knew by now that I would walk out if their questions got too nosey. I figured I would let Elaina get used to things around here for a few days and then we would have to talk about doing a joint interview. Freddy had already set one up with a credible entertainment nightly news show. I knew she would hate every minute of it but if I asked her to, she would do it for me. I felt guilty knowing that.

In two days, I had been going nonstop with work; in another few days, we were scheduled for the interview that would hopefully make things better with the press and make things easier for Elaina. There was just one problem: Elaina hadn't signed on yet.

I hated that I had been keeping this from her, but I knew that telling her the first day we got here would not go over well at all.

Tonight I was going to ask her. We had to talk about it now; my time had run out. Freddy had dropped off the contract earlier in the day. It was sitting on my desk in my home office, the room neither of us ever went into.

When I got home, she was sitting on the back deck with a drink. She was lounging in the chaise, gazing off into the ocean. Her face was calm and relaxed; she didn't hear me come in. The ocean noise filled every part of the air around her. I stared at my wife in amazement. I had been so lucky to find her, so lucky she came to find me after I had left her. She had become my wife and made me a proud and happy man. There she sat with her perfectly bronzed skin that seemed to glow under the afternoon sun. Her hair blew all around her face and shoulders, and I laughed as she tried to tuck long strands behind her ears tirelessly. She wore a white linen sundress that fluttered with the strong wind. Her eyes were closed and her face wore a smile. This vision of her reminded me of the way things had been in Belize—so simple and easy. I never worried about coming home to her there. There was no need. I shook my head, hating Freddy and my career momentarily, but I had to get this over with. The press would never stop bothering her or us if we kept hiding. I slid the door open and walked over behind her. I lowered my hands and dragged my fingertips across her jaw, and she smiled without opening her eyes. I was home and now she knew it.

"Hey baby," she whispered. "You wanna drink?"

"No, love, not yet. How was your day?" I asked.

"Uneventful. Just listened to a guy talk about himself all morning then I came home," she sighed with a smile.

"Is that so? Well, I hope the guy was at least handsome then." I laughed. I didn't remember talking about myself that much.

"He was okay, my husband is much more handsome." she answered. I kissed her again and again and then went back inside to make myself a drink. I hoped she couldn't tell how nervous I was. Before I could come back out to her, she was suddenly behind me, wrapping her arms around me. "I missed you today," she whispered into my back.

"That's good," I chuckled. We hadn't made love since getting here three days ago. It wasn't like us, but things were different here. For one thing, I was working nonstop and didn't have much energy or time at the end of the day. Another reason was Elaina. She hadn't been the same since we got here. She was nervous and anxious. She couldn't relax, but today she seemed different. She was content to be here now, and I silently cursed Freddy and my career again. What I was about to say was going to change all of this.

I took a sip of my bourbon and turned to face her. Before I could say anything, she grabbed my face and pulled me to hers. Her lips urgently pressed against mine and I forgot what I was supposed to do for a minute. I lifted her up and propped her on the counter, but then I did something I would never normally do—I stopped kissing her and pulled away to face her. Her face was confused and torn, and she tried to grab my face again. My hands gently pulled her hands away and she finally gave up with a huff.

"What is it?" she asked warily.

"I'm sorry, love. There is something we have to talk about tonight."

"Can't it wait? Just a half an hour or so?" she asked, and her lips turned up into a devilish smile.

"You're making this harder than it has to be, love," I warned her gently.

She laughed, not understanding my seriousness. When I didn't laugh back, she stopped, crossed her arms, and waited for me to start. I couldn't say anything. This time she warned me. "Gray?" she pushed.

"There is something we have to do this week. You're not gonna like it one bit, but I think we should do it, get it over with." I struggled to find the right words to make it sound easier than it really was.

"What?" she asked.

"It's an interview, a joint interview with *Nightline*. Freddy has already set it up. All we have to do is sign on and it's done.

She sat across from me as her feet dangled from the counter. Her eyes cast down and her brow furrowed in anger, or maybe it was disappointment. Whatever it was, it was directed at me and I knew I deserved it.

"How long have you known about this?" Her voice was low and even, not a good sign.

I wanted to lie, it was my first thought, but I didn't want to lie to her. "A while, since before we got here. I guess a couple of weeks or so."

She still wouldn't look at me, but I watched her every move, studied her every breath and frown. She was angry, probably more angry than she had ever been at me. The crease in her brow eventually smoothed, and she lowered her serious gaze on me.

"Do you want me to do this?" she whispered, but then raised her head and looked at me straight in the eye. Her brown eyes were sad but willing. I hated myself a little bit for making her look that way. "Do you, Gray?"

I wanted to say "No, not at all. Please tell me no." But I didn't. "I think it would make things a bit easier for the next two weeks if the public finally got to see the unknown—if their hunger was a bit more satisfied. Yes, I think we should do it." My voice was shaky and didn't sound very convincing.

She put her hands on either side of my face and her warm touch gave me goose bumps. She stared at me for a moment, searching for a reason to say no, but I guess she didn't find one.

"Okay. If you want me to do this, then I will," she finally answered.

That night, I watched her sleep, like I had so many times in Richmond. I watched her chest rise and fall. I watched her eyes twitch slightly as she dreamed of whatever she was dreaming of. I listened to her soft snore against the sound of the wind and the waves of the night. The interview was in two days. We would shoot it here in LA, but it wouldn't air for another week after that. I hoped that Freddy was right and that doing this would ease the rabid hunger of the press and the public. I knew there would be questions about us and our personal life. They would want to know about our wedding and our life in Belize. There would be questions about the photos and the settlement. I wondered how far they would dig on Elaina; how far back they would search on her—her first husband, the daughter she lost, her suicide attempt and stay in a facility. I wondered if this was the same stuff she was worried about. I hoped that in doing the interview, the frenzy wouldn't double or, even worse, reach a new height. I tried to figure out a way to protect her during the interview and how to prepare her for hard questions. I hoped that the interviewer would be kind and respectful.

In all my years of acting and relishing the fame and attention, I had never worried about an interview. I had never cared who I offended or if I said the right thing. I had never been so publicly vulnerable before. For now, I had to wait and worry just like Elaina. The way that woman could sleep through anything amazed me.

Chapter 20

Was it Worth It?

The day of the interview had arrived. We woke up early. She made breakfast—fruit, eggs and toast with coffee. We talked about everything but the weird thing we were about to do. We had to be at the studio for taping by nine so they could do makeup and lighting on the set. Freddy was going to meet us there to brief us both on the questions they planned on asking.

The interviewer was Scott Donovan. He was a big-time news reporter for JBC, the biggest runner of the television bunch. He was young, arrogant, and nosey as hell—my personal nightmare. Elaina was going to hate him, too, so I would have to try extra hard to help her control her temper. After Freddy's briefing, I felt no better about the taping. It seemed Freddy had made us available for any and all questions. We didn't have to answer everything, but we did have to hear every question.

By the time we sat down, I hated Freddy again, and Elaina was a mess. I could feel her hand shaking in mine.

"Just breathe, love," I whispered in her ear.

Scott Donovan was an average-looking guy—salt-and-pepper hair, cut short, with a fancy suit on. His nose was long and straight, and his lips were thin. When he met us earlier and shook my hand, his palms were sweaty. He pretended to kiss my arse and act like he was impressed with me. I don't know why they do that; it just makes them look like idiots if you ask me. They only care about if people watch the show, not me. He was already there when we came in from makeup to sit down. Elaina froze in the doorway when she saw the lights and different cameras set up everywhere. We had been in here before, but I guess this time it was too real for her. I wound my fingers through hers and walked my wife into the room.

"Well, I guess we can get started." He looked up with a look of relief and then a bit of nervousness.

"Sure," I answered, giving him a look of warning that I'm pretty sure he understood. Elaina took a deep breath and sighed. I wound my right arm around her waist and pulled her tight to me. She was as stiff as a board beside me, completely lifeless. I got really worried then. The good thing was that this was taped, not live. If we needed to stop at any time, we could at my command.

"So, what's new with you?" he asked and then laughed his cheesy TV laugh. Elaina and I chuckled. I was a bit relieved but not enough. I hated making her do this.

"So everybody has been talking about the two of you for months now. Hollywood's most eligible bachelor is off the market and happily married. So tell me, how's married life?"

"It's great. I found someone that I love and who loves me back, and I couldn't ask for anything more." I answered, already knowing it was Elaina's turn now. I hoped that she was ready. I turned to her and waited like we had talked about. She said nothing.

"And you, Elaina? Or should I call you Mrs. Sparks?"

She laughed and I squeezed her hip. We both knew that that wasn't her real name, or mine.

"Gray is amazing and I feel lucky to have found him," she answered perfectly. She was better at this than I hoped.

"That's wonderful. Some months back, the world was rocked by some photos of the two of you together, taking part in some intimate moments. What was that like for the two of you?"

"It was awful. I felt horrible for her because she's not used to that kind of thing, but we handled it," I answered as I turned to her again.

"It's behind us now," Elaina chimed in with a sigh.

"What do you think of the photographers that did this, Elaina?"

"I know they have a job to do, but we have a life to live. Personally, I think they are disgusting."

Donovan smiled a fake smile, realizing we weren't giving in. I knew that these short and boring answers would not do for him and he would dig a little deeper for more.

"So, Elaina, tell me how the two of you kept your romance a secret for so long."

"I wasn't aware it was a secret. We just didn't want to share it with the world. We weren't sure what was happening either." Her tone suddenly turned reproachful now. "I am a very private person and so is Gray. Our life is ours."

"There's been a lot of talk in the media lately about you two, especially you, Elaina, about your past. Your first husband and child were killed in an accident while you were driving. That must have been hard for you?"

"Yes, it was. It still is." Her voice was shaky and I shot Donovan a look.

"Do the two of you want children of your own?"

"Maybe. We have never discussed that, actually," I answered honestly. She glanced at me with the same look. We both shrugged our shoulders. We already both knew that Elaina could not have more children, but the idea of adoption was something we never discussed.

"You seem open-minded about it."

"You never know," I answered.

"How does it feel knowing there are many women out there that hate you, Elaina, because you have snagged one of the most wanted men out there?"

"Hate is a strong word, but I'd have to say that I'm just as surprised about it as anyone else, I guess. I kept telling him to leave me alone, but he wouldn't go." She laughed. "So here we are." I squeezed her with my arm, giving her what support I could.

"How are you handling the press and the paparazzi? The recent photos of you two arriving in LA showed a scared woman and very protective husband. Why not just let the world see you? Why are you hiding?"

"She's not hiding," I answered for her. "This is not part of our life together. Those photographers were yelling obscene things at my wife to get her to look for one measly picture. This is my job, a job that I'm ready to retire from." I hoped that I could deflect his attention away from Elaina and back on me and my future plans with acting.

"Oh yes, that's another question." Donovan quickly jumped with a fire in his eyes. My sudden change of conversation had reminded him of something he obviously wanted to discuss. I hoped that his focus would stay on me, but he quickly turned back to Elaina instead. "Many reports are saying that you are making Gray retire. Is that true?"

"No. Gray makes his own choices. I won't miss this part of his life though. I support his decision to move forward."

"I just want to get away and enjoy life. Take a break for a while," I followed.

"Are you happy here in LA, Elaina?" he asked, and she stiffened beside me again. My arm loosened around her enough to raise my hand and rub the base of her back.

"She's getting used to it. We've only been here a week," I answered.

"I haven't seen much of it. We are hounded everywhere we go, so usually I stay at home," she whispered softly. Donovan's face softened when she said that, and then one of his eyebrows cocked up.

"A lot of people are saying this marriage won't last, that you married too soon before really being able to know each other or that you may have married for ratings. There are reports of divorce already. How long did you actually date before getting married, and what do you say about the divorce rumors?"

"Divorce?" Elaina gasped. "There is no divorce or anything like that." She laughed. "We are happy, very happy, and we were together long enough before getting married."

"What about the rumors of Gray getting close with his costars?" Elaina stiffened again. I could tell she didn't like that question at all.

"Not true. I have never had affairs with any of my costars; and if I did, it wouldn't be a matter of media concern," I blurted.

"Tell me about your suicide attempt, Elaina? I ask because the acting world is stressful and taxing. Obviously you have gotten a taste of that with Gray. Do you think you will be able to handle it?"

"I will not discuss that time in my life. It's private."

"Nothing's really private now, Mrs. Sparks," he chided.

"That's up to me now, isn't it, Mr. Donovan?" she snapped.

Donovan laughed out loud in spite of himself. "She's good, Gray. I think she'll be fine."

"She can handle herself; don't let the beauty fool you," I warned.

"Okay, another question that Americans want to know is, is it true? Are you guys really even married?"

Elaina started laughing hysterically. "Let's not tell him," she chuckled and then rolled her eyes.

"Of course, we are married," I answered, not very amused.

"What goes on with you two when you are alone? What is Grayson Sparks really like?"

"He's not Grayson Sparks!" Elaina promised as she turned to me to wink. "Seriously, he's a normal guy with normal hang-ups and bad days just like everyone else. He is a bit messier than people would think."

"Any acting debuts we should look for, Elaina?"

"God, no!" she answered.

"So Gray, tell us about the new movie…"

The interview went on and on. For the first time, I hoped that every question was about the movie and not my personal life. By the end, Elaina was more relaxed. She still gave very little to Donovan. He pushed when he could, but whenever he got too personal, I gave him the look and he backed off. We were there for hours, and I could tell that Elaina was getting sick of it all. I motioned to Freddy and he swooped in like a hawk to its prey, and the interview was over. As soon as Donovan was out of earshot, Elaina relaxed in my arms.

The car ride home was silent. Neither of us wanted to speak another word. I needed a drink, and I assumed she did too. We hadn't seen the two cars following us or getting closer by the mile. I had lowered the window to smoke a cigarette, and I guess the paparazzi had seen it. It was all they needed to turn into hunters. I suddenly heard the screeching of the tires and the revving of another car's engine.

"Do you really think us doing that today will help, Gray?" Elaina whispered. I was listening to her but also distracted by the loud car coming up on us.

"I hope so, love," I answered. Now I was looking for the car that I could hear loud and clear. My heart started to pound when I saw the two small sedans weaving in and out of traffic. I sighed out loud and rolled my eyes as I flicked my cigarette out into the road.

"Hey, driver, you think you could pick up the pace a bit?"

"Gray? What's wrong?" she asked with a bit of panic to her voice.

"Just two jerks back there. I think they're following us."

"Where?" she asked, in full panic now.

"Back there." I motioned to the back and left of the car. "Hey, driver?" Then I saw him close his phone just to the side of his ear. I guess everyone has a price. Every pap's got their own way of getting information. Some bribe, some have friends, some just follow us around for days. I guess this guy got paid enough. He must have seen me see him, 'cause he started picking up the pace a bit, but not nearly enough.

"Gray?"

"It's okay, baby. We aren't far from the house." She closed the already nonexistent gap between us and buried her face into my chest.

I called Freddy to let him know what was going on, so he knew never to hire this driving company again. For the first time in six years, his phone went to voicemail. The engine was right beside us now and I turned to look at the driver just to see which jerk it was this time. I hoped it wasn't who I thought it might be. He was already looking at me with blank eyes. There was no life in them, just death. He smiled at me with his beady eyes and then he accelerated and jumped up a few car lengths ahead of us. I swiftly turned to Elaina and swung her seatbelt over her lap and buckled her in and then stretched mine out and across me to buckle it. For some reason, I knew this was bad, all of it. Then the small silver car slowed and shifted into our lane and in front of us. Then he did what I was praying he wouldn't do—he slammed on his brakes. Elaina must have heard the screeching of the tires, or maybe she felt my arms tighten around her like two steel vices, but she screamed out my name.

"Oh, God. Oh, no," was all I could think or say.

Chapter 21

The car flipped and flipped until I didn't know which way was up and which way was down. After we hit the ground again, everything was a blur. I knew that Gray was not beside me anymore, and our car was no longer a car but a death trap. I was dizzy and having a hard time breathing, but I was alive. I knew I was alive because I felt pain. I could hear echoes of rushed voices all around me. My head felt trapped in a long tunnel. I could see blurry lights flashing all around in the early evening light. There was chaos everywhere. I realized I was bound down to a board of some kind. I couldn't move my head or my arms and legs. The sensation of panic set in and I struggled against the straps, but a heavy hand gently pressed my forehead back down to the board.

"Stay still," the angelic voice said. "You're gonna be okay." It echoed out and away from me. I tried to follow it but I couldn't. I tried to find the face from the voice but I couldn't see. My eyes were burning, and no matter how many times I blinked, the pain was still there. I was tired and weak. My body felt like one big weight, and I was sinking farther and farther away from the red blinking lights. My eyes were wet but not from tears; something else. Then I noticed something new—my chest was not only heavy but it hurt to breathe. Each breath felt like I had arrows all though my chest. One of my arms was throbbing in pain, it was probably broken. I kept blinking my eyes trying to get whatever was in them out, but more of the slime kept creeping in. It burned like fire in my eyes. My head was pounding as the blood rushed in and out through the capillaries and vessels in my body. I slipped down into the darkness that was pushing down on me and drifted off.

~~~~~~~~

I could hear two voices close to me, whispering back and forth. It took me a minute to figure out who they were. I recognized them, but there was a ringing in my ears. My body tensed with pain as I tried to listen. It was Harris and Mandy. They didn't know I was awake yet, and I wasn't really sure if I was awake at all. I knew where I was—the smell was all too familiar—hospital. It never mattered where or what hospital you were in, they all smelled the same—sterile sheets and dry air. My head pounded as things slowly started coming back to me. We had been in an accident. That small silver car had caused it. We had flipped through the air on the highway and then slammed back into the earth. Gray had been holding me tight but then he was gone. I tried to open my eyes and I sucked in a huge breath of air. It burned mildly, and my throat ached. My chest tightened in agony, making me moan.

"Gray? Where's Gray?" I managed to croak out softly. I tried to open my eyes all the way, but I couldn't. They felt as if they had been sewn shut back.

My two best friends swarmed me like bees to honey. Harris was the first to speak. "He's fine, Laina; he's just down the hall."

"Is he okay?" I croaked again, this time more clearly.

"He's fine, just resting." Mandy answered this time in her motherly voice. "Just go back to sleep; we'll be here when you wake up." I heard another set of feet scuffling on the floor and then a watery sloshing sound. Then the same feet scurried out again.

"No," I whispered. "I want to see him, please." I begged, but my body started getting tired again. My limbs were heavy like they had been on the board in the highway. Nothing seemed to work. "Am...am I paralyzed?" I asked breathless with a shaky voice.

"No, you're just hurt pretty bad. The doctors don't want you moving too much. You're all right, Laina. Don't worry, get some rest…"

My head drifted away before she could finish her sentence. Before I knew it, I was asleep again.

~~~~~~~~

After that, whenever I woke up, it was the same routine. I was never allowed to stay awake, and then, eventually, time stopped meaning anything at all. I had no idea how long I had been in the hospital or how bad I was injured. When I dreamed, I saw John and Georgia. They were always smiling at me. Then sometimes Gray was there shaking John's hand and hugging Georgia. In every dream, Georgia was happy and running around. John and Georgia eventually disappeared in my sleep, and the only one there was Gray. He talked to me and cried a lot. His voice was distant and hard to make out, but I heard him. The hours went by fast and sleep came easily. I felt weak and queasy. I was starting to forget what was real and what was a dream. It was getting too hard to distinguish them.

I could hear his voice whispering and his hand holding my hand. His fingers caressed my hand softly. He was talking to me, telling me he loved me, telling me to get better. I could almost smell the cologne he wore. I wasn't sure if I was dreaming or not, so I slipped back to sleep.

The rain was pounding down outside the window. I could hear him breathing heavily beside me. My eyes were still heavy, but something had changed. The weight that had kept them closed had lifted and I tried to open my eyes. I struggled to remember how to part my eyelids open. Had it really been so long that I had forgotten how to open my own eyes? Finally I managed to lift them open.

The room was dim; it must have been late in the afternoon. My room was small and I could see the blurry walls around me.

The rain slid down the walls just like the window. I took a deep breath, and for the first time it didn't hurt anymore. There was no pain, no burn, only a mild discomfort. I felt fine, just groggy and confused.

"Gray," I breathed out so gently that it was more of a cloud than a word. His hand around mine tightened and I heard a chair kick down to all four legs again followed by his own feet.

"I'm here, love," he answered in amazement. "Are you in pain? Do you want me to get a doctor?"

"No, I'm fine," I muttered. I couldn't understand why everyone was fussing over me so much. I cleared my throat. "Can I sit up?"

"I...I'm not sure love, do you want to?" he asked with worry thick in his voice.

I struggled to sit up despite his wary tone. I had felt much worse than this before. Gray tried to get me to stop, but I reached over to the side of the bed to find the button that raised the bed up. I found it finally and pressed it. The button was hard to push in, and I realized my strength was much less that it should be. Slowly, I came back up to the world again. I wanted to see Gray's face; I wanted to make sure he was okay. Everyone had said he was fine, but it wouldn't be the first time I had been lied to. Suddenly, a nurse opened the door and came in quickly.

"She's awake?"

"Yes, just now," Gray answered.

"How are you feeling, honey? How are you?" the nurse asked.

"I dunno. How am I?" I mumbled.

The nurse laughed. "Sense of humor, that's a good sign. I'll get Dr. Stevens." She was gone in a few seconds, and it was just Gray and I again.

Gray came over and sat beside me on the bed. He was grinning but still unsure of what to do or say.

"What?" I whispered. I tried to sit up straighter and pain shot across my chest and shoulders. I winced slightly.

"I'm just…I can't believe you are already awake. The doctor said it would take days. How's your head?"

"It hurts," I grunted. I raised my hand up to rub my forehead and felt the stitches holding a huge wound together that started at my hairline and down my part. My arm was covered with bruises and my hand was still in some sort of brace. "How long has it been?" I questioned.

"Almost two weeks now. They had to sedate you; you kept trying to come see me," he chuckled softly. He leaned forward and kissed my forehead, and his fingers tucked my hair back behind my ear. His fingers lingered on my cheek and he gazed down at me. "You're gonna be okay though."

"How bad is it?" I asked. I started to feel my head throbbing away. My eyes smashed shut and I tried to wish the pain away.

"Elaina?" he asked with worry. His face fell into concern again.

"I'm fine, really. Please stop babying me." I cracked a smile and I could feel an old cut on my lip fight from splitting open again. "How bad is it?" I whispered.

He took a deep breath and tried to relax. I could tell he was fighting back a much stronger emotion, trying to hide his feelings from me.

"Well, you were really hurt. You knocked you head pretty good and then there was some swelling in your brain; the induced coma helped that. That was the worst thing. Other than that, you have a broken wrist and some cracked ribs. You were lucky; it could have been much worse." His voice broke at the last word, and his head dropped as he rubbed his head with both of his hands. He sighed loudly. "I thought…I don't know what I thought," he muttered out in a broken voice. He sounded tired and defeated. I reached my hand over to him with the brace still firmly gripped around my wrist. My fingertips touched his hand that was still holding his face. He looked up with a guilty face; he had tears falling down his beautiful face. His face stubble was thicker than usual with extra growth, his eyes bloodshot. He had a few cuts and bruises on his face as well. His arm was covered in cuts and healing wounds. He looked like he hadn't slept for days. "I'm so sorry, love. I never should have brought you here. I never should have forced you into that stupid interview. I thought it would help things. All I did was put you at risk and …now… look at you, look what I've done to you."

"You didn't do this, baby. I chose to come with you, remember? This isn't your fault. It's okay." I tried to comfort him, but he was a wreck. I decided a change of subject might work. "What about you? Are you hurt?" I asked in a groggy whisper.

He sniffled and tried to clear his throat. "I'm fine, just a few scratches here and there. I'll be good as new. Please don't worry about me."

"Why did this happen anyway? Why did that guy cut us off?" I asked. His eyebrows lifted in shock.

"You saw that? You saw him?" he asked in astonishment. Then his face turned sad again. His brows came together in anger. Maybe it was hope that he wasn't crazy because I had seen him too—the same creep that had been at my house in Richmond; the same guy that was forced from his job with the trash mag that published his pictures of us; the same man we had ruined by fighting back.

"Yeah, I saw him," I grumbled.

Gray sat back in his uncomfortable chair and sighed loudly. He shook his head back and forth and then started to stare at the ceiling. He was angry but trying to control it. He sat up and rested his elbows on his knees and clasped his hands together.

"What is it, Gray?" I whispered hoarsely.

Dr. Stevens rushed in holding a clipboard with a bunch of notes on it. He was young and handsome but not at all my type. He looked more like a Ken doll. It seemed that everyone here looked like a doll. No one looked their age and no one seemed to act their age either. Gray leaned over and whispered in my ear,

"That's Doc Stevens. He takes a little getting used to, but he's the best."

I smiled and then turned my attention to Dr. Stevens.

"Mrs. MacNally, I'm glad to see you are finally awake. I must admit, we weren't expecting you to wake back up from the coma so fast."

"Is that bad?" Gray asked for me.

"No! Not at all. It's actually great. We like fast healers around here." He smiled at me but it didn't ease my tension. He looked like he was all of twelve years old, not nearly old enough to be practicing medicine. That must have been what Gray had meant about "takes some getting used to." I could tell Gray was hiding something from me. Something he knew that I didn't. I didn't know if I should be mad or not, but nonetheless I was confused again. He looked nervous as the doctor looked over the medical notes on his clipboard.

Dr. Stevens explained all my injuries and that I was very lucky to have survived at all. In laments terms, I had suffered a pretty bad head trauma and should have died from the swelling it caused. Gray had skipped over that part. I was bruised and battered but he was confident I would be okay in a few weeks' time. I wouldn't be able to leave the hospital until all my tests came back okay.

Gray had dropped out of all press for his movie to be at my side. Luckily, everyone involved with the movie had been understanding and patient. I wish I could say the same about the media. There was a new story about the accident every night making our injuries sound much worse than they really were. The media was hungrier than ever and always present at the hospital waiting for me to leave with Gray. The press tour had gone on without him, but now that I was okay, I knew he would be going back to the tour soon. Harris and Mandy agreed to stay with me in LA until I was back to normal again. Thanks to the bump on the head and cracked ribs, I would stay pretty fragile for a while. I didn't like hearing that at all. Gray hadn't mentioned the man that caused all of this since that first day I had woken up in the hospital. I guess he was afraid of how I would react.

A week after waking up, I was told I could finally go home. The ride home was terrifying but not as scary as it had been actually walking out of the hospital. There were people everywhere with cameras, yelling and snapping photos. They called my name and Gray's, and there, of course, were the slime balls that yelled insults and disgusting things in an effort to get me to look up for a picture. That had been something I had never realized when looking through magazines. The pictures of the celebrities seemed harmless enough. I never realized how they got them to turn around or look into the lens for them. I was no prude, but some of the things they said were downright disgusting and cruel. Gray had almost gotten into a few fights with some of them with me at his side since coming here. I understood why he had been so happy the day he arrived in Richmond so long ago—the way he breathed, the way he smiled. He was relaxed and worry-free. He knew there were none of the paparazzi around to hassle him. I longed for those first weeks and the comfort of Belize and the escape from photographers.

Gray's house was the same as it had been the last day I'd seen it. Harris was not there; she had stayed in her hotel that night to give Gray and I some time alone. Mandy had flown back to Richmond a few days earlier; one of her kids had come down with the swine flu. Gray walked me up to the bedroom and helped me into bed. I didn't need to be babied anymore, but he insisted. He was still giving in to his ridiculous guilt and somehow still blaming himself for everything that had happened.

Surprisingly, I fell asleep quickly even though it was the middle of the day. I slept through the afternoon and most of the night. I woke up around one in the morning to find myself alone. I pulled myself out of bed and threw on my favorite grey-colored robe and made my way down the stairs. I felt good and strong now that I was back in somewhat familiar surroundings. I searched the whole house for him, even the office he never went into, but I couldn't find him. When I found Gray, he was in my favorite spot—the back deck overlooking the ocean. Of course it was dark now so there was no ocean to see, only to hear. He was lounging with his feet up, his head tilted back gazing up at the moonlit sky with his bourbon nestled in his hand. The moon was full and the light lit his face with a glow that resembled an angel's. I noticed something glistening in the corner of his eye. I slid the door open and sat down beside him. He smiled and shook his head when he saw me, but his eyes were tired and overwhelmed.

"What are you doing out of bed, love?" he asked as he rubbed the glistening mystery-something from his eye.

I shrugged my shoulders. "My husband was gone so I went to find him."

He chuckled, but his face tightened again, hiding something. "You should get back to bed. It's late."

"No. I've slept enough," I answered sternly.

He sighed and grabbed my hand in his, allowing them to dangle between us in the ocean breeze.

"What's wrong?" I asked in a way that he knew I was sick of the charade.

He huffed a breath of air through his nose in almost a snort. "Aside from almost losing my wife? Nothing's wrong."

"I'm gonna be fine. You heard the doctor," I assured him.

"Yeah, I know."

"Then what? What's wrong?" I pressed.

He was quiet for a long time. His breathing was rushed and unsettled. "This is all my fault. I meant it before; I shouldn't have brought you here."

"Why? I wanted to be with you," I encouraged.

He turned to me and smiled, but his eyes were still sad. I could see his eyes were beginning to well up with tears. Whatever he was trying to hide was struggling to fight its way out past his wall.

"Gray, please. Just you and me, right?" I reminded him.

He sighed again and let go of my hand. He stood up from his chair, walked in front of me, and kneeled down.

"That guy, the one who did this to you—to us—he's the same guy who was in the woods that night, remember?"

"Yeah, I remember," I answered, feeling nervous now.

"He's been a problem for a while now, even before I came to Virginia. He has been following me for years. He's...well... he's crazy, Elaina. I thought that after the pictures and then everything we did to get rid of him...that he was gone...for good. I was wrong. I completely misjudged him. Now, obviously, he was really pissed at me for what I did."

"What do you mean 'get rid of him'?"

"That's not what I meant, although the thought did occur to me more than once. I meant the legal action we took. Freddy made sure we took every precaution we could to...punish him. Apparently, he lost everything after the settlement—his job, his home, his family...everything. Now, he is—well he was—a bit more than bitter."

"Do the police know?"

"Sure they do, not that it matters now. The little son of a b... he died instantly in the accident"—he paused and caught his breath—"but you are still hurt. I can't help but feel responsible for it. I promised to protect you, and I already failed."

"This wasn't your fault, Gray. Besides, something would have happened eventually anyway. It was only a matter of time."

His face turned serious with anger. "You expected this to happen?"

"No. It's just that people want to know you; the public feels like they own you and they have the right to know about every aspect of your life. That includes me. Who am I to try to stop them? Who are you to try to stop them?"

"What are you saying?" he asked, confused.

"I'm saying that you should be who you are and stop fighting them so much. Stop hiding. Stop worrying about me so much and do your job. Give your fans what they want. *Be* the big movie star that you are. Our life is separate from this and it always will be, but I need to figure out a way to be a part of it, too, if I want to be with you. I know that now."

"No, you don't," he answered quickly, shaking his head emphatically.

I laughed, and the soreness of my ribs reminded me that I was far from healed.

"Don't laugh. I'm serious, Elaina!" he insisted.

"I am too. If we're gonna do this together, then we both have to accept who you are—whether you are in front of a camera or alone with me. You can't protect me from the public. I do exist and they know that. I never saw you the way they do, I only ever saw you as Gray, but now I see what they see. I see what you become in front of the camera and your fans. You shine. I can't make you choose between me and that other part of your life anymore. It's wrong."

He was quiet for a moment, letting my words sink into his stubborn head. Then he shook his head swiftly again. "No. None of this matters cause I'm retiring! After this movie, I have one more to promote, and then I'm done…for good. No more press, no more interviews, no more of this place, just you and me." He put his hands on either side of my face and gently pulled me toward him for a kiss. His lips were soft and gentle. He was being careful with me. I kissed him back with more force, and he pulled back to look at me. "Easy love, you're still hurt," he reminded me.

I sighed and leaned back in my chair. "So what are we going to do then?" I asked.

"Well, first I'm taking you back to bed."

I rolled my eyes and huffed while giving him the annoyed look he knew well.

"Okay, okay. I'm going to Paris in two days, and you are staying here with Harris until the doctor says you can come to meet me." Then his face turned serious again and he raised his finger to me.

"But if things get too crazy, you are coming back here to stay until I'm done."

"You act as though you can get rid of me so easily," I teased.

"I mean it, Elaina. If anything goes wrong, if things get too out of hand, you are on the first flight back here."

I smiled at him with one eyebrow arched.

"Promise me, or forget the whole deal," he warned.

"Okay, you win. I promise."

He finally smiled back at me and then he leaned in closer to kiss me again. This time he wasn't so gentle or careful. "I will not let anything else happen to you, I promise you," he whispered into my ear. A flush of heat flew over my body and settled in my stomach. He turned his head and pressed his lips to my neck and throat. He moaned into my ear again, and the fire returned to my skin.

"Look who's starting something now?" I pointed out breathlessly.

"I'm just giving you a goodnight kiss, Elaina," he whispered into my ear.

He managed his arms under my legs and lifted me up gently into his arms and carried me up the stairs and into the bedroom. He sat on the bed with me still in his arms and kissed me again. Then he pulled away and gazed at me. His hand reached up and his fingers grazed the healing wound on my head. His brow furrowed as his fingers slid across it, his mouth turned down. It didn't hurt me anymore, but I could tell that it hurt him to see it there. I grabbed his face in my hands and kissed him, trying to pull his attention away from it. It worked. He lifted me up carefully and placed me on the bed and then he climbed over me and lay down next to me.

"Good night, love," he whispered in a husky voice.

"Good night."

Chapter 22

Two days later, Gray boarded his flight headed for Paris. We said our good-byes at home that morning. Neither of us wanted to deal with the circus that would surely be at the airport. I had meant what I had said to him about changing. I couldn't hide from what he was and what he meant to the public. I had his heart, but I would never have met him if he hadn't been famous. He never would have stayed at my house. I owed his career to our ever meeting in the first place. So from now on, I would stop fighting the reality and go with it whenever I had to. I would not be scared the next time we walked through an airport or down the street. I wouldn't worry about photographers lurking around every corner. I would try very hard not to pay any attention to rumors and false reports. I would have to really trust Gray now. I thought I had fully trusted him before, but it had never been tested like this. We hadn't had to be apart or deal with any of this as a couple yet. I knew for sure that I loved him and that I needed to do whatever I could to be there for him. If we were gonna make it, we both needed to trust each other.

Three days after Gray left, he was on TV again. It was a brief clip of him in Paris walking the red carpet for his movie. He looked so handsome in his tuxedo. An interviewer had gotten him to stop, and he was being his movie star self.

"Thanks for stopping, Grayson," the female interviewer said.

"Sure, anything for you, darlin'" he smiled and tried to put the girl at ease.

"Are you enjoying Paris?"

"It's been great. The fans are wonderful here," he answered her with his stock answer.

"How has it been being so far from your new wife?"

His face fell ever so slightly showing the healing cut over his eye. "I miss her terribly, but she is still on the mend, I'm afraid. Hopefully, she will join me soon."

"Anything you want to say to her if she's watching?"

He knew I was watching; he had told me to right after he had spoken to the woman.

"I love you, Elaina. I miss you, love!" then he laughed at how corny he sounded.

Harris snorted from the other end of the couch. "Cheesy."

"Shut up, Harris, it was sweet," I snapped.

"You two are gross, you know that?" she added.

I rolled my eyes at her and ignored her with a smile.

After Paris, Gray was going to London, then Tokyo. Australia was in there somewhere too. He was pretty much going to every major city a person can think of. I was hopefully going to meet him in another week or so, and then we would be together again. I missed him so much. My heart felt heavy and alone. He called me throughout the day every day whenever he was in-between meetings or events. We e-mailed, skyped, called and waited patiently for the doctor to give me the go-ahead. My ribs hardly bothered me anymore. I still wasn't one hundred percent healed, but my bruises and cuts had all healed. From the outside I looked good as new.

I had two days to fill until my doctor visit. Gray had been gone over three weeks. His press tour would only be another week. It almost seemed pointless to join him now, but I was still gonna go. I missed him too much. We hadn't been able to be close since the accident over a month ago. It was the longest we had been apart since being married. Gray had called me late in the afternoon to check in on me and make sure I was taking it easy. He told me that he was doing press nonstop for the rest of the day and that he would call me late tonight and to not wait up for his call. It was a bummer but I understood. I missed his constant phone calls, but by ten o'clock that night, I was exhausted. I went to bed with a a cup of hot tea and watched a little TV. I didn't realize I was asleep until someone was trying to wake me up. I felt familiar fingertips sliding down my shoulder to my arm. Then I felt more fingertips on my face tracing my jaw and lips. I knew who it was before opening my eyes. I started chuckling under my breath as his fingers tickled my lips. I opened my eyes to see his face only inches from mine. He was smiling my favorite smile.

"You better go. My husband could be here any minute," I teased with a whisper.

"That dumb movie star is halfway across the world; he'll never know," he teased back in his thick accent as his fingers traced my face with his thumb. I smiled back at him and he leaned in to kiss my lips gently. My hands found his face in the darkness and my lips moved feverishly over his. He moaned quietly in his deep husky voice. "Mmm, I missed you," he murmured over my lips. I got the feeling he wasn't just talking about being apart.

"How long can you stay?" I sighed as his lips moved to my neck.

"We have an appointment in two days, remember?" he teased. "Then we are going to New York." He moved from his knees and slid onto the bed beside me to wrap his arms around me. "I spoke to Dr. Stevens yesterday, and he said there's no reason why you can't go with me."

"Really?" I asked, suddenly very happy.

"Yep. Ever been to New York?" he asked as he moved over me to hover. He ducked his head back down to my shoulder and kissed it.

"No, never," I answered, acutely aware of how long it had been since we had been alone together. "Is it nice?"

"You'll see, I suppose," he murmured against my skin. His hands wandered from my face down to my neck and throat. They slid past my cotton tank top and over my breast. Then his hand froze and he sat up on his knees straddling me. "How…umm… are you feeling?"

I chuckled, "As long as you don't make me laugh too hard, I'll be fine."

"So it's all serious business then?" he spoke in his lower husky voice. My body had another physical response to his voice with a flash burn of desire. His hand slid down my chest and across my stomach, trying to delicately remind me of my injuries. "I don't want to hurt you," he whispered.

My hands found him in the darkness and tugged at his T-shirt. My fingers slid under his shirt and found his bare skin. My hands traced his body upwards to his chest and then back down to the top of his jeans. I grabbed the waistband of his jeans and used it to pull myself up and closer to him. "I don't care." My mouth found his, and that was it for conversation that night.

~~~~~~~~

Waking up next to my husband was perfect. He was still beside me, just as he had been when he drifted off to sleep the night before. He hadn't moved an inch. His arms were still wrapped around me, careful not to put any weight on my ribs. I moved his hand away so I could get up. When I stood up, I noticed an ache in my chest. I grinned, remembering the night before. I went to the bathroom and started the shower. Suddenly, he was right behind me.

"Are you okay?" he asked, wrapping his arms around my waist.

"I think I'll be fine." I smiled.

He looked in the mirror at our reflection together and slid his hands up my arms. He was looking at the new scar I had on my forehead. It was slowly disappearing into my hairline. His fingers delicately made their way to it, and we both looked at.

"It's not that bad," I whispered.

"I can barely see it anymore," he answered.

I could see it, and I know he could too, but he was right: it had faded fast, and he seemed to be relieved. It was a relief because I was pretty much healed, and we were both okay. Things were going to finally get better, and we both knew it.

"I promise you I will never let anything happen to you ever again," he vowed.

"That's a pretty big promise."

He smiled back at me in the mirror before turning me around to face him. He pulled my hair back off my face and kissed me gently. He tugged at my tank top, sliding it up and over my head. "You want a shower?" he asked, a smile spreading across his face. The seriousness was suddenly gone, and he was interested in other things.

When we got back downstairs, Harris was already there. When she saw Gray, her eyes widened in shock.

"What the hell is he doing here?" she asked, shocked.

"Sorry to disappoint you, Harris, but I missed my wife."

The two of them had developed a strange kind of banter. They liked each other but never liked to show it. I was too happy to scold either of them for being rude.

"Just put the lid down, okay," she warned. "I'm going to the beach for a while."

Chapter 23

Two days later, we were waiting to talk to Dr. Stevens in his office. It was a huge office with floor-to-ceiling windows. I was nervous, but Gray was even more unsettled. His foot kept tapping on the floor as he impatiently waited for the doctor to come in. Suddenly the door opened and the young, tan man walked in. Gray's grip around my hand tightened as he raised it up to his mouth and kissed the back of my hand. What did he know that I didn't? What had frightened him so much?

Dr. Stevens had a serious face today—no smiling or goofy jokes like usual. When I saw the strain on his face, a lump settled in my throat.

"Good morning, guys. Sorry I'm running a bit behind today; it's been one of those days." Great, maybe this meant his mood wasn't about me or my latest tests. I took a deep breath and braced myself for anything. He began with my head injury. The technical crap was annoying, and after a while I drifted off and instead listened for key words like *hemorrhage* or *stroke*. I didn't hear any of those words, but I did hear the words *memory loss* and *brain damage*. I didn't like those either, so I started listening again to the mumbo jumbo that is medical science.

"...so in other words, you could experience short-term or long-term memory loss or nothing at all. The damage done to your brain was minimal, thankfully, but you did suffer some brain damage, so things could still happen in the future. The good news is the swelling is gone."

"So what about the memory loss then? Is she gonna start to forget things?" Gray asked in his serious tone.

"She could forget things that happened right before or right after the accident. She could forget other things as well. We won't know unless it happens." He turned to me. "Have you experienced anything unusual, Mrs. MacNally?"

I thought about it for a while as I retraced my last few weeks. Nothing seemed unusual or odd. I was still getting headaches, but that was part of the injury I sustained. The doctor had already told me that before. Eventually the headaches would lessen in pain, and then one day they would stop coming altogether.

"No, just the headaches."

"Are they still as bad as they were in the hospital?"

"No, and they seem to be getting less frequent."

Gray rolled his eyes as he got more and more impatient. "Hey, look, Doc, is she gonna lose her memory? Is there a chance of that happening or not?"

Dr. Stevens took a breath and answered, "Yes, it's happened to patients with similar injuries. In more severe cases they suffer from anterograde amnesia, meaning they forget everything that happened to them before the injury. Elaina's temporal lobe was affected in the injury from the swelling to her brain. Sometimes it takes weeks, sometimes months and sometimes, hopefully in this case, it never happens at all."

"In those other cases, how bad was the worst case?" Gray pressed.

Dr. Stevens had tried unsuccessfully to avoid this question. I knew as well as Gray that this was not going to be an answer that we wanted to hear.

"Okay, fine. The worst case was a thirty-two-year-old woman who suffered nearly an identical injury as Elaina. At first she was fine, just headaches and the usual things like dizziness, nausea... stuff like that. I was pleased with her recovery and had enough good tests back to assume she was fine. Of course when ever you are dealing with something as complicated as the brain, there are no guarantees. About four months after her injury, her husband called me. He told me something was wrong with his wife and he was concerned about her. He had woken up in the middle of the night to find his wife huddled on the floor in the corner. She was terrified and couldn't remember who he was or who she was even."

"How long did it take for her to recover?" I asked stupidly as Gray tightened his fingers around mine. No one answered me and Dr. Stevens just waited as I thought about that question again. His brows furrowed and his face was filled with pity. "Oh"—I said suddenly—"she didn't recover, did she?" I whispered.

"No, she didn't. Her husband wanted to put her in some sort of facility. We were looking into a few, but she committed suicide before we got her there." My eyes widened in fear and shock. "But listen, she was a severe case as well as the only case I have ever seen something like this happen. There is no reason to think that you will have any problems at all, Mrs. MacNally, none at all."

Those words kept coming into my head like lightening; *She didn't recover, did she?* As we drove home through the traffic that was LA, I tried to imagine forgetting everything I had ever known: Never meeting John or having Georgia and then losing them. Never meeting Gray or ever knowing him at all. Forgetting Mandy and Harris too; my nieces. How could I do that? How could I forget who these people were? My whole life I had held on to every waking moment of everything. I remembered details I probably shouldn't have—smells, colors, what clothes people were wearing. I could tell you the exact smell of Georgia's hair after a bath—it was the smell of baby powder and candy. I could still see in vividness the look on Gray's face when he saw me in the water at the end of his pier that day—the way his lips were turned up to one side with his hands at his sides; the way his head shook slightly from left to right as he tried to hide his shock and then happiness. I remembered the day John died; even though I was asleep, my body sensed him leaving. The way that the new lumber smelled in the house John and I were building together before he was taken from this world. I remembered being a child and running through the wet grass and sprinklers as my distant mother looked on. I can still smell the grass and flowers that circled the yard at my aunt's lake house. Both times I have said I do in my life to two of the most extraordinary men in the world are clear-cut memories in my head. The very first time I held Georgia in my arms and how exquisite she looked and smelled to me. I remember the way Mandy told me that my baby had died. While there are many things that I have experienced in my life that I wish I could forget, I am still acutely aware that I need them all. All the memories I have made me who I am. They have brought me here, so far. Without them, I am a ship without sails heading into the dark and stormy waters. I tried to imagine looking at my new husband and not knowing him. I couldn't imagine it, not even close. Then I remembered the doctor saying that I could be fine, that I may never have any more problems. Then, I was determined to be that person. Over the next few minutes, I resolved to be the healthy patient and not the sick one that kills herself. After all, who would take care of me if I couldn't remember anyone? I was pretty sure the sight of Gray would always be appealing to me, but I wouldn't love him like I do now. I wouldn't even know who he was. Not just him, Mandy and Harris too. My nieces and brother in-law. Even my mother and late father would be a mystery to me.

Gray sat beside me gripping the steering wheel with his large manly hands—the same hands that couldn't save me the day our car flew through the air any more than stopping me from forgetting whose hands they belonged to now. He gazed out the windshield as the wipers went back and forth, removing the few droplets of rain that started to fall. He didn't say much of anything at all. He sighed a few times and grabbed my hand in his. He was still careful not to take his eyes off the road—never again.

"This isn't a death sentence, you know," I reminded him.

"Don't do that Elaina, not now."

"Well, it's not," I repeated.

He said nothing else the rest of the drive home. When we got home, he parked the car and pulled the keys from the ignition with one swipe of his hand. He sat back in the seat and stared off at nothing. The news today had not been what either of us had expected. I started to wonder how much one man could take.

"Are we gonna talk about this?" I asked.

"I don't think I can right now, love," he answered as he turned to me with a pained look across his face. His hand rested on my cheek for a moment and then slid down off my face.

"Okay. Whenever you're ready, I'll be here, okay?"

He smiled tightly and nodded his head. "Okay love."

I rushed out of the car and flitted up the stairs so I could cry inside where he couldn't see. After I cried for almost an hour, I decided that I would have to be prepared for whatever happened. I made myself some tea and turned on my computer and started to write everything I could remember. I found that once I started typing, I couldn't stop.

Gray eventually came inside and sat down beside me. His eyes were bloodshot and puffy. I knew he had been crying. He looked at me in confusion.

"What are you doing, love?" he asked scruffily.

"Nothing, just messing with something," I answered with a forced smile, and I quickly closed my laptop with a snap.

Chapter 24

The day after the doctor appointment, we were set to leave for New York. I was a mess, and Elaina was definitely up to something and typed through the whole flight. I didn't ask her about it again since she seemed reluctant to tell me. Without her talking to me, the flight was long and boring. It gave me more time to think, which I hated. The idea of losing Elaina was something that kept creeping into my head.

It had only been weeks since I thought I would lose her from the accident. After she recovered so quickly, I assumed that things would get back to normal again. I never would have thought that something else could happen to us, especially so soon. Our life together had been so perfect until now. Now all I did was worry—worry about her getting hurt, worry about her drifting away and forgetting me.

I wondered how it would happen and if it would even happen at all. The thought terrified me. For now, she was fine and still the Elaina that knew me. She still looked over every now and then and smiled at me. Her face was as beautiful as it ever had been. Her fingers swept over the laptop keys as she typed feverishly. I wondered again what she was doing. She seemed like a woman possessed; as if she knew her time was running out. Every so often she would stop; in her pause she seemed in deep thought. Her brow twisted and turned as if trying to remember some distant time in her life. As soon as she had stopped typing, she started up again with a lit-up smile across her perfect face. It was the smile I loved and missed whenever I was away for too long. It dawned on me that she may never smile at me with that love again. She may not know me anymore. I had to turn away so she wouldn't see the sadness I was feeling.

In our hotel room hours later, I had managed to pull her away from typing long enough to get her ready for another red carpet for my second to last movie. She had made me promise to try to have fun tonight. A team of workers had arrived to do her hair and makeup, which she hated. There was a dress hanging up for her to wear. I had picked it up weeks before while crossing through Paris. I knew it was for her when I saw it and I had bought it immediately, positive that she would be well enough to wear it eventually. One of the team members came out of the bathroom and grabbed the dress with a swoosh.

I sat and waited with a drink, knowing she would be perfect. I was nervous for her; this would be her first red-carpet event. This would be her first time getting blinded by flashbulbs and spotlights. She would have to ignore the screaming and the yelling. I would hold her hand the whole way through and then try to enjoy the night afterwards. I worried about her again and tried to stop myself.

Suddenly she emerged from the bathroom with a drink of her own in her hand. Her hair was down and straight, hanging nearly to her buttocks. Her face was flawless—not that it wasn't always that way—but she looked so regal and beautiful. Then there was the dress she was wearing. It was black silk and fell down to the floor. My eyes traced her body as the silk clung to the curves that I loved. She turned and pivoted to show me the dress. Then her eyes met mine and she gasped pulling her hands to her mouth.

"Wow! You look so handsome," she commented me. Of course she did. She never thought of herself, only me. That was one of the things that I loved about her—her selflessness and her heart.

"This is nothing, love. Have you seen yourself though?" I asked her.

"Me? No. They just shellacked and sprayed and stuck me in a dress." She laughed. I couldn't help but chuckle as I turned her around and stood her in front of the huge mirror. She tried to turn away but I wouldn't let her.

"Look at yourself," I whispered in her ear. "You're so beautiful."

Her face flushed with red and she turned to kiss me on the cheek. "No, you are." She chuckled.

Suddenly Freddy stormed in grabbing his phone and some notes and passes. When he saw Elaina, he froze like a deer in headlights. "Are you guys...umm...ready to leave? The car is already downstairs."

"Breathe, Freddy, and tell her she looks nice," I instructed.

"You look wonderful, Elaina, really," he stumbled out.

"Thank you, Freddy," she answered bashfully.

"All right, that's enough, lets get this over with," I ordered.

~~~~~~~~

On the way to the movie opening, we sat close in the car, my arm around her and her hand resting on my knee. She wasn't nervous or scared. She was calm, and that made me feel calm. We had to circle the venue twice so we could hop right out and get going.

"Try not to look at the flashes too much. Remember, I love you."

"Okay," she promised.

"Yeah, yeah, love, love, love. It's time. Gray, you first so you can help Elaina out of the car," Freddy ordered, rolling his eyes.

When I opened the door, the noise was deafening. This was the last stop on the press tour for the movie and people were excited. Pressure had been building and the studio kept releasing more and more trailers of the movie. I had seen it, I didn't think it was that great, but I never did think they were all that entertaining. I never understood why people got so crazy at these things, but it was part of the job description.

I crawled out of the car and stood at the curb. The screaming was loud and borderline migraine inducing. I waved to the crowd and turned to help Elaina out of the car. Her face was that of total fear and panic. I smiled at her and kissed her as I helped her onto the curb.

"Just breathe, love. It'll be fine. Well, later anyway. We are just taking a slow walk in the park."

She smiled back at me and took my hand in hers. We walked down the carpet slowly, stopping along the way for pictures and interviews. People shouted out my name and hers, and her hand gripped mine a little bit tighter. We made our way through the press and photographers. It was easy and fun like I remembered it being years ago. I almost wondered why I would ever retire if it could be this fun. Elaina smiled and posed for pictures like a pro. Her hand loosened a bit more, and when we were asked questions, she answered with grace. I couldn't be more proud of her and relieved that she was doing so well. We had only fifty or so feet to go. There were about ten people left to talk to.

We walked hand in hand down the carpet after stopping to talk to everyone we saw. I felt like I had done my job well enough, so I gently tugged her onward to the building so we could get inside. As we walked, she started to lag behind—it wasn't like her—and then she stopped suddenly. Someone was shouting her name and she had actually stopped for them.

"Elaina, please let us have one picture without Grayson!" the voice shouted. She was already looking at me when I turned to her. Her shoulders shrugged and I motioned with my chin for her to go ahead and I smiled. I reluctantly let go of her hand and she backed a few steps away and started posing for the photographers. In truth, as much as she hated the camera, it loved her deeply. I had never seen a bad picture of her. She didn't pose like other women do at these things. She stood up straight and turned just a bit so that her body looked as best as she could get it. Not much work in that department was needed as far as I was concerned.

Still, she looked real and natural standing there, trying to smile as calmly as she could. Her eyes were lit up and she seemed to be enjoying this moment if only for tonight.

Suddenly she dropped her handbag and her face changed, as she rubbed her forehead with an abnormal force. Her eyes turned confused and distant. I made my way over to her thinking it was the lights. When she turned to me, she was still confused. I grabbed her hand and tugged her to me, but she stayed planted looking at me strangely.

"Elaina? You okay?" I shouted over the screams and shouting. She didn't answer and she looked scared; terrified is more like it. "Come on, let's get you inside, love," I shouted and tugged her inside the building.

When we got inside, she was still unresponsive and acting strange, so I called Dr. Stevens. He instructed me to bring her in immediately so he could run a string of tests. He didn't say that she had lost her memory or that anything else was as bad, but he sounded worried. Freddy accepted my leaving early. He knew better than fighting me when it came to Elaina. She was more important than anything else.

The flight back to LA was long even though we were on a private jet. She didn't speak the entire trip.

On the way to the hospital, I tried talking to her, touching her, anything to get some sort of response, but she was gone somewhere else. She clutched her hands together tightly and stared out the window spinning her wedding band around her finger.

Dr. Stevens was at the emergency room entrance when we got there, and he quickly ushered us into the third floor where his office was. He didn't ask any questions or say much until we were in his office.

"They are getting her a room ready now, Mr. MacNally, just be patient."

"Be patient you say? No, what the hell is going on? She was fine and then something happened."

The nurses arrived and took Elaina to her room quickly. Elaina said nothing, and when I tried to kiss her good-bye, she turned her head in fear. Her eyes were blank and distant. She almost looked like someone else all together. That's when I realized she didn't know who I was anymore.

Chapter 25

Come Back to Me

After Elaina was gone, I sat across from Dr. Stevens. I was in shock and I didn't know what to do or say. The doctor said nothing; he was waiting for me to gather my thoughts, I suppose. All I could hear was my heart pounding and the air-conditioning running through the office. The smell of stale air all around me and Elaina's perfume was still lingering on my clothes. Then all I could see was that blank look she had on her face.

"She's gone, isn't she?" I whispered.

"I think she may have had an episode, but I can't be sure; not without tests," he answered.

"I saw her face, Doc. She doesn't know who I am…her eyes, they were different," I explained, still in shock, unable to believe it myself.

"Let's not think anything rash until the tests come back. Some patients can remember again. Just get some rest and we'll know more in the morning."

Where was I supposed to go? Home? Not without her I wasn't. I was staying here, and when they found something out, I would be here waiting. The doctors ran their tests all night. Elaina was still unresponsive by morning. Nothing had changed. Around eight in the morning, they let me see her. She had been sedated and was lying in the bed with her arms at either side of her body. She looked unnatural the way she slept. Even the way her face looked while she slept was different and somehow not right. I sat beside her and grabbed her still hand.

"Elaina? Can you hear me, love?" I looked at her hoping for a response but knowing she was asleep. "Well, I promised you that I wouldn't ever leave you, and I'm not. I'll be here waiting for you when you wake up, love. Whether you know me or not, I'll be here. If you forget me, then I will make you remember. If you can't remember, then I will have to try to make you fall in love with me again. Whatever it takes, we will find each other again. I promise. I won't leave you alone."

I sat with her for an hour or so until the doctor came in with his little clipboard. His face was grim and he looked tired.

We sat down in his office and as the rain came crashing down outside, he told me the news. It had happened; the worst case scenario that wasn't supposed to happen, did. She couldn't remember anything at all. She was gone in almost every way. How could this be real? She was my wife, my partner, my everything. No time had changed that. I still remembered her in every way, and everything we had ever shared. But where I saw my best friend, she saw a total stranger. I was someone she feared; someone she didn't know at all. I dropped my head in my hands and I could feel the tears coming. My stomach twisted into a million knots as I tried to settle in my mind what this all meant.

"What do I do now?" I asked through choking tears.

"We don't give up. Sometimes they do come back around; sometimes they remember enough pieces to get back to their lives. Just not normally in—"

"Cases like this," I finished for him.

"Yes. In cases like hers…normally, nothing comes back. Just remember this is the brain we are dealing with. There are really no rules here."

"And if nothing comes back, then what?" I asked.

"There are places that handle these types of cases, Mr. MacNally—places that can care for her—living facilities."

My blood shot through my veins. "I'm not sending her to some... home so she can rot away somewhere!" I yelled.

"She will require a lot of care, Grayson. I don't think you realize. She doesn't know who you are. She doesn't know who she is. This is not likely to repair itself, ever."

"I'll take care of her!" I pointed to my chest.

"I'm afraid you can't. She is terrified right now. She has no idea who or what she is. She is much like a child or a baby. She doesn't remember how to do anything or what some things even are. You can't just take her home and expect her to understand what your intentions are. It doesn't work that way. The episode she had is much like a stroke. She will have to relearn most day-to-day things. Walking, talking, eating...these are things she will most likely have to relearn. You cannot possibly be in the position to care for her now."

His words cut through me like a knife. As much as I hated that doctor right now and wanted to smash his brain through the back of his skull, I knew he was right. But I couldn't just send her away; not like this. I promised her I would never leave her. I promised her I wouldn't let her forget.

"Where will she go?" I asked shakily, trying to control my body from jumping across the table and murdering him right then and there.

"I know she has family in Virginia and there is a great facility there in Richmond. It's one of the best actually. She can be with her family there. When she recovers a bit more, there are apartments there as well. Patients who suffer from this type of injury do manage to have normal, healthy lives."

"I'm her family too," I pointed to my chest, trying to steady my voice.

"You can all be there for her."

"When?" I whispered through tears.

"As soon as they can take her, I would like for her to go."

My head filled with pain was now replaced with fire. I went home and tore the house up, throwing things everywhere, breaking everything I could get my hands on. I was in a total rage. When I woke up the next morning to broken glass and plates, I made a decision. She would go, but I was going with her. I promised her I would be there, no matter what.

Things were turned upside down after that. She had been moved to her new home called New Beginnings. It was a nice place and Elaina seemed to do well there. I was not allowed to see her much and only really saw her when she slept. I would sit by her side every night, whispering to her about her old life. She never woke up but sometimes she would smile. Harris and Mandy were there too.

Days slipped into weeks. Things seemed to make their own way. I retired from acting for simple reasons. There was no way I could leave Elaina alone, and there simply wasn't enough time for anything else in the first weeks and months of her recovery. I didn't want to miss anything. Basically, I just disappeared from my old life. I was called a recluse by the media; and even though there had been minimal coverage of Elaina and my reasons for stepping out of the public eye, rumors still circulated. Some said she was a drug addict or that she had some horrible disease. I never even responded to them; Elaina was all that mattered now and her safety. My day-to-day life was a routine of thoughts and motions that blended into my life now. I woke every morning to find Macbeth waiting beside me, her soft furry little head resting on my pillow waiting for me to open my eyes. She would look to the other side of the bed and make the same sad face every morning. We were both lost without her it seemed. Always I awoke to the same disappointment—that today was going to be another day of hoping and waiting. Breakfast flew by in a matter of moments with mindless movements that seemed to happen on their own. Somehow, the coffee was brewed and poured in my cup that she bought me in Belize; the eggs were cooked, eaten, and dishes were cleaned before I knew it. Macbeth was fed and let out by some machine working on autopilot. Even driving to the place Elaina now resided was just a certain number of mindless motions that somehow seemed to get me there—only to see her there, sitting with her sketch pad and pencil in the shade of a huge weeping willow tree, staring off into the distance. She would turn in my direction and see me, only to turn away without any recognition of who I was or what I was to her. Lunch was another set of calculated events that involved me waiting for her to notice me, a stranger now, and see me sitting on my usual bench under a huge oak tree by the main entrance to her apartment building. She would always see me, smile politely, and then turn to her drawing pad with a vengeance. She was gone, the woman I knew and loved. Seeing her now was a painful time, not a joyous one. She didn't know me, or like me. I was a stranger now that was always around.

Elaina was in many ways like a newborn infant that was learning at an incredibly fast rate. For a long time, none of us were permitted to get too close to her. If she was frightened, she could regress even more. Finally, I had developed a good relationship with both her best friend and her sister. After months of fighting and disagreements, we were finally a team, and honestly I don't know how I would have ever survived all of this without them. It had been three years in this place and still no change.

Slowly, the three of us started to visit Elaina; at first just once a week, then two, then three. I finally got to talk to her by way of her sketches. It was just a matter of getting her to talk to me about them and show me her drawings, and suddenly she was talking to me. I was in shock at first and most likely looked like a cuckoo. I thought I couldn't be happier to just talk with her until she showed me her drawing that day. It was of the ocean. The view was almost exactly the view from our house in Belize. I nearly said something along those lines but quickly caught myself, remembering she didn't know that place at all. After that it was a little simpler to strike up a conversation with her, and Harris and Mandy eventually got worked in, too. It was a long process but eventually we were there almost every day visiting her. Elaina actually really liked Mandy the most. It was probably her mothering ways or how kind she was to her. Elaina had no idea who we all really were. Mandy liked to draw with her sometimes, and Harris mostly just listened to her talk about different things. It didn't really matter to her what Elaina said, just that she could talk to her was enough for Harris. The doctors didn't think it was a good idea to let her know who we were. Still my life hadn't changed in the sense that I was still her husband, Mandy was still her sister, and Harris was still her best friend. Elaina just didn't know it.

She was different now, not at all the Elaina I knew, but she was still the love of my life. There were certain aspects of Elaina that would forever be there, but she was a new person. The doctors had all told us after the first-year mark that she would most likely never regain her memory again and that we should try to find a way to accept things for what they were. We all tried. That was the worst time for me—trying to give up the faith I had in my heart for her to remember me.

Still there were things she would do that kept us all wondering—the sketches for one and then there was the way she would hear a song that she used to love and actually start singing every word of it from memory, a memory that according to the doctors was lost. She knew how to knit; she had remembered that. She still loved fruit and hated oatmeal. She still cleaned obsessively and her room was kept in a meticulous state all the time. Then there was the obvious—that she didn't know me, Harris, or Mandy. She thought we were nice people that liked to visit her while we were here supposedly visiting someone else. Still sometimes I would catch her looking at me in a peculiar way. It wasn't recognition, it was something else altogether, something stronger—like, dislike, or maybe, hopefully curiosity; I couldn't tell. Mandy and Harris swore that she seemed more excited when I was there during our visits. I didn't believe them. Believing that was false hope—hope that I was running low on more and more every day.

Elaina wasn't mentally ill or unable to care for herself, but the first days being here she was completely at a loss. She would look at things like tying her shoes and want to pick up the laces and twist the laces together into a bow, but she couldn't remember how. She knew a fork was a fork but couldn't figure out what she was supposed to do with it. The things she learned now, she remembered easily. Her brain was like a sponge whenever she was learning something new. She smiled differently, she talked differently, with more of a southern country accent like the nurses who worked here, and slowly I started to merge the old Elaina with the new one. I was starting to fall for my wife all over again.

Years before, on a trip back to LA to settle some matters, I found her laptop. It was right where Freddy had left it beside the bed on her side. I remember being amazed that it was still in one piece after my tornado-like behavior. I grabbed it mindlessly and took it with me to my new house in Richmond. It was an old farmhouse near the facility she now lived in. Macbeth had been delivered back to me shortly after moving back to Richmond, and we tried to get on with our lives. I retired years ago and had no desire to ever return to the movie business. My whole life now revolved around Elaina and being with her as much as I could. I wanted to be the best person I could for her. I quit smoking and rarely drank anymore. I spent most of my time alone with Macbeth or running up and down my old dirt driveway, and then one night, out of boredom, I turned on the laptop. Her background picture was of us together in Belize. We were both smiling and happy. Those days were now gone. I wanted to slam it shut and throw it across the room, but I didn't.

I had remembered her typing obsessively on the plane to New York that day. I remembered wondering what she was doing. I never would have believed she would do what she did though. I opened her files and found something entitled *Don't Forget*. When I saw it, I felt a shiver down my spine. I was scared to open it, scared of false hope. Would this be something that would help her find her way back to me? The doctors had advised me not to tell her who I was, that it would be too much for her. But this was new—this was something she had done, for herself.

I opened the file and read the hundreds of pages she had managed to write. It was all about us—how we met, how we found love with each other, the accident, the recovery, and then the bad news that followed. There were also notes and instructions for where to find everything she still had of John and Georgia. She'd written notes on where to find the photo albums full of their memories as well as her saved treasures of us that she had kept hidden away. On the last page, she had written something else, something to me:

> Gray, I know if you are reading this, then what I was terrified of happening happened. All I can think of to say is that I'm so sorry for leaving you. I'm sure that you will disagree with me when you read what I am about to ask of you. Please remember that this is for me, but also, maybe for us too. I know that I have forgotten everything, and if I know you, you're still right there with me in some way. Please know that I loved you more than anything in the world. Even if my head doesn't know it, my heart does. The time you gave me with you was the best time in my life. You taught me how to love and live again, and for that I'm eternally grateful. But if I never remember you again, I want you to know that it's okay for you to move on. If you have given up, I understand. But before you leave me in my new life, there is something I'm asking you to do.
>
> So here's the big question or, really, request I have of you: Before you leave and try to start over, please let me read this if I have forgotten, because I want to remember you—all of you. Just you and me, remember.
>
> I love you so very much.
>
> Your Innkeeper,
> Elaina

I cried and cried as I read it over and over. She knew it was over. She knew it was going to happen. I don't know how she could have known. It was time to show her this. I had held on to it for over two years waiting for the right moment to spring it on her. I wanted to wait until I was sure there was no other way. After the past few months, I was sure she was lost forever. I decided now was as good a time as any to try, just one more last thing. If it didn't work, then I would move on like she asked and the doctors had told me to do. I would try to find someone else to spend the rest of my life with. I knew that I would fail at that, but I would try for her because it's what she would have wanted me to do. I discussed it with Mandy and Harris. They agreed that it was most likely going to upset Elaina, but they also felt like she needed to know who we all really were—that we weren't just strangers, but her family. They both read what she had written and told me to go ahead and give it to her, but how? How do you go about something like this? "Hey, read this and tell me what you think…You wanna go on a date or something?" No, this would have to be handled delicately and with the most care. If I did something wrong, I could lose my chance. It took me months to figure it out.

While I was figuring things out, however, Elaina was becoming more and more comfortable with me. Harris and Mandy arranged for us to start meeting by ourselves more and more. Things were going well and she was more than receptive to me. She did seem to smile more often whenever I was there. Her actions scared me even more. I was starting to fall in love with her again. I was allowing myself to hope, and that was a dangerous game. We usually went for walks every day, but one day she grabbed my hand suddenly and twined her fingers with mine. It startled me because she usually acted so shy around me. But I let her hold my hand, and a small part of my soul was reborn.

"Your hand is so soft," she announced with surprise.

"So is yours," I answered with a chuckle.

"I like your laugh. It reminds me of...someone," she continued. Now, I know most people would have been shocked by that comment, but she said stuff like that all the time. It was comments like that that kept me here and trying.

"Thank you, I think," I answered with another chuckle.

She covered her mouth and laughed quietly, embarrassed like a little schoolgirl.

"I like your laugh," I answered.

"What is Scotland like, Gray?" she asked trying to take the attention from herself.

"Scotland? Well, it's a lot different. Honestly, I haven't been back in a long time," I answered sadly.

"I like your accent," she complimented.

"Thank you, again," I said. *I know you do* is what I thought.

It was days like this that I went home feeling positive and hopeful. I couldn't help feeling like we were all lying to her though. It really burned me that I couldn't tell her who I was and that I loved her. The past years had changed me. I was quieter now, too, and not as confident as I once had been, especially when it came to her.

"Come for lunch tomorrow?" she asked every day.

Over the next few weeks, we met every day for lunch and walked the same path around the grounds afterwards. I loved every minute of courting my wife all over again. Each day we grew closer and closer. Her hand didn't hesitate to grab mine anymore. She looked into my eyes with less shyness. When she spoke, her words came more easily. She laughed more and was actually pretty funny. There were things that were different about her too. Her spunk that I had loved about her before was gone and replaced with an uncertainty that was just as endearing. She asked me all about Scotland like she had when we had gotten to know each other before. She wanted to know about acting; the craft, not the crazy photographers that had chased us around for years. I was obliged to tell her all about it. Then there were certain things she didn't ask me about. She never asked me who my friend was that I was supposed to be visiting. It was like she played her own part in that charade. Instead she asked me things that were easy to talk about. She didn't really care why I was there, as long as I was there for her talk to. I was seemingly her closest friend, and she relied on that friendship almost as much as I did.

"Why did you stop acting? It sounds like such an exciting life."

"I didn't love it anymore," I answered, shrugging my shoulders and stuffing my hands in my pocket. "It's not all it's cracked up to be." She wound her arm around mine and leaned her head against my shoulder as we walked along. It was just another thing she did now that she had done exactly the same before, and it was hard to remember what time we were actually in.

"You talk about it as if you do still love it," she stated plainly.

"Sometimes things change," I said. She looked at me with fiery eyes as if she knew I was holding something back, and it reminded me of the old Elaina. "Something happened to me that changed everything," I whispered sadly.

"I wish you would tell me," she encouraged.

"Another time," I answered.

~~~~~~~~

More weeks passed and she actually asked me out on a date. Well, it was more like she begged me to take her out somewhere else other than her place. I was excited but nervous. She had made me promise to pick her up at seven sharp and take her to a steak place. The steak at the cafeteria building she lived was horrible, she had told me.

When I picked her up, it was seven exactly, and she was waiting for me, sitting on the steps of the apartment building she now called home. Her hands were resting on her knees and her fingers were rapping on top of one another. She was nervous, I recognized that. Even if she was a totally different person now, I could still see that.

"You're right on time," she announced as she stood from her stoop.

"You said seven on the dot, so here I stand, my lady," I answered. She was wearing a dark-blue sundress with sandals. Her hair was longer now, passed her waist. Her brown eyes burned me through the late afternoon sun. I reached my hand out to her. My, she was gorgeous. "You look lovely," I said as I tucked a strand of hair behind her ear.

The blood rushed to her cheeks as my fingers grazed her face, and she turned away but blindly took my hand. "Thank you." She blushed.

We drove off and she continued to rap her fingers on her lap.

"Is something wrong?" I asked her.

"No, not really...so, where are we going to eat?" she tried in vain to change the subject.

"Well, I have something different in mind, if that's okay." I flashed a smile her way and hoped that it was.

"What do you have in mind?" she asked, sounding a bit nervous.

"Well, I have a house. It's kind of on a lake. I was thinking it would be nice to eat there...outside...tonight."

"You mean *you* are gonna cook?" she asked, surprised.

"Trust me, you'll like my cooking," I assured her, hoping that she would.

"How do you know?" she asked curiously with an eyebrow raised.

"I just do," I answered.

When we got to my house, she got out of the car slowly. She was still unsure of me, I could tell. I walked up to her and grabbed her hand to lead her to the back of the house. There was a porch there with two rocking chairs waiting to the left of the backdoor. To the right of the door was a round table, dressed for company. I left her in a rocker and lit the candles all around the porch, bringing it to life from the dark of the night. She was content to rock and watch me. She laughed quietly as I readied everything and poured us some wine.

"Are you laughing at me then?" I asked.

"Sorry, you just remind me of someone." Her brows were relaxed but then tensed up in confusion.

"Who?" I dared to ask.

Her brow furrowed in deep thought and she answered, "I don't know."

I poured another glass of wine that she said she didn't want, but after refilling it three times I realized she did. I served her a filet mignon with a creamy pepper sauce that she all but licked from the plate. She left the asparagus on the plate, crunching her nose at them, which made me laugh.

After dinner, we had some more wine and held hands a little more. She was smiling up at the stars. Then her smile turned somber and she sighed out loud.

"Do you ever get the feeling that nothing is what it seems? That people are lying to you?" she asked without looking at me. I said nothing. "It's like I know you already, like Mandy and Harris."

"You do know Mandy and Harris. They visit you every week, like me," I offered.

"No, it's different, it's…more," she pressured. "Sometimes I think you know me better than you let on."

"I can't talk about this," I whispered and started to rise to my feet.

"Why not? I know that I'm different. I can't remember why or how I got this way, but I know I'm different. The doctors have told me about my brain injury," she shouted. She grabbed my arm and forced me to look at her.

"I'm not supposed to say anything about that, you know that," I answered, looking her deep in the eye.

"Please," she begged quietly. "I want to know. Just stop lying to me, please. You are the only one that doesn't treat me like a…a patient."

I was quiet for a long time thinking about what to say or what to do. Her face softened and she tried turning on some sort of teenage-like charm. Her eyes changed, rounder somehow, and her touch now seemed different, more affectionate than before. It all made me feel dirty and wrong for lying to her. I could see the desperation in her face, hear it in her voice. Ah, damn it, she was just as powerful over me as she always had been.

"I knew you before, didn't I?" she asked.

"Yes," I whispered without looking at her.

"Ugh! Just tell me already!" she shouted.

"I think I should take you home," I said calmly.

"No, please, just tell me who I am. I need to know," she begged.

"You're Elaina, that's who you are. That's who you will always be." I stood up and darted into the house, grabbing the printout that she had written years before that I had bound and made into a book. The pages were worn from me reading it over and over and the binding was cracked. When I came back out, she was crying into her hands.

"It's late. I should get you home," I announced in a whisper.

~~~~~~~~

She stared out the window into the darkness the whole way home. She was mad and not speaking to me. It was our first fight the second time around, but it felt very familiar to me. Her arms were crossed and the space between us large. When I pulled in front of the building, she moved to get out of the car.

"Elaina?" I called out softly.

"What?" she answered, annoyed, with a sigh.

"There is something that I want to give you. I'm not supposed to, but I'm going to anyway. You wrote it a long time ago. I think you should read it now," I whispered.

"Okay," she answered in confusion, reaching out to grab the small booklet. "What is it?"

"Just read it, okay. It will answer your questions, I think. Whether you want the answers or not, it's all there."

She took the bound pages and smiled warily. She turned to step out from the car and a sudden breeze blew a few strands of her hair from her ponytail. She slipped the hair back behind her ear and turned back to me. "Thank you, Gray."

I was still mesmerized by her fingers lingering on her neck behind her ear when I finally answered her. You're welcome was all I could say. She was going to finally read about her life and who she really was. The doctors couldn't protect her from it anymore. Whether she liked it or not, she would know who she was when the sun rose tomorrow.

"I'll see you tomorrow then. Good night, Gray," she answered sorrowfully.

Chapter 26

In the morning, it was hot and humid. It was full-blown summer in Richmond. The bugs were out, the air was sticky, and everyone was trying to beat the heat. I had sat up most of the night wondering what Elaina was doing and thinking. For a while, I had deeply regretted giving her the notes she had written so long ago. Eventually I had decided to accept whatever she wanted to do. The Elaina I knew now owed me nothing, I knew that. And yet, a tinge of hope still resonated in my broken heart.

I was making some fruit for myself and throwing Macbeth some bacon when I heard the car speeding down the long driveway to my house. I had no idea who it could have been. Mandy was at home and so was Harris. Elaina didn't have a car, or so I thought. That was it for me. I didn't have any other friends here. I ordered Macbeth outside the back door, popped a strawberry in my mouth, and strode to the front door, curious.

I stepped onto the front porch to see her sitting in her car, unsure of what to do. Her hands were still resting on the wheel and she was staring off into the trees. The engine was still running, so I made my way out to her car.

"Usually people turn off the engine after they park," I teased.

She looked up at me through tears. She turned the key, cutting off the engine, and opened the door to her borrowed car. She climbed out and leaned up against the hot, dusty sedan. She had managed to find a spot in the shade so her eyes didn't squint so much and I could see their true beauty.

We stood for a bit in silence, waiting for one of us to speak, but neither of us did. We didn't risk a glance at each other either. A summer breeze settled over us and brought with it a renewed confidence in me.

"Do you want to come in for a bit?" I asked.

She glanced and sneered at me, and her eyes tightened.

"Maybe not then," I offered. She lost her anger for a second and smiled with a sigh.

More silence and staring at the grass, the trees, the sky; anything but each other. The wait was excruciating. She ran both her hands through her long hair and let her head fall back to gaze at the summer sky with another long and heavy sigh.

"You know what the crazy thing is?" she asked.

I thought it had been rhetorical so I hadn't answered immediately. "What's that then?" I answered.

She finally lifted her head back up and leveled her eyes on me with a smirk. "I knew it. I knew it all along that you were someone I had been very close to. Three years you sat there and you never told me. All these things that I wrote then and I can't remember one of them. I had a whole life before this but nobody ever told me. All this time you could have told me who you were, but you didn't. A car accident changed my life and took away every memory I have ever had and yet nobody tells me about my past." She shook her head angrily. "Why?" she demanded with her hands crossed across her chest.

"I'm sorry. The doctors thought it was best that way," I explained.

It was the only reason I had.

She shook her head, unable to understand. "How could you do that? Watch me day after day, not knowing who you were. How could you do that every day?"

I grabbed her hand in mine and pulled myself closer to her. "Because I love you. I figured I could still be with you somehow, even if it wasn't how we used to be, how we were meant to be. I could still see you."

Her head hung down and I watched as her face grew angrier and angrier. I let go of her hand. I had seen that face before, years ago. I knew it was time to back off. But then her expression changed again and she seemed more curious than angry.

"How did it happen?" she asked.

I sighed, not really wanting to relive that horrible moment, but I did anyway. "One minute you were holding my hand and the next minute you were looking at me like I was a stranger. It was no more time than a blink of an eye really."

"Were we happy?" she questioned.

"Yes. Very," I answered. My breath was becoming uneven with nervousness.

"Why can't I remember you? I mean, I know why, but why can't I remember anything about you?" she asked, getting flustered.

I laughed silently at that question for two reasons: one, because she was so cute, and two, because she did remember things. "You do. You just don't know it. Like my hands, you always loved how they felt. You used to tease me that they felt more like a woman's hands." She laughed at that. "And my laugh, you always loved that."

She suddenly blushed to bright red. "That person is gone, Gray. She doesn't exist anymore." She spoke through her teeth. She was angry but I couldn't tell if it was me that she was angry with.

"Don't you think I know that? I've been watching you for three years become somebody completely different. I see you every day and look at you and know that you have no idea who I am. That doesn't matter anymore to me. I just miss you, and I've learned that it doesn't matter what form of you I have now. You are still in there somewhere. I see you even if you don't. I hear you even if you can't. I remember even if you've forgotten." I grabbed her by her arms. Feeling her under my hands reminded me of how much I missed her. I kissed her gently, and like our first kiss, she shied away at first, leaning back on her car. She looked away and started to smile, but then she looked me in the eye.

Her hand touched my face and her fingers caressed my cheek. There was something there that she recognized, something she remembered, and suddenly she kissed me back.

She pulled away after a moment and then leaned into me again, resting her face against mine, cheek to cheek. Her hand was still resting on the other side of my face and she whispered, "But I don't know you."

I put my hand over hers with a smile. "You can get to know me, again, if you want to. We can get to know each other again," I whispered back in her ear.

She was still unsure, so I grabbed her other hand. "Come with me. There's something I want to show you. I think you'll like it."

"I lost my memory, Grayson, not my mind. I'm not going to your bedroom. As much as I am attracted to you, I'm not going there just yet," she snickered.

"It's not in my bedroom," I promised. "Just yet?" I asked, surprised, realizing she had thought about being alone with me. She rolled her eyes, just like she used to, and I laughed.

"What?" she asked in annoyance of my laughing at her.

"Nothing. You just used to roll your eyes at me like that all the time. It never got old." I chuckled.

"Oh," she answered oddly. She seemed thrown off guard by that, but I didn't let her reaction deter me.

"Come on," I tugged her along.

I led her into the house and down the hall past the kitchen and into the office. When I opened the doors, there was everything: All the pictures she had hung in LA and in Belize. All the memories we had made and shared. I had kept all of her photo albums from her childhood and beyond. When she saw all of this, her eyes lit up like a child's. Immediately she began circling around the room; her eyes were bouncing from one thing to another. I watched her wonder through the past. She eventually came across a picture of Belize. It was just of the ocean sitting from our house looking out at the water.

She paused to stare at this picture in particular. "This place"—she ran her fingers over the water in the photo—"I dreamt about this place," she said in wonderment. "A lot," she added.

"That doesn't surprise me at all. It was your favorite place in the world. It was ours. I still have the place. I didn't have the heart to sell it," I confided.

She smiled in delight as her eyes drifted over the room.

"You said you wanted to know who you are, and this is everything," I offered.

She came across another photo of the two of us at the last red carpet premiere event in New York. She had been so stunning that night. Freddy had framed it after her mind had gone and dropped it off the day he quit.

"Where is this?" she asked.

"That's...umm...New York," I answered shakily. She turned to face me, hearing the sadness in my voice. Her confusion suddenly changed to realization.

"Is this when it happened?"

"A few minutes after that was taken, actually," I answered.

Her finger rubbed across the frame mindlessly. "I wish I could remember."

"That's okay. I do."

We spent the rest of the day going through photo albums and cards; things she had kept when we were dating in the beginning; letters I had written her and left for her in the mornings; places we had gone to. She laughed when she saw Macbeth barge into the room. She didn't remember the dog, but Macbeth remembered her for sure. She put her head under Elaina's hand and waited as Elaina mindlessly scratched her head exactly the same way she had before. When she did things like that automatically, I wondered if she did remember some things. *Could a habit actually survive a head trauma?*

"I think someone missed you," I chuckled. "Her name's Macbeth. You two used to be pretty close."

She knelt down to the dog's level and wrapped her arms around her. "I'm sorry, Macbeth."

Macbeth licked her repeatedly until Elaina stood out of her reach. She laughed, "I think you're right."

She sat down at the kitchen table as I poured her some coffee and offered her some fruit.

"You still like pineapple and strawberries, right?" I asked, realizing I was usually not with her at breakfast time.

Her eyes flitted up to me in surprise and then she laughed covering her face. "Yes, it's my favorite. How did you kn..?" She stopped short when she saw me smiling back at her.

I sat across from her and watched her eat. There was something new but also familiar about all of this. She knew the truth but she was still someone else. No matter what I told her or showed her about her old life, it was over; and although we could try to know each other again, I was still sitting here with a stranger. I didn't know much about her now. It was sad but I was grateful to have her here in my kitchen with me. I wondered what Mandy and Harris would think about this.

We talked for a while about mindless things, but eventually she started to get quiet again. I knew this was something she did when she was thinking deeply. It seemed unfair that I knew so much about her habits and she knew nothing about me at all. I stared at her, waiting for her to ask her question that was so obviously on the tip of her tongue.

"Go on, ask me then?" I encouraged.

"So, we are married?" she asked teasingly.

"Yep," my lips popping on the *p*.

We sat across from one another and smiled uncomfortably. Neither of us knew what to say.

"Mandy is my sister and Harris is my best friend?"

"Umhmm." My eyebrow arched.

"Macbeth used to my buddy?"

"That about covers everyone," I chuckled.

"What do we do now? Live as husband and wife? What?" she asked, suddenly sounding anxious but curious at the same time.

"I thought we could start with a date and maybe some more hand holding, kissing, and the…umm…other stuff, well, as much as I wish I could kiss you now, it can wait." I smiled. "I'm sorry about that earlier by the way, I shouldn't have done that."

She blushed. "No, no, it was nice…kissing you. I have imagined it for a long time actually. As far as the 'other stuff' goes, well I don't even know what to do. I am basically…Oh God, I guess I'm a virgin when it comes to all that. I have no memory of any of that at all. Sorry." Her face was full of worry and confusion. "You already know about that part though. That's not very fair."

I chuckled again, making her blush. Then she shook her head back and forth.

"What?" I asked.

"Was I any good at that stuff?" she asked bashfully.

"We were both very happy, Elaina. That was just another reason for us to be happy."

She smiled and tightened her arms around the book. "I'm gonna read it every night, that stuff she…I wrote about us. I may not be able to remember, but that doesn't mean I will let myself forget."

I smiled widely and she smiled back, comfortably. I was happy now sitting with her, confident that she would learn to love me again, that she wanted to. I grabbed her hand that was resting on the table beside her fruit. She smiled again as I examined her hand in mine. She smiled up at me.

"Nice hands," she whispered.

Chapter 27

Tell Me Everything

Every day after that was different and new. I learned more about the new Elaina every second of each day. She was new and energized. She wanted to read every book, hear every song, and do all the things we had done before. I tried to oblige her every request. She went through box after box of her old things, hoping for some shred of a memory, but nothing came. It was frustrating for her. I, however, was used to it. She asked me all about Belize and wanted to go there again. She asked if she could swim or even scuba dive, which she could before. I wasn't sure at first if she could still swim or if she would have to learn it again. When I showed her all the gear, she knew how to do everything. It seemed another small detail had crossed over into her "new brain." She made me take her to a pool to really test out her knowledge. She did fine, of course. She would start to read books and after a few days put them down with a frustrated sigh. "I already know how this one ends," she would say, and after telling me the ending correctly, I would sigh and tell her I was sorry. She wanted to try eating things she had loved. She discovered that she hated fish now, when she had loved it before. She hated coffee, which was really strange because she never could get through a day without her cup of java before. She figured out that she could not cook at all after several attempts. She hated liquor now, especially vodka. She told me how she hadn't known if she could even drive that day that she came over after reading the "book," but when she got in the driver seat, everything came back to her. She explained it like being on autopilot—that her body just took over and showed her that it remembered. We talked for hours and hours about why this could be happening, why she could remember such mindless things but not anything important. Sometimes it seemed that her "old brain" was fine, just in hibernation, blocking certain things from coming through. The doctors were also clueless. They explained this as a blip in her brain. Much of the time Elaina was frustrated with her doctors. She seemed annoyed that they couldn't fix her. I was getting tired of her living there; it didn't seem to be helping her at all.

Day sixteen, she saw Harris and Mandy for the first time since knowing who they really were. At first it was awkward and strange, but by the end of the day, the three of them were laughing. By day seventeen, Elaina started asking me about John and Georgia. She asked about their lives and who they were to her; why they had disappeared in the photo albums. That was a bad day for her. I never knew if it was really right telling her so soon after everything else, but she insisted that she know everything one day at a time. I tried to tell her that some things can't be relived in one day but she ignored my warnings and pushed on anyway.

Day twenty, Mandy came back to see her. That day, Elaina wanted to know about her mother and father. That was not something I was equipped to offer to her. She had separated from her mother way before I came into the picture. Her father had died shortly after John and Georgia of cancer, something Elaina had never told me about. After her father had died, Elaina's mother's anger over how Elaina handled her own family's death intensified. She eventually moved to her river home and cut Elaina out of her life. I had never met Elaina's mother, and the more I heard about her, the less I wanted to. She seemed like a cold woman that never really loved or cared about her children. The way she abandoned them bothered me greatly.

As horrible as this woman sounded, Elaina still wanted to meet her. When Mandy told her she couldn't because she was now suffering from dementia and had been placed in a home years ago, I was relieved, but Elaina was saddened by the feeling of never having had closure.

Through all the information, Elaina was very aware that we also weren't telling her certain things. I kept things like her attempted suicide and how John's mother had died two years ago to myself. She was essentially an orphan now with Mandy. I had a feeling that Mandy had always been more of a mother to Elaina anyway, and I didn't worry about that.

On day thirty, Mandy brought her husband and four daughters to meet Elaina. It was funny the way they hugged her like not a day had gone by. It was a good day with lots of laughing and giggling. Elaina's doctors were impressed with her progress and eagerness to learn about her past. They apologized over and over for refusing us to share these things with her sooner. I couldn't get mad, three years had passed; and even though they had been hard, I had gotten through it, and now I was the one winning. I had Elaina back in my life without the secrets, well, maybe one.

Day thirty-three was also date number thirty-three for Elaina and I. We had been together every night since she had read the "book" of her past. We went to a different place for dinner every night. I had even taken her back to our park where I had told her how I felt about her the first time. We walked for hours that day with Macbeth by our side. I drove her to her old house, where we had lived together in the beginning. She was more like a girlfriend now, a serious one. We liked to do lots of different things, but kissing was definitely still one of our favorites, and we did that often.

When she opened the door to her apartment at New Beginnings, she smiled. "Hey" she whispered as she wound her arms around my neck and pulled me down to her lips. She kissed me gently for a moment and then pulled away and smiled.

"I'm guessing today was a good day with Mandy then?" I teased.

She shrugged her shoulders, just like she used to. "I just missed you."

"That's always good to hear. Where to tonight?"

"Can we stay here tonight? I kind of umm…I cooked," she offered, raising one lone eyebrow.

"You cooked? Well, we can always order a pizza, I guess," I teased.

She rolled her eyes and then laughed. "That's not fair. You haven't even tried it yet. You should know that I have been practicing, and well…Mandy helped a little."

"In that case, where's the food?" I teased again. She punched my arm playfully and took my hand to lead me through her place.

Elaina's place was on the ground floor. She had her own patio and deck. I had made sure she had the best. She opened the door to her living room. My eyes drifted past the couch and over to the dining room table. It was lit up with candles and fancy plates— obviously not Elaina's, most likely Mandy's.

"You and Mandy have been busy. What is all this?"

She rolled her eyes again with a grin. "Just sit down and be quiet," she commanded.

"Yes ma'am."

Elaina served me my dinner, which was really great. She had cooked crab-stuffed fillet with roasted potato fingerlings. She knew what I liked, even now. We had gone through nearly two bottles of wine before dinner was done. She seemed a little nervous and I couldn't quite figure out why. She kept smiling, though, and I liked that. I grabbed the dishes and followed her to the kitchen when she got up.

"You didn't have to get those, I was coming right back," she said as she turned on the faucet.

"It's no problem." Then I saw it—a huge chocolate cake with a shiny chocolate glaze smothered all over it. "What..is..that?" I asked excitedly, pointing right at the delicious-looking dessert.

"Oh, that's dessert. Doesn't it look good? I was tempted to just have that for dinner, but Mandy convinced me otherwise."

"Dinner was great, but that cake would have done the trick just fine," I chuckled.

We each had a huge slice and sat on her front porch with another glass of wine. It had been a great night.

"So I've been meaning to ask you something." She paused until I looked back at her. "What's with my old nickname, Innkeeper?" she asked.

I chuckled. "I started that. You know how we first met, right? Well, I called you that because you were my keeper of…well, my heart. You were where my heart belonged from the moment I saw you."

"And now? What would you call me now?"

I thought about that for a moment but couldn't answer.

"We do have a second chance, you know," she answered softly.

"Is this what this is all about tonight?" I asked gingerly.

She smiled and shrugged her shoulders. "Do you think it's possible to fall in love with the same person twice in one life?"

"I certainly hope so," I smiled, still not seeing where she was going with all this.

She inched a little closer to me and grabbed my hand in hers and raised it up to her lips to kiss the back of my hand. I felt a shudder down my back when her lips made contact with my skin. I looked up to the sky to steady myself. It was always hard to control myself with Elaina when she was this close. So far nothing much sexually had happened between us; sure a lot of kissing and some heavy petting, but nothing more than that. I was content, but it was getting harder to control myself with her. I sighed up at the moonlit sky. When I looked back at her, she was gazing up at me. Her eyes were gentle and round. She seemed to be waiting for me to say something. I was just so nervous.

"I do still love you, Elaina, of course. Is that what you are asking?"

She smiled again and her other hand reached around my neck and pulled me closer to her. Her lips pressed against mine. My hand found her face, while my other hand untwined from hers and wound around her waist. I pulled her over onto my lap and her legs wrapped around my waist; this was all still normal for us. My hands cradled her face as I kissed her. My hand eventually drifted to her waist and then found its way to her backside and pulled her even closer on impulse, and suddenly she stopped breathing.

"Ahhh, bollocks, I'm sorry." I offered as I pulled my eager claws off of her. "I should probably go," I offered breathlessly realizing I may have misread her and pushed her too far.

"No, don't go, please," she answered back, just as breathless as me as she pulled my arms back around her.

I chuckled quietly and tucked some of her hair behind her ear. "We don't have to rush this, you know."

Her mouth twisted up into a sneaky smile. "But we've already done this, remember?"

"I have, but you…haven't," I answered with confusion thick in my voice. Sometimes it was hard to distinguish these two very different women. Even though they were the same person, neither had any recollection of the other. It was a slippery slope sometimes trying to word things just right.

"Don't you want to?" she asked with a smile, and then her head ducked under my chin. As her lips found my neck and my ear, I could feel my blood racing and my body starting to react to her again. I tried to steady myself as she continued kissing my neck and jaw.

"Of course I want to, but…"

"But what? I'm already your wife. It's a done deal, isn't it?" she whispered into my neck. "And I want you." Hearing her say that took all of my self-control away. My lips found hers instantly and she was all too ready for me. I lifted her up, with her legs now tightly wound around me, and carried her back into the apartment and into her bedroom. This was something I wasn't prepared for or even thinking she would do. I remembered how she had done the same thing to me the first time we had made love. She had taken me by surprise by taking over, just like she was now. Nothing about this had changed—the kissing, the touching. Her skin was the same against mine. I tried to take my time but I couldn't wait any longer. She didn't seem to mind much. She was just as eager to get to me as I was to get to her.

She whispered into my ear that she loved me afterwards while we were lying in bed. In many ways, it was like we were starting all over again, but completely different than the first time. She was different, but then again, so was I. I wasn't unsure about love like I had been the first time. I knew what it was to have loved and then to lose it. I was much more cautious than I had been. The night was very young and her whisper only lead to more kissing, and when we finally fell asleep, we had made love four times.

I drove home early the next morning. She had kicked me out of bed so that her neighbors didn't know I had stayed the night.

"We are married, you know," I gruffed at her.

"Just go. I'll call you later," she whispered with a laugh.

When I got home, there was a familiar car in my driveway with a very irritated-looking woman leaned up against it.

I parked my car and approached the fuming female. I raised my hands up as if I was turning myself in to the police.

"Whatever it is, I didn't do it!" I offered. But as I got closer, I saw that she wasn't in the mood for my crap. "What?" I asked.

Mandy was not happy. Her face was twisted up into a frown that I couldn't quite understand. She shook her head. "What?" she asked back, although it wasn't really a question. "Where the hell have you been all night, Gray?" she asked with accusation.

"You know where I was, Mandy. The same place I am every night." I answered with a bit of annoyance in my tone. I walked on by her and into the house to make some coffee to burn off my tiny hangover. Too much wine, I guessed. "Want some coffee?" I asked.

She followed me, letting herself into the house after the screen door slammed into her behind me.

"What are you doing?" she asked a bit more calmly.

"What do you mean? I'm trying to get to know my wife. She cooked me dinner last night, we had a great dinner and a lot of wine. What are you doing?" I asked, still trying to figure out why she was in my house at seven in the morning and why she was so mad.

"You spent the night there?" she asked, but again it wasn't really a question; it was an accusation.

I froze when I realized what this was about. "Yeah, I did. So? Too soon for that then, *mom*?" I answered sarcastically, crossing my arms over my chest, almost daring her to continue her tirade.

"Did you tell her?" she growled.

"Tell her what?" I demanded back.

"You know exactly what!" she hissed back. "You and Harris have been very close for a while now," she sneered.

"It's not what you think, Mandy. We are just friends," I explained desperately.

"I know what happened, Gray." She spit my name out. "She told me."

"It was just one night, Mandy, it never happened again. Please, it's not what you think!" I shouted back. This interrogation was infuriating.

She was quiet for a long time. "Are you gonna tell her or not?" she asked, slightly calmer.

"She doesn't need to know about that. Harris doesn't want her to know anyway," I answered.

"You should tell your wife that you cheated!" she growled.

I turned around to face Mandy—good, old, overreacting Mandy. The blood was pumping through my veins and I could feel the anger seeping up to the surface, anger that had been festering for years.

"That woman isn't my wife! My wife died over three years ago! You can't cheat on someone who's not there anymore! How dare you come in here and tell me what I should and shouldn't do or even judge me! I was lonely, I was all alone with nothing! I needed someone, okay! It was just one night, that's all. She didn't even know who I was, Mandy! She had no idea who I was. Do you have any idea what that's like?" I yelled.

"Yes, actually, Gray, I do."

"No you don't! Your husband knows who you are; he hasn't forgotten you!" I shouted.

"Gray?" I heard the softer voice in the middle of yelling and shouting. It wasn't Mandy's voice, it was Elaina. I spun around and there she was, standing in the doorway of the kitchen. She had come straight from her apartment this morning. Mandy and I hadn't seen her or heard her over our yelling. She wasn't smiling like she had been this morning. She was sad and hurt, her eyes filled with confusion and pain.

"Elaina, I'm…so sorry—" I started, but she cut me off.

"No, I'm sorry," she hissed under her breath. She turned and ran to her car and jumped in. I was frozen, speared to the floor. It felt like the life had just been sucked out of me. I was dizzy from the arguing and then the abrupt ending.

"Oh my God," Mandy whispered. "Gray…I'm sorry, I'll talk to her…I promi—"

"Just go, Mandy, please," I managed.

Chapter 28

Companionship?

It was two years ago when it happened. Neither of us had planned it or even expected it. Every day we went to the apartments at New Beginnings, hoping for a miracle of some kind. This morning was the meeting we had all dreaded. I got there first. Harris pulled up right behind me and parked her Lexus sedan beside my Range Rover. She stayed in the car for a bit, talking on her phone. We had become pretty good friends in the past year. I had grown to really like her and she was a great friend, maybe one of my best friends. She cut her eyes over to me and rolled her eyes as she opened and closed her hands like a talking mouth. I smiled back at her and then I turned back to see Mandy pulling into the lot in her minivan. She parked and then hopped out of the car speedily.

"Sorry! Sorry I'm late. The girls all have the flu and my husb—"

I lifted a hand to stop her. "It's okay, Mandy, Harris is still on the phone anyway. And, you're not late, you're right on time."

"Oh," she sighed. "Good. Let's go on in. Dr. Reynolds is probably waiting for us."

"We can wait for Harris," I answered. Mandy rolled her eyes. I could never tell if she was annoyed by Harris out of jealousy or because she truly disliked her. Mandy grew more and more impatient as she made her way over to the gleaming white Lexus and slammed her opened hands on the hood.

"Let's go, Harris!" she shouted.

Harris snapped her phone shut a few seconds later and roared out of her car in a huff.

"Somebody woke up on the wrong side of motherhood this morning," she grumbled.

"Can we just get going, please? I don't want to be late!" Mandy shouted back and started walking briskly toward the building.

I noticed Harris's eyes were puffy and red before she pulled her huge sunglasses over them. Her face was turned down and she looked sad as we walked to the apartment building. We both shook our heads at Mandy's warp speed walking and lagged behind.

"You okay, Harris?" I asked.

"We can talk about it later," she huffed in annoyance. "Drinks, later?" she asked.

"He dumped you, didn't he?" I blurted out before even thinking.

She froze in her tracks and looked up at me with her mouth slightly hanging open. "Did you really just say that?" she hissed.

"Sorry, I'm just really distracted this morning," I apologized, shoving my hands into my pockets.

"We can talk about it later over the drinks you are now gonna buy me," she answered as she mock-punched my arm.

Harris and I usually went out for drinks two or three times a week. Her job gave her tons of free time, and she made her own hours, and I had nothing but time now that I had retired, too soon, from acting. We walked onward to the building were Elaina was living now. It was a really beautiful old Georgian-styled mansion that had been converted into about ten large apartments. The middle of the old mansion held two doctors' offices. A few miles down the road was a larger medical facility in case of emergencies. It was elite—only the best for Elaina—and not many people were even aware that this building housed "patients." I had made an incredibly generous donation to get her in.

Dr. Reynolds was standing at the front door on the front wraparound porch. My eyes drifted to the left like always, all the way down to the end of the front of the building where Elaina lived. I sighed as I wondered what she was doing right this minute. Was she cooking? Was she cleaning feverishly? Was she remembering me? I had no idea and it sucked.

"I'm glad you all could make it this morning. Please come on in." He spoke as he gestured his hand to follow him. I could hear Mandy hiss under breath. "Don't know why she has to be here too." She was clearly annoyed by Harris's presence.

I poked her arm to let her know that she was being mean. She sighed again and we followed the doctor into the house and down the main hall to his on-site office. All of us were a mess this morning, all on edge, all worried; all for good reason. We all filed into the smallish office and sat down across from Elaina's doctor that none of us really liked too much.

"So, we have been trying to be patient with Elaina, to see what she might remember on her own. I think you are all aware that she hasn't regained much of anything, just some random things that she remembers how to do. It's been a year since the episode without any change. Gray, you told me that you recently traveled back to LA to retrieve some of her belongings?"

I was still stumped by his choice of words—*episode*. Mandy elbowed me and I tried to answer the doctor. "Yes, I did. I found a diary she wrote to herself before she lost her memory...or the episode," I snickered. "In the diary, she asked me to let her read it." I could feel Mandy's eyes on me.

"You didn't tell me that," she chastened.

"I don't tell you everything, and besides, I was going to," I answered, reminding her that I was a man, not one of her children. I could hear Harris chuckling on the other side of me.

"I'm going to advise that you not show that diary to her. If she hasn't remembered anything by now, she most likely isn't going to. Reading that diary could do more damage than good. It could send her over the edge," the doctor advised.

"But she asked me to let her read it. It's kind of like a last request," I insisted.

The doctor paused with his hands bridged together. He was about to tell us some more bad news, and I suddenly wished I were deaf. "I'm sorry, but I think it's time the three of you tried moving on with your lives. The old Elaina is gone, and she isn't coming back. The new Elaina is who she is now. That other person is gone. Elaina has no idea who that person is. She doesn't know any of you. Gray, maybe you should try acting again; Harris, you could try to build up your client list again; and Mandy, you could focus more on your family," he offered. As annoying and full of himself as he was, I knew he was only trying to point out the obvious. He was completely lacking in any bedside manner in his attempt, but he had a point. Still I was pissed and didn't appreciate his opinion one bit.

"Don't try to counsel me, Doctor. We are her family and we aren't going anywhere," I huffed, suddenly feeling Mandy's hand on mine, trying to give me support.

Dr. Reynolds looked at the three of us to see our furrowed brows glaring back at him. "I'm sorry. I didn't mean to offend any of you. It's just that this is not going to change, and I feel like you are all waiting for something that isn't going to happen."

"Are you saying we should give up?" Mandy demanded.

"I'm saying you should all be realistic and try to move on with your lives," he answered evenly.

~~~~~~~~

"That doctor's an idiot!" Mandy shouted as she stormed toward her dusty blue minivan.

I walked alongside her. I grabbed her arm to stop her. "I agree, but...damn it, Mandy, he's got a point."

"What?" she asked in shock. "You think we should just give up and move on with our lives?"

"No, of course not. I was talking about you spending more time with your family. All this driving back and forth, it's just crazy. I'm right down the road and Harris doesn't have your crazy schedule with kids and a husband." Harris grimaced at me and I grinned back at her apologetically. "Why don't you let us take on the load for a while; spend some time with your family," I suggested. Mandy looked furious as her glare bounced back and forth between Harris and I.

"What is this? Are you guys like…teaming up on me or something?" Her eyes started to water and she looked hurt.

"No, not at all, but you look exhausted, that's all. You can't do everything, you know," I offered.

"What's going on with you, Mandy? You are really emotional these days, kinda like you were the last time you were pr—" Harris cut herself off suddenly. "Oh my God, you're not pregnant again?" she asked.

"Are you?" I asked, surprised.

Mandy's eyes softened, and she wiped a tear from her cheek. She looked guilty. "I wasn't gonna say anything, you know, with everything that's been going on. It was a surprise; we didn't plan it."

"Four children?" Harris huffed.

I elbowed her and turned back to Mandy. "That's great, congratulations. You could have told us; it would have explained things," I said.

After congratulating her again, I helped her to her car and watched her drive off. She agreed to take it easy, and that meant that she would keep her hormones and her outburst safely at home.

Harris drove us to a nearby bar named Willy's. It was small and quaint, but it did the job after a hard day. We ordered some fried mushrooms and steak fries along with two bourbons. Harris excused herself to the ladies room, and I automatically watched her as she walked away.

I wasn't attracted to Harris, but I did admire her beauty. She was a rather sexy woman. I had always skipped over her before because of Elaina, but she was a very attractive woman. Her red hair and freckled skin gave way to her unbelievable figure. That's not all that was attractive about her though. She was funny and spunky like Elaina had been. In many ways, she reminded me of how Elaina was. She spoke her mind and stood behind her opinions. She could drink me under the table, and she never apologized for telling it like it was. I knew now why Elaina had loved her.

She reappeared from the bathroom and strutted back to the table without even knowing what she was doing with her hips and sat down with a huff.

"Can you believe she is having another one? Jesus! Is she trying to populate the whole world or something?" she growled.

I laughed. "I think it's pretty cool actually." I lied, but I had secretly always wondered what it would have been like to have a child.

She rolled her eyes and speared a mushroom with her fork and jabbed it into the ranch dressing to the side.

"So what happened with you and Jeff? I thought you two were doing okay," I asked.

"Jeff is great, just not with me," she snorted. "He's just not what I want right now. Relationships—they just aren't for me right now." She sighed and she shoved a french fry in her mouth.

"I'm sorry, Harris, really I am." I reached across the table for her hand and squeezed it. She smiled back at me but there was nothing more behind her smile. She looked tired and down. She pulled her hand away and took a gulp of her drink and looked back at me sheepishly.

"Mandy doesn't like us...you know...hanging out like this. She thinks it's dangerous; that things could happen. I know I call you a lot but it's just because...I miss her so much."

"I know," I answered. "We aren't doing anything wrong here. We are just friends and I...miss her like crazy too." It felt weird explaining our need to hang out with each other so much. I was annoyed that Harris had said anything about it at all, but I knew she was just drawing the line between us.

We ate and drank for a couple of hours and then she drove me back to the apartment building. When we pulled up, I wasn't ready to be by myself yet. Elaina's light was out at her place and I felt a familiar feeling sinking down on me—loneliness. Harris parked the car and waited for me to get out as she gripped the steering wheel looking to the same window I was. She sighed loudly and turned to me.

"You wanna come over and read the stuff she wrote? You are in it too," I asked.

Harris twisted her lips up and to the side thinking that she probably shouldn't but knowing nothing would happen that shouldn't. "Sure, I'll follow you there," she answered.

~~~~~~~~

Harris sat at my kitchen table like she had so many times before reading Elaina's diary of thoughts and memories. I poured us both another drink. If she couldn't drive, she would stay on the couch like she had a few times before. I caught myself looking at her again and silently chastised myself for thinking of her that way.

I hadn't dated or even looked at another woman in over a year. I was still married to someone who didn't know me. After today, I felt sunk. The doctor had informed us that Elaina was gone and not coming back. It was like she had died twice now, and I was feeling reckless and angry about it all. It had been a long year—a lonely year of hoping and praying. Nothing had come of my dreaming and wishing. She was still the same person she was when she came here. Sure she thought I was nice, but Elaina had no clue who I was or why I stared at her so much; why I tried to find any excuse to come to see her every day. Harris's voice broke my thought and I was grateful.

"It's funny, her words are just so familiar," she said softly and then drifted back the pages. "Do you think she will ever remember us?" she whispered as her hands trailed Elaina's typed words.

"I don't know. Sometimes I think she remembers, but then nothing," I answered somberly and sat down beside her.

"Do you think that I should have given Jeff another shot? Maybe I was too hard on him," she asked.

"Jeff's an idiot if he doesn't fight for you," I told her.

She laughed but then she looked at me and her eyes turned down. "You miss her so much, I know," she said as her eyes started to water with tears.

"Yes, I do," I answered through the ripples of tears in my throat.

She leaned over and wrapped her arms around my neck and hugged me. "I don't know what to do without her around, you know. It's like I lost my best friend, my sister." She wept into my neck. I wound my arms around her tightly and embraced her as we both cried.

"I can't let go, Harris, I just can't," I wept.

Her hands grabbed my face and she whispered, "Then don't."

Then she did something unusual that she had never done before. She kissed me gently on my lips. It was a peck, nothing more, but there was something more there that she was holding back.

"Harris?" I whispered in a lecturing tone.

"I'm sorry. It's just been so hard lately and we've been spending so much time together. I'm just confused and upset about everything…" she rambled on, and I started thinking, *What's the harm anyway? My marriage is over for all intents and purposes. I hadn't been with a woman in over a year. I am lonely, too, and upset.* The idea of being in a woman's arms was a comforting thought.

What the hell, I thought to myself, and I grabbed her face and kissed her back this time. We didn't talk anymore after that.

She stayed the night, and finally I woke up in someone's arms and not alone. I realized in the morning, however, that she wasn't who I wanted to wake up to. She wasn't the woman I was in love with. I rolled away from her and faced the window. The birds were singing and chirping loudly, and I could hear Macbeth barking in the distance at some furball she was probably chasing. Elaina had always laughed at Macbeth.

What had happened between Harris and I was wrong, but I hoped that we hadn't ruined our friendship too severely. I got up and got dressed as she slept in. I went downstairs and made some coffee and waited for her to come down. An hour later, she emerged from the staircase and walked shamefully into the kitchen. Her eyes avoided mine completely, and I wondered if she was gonna say anything at all.

"Good morning," I said.

"Morning," she grumbled.

I offered her a cup of coffee, and she sat down at the kitchen table and drank it hesitantly. I had no idea how to fix this or make things normal again between us.

"Look, do you wanna talk about what happened?" I asked gently.

"It was nice, but we both know we don't want each other," she answered, and suddenly I was a bit offended.

"Jesus, I've had better reviews from my high school girly," I grumbled.

She laughed, and suddenly I knew it was okay.

"I'm sorry, but you know what I mean. We don't love each other; we're just lonely. This will not happen again. Agreed?" she asked.

"Agreed. Only a two-drink maximum for us from now on," I answered.

"We can't ever tell her about this, no matter what happens or what she remembers. She never needs to know about this. Agreed?" she asked.

"Agreed," I answered seriously.

I should have made her promise she would never tell Mandy either, but at the time I really thought Elaina was lost to us. I didn't think it would ever matter.

After that night, we kept our word. It was strange that I never thought of her that way again, and she didn't seem to either. The night we shared only seemed to make us grow closer as friends. It seemed to cement that we were just friends. Maybe we had just tried to see if it would ever work. Nevertheless, it never came up between us, and we behaved naturally as if nothing had ever happened.

Chapter 29

Elaina

I drove home in a hurry, wanting to be back in my apartment where I felt most safe. When I got back, I ran straight into the shower and scrubbed and scrubbed at my skin. I wished I could rip this strange skin off my body. When I got out of the shower, I ripped the sheets from the bed and threw them in the trash can. I wanted every possible part of him away from me. *That woman isn't my wife…* the way it came out of his mouth in reference to me—it was all I could think of when I thought of him. Why had he talked about me that way? Why was he so angry with me? It was true I didn't remember him at all, but I thought that we had been getting very close in the past months. I actually thought that we could make this strange thing between us work.

I heard everything they had argued about. Surprisingly, his sleeping with Harris didn't bother me as much as what he said about me. It wasn't even fair of Mandy to make him feel so badly about what had happened years ago when he thought he had lost his wife, but for him to spit those words about me; the fury that he felt, the pain that he was still carrying. Why was he still so angry? My head started to ache, and I twisted my fist to the side of my temple trying to will it away.

I didn't know who I really was anymore. I had no idea who I was or what I was doing. It was horrible what had happened to me, but I was trying to make it work. When Gray and I started spending more time together, I was happy about it. I felt so safe with him and natural. It just felt right. I had had a crush on him for over three years. He would come almost every day and pretend to do other things while smiling at me from a distance. He was so handsome, almost irresistible really. His eyes were so gorgeous and warm. His smile was adorable and loving. I was more than attracted to him. My head pounded with thoughts and worries. I liked him—I really liked him—I was sure that I loved him. But now, he was someone else I didn't know. I had never seen him that way before.

My head started pounding harder, and I grabbed my forehead and closed my eyes. I took some aspirins and tried to lie down for a while. The headaches had been coming on quickly these days. When I slept, I dreamed about the ocean—always the ocean, with crystal-clear water and white beaches; a purple house with a weird blue roof. I heard laughing and splashing and barking. I could almost smell the perfume of the red flowers and the salt of the ocean. Images came in and out of focus as I woke to a light tapping at the door. I recognized it immediately and bounced up from the couch to answer the door. My head was still aching mildly.

When I opened the door, he was standing there with apology thick in his eyes. His eyes were filled with tears, and they were red and puffy. Suddenly, something flashed in my mind. It was recognition. A foggy thought emerged in my brain of him kneeling before me with the same cried-out eyes looking up at me. Then it was gone as fast as it had come into my mind, like a flash of lightning. I sucked in a breath of air and grabbed his hand. He had no idea what was happening in my head.

He wasted no time with his apology. "I'm sorry, Elaina, I didn't mean it, I promise you. It was nothing; it was so long ago…"

I put a hand up to stop him. "I'm not upset about that," I insisted. My mind was spinning and my ears started ringing.

His brow furrowed, then they lifted again thinking of something else to apologize for. "Oh, then the yelling and screaming then? I was upset with Mandy; I didn't mean for that to come out that way. Mandy and I will work it out, don't worry…"

He rambled on, and then another flash of him by a pool, grabbing plates and glasses from an outdoor couch. A laugh echoed in my head as he was smiling at me and then the image was gone again. I didn't realize I had been staring off at nothing or that he was even done talking until he said my name.

"Elaina? Are you all right, love?" he whispered with concern.

Then another moment, deeply blurry, of him standing across from me on a pier saying I do, then another moment with us unpacking our stuff in LA and then he turned to me and winked. Then suddenly, I could hear him talking to me but there was nothing to see, only darkness. I could hear him saying in a grunt of a voice filled with pain, "I won't ever leave you, love." I closed my eyes tightly and gasped.

"Elaina, what's wrong?" he asked again, this time with more worry.

"It was you, wasn't it? The voice I heard. You talked to me all the time; you were there. You told me you would never leave," I whispered, talking very fast.

His eyes widened into shock. "How did you know that? I never told you about that?" he whispered as he remembered his vow to stay with me whether I remembered him or not. "I talked to you while you slept."

"I heard you and just now…something you said…I don't know, something triggered it…I remembered hearing you talk to me."

"You…remembered?" he asked. "Anything else?" he asked as his eyes lifted in surprise.

I closed my eyes and waited for anything to come. "We were married on our pier I think it was in Belize. I remember I had a pretty flower in my hair with a silk dress…and you liked to wink at me; I think you thought it was funny to make me blush," I answered.

Gray's face changed. He was stunned but happy at the same time. Suddenly, more things started rushing in.

"It's weird; they are there but still so fuzzy. It's almost like a dream I had that I can't quite remember fully...You used to drag your fingers down my side to wake me up... and you liked egg whites instead of real fried eggs...yuck, nobody likes egg whites," I added.

"You... remember that?" he asked in a barely audible voice, still in shock.

"I remember...parts of things," I insisted, and then I threw my arms around his neck and hugged him. "I remember...you, I think." He chuckled at my shoulder.

"Is this real?" he asked through his laughing.

"I think so. It feels real and it all...looks real in my head," I answered, still unsure but growing more positive. "You and me, right?" I asked, remembering something else in my cloudy past memory.

But he pulled away suddenly to look at me. His arms dropped from around my body and they found my face. "I knew you would come back to me. I knew if I didn't give up you would come back to me," he whispered through his tears of happiness. He kissed me passionately for a long time, and I enjoyed every second of it.

I opened my eyes and sighed, "I remember this, your hands on my face, your mouth on mine, your lips," I whispered and closed my eyes, remembering more. His arms dropped again down to my waist but his lips found mine again as he lifted me up and into his arms still kissing me eagerly and fervently.

When he moved his lips to my neck and I was able to speak, I whispered, "I love you, forever." I could feel him smile into the curve of my neck. "Gray?"

"Yes, love," he whispered.

"I want to go home," I requested.

He chuckled again and grabbed my face to pull my lips to his. He kissed me for a long moment and then pulled away to look me in the eye. "We can go wherever you want."

~~~~~~~~

Weeks later, I woke up in my bed with Macbeth sitting right beside my head. Gray was gone, already up and out for the day. I reached my hand up to pet Macbeth's cute face as she licked my cheek. I sat up and swung my feet to the floor, the cold wooden Belizean floor that I loved. The windows were covered in sheers that flew across the room from the strong breeze. I brushed my teeth and hair and moseyed out to the kitchen for some fruit. I could see Gray on the pier messing with his boat under the bright sun. He turned to me and waved with his crooked smile. On the counter was a bowl of fruit and a note. I smiled, knowing it was from Gray. I picked up the stark, thick paper and opened it up to read. There was his handwriting and it read,

Welcome home, my innkeeper.

Lightning Source UK Ltd.
Milton Keynes UK
UKOW07f2120141214

243121UK00014B/171/P